To Willow~

May you feel the touch
of Jesus in this book!

All Gods Best!

Catherine

They Call Me
Mary *of*
Magdala

*The Story of
My Seven Demons*

CATHERINE L. TERRIO

WESTBOW
PRESS®
A DIVISION OF THOMAS NELSON
& ZONDERVAN

WestBow Press books may be ordered through booksellers or by contacting:

WestBow Press
A Division of Thomas Nelson & Zondervan
1663 Liberty Drive
Bloomington, IN 47403
www.westbowpress.com
844-714-3454

Edited by Kevin Fanning

ISBN: 978-1-6642-9641-1 (sc)
ISBN: 978-1-6642-9640-4 (hc)
ISBN: 978-1-6642-9642-8 (e)

Library of Congress Control Number: 2023905893

Print information available on the last page.

WestBow Press rev. date: 07/14/2023

This book is dedicated to the two great loves of my life.

To my one and only Glorious Savior Jesus Christ of Nazareth. Meeting You at the age of twenty-five was the best thing that ever happened to me and walking alongside You for these last thirty-two years have made me who I am today. Without You, my life would have no meaning. You are my Savior, my Redeemer and my Healer. My heart overflows with gratitude every day for who You are to me. I will praise You as long as I have breath in my lungs…

To my beloved late husband, Michael Joseph Theriault. You showed me what true unconditional love looks like. You believed in me and inspired me every day of our fifteen and a half years of marriage. Though leukemia cut your life short, your legacy lives on in my heart. You continue to inspire me even after being gone these many years. Our life together was a gift from God, and I loved being your wife, your True Companion and your Flower of the Son. I miss you every day and I look forward to our glorious reunion in heaven where we will never have to say goodbye…

CONTENTS

CHAPTER 1

Mary

Where It All Began

MY NAME IS Mary, a common name, and *common* is what many have called me. I've known horror and torture at the hands of many people in my life. I've known sorrow and pain as well. But it wasn't always this way, and ever since He walked into my world, nothing has ever been the same.

When I first saw the one they call Yeshua, something fluttered in my heart, for He was so familiar to me. Battling the demons in my mind as the faces of the men I'd encountered in my life flashed before my eyes, I couldn't figure out where He fit in. And then I remembered. Nazareth—it's where I would go whenever my father would leave and not come back for many nights. It's where my mother would send me, to the small village a day's walk from our home, to stay with my sweet Auntie Naomi, her only sister. Now all these years later, standing here staring up into the cloudless blue sky, my mind rewinds and I am transported back in time ....

I see only glimpses of our life before we came to live near my mother's family. My father was a fisherman on the Sea of Galilee. He was from the town of Magdala and would sometimes take me with him in the early mornings before my mother would wake. "Shh, let's not wake your mother," he would say as we gathered the supplies to go out and catch the fish that would pay for our food and make my father smile. But one day he didn't come back at the usual time and my mother was frantic with worry. She did not know where he fished, but I did, and even at five years old, I could find my way in the dark.

"Run," she said. "Go and find what has happened to your father." So,

I ran as fast as my little feet would carry me and it was then I spotted the crowd around my father's boat. He lay on the shoreline, still and lifeless.

"Father, Father!" I screamed as the people let me through. He was barely breathing, and the men did not know what to do, thus they did nothing.

"Papa, can you hear me? Papa! Open your eyes," I pleaded through my tears. His eyes fluttered open, but he looked right through me. It was only later after they carried him home to my mother when I heard the whispers of what happened to him. Somehow, he had fallen overboard and got tangled in his nets. The ones who saw him first did not know how long he had been under the water. When they dragged him to shore, they feared he was dead.

My father was never the same after the accident. He became a mean and hateful man, yelling and hitting my mother, though she tried only to help and care for him. A part of his mind had died that day on the shore, and I did not know the man he had become. He took to the bottle to find the comfort he used to get from fishing. Life as I had known it was forever changed.

It was not long after that fateful day when we moved south so we could be closer to my mother's family, to a village just north of Nazareth. My father would not allow us to live too close, but my mother insisted we needed to be nearer to family until he could get back on his feet. He never did. He started drinking more and more, often staying away for many days at a time, sometimes longer.

I was a shy child always trying to stay hidden, for it seemed I always drew the attention, stares, and comments from all of my father's fishermen friends, my "uncles," and the men in the villages. With my dark auburn hair, and my golden emerald-green eyes, I was different than the other girls my age. Those men would often beckon me to them with a wave of their hand while holding a piece of sweet candy to get me to come closer. I could then feel their rough hands underneath my chin, pulling my eyes up to theirs where I could see untold evil in their smiles.

I learned to run away, though sometimes they found me. I tried to stay hidden behind trees and bushes or the beautiful scarves my mother wrapped around my head to hide my unusual hair. But sometimes that was not enough, and I became the object of their unwanted affections. I learned never to make eye contact with the men whose breath was foul and whose bodies hadn't seen soap for far too long. I learned fear and shame at a very young age.

I was the only child of my mother and father, a disappointment when they realized I was but a female. After many years of being barren and enduring loss after loss of unborn babies, I arrived only to be greeted with the words of my father: "After all this time, a girl." My mother reminded me of this often and her pain was passed on to me as she nursed me and kept me close by her side.

After we moved south, it was just her and I, both hungry and waiting for my father to come home. Sometimes we waited weeks and only the kindness of a nearby neighbor would keep us alive through the gifts of stale bread and dried fish.

When the days stretched into weeks, it was then my mother would send me on the day's journey to my auntie's house in the next village. At six years old, I was resourceful and could run faster than all the boys. I always knew I was near to my destination when I heard the sweet sound of my auntie's voice singing the *Love Song to Yahweh*. I would begin humming as I entered the house that always smelled of baking bread and cinnamon. She would turn with sun-kissed arms outstretched and scoop me up to softly kiss my wind-burned cheeks, declaring how beautiful I was to God and to her. She would sit me down at the table and feed me a meal of fresh goat cheese, sweet dates and warm bread, straight from the brick oven. I would eat as fast as I could to fill my empty stomach as she said over and over, "Slow down, Sweet Mary. There's plenty more where that came from." My cousins would then run into the house with joyous laughter when they saw me, their faces, hands, and feet filthy from playing in the Nazarene streets. My auntie would bring more dates, cheese, and bread; but not before she scolded my cousins to wash up before they dared touch the coveted food.

"Eli, take your brothers back outside and make sure they wash well," she would say.

"Yes, Ima," was always my eldest cousin's reply.

When we all had our fill, my cousins could not get outside fast enough, always trying to entice me to come out and play with them. I was always reluctant, preferring to stay in the warmth of my auntie's kitchen within the sound of her sweet voice. More often than not she would shoo me out the door, and I would find myself trying to stay invisible.

At night we would all gather on the straw pallets as my uncle shared from the ancient parchments that he held so sacred. We would listen attentively to his deep, rich voice recite the words of my ancestors, the Shema, while my auntie would brush and braid my thick, long hair.

Then each of us would take a turn recalling from memory the words we had heard our whole lives: "Hear, O Israel. The Lord our God, the Lord is One. Love the Lord your God with all your heart and all your soul and all your strength."

We would then all lie down together. I always stayed as close as I could to my auntie, the source of my comfort. The sleep would come swift and sweet, for I was safe.

In the morning the smell of baking bread would wake me up before my cousins would rise, and I would join Auntie in the kitchen to help her and to hear her tender voice humming in worship to our God.

After breakfast and chores, we would be ushered out the door to play, not to return until our bellies told us it was time for the noon day meal.

The girls in the village were mostly kind to me, probably because they wanted to be near my handsome cousins. The boys were disinterested because I always kept my head down and would hardly speak, even when someone spoke to me. This ensured they would leave me alone.

All too soon, I would hear my own mother's voice calling to me: "Mary, my little Mary, it's time to go home, my love." My heart was always torn, for I loved my mother with all I had, but I longed for the safety and security I found in my auntie's home. The heart that beat with love for my mother always won out, and I would run with all I had into her outstretched arms. She would smile and tell me excitedly that Papa was home and that everything was going to be better now. I desperately wanted to believe her, but I could see the doubt betraying her as tears gathered in her own golden green eyes.

We would say our farewells with my auntie holding me just a little longer than was expected so she could whisper in my ear "This too, is your home. Come here anytime." I would search her eyes and see the truth in her smile, and I found peace in my heart. She would look at my mother with sadness and embrace her tenderly, inviting her to reconsider staying for the evening meal. My mother always declined even as I pled with my eyes to stay for as long as we could. I now know that the jealousy my mother felt ran deep, for while her sister had given birth to five sons, she was only able to bring one lowly girl into this world. Though the sister bond they shared was true, the envy pierced through my mother's damaged soul.

My father was sometimes happy to see me at first, and then he would be reminded I was but a female and was really of no use to him. For the first day or so upon my return, he wouldn't drink from the flask that was never far from his reach. But after a few days of my quiet reluctance to engage him, he would start drinking again and then retreat to the fields to gather the stones he used to grind into arrows. He would then send my mother and I to the market to try and sell his wares. When the days turned into weeks, my mother and I could sense his restlessness. She would desperately try and make our shabby hut a little cleaner and hang the lavender that she dried from the windows to take away the smell of his unwashed body. She would smile a little brighter and hum a little louder all in the hopes he would stay. At six years old, even though I had no schooling, I was already learning the ways of the world. My father would leave and the whole cycle would begin all over again.

I began to look forward to the times when he would leave, for soon I would be told to begin the day's journey to my beloved auntie's house. Though each time I was told to go, I felt like I was betraying my dear mother, and the tears would stream down my cheeks for the first hour of my walk. I could feel her eyes boring into me as she told me to walk and not look back. I obeyed and wondered each time what she would do while I was away. How would she find food? Would the neighbors care for her even though I was not there? I prayed to Yahweh to protect her and keep her safe until we could be together again.

CHAPTER 2
Mary

Life with Auntie

THE ROUTINE AT my auntie's house was familiar, and because I knew each day would be the same, I was able to find peace and joy. Each season gave way to the next, and though I missed my mother deeply, I began to feel the security grow in my heart. I had now been there for many months, with no sign of my mother. I felt safe for the first time in my life and learned to smile and actually laugh when my cousins would tease me. I felt stronger as I carried the sloshing buckets of water from the well. I began to hold my head up as I was spoken to and found my voice for the first time. I was now almost eight years old and the days of my father's visits were few and far between. My mother would come and take me from my auntie's home for only a week here and there. I began to smell the familiar scent of my father's breath when my mother would bend down to kiss me. I could see that she was becoming numb to the hardships of the life that had become hers.

With no real husband and no friends, she was alone. The village women would turn away from her when we went to the market. I could hear them whisper behind our backs when they thought we weren't listening. But I was always listening, and what I heard broke my young heart. The lies these cruel women were sharing about my mother could not possibly be true. I refused to believe it and covered my ears when I heard the words harlot and loose woman spoken about my dear mother.

It was harvest time of my ninth year and I had already been in Nazareth for many moons. I had learned the skills of how to knead the bread dough just enough, so it was not tough when baked.

I spent hours watching my auntie's most treasured friend, Mary, weave the soft sheep's wool my cousins would bring in from the shearing rooms, or the fine silk threads purchased from the traders at the market. She was the most skilled weaver in the village, and I was mesmerized as she created beautiful robes for her sons Yeshua, Jacob, and Simon. I longed to be as masterful at the art of weaving as she was and begged her to teach me. I sat at her feet and could not tear my eyes away as she created one lovely shawl, robe and blanket after another.

One day as I watched, she began weaving the most beautiful gold, red and emerald green threads together into the most magnificent shawl I had ever seen. I reached out to touch the hem, and then she lovingly placed it around my shoulders. For one glorious moment I was transported in time to a place where I was a beloved princess of my father, and my auntie was my mother. I closed my eyes and breathed in the scent of the freshly dyed threads which made up such an incredibly soft garment. I felt a tear slip onto my cheek as her hand touched my shoulder and the garment was removed. I felt alone and naked as though I had been stripped of the one item that had ever made me feel like I had any real value. Her smile warmed my heart as she gently wiped the tear from my face.

I learned how to tend the fire so that it was perfect for baking the sweet treats my cousins loved. But best of all, I learned how to pray and how to worship the God of my ancestors, the great and almighty God of Abraham, Isaac and Jacob. I learned how to read from the parchments and study the stories of old. I got lost in the lives of Noah, Moses and Joshua. I dreamed about being like Esther, Deborah or even Ruth who became the great grandmother of King David. I would spend hours secretly listening behind the closed doors while my cousins were being taught by the Rabbi's. I yearned to be able to go on the upcoming journey to Jerusalem for the Passover and prayed that my mother would not show up to take me away before we soon began the three-day procession. Though I prayed desperately for my dear broken mother, as the months stretched on, I felt my heart had found its true home with my auntie, uncle and cousins.

The preparations were made, and we were to leave at dawn the next day. As we prepared to lie down for the night a soft knock on our door was heard. My heart seized in panic and I prayed it was not my mother who had come to take me away. My uncle got up and opened the door to greet my auntie's friend Mary. Though I could not hear what was being spoken, I breathed a deep sigh of relief as I knew her soft voice and wondered what could be happening. After a several moments, my uncle came in carrying something in his hands. He held out the exquisite shawl I had admired days before, and he stated that Mary wanted me to have it for my own. Indeed, she had made it especially for me as the colors were similar to the shades reflected in my eyes and hair. Though my uncle repeatedly declined, saying it was far too extravagant a gift for a child, Mary insisted that I have it for our journey to Jerusalem for the Passover. She would not take no for an answer, stating it was necessary that I have something to cover my head and to protect me from the prying eyes of men. That was what had convinced my uncle to allow me to receive the most beautiful gift I had ever seen.

I sat trembling as my uncle told my auntie to make sure I took good care of it. She looked at me with the tears streaming down my face and understood there was no need to tell me that. She knew deep in her heart this gift would be my most treasured possession and that I would never allow it out of my sight.

My uncle held it out to me, and I reached up and took hold of a lifeline. I now held in my hands a beautiful piece of art that was solely mine, no one else had ever worn it, and no one else ever would. I would guard it with my life for as long as I had breath in my lungs. Perhaps I was a princess after all, beloved of my Father in heaven.

The donkeys were loaded and weighed down with the supplies. Our family was ready, and our offerings were prepared. We, along with hundreds of other faithful Jewish believers, were anxious to travel for many days in order to participate in our annual Passover traditions. We would caravan together for safety and sit around the fires when we camped at night. I would drink up the stories of how my ancestors had gathered up all their belongings before leaving Egypt in the middle of the night. The story of the Angel of Death passing over the homes of the faithful Hebrew's who had painted the blood of the sacrificial lamb over their door frames in order to escape death. These stories and others kept me awake long into the night wondering what kind of Mighty God could rescue his children from slavery and deliver them into freedom. Each day would bring us closer to the City of David, where the history of my people was embedded deeply in my heart.

Upon arriving, the atmosphere was electric. People crushed together pushing towards the sacred city. Other people set up along the roadside selling freshly roasted lamb shanks, bread, hot from open fires, prayer shawls, brightly woven carpets, as well as lambs, doves, or pigeons to be sacrificed. The sounds of sheep bleating in their pens, and the smells of fresh manure from the many cows, camels and donkeys that littered the roads overwhelmed me. My senses were on overload as I absorbed all the sounds, sights and smells to later recall and treasure in my memories.

It was easy to get separated from my clan, so I stayed always within arm's reach of my auntie or uncle. Since my cousins were older, they were permitted to run ahead, but warned not to get too far so as to not be able to turn and see our family. My heart feared separation more than adventure, yet at almost ten years old, I longed to run ahead with my cousins and their friends to be in the middle of the festival. My shy, timid nature kept me safely holding onto my auntie's hand while we made our way to the area where we would set up camp for the days and nights until Passover.

It was only my second festival. My mother had refused to allow me to travel with the family until after my eighth birthday when my uncle assured her that he would care for and protect me with his life.

I had not seen my mother for many months, and I suppose it was understood I would travel again with our clan to celebrate the greatest feast of our faith. I had not remembered how beautiful all the brightly clothed women were, or how many little children were unaccompanied in the streets. I was old enough to see past the facade of thinly veiled holiness to what was barely hidden in the eyes of the men leering lustfully at the lovely women that surrounded us. It seemed this was a curse that always followed me; I was able to peer deep into the souls of others whose hearts bore the sin and shame I often saw reflected in my dear mother's eyes.

It was almost impossible to fall asleep at night with the festive sounds echoing off the tent walls in the crowded camp site. I tried to block out the noise and keen my ears towards the singing in the distance. It was the favorite tune from my childhood, the *Love Song to Yahweh* my auntie had hummed for years and had penetrated my heart. I hummed along softly as I drifted off to sleep each night.

The days were consumed with sacrifices, the temple worship, and the reading of the Law. From morning until dusk our family, friends, neighbors and faithful Jews from near and far celebrated the Great Feast of the Passover. It was a magical time in my life that I would treasure in my heart for as long as I lived.

CHAPTER 3

Mary

Return from Jerusalem

AFTER THE FESTIVAL ended, we packed our tents and began the long journey home to Nazareth. Many neighboring clans had joined our caravan and the celebration continued as we recounted the highlights of the last several days. Donkeys and camels were heavy laden with new treasures bought in the city: carpets, robes, and animal skins dyed the color of the Sea of Galilee.

The festivities continued as we traveled all day and all night through the treacherous terrain until my auntie's beloved friend, Mary, came running toward us waving her hands in the air shouting something over and over. As she neared, we heard "Yeshua, we can't find Yeshua," repeated at the top of her lungs. My auntie took hold of her hands to still Mary's frantic ravings and then placed her hands on her friend's face calmly telling her to explain what was happening.

By this time the whole caravan was in an uproar, for one of its own sons had gone missing. Mary described how she had thought Yeshua was with her cousin when we all started off together, but upon looking for him, no one had seen him. He had not left with Elizabeth and Zachariah. Even their son, John, had no idea where his cousin was.

At twelve years old, he was far too young to be left alone, even though Yeshua always seemed so much more mature than all the other boys. He was often found sitting off by himself when the boys were playing or rough housing with each other. He was always kind to everyone, and though I had never spoken to him, his eyes held a depth and wisdom that

11

transcended this world. Once I heard him talking with the Rabbi's long after all the other boys had been dismissed, and when he saw me crouched down and listening behind the door to the tent, I'm sure he smiled at me.

The frenzy grew when it was discovered that he was not to be found in the entire caravan. His mother and father quickly made preparations to return to Jerusalem to find their son. The decision was made to make camp and remain where we were until the boy and his parents re-joined our group. The elders prayed and blessed Mary and Joseph as they hastened back to the city.

On the third day, they were seen in the distance making their way toward us, all three of them with the young Yeshua lagging behind his obviously irate parents. Upon arriving, Mary offered her heartfelt apologies for holding up the caravan while Joseph expressed his gratitude at our waiting for them and looking after his other children. My auntie embraced her friend, thanked Yahweh and tousled the hair of the boy, eliciting a smile from his wise eyes. He seemed even more confident as he was embraced by the many in our clans. He graciously endured the scolding of the several adults who felt compelled to tell him that his parents were worried sick about him.

As we traveled on, I decided I would follow as closely as I could to hear what great adventures he must have experienced while back in Jerusalem all by himself. That night, while sitting around the fire with the other children, he shared about how he had not intended to cause his parents any alarm but had gotten so engrossed in the teachings at the temple that he could not pull himself away. When he realized his family had departed early the day before, he reasoned that it would be better to stay where he was rather than risk getting lost trying to find his way back home alone. Knowing his parents would come in search of him, he settled in and gleaned as much wisdom as he could from the Rabbi's, who were patient, and intrigued by his thought provoking questions. As he spoke, my heart broke a little more with the realization that I had no parents who would travel several days journey to bring me home. Indeed, I wasn't sure if my own parents even realized I had been separated from them for so very long. As the tears slipped down my cheeks, I stared into the fire and then realized that his mere twelve-year-old eyes were staring into my broken soul. Embarrassed at my weakness, I found comfort in his stare and finally had to look away for fear of being discovered.

Back home in Nazareth, the stories continued at the well, at the market and just about everywhere I went. The recounting of the festival, the countless stars in the stunning night skies, the worship, and of course young Yeshua getting left behind. Life went on as usual in our sleepy village. It was now where I called home as I had still not seen or heard anything from my parents. They had stayed away for two whole harvests, and I wondered if they were even alive.

I was growing up and learning the art of weaving from my auntie's beautiful friend Mary. Each day when we visited, she would teach me something new, and I cherished those special times together.

My cousins kept a close watch over me, and my heart was secure in the family that loved me. I missed my mother and the dreams I had of us being a real family. However, I found contentment in the life Yahweh had chosen for me. I was still a shy girl and stayed close to my auntie as this is where I felt safe.

I learned more and more about baking bread and roasting the meats with just the right amount of spices to illicit praise from my uncle and cousins who loved to eat. Auntie often allowed me to prepare our evening meal and complimented me that I could make some of the lightest and fluffiest flatbread in the whole village. I loved to stand by the window and watch the boys playing while I kneaded and rolled out the dough. I began rolling spices and even sugars into the sticky substance and would serve the cinnamon and sugary bread for a treat after supper. My uncle would smile at me when he bit into the warm sweet dessert, dripping with honey. He would lift my chin so that my eyes would meet his and say, "You will make a fine wife someday, my Sweet Mary." His compliments made me smile as warmth rose to my cheeks.

Sometimes, I would even get my cousins to do my chores for me. If it was my turn to clean out the stable stall, all I had to do was promise to give them my share of the dessert that night. They were happy to do whatever they could to earn some more of the delicious treats I had become so good at making. I loved to make people happy and only wished that somehow, I could make my mother and father happy enough so they would not crave the poisonous drink which made them stay away for so long.

I grew in my love of the Torah as well and vowed I would continue to study and learn as much as I could for as long as Yahweh allowed me to walk on the earth.

Another Passover had come and gone and this time I was able to sell one of the shawl's I had woven with Mary's instruction. I was allowed to keep the payment but insisted that I give a tithe to Yahweh as an offering at the Temple. This seemed to please my auntie and when my cousins begged me to share my bounty with them, I was able to purchase the sweet treats that they loved so much. I also found a beautiful polished stone in the shape of a heart that I bought for my beloved auntie. Our secret sign that she had adopted me forever as the daughter of her heart.

I knew God had blessed me with a gift to weave and that I would steward and cherish this gift forever. I showed my gratitude to Mary in whatever way I could, carrying water or picking flowers for her when she came to our home. I desperately wanted to please my auntie and tried to make sure she knew how grateful I was that she treated me as the daughter she never had. I settled in more and more and my heart was at peace. The faces of my own parents were hard to bring to my mind, and the memories were fading to the point of not being quiet so painful. I was beginning to show signs of growing up, and the little girl I once had been was now replaced by a slightly more confident young lady who was thriving in the love and teaching of my auntie and uncle; my heart was finally at peace.

We had now been home from the Passover celebration for several weeks. One day, while filling my jars at the well, I was told by my breathless cousin to hurry home because my mother and father had just arrived. My mind raced and my heart squeezed inside my chest as I prepared to see my parents. It had been more than two full years since I had seen my father and countless moons since I had laid eyes on my dear mother. I was a shaky mixed bundle of confusion, joy, fear and dread as I approached my auntie's home. It was then that I heard the shouting. My father's voice was raised, slurring his words and my mother's shaky voice trying to calm him down. My auntie and uncle were trying to be heard but my father would not listen to any of it. He demanded to see his daughter. I paused just out of sight while I heard my auntie say, "Truly she is thriving here, Jonah, and is welcome to stay as long as she desires. She is no bother at all and has learned how to read and write, to weave and bake. She is the sister that my sons never had. Please do not take her from us," she pleaded.

My father shouted that I was his possession, and it was time for me to come home with them. As I approached the house, I had the sinking sensation my life was about to change, and nothing would ever be the same again. Fear gripped me in the depth of my being, and I could feel the anger, hatred and the rage that poured out of my father. Oh, how I wished I never had to lay eyes on him again. But my duty as his daughter was etched deeply in my soul. I needed to spare my beautiful auntie and uncle, who were the parents I wished I was born to, from any more abuse from this wretched man. I raised my voice to be heard over the arguing. "I am here father, no need to shout, I will gather my things and be ready soon." The familiar smell of my father made my stomach turn and my mother's awkward embrace confirmed that she too had been drinking the dark liquid in the flask my father always carried. I could smell the sour stench of the drink and knew I would have to lock away the person I had become and try to ignore the resentment growing in my heart by the moment. I rushed in and gathered my things, making sure to put on my beloved shawl underneath my robe so it wouldn't be taken from me. The softness reminding me that no matter what happened from here on out, I was a beloved princess of my Heavenly Father.

I walked out and ran to my auntie's embrace. I heard her whisper into my ear, "Never forget, Sweet Mary, you are dearly loved by Yahweh. You are loved by all of us and you always have a home here."

I barely got to say goodbye to my cherished family before I felt the rough hand of my father around my arm tearing me away from what I feared might be my last tender embrace.

The tears burned in my eyes as my throat constricted. I could not show weakness, or my father might punish me in front of everyone. I swallowed hard and bid them all farewell. My heart shattered into a million pieces and I left them all lying on the dusty ground in Nazareth—the only real home I had ever known.

CHAPTER 4
Mary

My Exile

AS WE WALKED, my father looked at me with eyes that said he hardly recognized me. The fear gripping me was as real as anything I had ever experienced. The terror in my heart began to grow as I looked at my mother, who would barely glance my way. Her once beautiful cream-colored robe was now a dingy brown and hung off her bony shoulders. Her auburn hair was tangled and wild. Her eyes, so very like my own, were now vacant and hollow in her once lovely face. It was hard to believe this was my dear mother whom I had longed for all these months.

The long walk back to our village was silent except for my father's heavy breathing. I dared not say a word for fear of his anger being unleashed on me or my mother. I felt myself begin to withdraw back into my shell. The heaviness in my heart was like a stone making it hard to put one foot in front of the other. I could sense there was something my parents were not telling me; this was not the typical family reunion most children would experience after not seeing their parents for so long.

The dread inside of me grew great as we neared our home. My mother had still barely spoken to me during the long, dirty walk. Together, they passed the flask back and forth and their steps became more and more labored the longer we traveled.

Upon arriving at what used to look like my home, I was shocked to see what appeared to be all of my belongings heaped into a basket in the yard. I dared not ask what was going on but kept my head down and my eyes averted whenever my father looked my way.

Before long, two men on donkeys appeared on the road and approached our home. The first man seemed older than my father with a wiry grey beard. The second, a short round man with greasy hair and beady, dark eyes. My mind was spinning out of control at the possibilities of what could be happening. It was then I heard my mother's slurred voice speaking my name through her tears.

"Mary, my beautiful Mary. You are getting old enough now and it's time we started thinking about your future."

Oh no, please no. My heart began to beat out of my chest, and I remembered the girl next door who was sent away when she was just a little older than me. I can still hear her screams as she begged her father not to do this to her; the sound of her mother's weeping as she said goodbye to her only daughter.

My mind frantically searched for answers. Were they going to sell me to some man to be his child bride so they could afford to continue to buy their drink? Is this what parents do when they despise the children they have brought into this world? The questions spun around in my head. Would I be married at barely twelve years old, only to die in childbirth at the age of thirteen? Would I enter into slavery and be beaten for not sweeping the floor correctly?

"Dear God, help me please," I whispered. I felt the air around me being sucked from my lungs, so I could not breathe. My hands began to shake. My knees went weak.

As the two men got close enough to see me, the bearded one asked, "Is this her?"

My father nodded and they both came so close I could smell that they too had been drinking the same dark liquid my parents shared.

The shorter man bent down and whispered into my ear, "My, my, you are a pretty little one. With eyes the shade of emeralds, green and golden, and hair the color of a chestnut mare; you will fetch a nice price."

My father interrupted him when he saw the tears running down my face. I thought I might have seen a glimpse of remorse in his eyes, but then it was gone. The bearded man asked him, "Has she started to bleed yet?" As if I was some type of barn animal.

My mother stifled a sob and ran into the house leaving me all alone with the evil in front of me. My father grunted and told him I was perfect and pure and that he expected the agreed upon price.

The shorter man with the hot breath told the bearded man to pay whatever he wanted, saying to only his partner, "We will make far more with this one than the cost of what we will pay for her."

The man walked over to his donkey and began digging through his saddle bag. It was a small bag of coins that he thrust into my father's hands and then the rough hands were on my shoulders. I was being pulled by my braid towards the road. My life was only worth a few coins in a leather pouch to my father. The shorter man picked up my slight body and threw me over the back of the donkey. My life as I knew it had come to an end.

With no farewells from my mother and father, I watched through my tears as the basket of my belongings disappeared from my sight as we rode down the dusty road away from what had once been my childhood home.

CHAPTER 5

Mary

The Journey North

I HAD NO idea how long I clung to the back of the donkey or which direction we rode. The terror in my heart was suffocating me and my tears had turned to deep body wrenching sobs. I tried to pray but the words would not come. Where was Yahweh when I needed Him the most? When would the God of Abraham, Isaac and Jacob come to my rescue and wake me from this horrifying nightmare?

The two awful men talked together as we rode and paid no attention to me, making plans about how they would spend the small fortune they would receive from selling me. I heard words like *bride price, house servant, temple prostitute.* They held my destiny in their hands and all they could think about was how much gold I would bring. My fate was sealed, and my childhood was over.

As the hours passed, I realized my tears had dried up and I felt a burning in the pit of my stomach. Was it fear, anger, rage, hatred or confusion that clouded my vision? I tried to fathom how a mother and father could sell their only child for a small bag of silver to total strangers and not care one bit about what was going to happen to their daughter. I began to build a brick wall around my heart, as all of my worst nightmares had become my living reality. I had known as a young child that evil was a very real and present part of my life, but I had learned to push that deep into the recesses of my mind. Now this took my fear to a new level as I rode on the back of a donkey into the darkness that was going to be my future.

As the sun was setting, we arrived in a faraway village where I did not

19

recognize the speech of the foreigners surrounding me. The women were dressed in brightly colored robes and their eyes were blackened with kohl, their lips the color of crimson. Two women took me from the donkey and examined me in the fast-approaching twilight.

They ushered me into a tent where I joined many other girls around my age, all huddled together in the corners of the small enclosed tent. I recognized the fear in their eyes as a reflection of my own, their faces stained with tracks of tears from the dusty ride. I was pushed into the corner by one of the women and stumbled before I fell over a little girl who was no more than a child. The burning that had been churning in my belly erupted into a raging fire and I screamed at the top of my lungs with everything I had.

A mean-eyed old woman rushed into the tent, came at me with arms flailing and slapped me as hard as she could sending me sprawling to the dirt floor again. I had seen evil in the eyes of men before, but never in the eyes of a woman; that is until this moment. She spit in my face and cursed at me in a language I did not understand. It was the last time I heard myself scream. I rubbed my cheek as it began to swell with her handprint. The other girls inched as far away from me as they could get. I was alone and terrified, so I crawled to the farthest corner, curled up into the tightest ball that I could, and cried myself to sleep.

The morning sun brought stifling heat into the tent. Even at dawn, I was able to smell the fear coming from sixteen young girls all ripped from their families and destined to a life of unknown horrors. My hair was covered in dust, my braid undistinguishable. My face hurt, my lips were cracked, and my mouth was as dry as a hot summer wind.

I was weak and hungry. Suddenly my stomach reminded me the last time I had eaten had been breakfast at my auntie's house the day before. Was it only a mere twenty-four hours since my world had crumbled into this evil darkness?

The thought of my dear sweet auntie threatened to bring on a fresh wave of tears, but I fought to keep them locked inside my eyes. I could not let anyone see me cry, for tears meant weakness, and weakness meant that I would not survive this inferno I was entering. I hugged my knees close to my chest and began rocking back and forth, as I looked around at the others, most of whom were still sleeping. When I turned my head to the left, I was met with the most striking violet eyes of the little girl I remembered falling over the night before. She stared at me with fear and confusion and then I saw the corner of her mouth turn up in an attempted smile. I nodded my head and tried to make my mouth show happiness, but my lips would not cooperate.

I gestured with my hand and patted the ground next to me. She tentatively crawled over on hands and knees and got as close as she could without touching me. I learned her name was Kiera and that she was but 8 years old. Her presence calmed my spirit and I realized I was not alone anymore. She gestured to her hair and my own, which were almost the exact same shade of auburn, and this time I was able to force my mouth to turn upwards. She rewarded me with a full smile that reached her eyes as the tears started to flow onto her cheeks. I wrapped my arm around her small shoulder and she silently sobbed while I held her. We were all in this nightmare together, and I wondered if her parents had sold her without looking back as my own parents had done to me.

When we heard the rustling at the entrance to the tent, she quickly moved away from me and wiped her face on her sleeve, filthy as it was. Two teenage girls that I had not seen the night before came in carrying trays of food. They set the trays on the floor in the middle of the tent and then turned to leave, but not before waving their arms and motioning for us to eat. Several of the girls were awake now and I assumed were as hungry as I was, so I moved forward toward the trays. Just then one of the oldest girls ran to one of the trays and picked it up and carried it over to the other side of the room. Several other girls attacked the other tray until it was empty. I could smell the bread and see the figs and grapes and was not about to go another day without eating.

I stood as tall as I could, gestured to my new little friend to stay where she was, and walked across the room. I stared into the eyes of the tray stealer and dared her to stop me from taking the food. She must have felt the intensity of my emotions, for she took what she wanted and pushed the tray towards me. I picked up the tray, carried it to my friend who took her share. I then made my way around the room, making sure each girl got a warm breakfast. I could feel the stares at my back and wondered about each of their stories. How far had they traveled? Did they have brothers? Were they loved and missed back home? As I served the last girl, the tray was empty, except for a scrap of bread and a small fig. I set the tray down in the middle of the room, took the scraps, and brushed the crumbs into my hand and went back to my corner. The minutes stretched on and I tried to chew slowly as possible so as to savor the taste of the fig. I closed my eyes and when I opened them, the tray stealer stood before me, hands outstretched, offering me a piece of bread and several grapes along with two more figs. Our eyes met and a peace was brokered in our smiles.

With food in our bellies, the girls began to whisper to each other, many in my own Aramaic language, "Where is your home?" one questioned. Another inquired, "What is your name?" Still another asked, "How many years do you have?" With fear in our hearts the main question on all our minds was, "What will happen to us now?" The power of unity holds with it a strength and confidence that cannot be found alone. We recognized ourselves in each other's eyes, and in our stories. Thus, we each grew just a tiny bit stronger. This is how friendships are born.

CHAPTER 6

Mary

The Preparation

AS THE MORNING sun beat upon the tent, the two teenage girls returned for the empty trays. Behind them came several women carrying pails of water. One pail was set in each corner of the tent and the women began beckoning us to them. As I approached timidly, I felt the material of my robe being torn from my body. Underneath I wore my beloved shawl and when undressed I clung to it as if it were priceless gold, which to me it was. I could see the envy in the woman's eyes and as she reached to take it from me, I growled from the depths of my soul, baring my teeth and daring her to take it from me. Another woman laughed and gestured for me to hand it to my new friend, (the tray stealer) for safekeeping while I was washed. I reluctantly handed over a part of my heart and trusted her with my most prized possession, reminding her with my eyes that I would fight to the death for that shawl. She nodded and took it from me.

Each of us was to be stripped naked and bathed right in plain sight of anyone who would enter into the tent. The rough hands began scrubbing my body with a rag and some type of soap that smelled of rosemary. When they began washing my hair, the matted tangles brought frustration and curses from the one who was washing me. My hair was very thick and hung all the way down my back, always requiring extra care and tenderness when trying to get the tangles free. The pain was unbearable, and tears fell from my eyes. Soon a dark-skinned young woman stepped in and took over for the angry one who brought me to tears. There was a gentleness in her touch as she patiently started from the bottom and worked the knots out until the comb could run freely down the length of my hair. I tried to block out my shame and humiliation while I was passed onto the next woman who then rubbed olive oil into my skin and hair. I was given a clean, brown robe to wear. We were given no undergarments, but I had my beloved shawl and it protected me from the robe that would chafe against my raw skin. I closed my eyes and remembered the beautiful Mary who had given me this priceless gift. I thanked Yahweh for the softness of my precious shawl which was now safely hidden under my new robe.

At some point, mats were brought in and we were motioned to sit down; we understood clearly that we were not allowed to get the new robes dirty. It was hours before we were all seated on our mats and left alone again, wondering what would happen next. I had learned the names of several of the girls, and my little violet-eyed Kiera would not leave my side. Most of them spoke in my native tongue, all victims similar to Esther who had been taken from her home as well. I had somehow gained the trust of many of them and they brought their mats close to mine to ask questions to which I did not have answers. I silently prayed to Yahweh to give me the wisdom of Solomon as I tried to bring comfort and ignite courage into my new sister's hearts. I told them about the beautiful, young Hadassah who later became Queen Esther. How, she too had been kidnapped from her home and family as a child. She was taken to the palace and given beauty treatments for one whole year. Then, because of God's grace, she went before the King and won his favor, only to become queen and save her people.

Before long, more food was brought in and this time the tray stealer took the tray around and served each newly bathed beauty before she ate. We all had our fill and then lay down on our mats to rest while we waited for our fate to be decided.

Early in the evening, the mean-eyed old woman came in again. I shrunk back as far as the tent wall would allow, still feeling the sting of her hand striking my cheek. She was followed by a man that looked like he was from my tribe, same robe, sandals, and head covering the men in my auntie's village wore. The old woman spoke to him and he began to speak to us.

We were told that in the morning we would be taken to the market where we would be put on display for the highest bidder to purchase as property. Some of us would be sold as servants, some as brides and others sold to the Temple for services to the gods. My mind raced to grab hold of what would be the best of the three terrifying options. When each scenario played out the unimaginable horror in my mind, I decided each possibility would be unbearable. I longed for Yahweh to come and take me into his arms, delivering me from what lie ahead. I would rather die than allow any of those nightmares to become my reality.

My eyes darted around the tent searching for an escape. It was as if the mean-eyed old woman had read my mind, for she came and stood in front of me and glared evil into my heart, daring me to attempt escape. I dropped my head and prayed again for mercy from my auntie's God.

Each of us was questioned at length by the man who spoke our language. Could we read and write? Did we know how to cook or tend the fire? What skills did we possess? Many of the girls were like me and had been taught to read and write. Several of them shared of their knowledge of herbs and plants. I wondered if I should tell them of my love for weaving and decided to keep my secret to myself, but then thought better of it as it may allow me a privilege the others did not have. I was so confused and could barely breathe much less make decisions I should not have been making.

The night seemed endless—none of us could sleep. Our hearts wept as each of us realized our fate and said goodbye to our innocence and our childhoods. Kiera cried quietly all night, her head resting on my shoulder. As morning dawned, it was obvious many of us had not slept a wink and our caregivers were none too happy about it. We were roughly treated to more hair brushing, more olive oil and a fresh new white robe. Then they loaded us onto a cart, and we began the trip to the slave market.

How strange it was that the last time I went to a market, I held my auntie's hand, and we chose the most beautiful pomegranates together while humming the *Love Song to Yahweh*. I wondered if my auntie knew what my parent's intentions were on that fateful morning only two days before. Surely, she would not have allowed them to take me had she known, would she? Is that what all grown-ups did to their children? I pushed the thought from my mind vowing instead to hold onto the love I knew my auntie felt for me. Perhaps she would go to my mother and father and demand that I be allowed to live with her forever. When she could not find me, perhaps she would start out on a search for me the way Yeshua's parents had searched for him. Maybe she was even looking for me right now in the neighboring villages, asking if anyone had seen her young Sweet Mary with the emerald golden eyes and auburn hair. The thought brought a little smile to my heart as I remembered her soft voice humming me to sleep at night.

CHAPTER 7

Mary

My Fate Decided

BEFORE I KNEW it, we had arrived at the market and each girl was helped off the cart as if we actually mattered to the ones whose calloused hands were helping us. What an ugly charade was being played out as we were paraded into a tent before being auctioned off, like cattle or sheep, to the highest bidder. My stomach was in knots and my breakfast threatened to come up as it was almost my turn. I could hear the whistles and laughter from the men as each of my new friends were taken to their new destinies. I was the last one waiting to be taken up on the stage. By now, my heart was hammering in my head and my knees were so weak I could barely stand. As they brushed my long wavy hair and pinched my cheeks, I was sure the God of my ancestors had forsaken me. How could He allow this to happen to me? Something slammed shut in my heart as the last brick was put into place around my heart. I was no longer Sweet Mary—I was about to become the human property of the evil that ran free in this dark world.

As I walked onto the stage, a hush came over the crowd. There were no whistles or laughter, only a few whispers were heard. The silence was deafening, and I wondered at what revulsion all of these terrible men must have felt for me to not even garner a single whistle. An older man dressed in a gleaming, white robe with a bright turban on his head stood up quickly and loudly said something that I could not understand. All eyes turned to him and the silence continued on for what seemed an eternity.

I was taken off the stage and into another tent. I had just become the property of a man who was obviously wealthy and had the power to silence everyone; therefore, no one dared bid against him. I have no idea what he paid for me or what his plans were for me, but in my wild imagination, I prayed he would make me as one of his own daughters and I would be raised in a palace as a princess. I held onto my hopes and dreams and would not allow them to rob me of my humanity, even if they took everything else away from me. I did not know what happened to my little Kiera and my heart broke a little more. I did not even get to say goodbye to her.

The journey to my new home took several days. It seemed like we traveled north because in the morning the sun was rising in the mountains and as the day came to an end, it set beyond the sea. The nights got colder. The days no longer bore the heat of my childhood summers. I had never been beyond Jerusalem and though no one spoke to me and I could not understand my captor's tongue, they treated me with care. No one harmed me. I was tended to by a young, black Egyptian who was probably about fifteen years old. She was kind and made sure that I was clean, fed and comfortable. Sometimes I could even get her to smile. Her name was Zara and I quickly came to enjoy her company.

The man who bought me was the age of a grandfather, not that I knew either of my grandfathers, but I had heard other children in our village call the old men "Saba", which I think meant Grandfather. Surely, he would not want to take me for his own wife; the very thought made my skin crawl even in the warm afternoon sun. If I was to be a servant, why would Zara be taking such good care of me? Wouldn't I already be working if that was going to be my role?

I was more confused than ever and tried to still my jumbled thoughts with memories of my past. I set my mind to pray, but could not reconcile my auntie's God, the Almighty God, with a god who would allow a barely twelve-year-old child to be sold into slavery by the very parents who gave birth to her. My heart was growing cold and as hard as the stones on the ground, and I questioned whether there really was a God in heaven.

When we finally arrived at the gates to what appeared to be the city of the grandfather, many guards and servants scurried around making sure the way was clear. They bowed down and made sure the old man had something cold to drink before he even passed through the entrance. Many people stared up into the cart that was carrying me while Zara tried to shield me from being seen through the open windows of our transport.

It became obvious I was entering a whole new world: a new language, new clothing, new food. There was nothing left of my old life. Even my given name of Mary was now pronounced *Myree*. I saw what appeared to be palace after palace as we continued further through the walled city. Trees that reached to heaven, sweet smelling flowers and gardens surrounded us as we traveled along. Perhaps I was to become a princess after all, treated as the daughter of this man and loved by all. My childish dreams would keep my hope alive through whatever came my way. I could not allow anyone to steal the precious drops of joy that still kept my heart from drying up and blowing away in the wind.

I was taken into a house so big I felt even smaller than I already was. The ceilings were taller than trees, the floors so shiny I could see my face when I looked down. The smells were of lavender, cinnamon, and spices of what auntie would call the Eastern people.

Zara led me down several hallways and up a staircase that overlooked a pool with fish swimming in it. I could not believe my good fortune. If I was to live here, maybe Yahweh was looking out for me after all.

Upon entering what seemed to be my new bedroom, I saw a bed bigger than I've ever seen with countless pillows piled high, and I felt soft fur rugs beneath my feet. I could not help the smile which spread across my face, forcing the memories of my abandonment to fade into the recesses of my mind. I was given more dresses than I could ever wear in a lifetime, and beautiful jewels for my hair. The slippers laid before me had sparkles and laces that tied around my ankles. I felt as if I was in a dream and I never wanted to wake up. A knock on the door brought me back to the reality of my new world and a young man entered and began speaking to Zara. He then looked at me and in perfect Aramaic, the language of my ancestors, he told me I was to be bathed and dressed in the finest gown in the wardrobe, for tonight I would meet my husband.

CHAPTER 8

Zara

My New World

IT SEEMED LIKE a lifetime ago that I was a mere kitchen slave, though it was not even one full moon since my fate had turned. I was ushered out of the hot cooking area and taken by an older slave to our quarters. I was then told to bathe and put on a clean robe, for soon I would depart with the patriarch of the family. He was the man who had kind eyes and never raised his voice, unlike his daughter who seemed always to be yelling at one of us. We were, after all just property to be bought and sold, treated as if we had no value at all. Now, here I was getting ready to get on a transport to unimaginable adventures I had only dreamed of.

I had never traveled, having been born in the dark hut where we all lived together. I barely knew my mother, for she died while being beaten in the orchards after trying to escape. My father was sold off after that, due to the fact that he was inconsolable after the death of my mother. I never saw him again, so at five years old I was an orphan slave girl passed around to any female slave I was told to work with.

As a small child, I was taught how to gather the crops, how the wash the robes and how to prepare the fire. So, when I turned fourteen and began to bleed, the masters kept a closer watch on me and did not allow me to wander as I had when I was a young child. Now this new adventure I was embarking on with Jidu, as the family called him, was so exciting to me that I could barely suppress my joy. As I practically skipped to the caravan which was being loaded, I saw a hint of a smile in the corners of Jidu's eyes and I felt a new-found peace. Perhaps I was not destined to be a kitchen slave for the rest of my life. We traveled for days, crossing the border into a new country where I heard different languages being spoken.

Finally, we arrived at our destination and I was shocked to realize that we were at a slave auction in the middle of the desert. People from all around the region had come to purchase people like me as property. My heart sank as I lost all respect for Jidu, not wanting to believe him to be like all the rest. I slid down in the carriage, wanting to disappear when I heard Jidu talking about the reason we were there. He said he was searching for a wife for his eldest grandson, Misha. This was the homeland of his own lifetime bride, Myriam, whom he had loved dearly had recently passed away.

He described in vivid detail the description of the girl he was searching for. She was young, between the ages of nine and twelve years old, with striking beauty and features which set her apart from the other girls. She must speak clearly with some degree of intelligence and be skilled in the ways of women's work. She must know how to read and write, know how to tend a fire, be teachable in the arts, and most of all, have a kind and endearing spirit. I thought it would be nearly impossible for a girl like this to be found here at a slave auction, but I kept my eyes open.

After several hours of young girls being paraded on and off the stage, we were near the end. The last girl to walk onto the stage had dark, auburn hair and golden emerald eyes that shone in the sunlight. The hush of the crowd was unnerving as each man stared at the child. She was stunning and I had to catch my breath. This was the girl that my master was looking for and he immediately stood to his feet and motioned to the man in charge. No one dared move, for my master had great wealth and no one would be able to pay what he was willing to pay for this extraordinary girl.

From there, we were ushered out of the big tent and I was told to take the child to the carriage while the price was being negotiated. We were guarded by another servant who was told not to allow anyone near the girl and to guard her with his life. She looked at me with fear in those mesmerizing eyes while I took her gently by the hand and led her away. She smiled shyly at me, squeezed my hand, and I knew this was the beginning of our friendship. I was given charge over her and told to care for and watch over her, tending to her every need. She was to be the bride of the heir to the throne. In my heart, I dared to dream that one day she would perhaps be so kind as to set me free. I vowed to serve her faithfully, and to cherish her for as long as I lived.

CHAPTER 9
Myree

My New Identity

HUSBAND? BUT I was not yet even thirteen years old. My world spun out of control again. The tears flooded my eyes and spilled onto my cheeks as he turned and walked out of the room without closing the door. Zara came over and sat next to me on the floor where I had collapsed upon hearing the word *husband*. She dried my tears with her sleeves and helped me to my feet. She set me on the bed and motioned for me to lie down. I crawled onto the massive bed and curled into myself and wept hot, salty tears.

When I awoke, it was almost dark outside. Zara had a tray of fruits, cheeses and dark warm bread that I had never seen before. After I had eaten, she led me to a room with a small pool of running water and what looked like a version of our outdoor toilet, but this was in a room of its own. She slowly brushed my hair, unbuttoned my robe and then motioned me into the pool. I clung to my beloved, precious shawl, not wanting to part from it. She was kind and gently took it from my shoulders, folded it neatly, and placed it in the bottom of a giant trunk underneath countless other robes meant for me. I decided that was a safe place for my beloved possession and allowed her to guide me into the huge pool. The water was warm and smelled delightful. For a moment I forgot why I was bathing and then the word *husband* slammed into my mind again. No! No! It could not be. I could not be the one that lie underneath a grown man while he panted, groaned and pushed up and down on me. I was only a child. Please, God, don't let this thing happen to me I prayed, as I slid under the surface of the warm water.

As the water grew cold, Zara had gathered all of the items that I would need for my presentation to the man I would marry. *How can this be my life?* I wondered again as I was treated with fragrant oils and dressed in the most magnificent garment I had ever seen. The gown I had chosen was a deep cocoa brown that enhanced the color of my long auburn hair which was now piled high on my head. Makeup was applied to my eyes, cheeks and lips. When I looked at my reflection, I did not recognize the face staring back at me. It seemed I had aged into a younger version of my mother, and the memory of the woman who had savagely betrayed me pierced my heart. I was no longer Sweet Mary, but rather the beautiful Myree now. Whether I liked it or not, tonight was the night I would meet the man I would spend the rest of my life with.

I forced the wall around my heart a little higher in an attempt to protect the young girl within me. My thoughts flew to the streets of Nazareth where I spent the majority of my childhood. I recalled the noise of the squeaking ropes as I raised the bucket of water from the deep well. I pictured the faces of the baby lambs, when they were just days old. I remembered the sound of my uncle's voice as he read from the parchments. I stored all these memories deep inside my heart, so I could bring them out whenever I needed to remember who I really was.

Walking down the staircase and into the banquet hall, I was assaulted by the smells of a great feast. The voices of probably thirty people were quieted and the sound of the grandfather was heard above all. "Welcome to your new home, Myree. We greet you as one of our own and wish for you to feel that we are now your new family. Please enter and allow me to present my children and grandchildren to you."

A sea of faces approached me and bowed down before me, some lingering far too long up and down the length of my beautiful gown. There were men and women, boys and girls and several young men who appeared to be as old as my cousins. They were all dressed in the finest clothing I had ever seen.

Grandfather was the only one who fluently spoke my native language, so he introduced each of them by name and position in the family. I was desperate to know which one was to be my husband. I prayed it would not be the one with the crooked mouth who seemed to undress me with his eyes, but rather the one who was introduced last of all. The one with the shy smile and eyes that shone with warmth and compassion. Surely it was not the youngest son who was not much older than I?

Grandfather Jidu gathered everyone together and told us to take our seats at the table, for the feast was about to be served. I was ushered up toward the head of the table with a lovely woman on my right and a man who appeared to be her husband on my left. Directly across from me sat the young man named Misha, the one with the shy smile.

The table was covered in exotic smelling dishes. I had no idea what many of them were. Others I recognized the aromas I knew from the market where auntie and I had spent many hours discovering new flavors and spices. She had taught me about saffron, nutmeg and cloves, all of which filled the air of the elaborate banquet hall. There were giant platters of stuffed eggplant, pistachio chicken, brightly colored melons, almond puddings, breads, cheeses and lamb shanks. My mouth watered as I stared at the feast before me. I had never dreamed of being seated at a table this lavish, much less being treated as the guest of honor. In my wide-eyed, dazed expression, Jidu asked if I was feeling well. I swallowed my trepidation and explained that I was simply a little overwhelmed, but yes, I was feeling fine and my hunger was growing by the moment. This elicited a smile from his lips and more conversation from the others, presumably to ask what it was I had said to make him smile.

It was explained throughout the dinner that Misha was the eldest grandson, the son of Avila and Samir. There were two other sons, Zain and the younger Jamal. Avila was the only child of Grandfather, whom they called Jidu, and his beloved Myriam. Myriam had passed away two winters ago when the cold came into her lungs and took her life. Grandfather described Myriam with great affection and tears shining in his eyes. He explained that Myriam was from a village not far from mine and was brought to him when she was just about my age. He said it was out of love and respect for his beloved Myriam that he had searched the region and came to find me for his grandson's wife.

Misha, being the oldest son, was expected to enter the military and go off to war for one year on his eighteenth birthday. Before he left, he was to take a wife so that when he returned, he could build his family while he prepared to assume the role of leading his grandfather's empire.

He continued by saying that he did not wish to find a wife for his eldest grandson from among their own people, but rather from a tribe which held to the ancient ways of Misha's grandmother. This young woman would then learn their Syrian ways of being a proper wife and mother when the time was right.

Jidu explained that we would not marry right away but take time to get to know each other, but by my fifteenth birthday, I would become his bride. I would be educated in the ways of their people, taught the language they spoke, and learn all the skills needed to become a model wife in order for the family dynasty to continue. I heard some of what was being said but took hold of the fact that I would not become a wife for over two more years. My heart exploded and I again wondered if my auntie was praying to her God, for me.

The voices around me got louder and louder as the children talked among themselves and the grown-ups passed the wine around the table. From time to time, I could feel the heat in my cheeks as I sensed the eyes of my future husband stealing glances at me from across the table. His eyes were a dark chocolate color that sparkled when he spoke. He had a strong jawline and perfectly straight, white teeth that were revealed in his frequent smiles. His hair was thick and wavy—black, the color of a midnight sky. He was tall with broad shoulders and a physique that seemed far older than his sixteen years. I barely tasted the exotic foods before me, but instead tried to wrap my mind around what the next few years would look like. I would be educated, I would learn a new language, and I would try to fall in love and entice my new husband to love me in return.

I was wondering how an almost thirteen-year-old girl falls in love when I heard a distant voice calling my new name, "Myree, Myree. Are you enjoying your meal?" Jidu asked, bringing me back to the present.

"Yes, yes, of course. It's delicious, thank you," I stammered, remembering my manners.

After what seemed like an eternity, I was ushered up the grand staircase again to the spacious room that had now become my new home. Zara undressed me and carefully wiped my face with cream to remove the make-up that made me look like my mother. I climbed into the giant bed and cried myself to sleep, remembering the soft voice of my auntie humming her favorite *Love Song to Yahweh*.

CHAPTER 10
Myree

My New Life

THE MORNING BROUGHT the sunshine streaming across the floor as my eyes tried to focus on the four posters which held together the bed I slept on. The fabric draped across the top was like a ceiling of soft pink clouds. I looked around my new surroundings and found them to be even more luxurious than I had dared to dream of the night before. Had it really been less than twenty-four hours since I had arrived, been welcomed into a new family and met the man I would marry in less than three years?

I rubbed the scratchy sleep from my eyes and sat up in the bed just as Zara entered the room carrying a tray of beautiful fruits and bread. The smell was heavenly, and I smiled at my new friend who was like an angel sent from God to keep me from bursting into tears every time my mind raced backwards or forwards. She clapped her hands and beckoned me into the bathing room. She rinsed me quickly in the scented water and gave me a dress to put on with a sash to tie at my waist. She quickly braided my hair and then set me in front of the large picture window to eat my breakfast.

I wondered what this new day would hold in store for me. Before I had time to swallow that thought, the young man from last night who spoke my language came in. He spoke with Zara and then told me this morning I would begin my language studies. I would then work in the kitchen learning the customs of Syrian cooking and then would be taken on a tour of the grounds with Misha and a chaperon, of course. I wanted to ask him a million questions but just as I opened my mouth, he turned and left the room.

How I longed to speak with someone who understood my words, who could tell me that everything was going to be all right and give me some measure of comfort that I desperately needed. I resolved, as I chewed the sweet and juicy red plum, to study hard and learn as much as I possibly could so I would not be at such a disadvantage. I was ever so thankful Uncle had taught me how to read from the ancient parchments but wondered if that would help me to learn a whole new language.

I gestured to Zara with my hands to try and get her to understand that I thought the food was delicious and I was very grateful to her for taking such good care of me. She only smiled and shyly looked away. One more reason to learn this new language that I would soon begin speaking; so that my new friend would know how much I appreciated her in every way.

After she cleared away the tray of food, we made our way down the curved staircase. I was taken by a middle-aged woman who pulled my arm just a little too hard as we walked across the courtyard to what appeared to be a school room. She did not smile but motioned me to sit in front of her as several other kids about my age gathered at the open windows. I could barely see them, but I could sure hear the whispers and the giggles. She shooed the children away and began writing on a wall what was probably the letters of the alphabet. She said them in a foreign tongue and then pointed to me. I repeated them dutifully and when I mispronounced something, she glared at me and made me repeat it over and over again until my throat was dry.

It seemed like I sat there forever until finally Zara came and took me to the kitchen where I sat at a small table in the corner and ate some roasted meat and cheese. My mouth was parched so the cool liquid I was served was like nectar, and I drained my glass again and again. Zara smiled as two more women my mother's age clapped and motioned me over to where they were rolling out dough on a flat surface. Finally, something I knew about, and I began expertly kneading the dough and forming it into small cakes. The women stood back and surveyed me with smiles playing at the corners of their mouths. I could have stayed there all day, remembering the way my auntie would dust my hands with flour and then sprinkle a little in my hair and laugh as I chased her around with flour in my hands.

The hours flew by too quickly and soon Zara was there again to take me back to my room to change for my afternoon with Misha. I had tried

37

not to think about it all day, but my mind kept drifting back to the time when I would walk beside the young man whose wife I would become. I was both utterly terrified and strangely intrigued. What would he be like? Kind and gentle or distant and harsh? I feared the worst but silently prayed that Yahweh would have mercy on me and send me a man like my uncle who was smart, kind, funny and tender all at the same time. A girl could dream, right? Who knew, perhaps Yahweh was still up there watching out for me. I realized it could have been so much worse had I been sold as a temple prostitute or a slave. I bowed my head and thanked Him for being so gracious to me, asking for just a little more mercy with this man who was to be my new husband.

CHAPTER 11

Auntie Naomi

My Broken Heart

IT HAD BEEN seven long nights I had lain awake and wondered what had really happened to my Sweet Mary, the niece who had become like a daughter to me among my five sons. Each night I wept and grieved, replaying the scene in my mind wondering what I could have done differently to keep my weak-willed sister and mean-spirited brother-in-law from taking Sweet Mary away from us. Should we have fought them, called the elders of our village, offered them money to keep her? What could we have done? The look on my sister Mira's face told me everything I needed to know as I confronted her three days after Sweet Mary had been ripped from my heart. I should have gone earlier, but my youngest son was feeling feverish and my husband told me it was none of my business. He said Mary was not our child, and I needed to let her go. He promised she would return, after some time like she always did. But I knew in my broken heart: this time something was different. I saw something dark and sinister in those black eyes of my brother-in-law. That, and the fact that my sister would not look at me made my stomach churn until I could stand it no longer.

I started out for the village next out ours to see my Sweet Mary and take her back with me once and for all. As I got closer, I could see the once neatly kept home had become a broken-down pitiful site. It seemed my Sweet Mary's belongings were in a discarded basket in the front yard and I could hear the sobbing of my sister from outside the home. I could barely make my feet move forward as the dread in my heart began to grow.

What had they done to my Sweet Mary? She was such a precious child with the golden green eyes and the long, rich chestnut hair; a child whose trust had been shattered so many times. Still, her joyful spirit shone in the golden flecks of sunshine reflected in her eyes. I had been crying out to Yahweh for the last four days since she had been taken from us, begging Him to keep her safe and hold her in the palm of His mighty hands. I prayed harder as I approached the door and peered in. My broken sister lay weeping in the corner of the cot, the stench of alcohol filling the room. The disarray of the place told the story of violence and poverty as well as pain and shame. Sweet Mary was nowhere to be found.

A sob caught in my throat as I imagined the scene the child was exposed to, and my sister was alerted to my presence. She sat up and backed away like a caged animal. My fury dissolved into compassion as I remembered the beautiful young woman she had once been before the darkness of the drink took hold of her. My mind flashed back to our childhood—the two of us sleeping side by side, running and playing together. I bent down and questioned her, but she could barely speak. She wouldn't even look at me, and then finally screamed, "Get out of my home and leave me alone!"

I wanted to shake her and demand that she tell me what happened to Sweet Mary. I feared the worst and already knew in my heart; they had sold her. The beauty of that twelve-year-old girl would command a high price. People who were imprisoned by the cravings that came when the drink was gone were capable of anything. I stifled my sobs until I was in the street again and then fell to my knees weeping for the loss of my Sweet Mary.

CHAPTER 12

Myree

My Future Husband

AS I TOOK each step down the staircase, the fear rose in my throat and I could taste the anxiety on my lips. There at the bottom was Misha, eyes downcast and feet shuffling back and forth. Perhaps he was more nervous than I was, but that could not be as he was a handsome teenage son of a wealthy family with a destiny to fulfill. I was but a child who had been sold by her parents. There could be no doubt as to which one of us was more nervous, and the heat I felt in my face betrayed my innermost feelings. I wanted to turn and run back up the giant marble staircase and crawl under the soft blankets of the enormous bed and never come out. Just then Misha held out his arm for me to take and I found myself in step with him moving along the cool, polished floor.

We were followed at a short distance by two women who spoke in hushed tones I could not understand. Just when I thought this was going to be a very long tour, Misha spoke to me for the very first time in broken but very understandable Aramaic. I was shocked and elated, jumping up and down with delight. My excitement was met with the glare of the two chaperons and I quickly quieted my soul and began asking Misha questions; "How do you know my language?" I asked.

He explained that as the eldest grandchild, his grandmother had taken him under her wing and spent many hours teaching him and telling him the stories of her homeland and her youth. He spoke of the love she lavished on him and how they would spend hours in the orchards together when she was still alive. He said his grandmother was more of a mother to him than his own mother. He explained that his mother, Avila, was always taking care of his brothers and having to perform required duties of the estate. Therefore, she often did not have the time for him.

"Of course, she loved me, but Father kept her very busy and then my brothers came along," Misha clarified. "Grandmother was kind and gentle and spoke of when she was a child and about her God, the God Yahweh, who made the heavens and the earth. She taught me about the soil and how I needed to tend it in order for it to produce fruit. Her love for all things of the earth has been buried in my heart, and someday I hope to be able to grow food that will feed the whole world."

My mind could not fathom what was being said by this handsome young man who knew about my God. Surely God Almighty was watching over me and had even brought me a husband with whom I could speak, as well as learn from. My heart beat a little faster as I asked question after question. Finally, he stopped to look into my eyes and smiled at my inquisitive nature. My heart did a somersault in my chest and I'm sure my face was as red as the apples on the trees we walked by.

The hours seemed to fly by and soon it was time for us to part ways and prepare for the evening meal. I could not believe my good fortune and silently thanked Yahweh for how He had smiled down upon me in this new turn of events in my life. We parted ways with Misha inviting me to join him on another walk the following day, which I gladly accepted.

I could feel his eyes upon me as I was ushered up the grand staircase and dared a glance backwards as I ascended. The warmth of his smile filled my heart with joy and I nearly ran the rest of the way up the stairs.

I danced into the room where Zara was waiting for me. I poured out the whole story to her, and though I knew she did not understand my words, she beamed at me with a smile that filled the room. We danced around the room together giggling and laughing at my exceedingly good fortune.

CHAPTER 13

Zain

The Fury Builds

I COULD SEE my brother and the Little Beauty from my hiding place behind the barn. I watched as she looked intently up at him while he spoke to her in her own language. Her smile lit up the sky and she was more radiant in the light of day than she had been the evening before. Though I was only one year younger than my brother, Grandmother had never paid much attention to me because she was too busy walking with Misha in the orchards. She never taught me the language of her youth the way she did to my brother. I was left with the old nannies while my mother nursed my baby brother and Grandmother doted on the favored son of my father. I seemed invisible and found ways to stay out of their path. I only spoke when I was spoken to.

Soon my heart was closed to those who called me family. I did not need them, nor did I want them to pretend they loved me. I would not receive the love that was lavished on my younger brother and the attention and affection that was poured onto my older brother. Just because I was born with a slight imperfection on my upper lip, they should not have treated me as if I did not matter, as if I was invisible. They pretended to show me affection, but I knew in my heart—the same way that I hated my reflection in the mirror—they all hated to look at me as well. I hated them too, especially Misha, the golden child, heir to the throne and Father's favorite.

There was a time when we were young boys and things like my appearance did not seem to bother him. We would run, play, and wrestle just like other families. As the years passed and my mouth twisted so that

43

my speech became difficult to understand, Misha always understood what I was saying and would try to speak for me. I began to resent my older brother when Father would question Misha about what I had just said. This allowed him to not have to address me personally or even look at me for that matter. I felt the anger being born in my soul and my brother became the target of my rage. When he tried to get me to play with him, I knew it was just pity he felt, causing more hatred in my heart for his perfectly formed mouth. I would provoke him into fighting with me, hoping I could smash his mouth bloody, and he too, would be imperfect like me.

Year after year he grew stronger, smarter, and more eloquent. At the same time, I fought with everything in me to speak as if my mouth was not misshapen and twisted, but rather perfect like his. Though they took me to different doctors to try and fix me, it only made matters worse. I was told it was hopeless—that I was hopeless—and I would never be perfect like my brother.

I found myself retreating more and more into my own safe darkness, a world where I didn't care what people thought of me, and I could be alone with my anger and envy. Even now I feel invisible, just as I have always been and that's the way I want it to stay. Someday they will see me—really see me—and then they'll be sorry. Now, hearing my brother speaking in another language, the anger again raged inside of me.

I flashed back in my mind to the night before when I first laid eyes on the Little Beauty. Her golden green eyes were shy as she felt my eyes upon her body, and she turned her head away. Was that revulsion I saw in those eyes before she quickly looked down? She would be no different than anyone else who looked at me and tried not to stare, but in disgust, averted their eyes. I was mesmerized and could not take my eyes off her. Now, in the sunlight, her hair was so shiny that my hands shook with the idea of running them through it. I could imagine her bare before me and I secretly smiled.

I watched and followed them as they walked in the orchard speaking words I did not understand. When she laughed, it was like the song of the birds singing in the trees. My brother was already falling for her. I could see it in the way he stole glances at her and quickly looked away. If she was mine, I would stare deeply into her eyes and never look away. I had to stay hidden, lest the two old hags who followed them saw me and chased me away. I would not miss one second of this show or any other opportunity I had to fix my eyes on the most beautiful thing I had ever seen. My brother was too weak, too timid for someone like her. She deserved a real man, someone like me to be her husband. If only there was a way ....

CHAPTER 14

Mira

My Shattered Soul

MY HEAD POUNDED as the night before came slowly into focus. I reached up and touched the side of my face that was swollen and tender. The air reeked of stale wine and the tangled sheets told me the story that had become my life. I lie in the filth, the shame and disgust waking up inside my heart once again. Last night the man who was usually decent to me was in a foul mood and took it out on me. He yelled at me saying I was nothing but a whore and I should have at least cleaned up a bit knowing he would be coming over. He finished the last of his bottle and struck me on the face before taking me by force. I was surprised to see the coins which were left on the table, and I imagined that his conscience had gotten the best of him. It was just enough for a little food and some more of the drink that would allow me to continue the lifestyle of selling myself for one more day.

Looking around my broken-down home, I was horrified to realize what my life had become. After I watched my only child being taken away on the back of a donkey, I wailed from the depths of my broken heart, begging my husband to go after her and get her back from the men to whom we had sold her. He cursed at me, slapped me across the face and finished the flask of dark liquid. He walked out of the door that had been our home and I haven't seen him since.

The only person I recognized in my drunken haze was the sister who had stolen the love of my only child. She stood in my home several days after I had sold my very own soul, expressions of hatred, disgust, pity, and compassion written all over her face. She tried to come near me, but I recoiled like a snake. I wanted to lunge at her, but instead screamed at her to get out of my home. I could hear her sobs coming from the window that looked onto the street where she fell in her anguish.

I can't remember how long it has been, but the shame in my soul demands that I keep drinking the dark liquid so I can forget. Since my husband left me, I have found the only way I can get the drink I need, is to open my door and my legs to the strangers who are passing through the village.

It was one day not long ago, a man at the market asked me where my husband was. I had no answer, so he followed me home and gave me more wine than I needed to lie down with him. He was kind and left me a loaf of bread and a few gold coins. I don't know how it happened but somehow the word got around. After that, it seemed the men were always showing up at dusk, holding the bottle I craved. In the morning, I could barely remember anything, except that the stickiness between my legs reminded me of my filthiness. I needed the drink in order to drown out the sound of my precious Mary's screams as she was thrown atop that grey donkey and taken away from me forever. My mind tortured me as I pondered her fate. Was she too being sold to dirty, disgusting men whose breath reeked of wine? Was she safe in the care of a husband who saw the beauty inside her? Was she even alive? These thoughts tormented my soul every moment of my pathetic existence. Each day it became harder and harder to get out of bed. My thoughts haunted me, wishing only for death to come and take me away.

CHAPTER 15
Myree

Sharing My heart

THAT EVENING, I knew Zara would take special care with my preparations before the evening meal where I knew I would again see my future husband. Since arriving back in my rooms, I replayed the conversations we had during our time together walking in the orchard. The fact that he could actually speak my language was nothing short of a miracle sent from heaven. Though he was shy at first in attempting to communicate with me as we walked, I could feel him relaxing and being more courageous to speak the tongue his grandmother had taught him so many years before. When he told me he was feeling like a *tree* whenever he thought about going off to war, I had to stifle a giggle and did not want to ask him about what he was really feeling, knowing he certainly would think I was making fun of him if I dared to correct his mistake. My heart wondered what it was he was truly feeling, as it was less than two years before he would have to leave his home and everything familiar and go to a foreign land. That thought pierced my soul as I realized I did, indeed, know what he was feeling as I too, had just left my home and been taken to a foreign land where my whole life had changed.

My mind wandered back to my auntie's home, and I could smell the fresh bread baking over the crackling fire and hear my annoying cousins arguing outside the window. My throat constricted and I blinked back the tears that threatened to escape. I could not allow myself to sink into the place of despair, but I had to remind myself of how fortunate I was to have been brought to this palace and treated with such kindness. I knew in my heart I was one of the lucky ones. I heard the stories of what had happened to girls like me who were sold into slavery or used as temple prostitutes by any man who had a coin to pay to satisfy his lusts. Other girls were sold and married off to men as old as grandfathers. They were beaten by the wives of the grandfathers and treated as household trash until the next time the grandfather needed to vent his rage on them.

No, I had to remind myself constantly that Yahweh was looking after me. Perhaps one day, when I was the wife of Misha, I could then return to my homeland and once again experience the warmth of my auntie's embrace. Yes, I would focus my thoughts on that day in the not-too-distant future when I would become someone. The day when I would have a voice, a time when my opinions would count. Until then, I had to have a plan to make sure nothing would get in the way of me becoming the beloved wife of the heir to the family dynasty. I had to make sure Misha would fall in love with me and treat me with the love and respect that was obvious in his parent's marriage. I would be demure, thoughtful, kind and loving to ensure my position was secure so that one day I would be able to be reunited with my own family.

This was my goal, and though I felt my cheeks growing warm at the thought of Misha falling in love with me, I had to make sure that I was in control of my emotions so I could guarantee my future.

My thoughts were interrupted when Zara beckoned me over to the warm water she prepared for me. I submitted to her care and then soon found myself descending the marble staircase to an awaiting Misha. He stared openly at me before averting his eyes. I realized I had achieved the affect I was looking for.

I smiled shyly as he escorted me to the dining hall. I was seated in between my fiancé's two brothers: Jamal, the youngest, was on my left; Zain, the middle son, on my right. The younger was probably just a couple years my junior and Zain, was just a year behind Misha. I tried not to stare and quickly looked away as I caught Zain leering at me. He was the one who I had felt was undressing me with his eyes the first night of my arrival. I thanked God that he was not the one destined to be my husband. I shifted in my seat when he leaned his body next to mine. When he tried to speak, he covered his mouth; but I could still feel his hot breath on my ear. I moved as close to Jamal as I could and desperately looked at Misha to come to my rescue. Suddenly, I heard Jidu's angry voice, and then Samir, Misha's father, shouted directly at Zain. Though I could not understand what was said, Zain's face grew red, his eyes narrowed, and his twisted mouth became a sort of devious smile that gave me chills up and down my spine. I was visibly shaken but tried to appear normal as I did not want Zain to sense the fear which had just taken hold of me. I placed food in my mouth and chewed, but tasted nothing.

The conversation was lively around me. Occasionally Misha or Jidu addressed me in my native tongue and I answered as politely as possible. I could not shake the feeling that evil was sitting right beside me and vowed to never be alone in the same room with Zain.

After what seemed an eternity, the meal was over, and I was allowed to return to my quarters. After Zara tended to me, helping me out of my gown, cleansing my face of the makeup and braiding my long hair, I climbed into the softness of the bed. Oh, how I longed for someone to talk with and share my confusion and fears. I lie on the bed and tossed and turned for what must have been hours.

Finally, I got up and went to the window and looked up at the night sky. I opened the door and inched out onto the balcony that connected my room with the trees and black canopy. The stars were twinkling in the same way they did in Nazareth. My cousins and I would often lie outside in the summertime when it was too hot to sleep. We would look up, trying to count each star until we ran out of numbers. A gentle breeze touched my skin and I wondered if Yahweh was up there somewhere looking down on me.

The hot tears started to flow, and I let them burn down my face onto my nightgown without stopping them. I felt the pain of my mother and father's betrayal; the loss of my auntie, uncle and cousins, who were the only real family I had known. I relived the scene of being dragged across the yard where my earthly possessions lie in a discarded basket, and then being thrown over the back of a grey donkey. I again felt the slap of the mean-eyed woman's hand across my face as the other girls watched in horror. My mind raced on without an end in sight. The fear, confusion, anger, dread, and sadness all came crashing down on me and I sobbed from the depths of my being.

When my tears had exhausted themselves, I sat for the longest time staring out at the night sky. Below me something moved and caught my eye. Was it one of the dogs or cats that roamed on the property? Was it something else ... or *someone* else? A chill took hold of me and I quickly retreated to my bed and pulled the heavy covers over my head and prayed for sleep to come.

CHAPTER 16

Zain

My Plan Begins

ANOTHER NIGHT OF being humiliated by my father as he reprimanded me in front of the family. All I did was lean over and whisper into the Little Beauty's ear and before I knew it, all eyes were on me—eyes of disgust and pity and now even anger.

"Do not dare to even think of speaking to Misha's future bride," my father's voice boomed across the table.

How dare he scold me in front of her, treating me as if I were a servant and not his second son. What was I supposed to do, pretend that she wasn't just inches from me, and I could not smell the fragrance of lavender and vanilla which rose from her skin? Her nearness was intoxicating. Even though I could feel my brother's eyes boring into me, I could not help but lean close and whisper in her ear that she was the most lovely thing I had ever seen. I knew she would not understand me, but my heart was racing, and I could not stop myself.

Though I wanted desperately to place my hand on her leg under the table, I knew that would be more than my father would tolerate, so I kept my hands above the table so I was not tempted beyond what I could bear.

After that, I did not hear another word being spoken around the table, my brain exploded in my head and I could see only red and feel deep hot anger coursing through my entire body. My mind was now set on vengeance. Someday, I would not have to take being treated like the dog they all thought I was. It seemed my family's only goal was to see me destroyed once and for all. I was the pitiful brother who was not even allowed to speak. How they must despise me and long for me to disappear.

The look in my father's eyes told me everything I already knew. He wished I had never been born and was too ashamed to even look at me with my twisted mouth, and deformed face. I was a disgrace, and everyone knew it. The rage inside of me blocked out the voices and I ate voraciously everything that was placed in front of me. I tried to focus only on the food, but her nearness was driving me to the brink of insanity. As soon as it was acceptable, I excused myself and hurried into the dark night. I walked quickly until I was out of sight, and then my feet began to carry me into the fields where the Little Beauty had walked only hours earlier. I ran until my lungs were on fire and then fell to the soft earth, screaming with all the rage left inside me. I hated my father, and the way my mother remained silent while I was shamed. I despised my perfect brother and felt nothing but contempt for the grandfather who would not even acknowledge me. I seethed with fury and vowed that someday they would all be sorry. Their treatment of me would not go unpunished and I would one day have the respect and admiration I deserved.

I lay on the cool dirt for what seemed like hours and then began to walk, aimlessly at first, but then as if a magnet were drawing me, I found myself in the one place my heart desired: as close to the Little Beauty that I could get. I sat below the open windows, hidden in the bushes where I could see the breeze moving the curtains in her quarters. As I stared up at the open windows, suddenly she appeared on the balcony as a vision. The gods must have been smiling on me to be this close and not have to move away or take my eyes off her. It was dark and still, until I heard what sounded like weeping.

I remained as quiet as I could and listened as my Little Beauty began to sob, deep cries of anguish that sounded like an animal who was wounded and near death. I listened and felt a stirring in my whole body. Her pain was powerful, and I understood her emotions. I had experienced the same raw pain, yet never allowed it to come out. All my emotions were stuffed so deep inside me they had hardened and turned my cold heart to stone. What she was allowing to pour out, I had locked away deep inside my soul and no one would ever see. Was it sympathy or disgust that had my whole body shaking? Did I feel a connection to her pain which so closely resembled my own? Her pathetic weakness sickened me, for she had nothing to cry about.

She was perfect, just like my brother and soon they would be married and live happily ever after. How dare she vent her emotions as if she understood what real pain and anguish felt like. She had never been tormented by her own reflection, never felt abandoned by the only people in the world who were supposed to love and take care of her … or did she? I listened for a long time until her tears were spent, and the air grew quiet. I moved to get a better view to see if she was still above me. The bushes shifted from my weight and she peered down as if looking for me before quickly retreating into her room. I crawled back under the cover of the branches and sat remembering the sound of her cries. My stone-cold heart began to beat again, and after a time, I walked back to the house confused, and yet more intrigued than ever by my brother's fiancé.

CHAPTER 17

Myree

Time Moves On

THE DAYS BECAME familiar, as each one tumbled into the other. Mornings would find me bathed, dressed, fed and waiting for my schooling to begin. I found myself eager to learn and enjoyed the approval of my teachers. I was proficient in math and took a special interest in the gardening as I knew it was Misha's passion.

Afternoons were enjoyed in the warmth of the kitchen where I excelled in the new-found arts of Syrian cuisine. My smiles were reflected back to me as I hummed the *Love Song to Yahweh* while I rolled out the dough, just as my dear sweet auntie had done. I found my tune being shared by my new friends in the kitchen, and together we created new recipes which were well received by all who enjoyed them. The hours flew by and before I knew it, I was strolling in the orchards with my soon-to-be-husband.

Though I wanted to share my growing talent for his own native language, Misha insisted we speak my native tongue so I would not forget the language of my childhood. While I shared that I desperately wanted to be as fluent in his language, he shared that he also wanted to be more fluent in mine. We smiled at each other and I came to the understanding that he did not want me to become something I was not, only all I could possibly be. With each step we took, my appreciation, intrigue and enjoyment of this young man grew, and I found myself eagerly looking forward to the hours we were able to spend together walking in the orchards and vineyards.

When Misha questioned me about my parents, he saw the look of horror on my face and when the tears glistened in my eyes, he regretted his questions, apologized, and quickly changed the subject. My heart was not yet ready to share the deepest shame of my short-lived life—the betrayal and abandonment which continued to haunt me day and night. I found myself instead talking about my times spent in Nazareth with my cousins and the auntie and uncle who were more like parents to me than my real mother and father. I spoke of how I knew the well-traveled paths that led from our village to theirs. I shared of how I would keenly listen for the sound of my auntie's voice as I neared the home, and then break into a run before being swept into her arms. I told him of my cousins teasing and how I learned to read at my uncle's knee, as well as the way I knew just where to hide so that I could hear the Rabbi's teaching without being seen. I talked of my love for the loom and how I adored the woman whose name I shared. I described the beautiful Mary, and how she wove the most exquisite garments I had ever seen with such masterfully skilled hands.

Misha listened carefully to my stories of the cousins pulling my braids, while trying to coax me outside to play with them. He was intrigued by their protective words to anyone who would dare to comment on my reluctance to speak or make eye contact. They would defend me fiercely saying I was too smart to speak or look at those who were so inferior to me. I recalled to Misha how my heart smiled, and my confidence grew under the watchful eyes of my tender cousins' care.

Then I spoke of our journey to Passover. Each time I paused to take a breath, Misha would stop mid-stride and fasten his eyes on me, as if terrified I wouldn't continue. He was mesmerized by the stories of my former life and questioned me about the sights, smells and sounds of every detail of the Feast of Unleaven Bread. I was thrilled to remember and recount every vivid detail of those glorious days and of the world I once knew. Yet later, when I was alone with my thoughts, the memories would pierce my soul and I would weep bitter tears of longing. I would never allow Misha to know how his questions often brought me deep heartache. Because in some small way, I felt with each telling of the stories, a little part of my shattered heart began to heal. His questions allowed me to trust that the God of Abraham, Isaac and Jacob had not really forsaken me, but had indeed been watching over me. I could believe Yahweh took delight in seeing me tell the stories of reading the ancient scrolls of the Mishna to this foreign young man who was hungry to learn about the God of my ancestors.

I too was filled with questions for my husband-to-be and would relentlessly ask about the customs of his parents, the laws of the land, and what the future held for him as the leader of his grandfathers' empire. He would regale me with tales of his mother and fathers' love as told to him from his grandmother. I was fascinated by their wedding feast which lasted for over a month and how people from faraway lands traveled to attend this most special event. Then Misha would shyly share his heart and his desire to have a marriage ceremony and relationship like his parents who seemed so in love even after all these years. My mind could not fathom what that would look like, and yet the reality loomed ahead in my near future.

Misha would speak passionately about his dreams to build a home of his own on the land above the vineyards and orchards, so that each morning he could awake and see the growth that the night had produced in each vine and branch. Whenever the subject of his brothers arose, Misha's face would cloud over when Zain's name came to his lips. He would beam when talking about little Jamal. He laughed out loud at the antics of his baby brother and the joy the child had brought to the family. He frowned and told me about the unfortunate disasters that had occurred when the doctors had repeatedly tried to correct Zain's crooked mouth. "The despair my mother and father felt was heartbreaking," he said. "They knew their middle son would be permanently disfigured." He paused and then continued. "This scarred the entire family and soon everyone began looking at Zain with pity and sadness instead of the love and acceptance he deserved." His voice was barely able to share his own heartache over seeing his once happy little brother begin to retreat and build a wall around himself so that no one could ever hurt him again. Misha shared how he had not been able to reach Zain for several years and now there was only a tolerated silence between them. He knew Zain was jealous and envied his chosen, favored position as the first-born son, but what Misha could not understand was the hatred he often saw simmering in his brother's eyes. Misha would wipe at his eyes while walking along recalling the close relationship he once shared with Zain, and then whisper how he longed to have the closeness with his brother restored. Though he tried to speak to his father about allowing Zain to have more involvement in the family business, his father would always change the subject and refuse to entertain the idea.

Misha shared that he did not comprehend how a father could reject a child of his own flesh and blood and treat that child with such distain. A dagger pierced my heart as Misha uttered those words and I too felt deep confusion as to how my own father could sell me to strangers for a bag of coins. As my body tensed beside him, Misha sensed that he had touched on something very fragile in his bride-to-be's heart and seemed to tuck this information away in his mind. He was always sensitive to my feelings and was beginning to recognize when he ventured too close to an area of my life that he was not allowed to enter. He was patient and did not want to upset me, stating that his only desire was to win my trust so that someday I would willingly share my deepest hurts with him. Until then, we would enjoy every moment of the time we had together before he was sent off to battle.

CHAPTER 18

Myree

Day at the Market

I WOKE WITH a smile on my lips and remembered today was going to be a very special day. Yesterday my future mother-in-law, the beautiful Avila, came into the kitchen to see me and as she watched my obvious delight in these familiar surroundings, she invited me to go on a journey to the market with her the following day. I had not been to the market since living in my new home, and though I was getting fairly familiar with the customs, dietary laws, and the culture; I was overjoyed to accept the invitation to experience this exciting place first-hand.

I remembered so clearly our markets back in Nazareth with my Auntie Naomi and how we would purchase the spices that would accentuate my uncle's favorite dishes. It was always a thrilling adventure to hear the vendors inviting us in to taste their wares. Smelling the familiar and not so familiar scents that came from all over the region was truly a treat and Auntie would have me close my eyes while she held something under my nose for me to identify the unique smell. Cinnamon, cumin, coriander and turmeric were all fairly easy to name, but Auntie always had one or two that she would introduce me to, explaining the qualities of the particular herb and allowing me to touch and smell it long before I could open my eyes. This was our special time together at the market and I cherished those memories.

I wondered what I would be exposed to today as I walked closely with Misha's mother, the beautiful woman that I so admired and wanted to be like. She would often catch me staring at her across the dinner table.

59

I would then smile shyly and look away, embarrassed by my own lack of manners. She rarely spoke to me whenever we passed in the courtyard.

Until today, I had not had any real opportunity to spend time with her. I was both elated and anxious at the thought of being so near to her and prayed a silent prayer that I would not make a laughingstock of myself by saying something ridiculous in front of her. Would she be pleased with the new language skills I had so painstakingly learned? Would she be impressed at my knowledge of spices? Would she ask me any questions about my past? If so, how would I ever answer her without being evasive or impertinent?

Zara helped me dress with care because of the importance of this day. She helped me to pick out just the perfect robe that was both ornate yet understated. I wanted to make my new mother-in-law proud of me and wanted to appear more grown up than my twelve years allowed. My body was starting to change, and the new robe was tied around my middle with a sash that accentuated my small waistline. The color was a burnt orange, the shade of the sweet potatoes I knew Misha's mother enjoyed. My hair was braided in front and left to hang loosely in curls down my back. I allowed Zara to apply a touch of color to my lips and cheeks and to smudge some kohl around my eyes. It wasn't too much, but enough to bring out the emerald amber flecks that reflected the sunshine.

When the time arrived, I was escorted down the staircase by one of the elderly women chaperons who often accompanied us on any outings. Whether leaving the compound, or within the walls of the home, I was never left alone. On this particular day, I was pleased to see it was the woman with the unruly gray curls whose smile came easily. The same one who would often reach out a plump hand to help me walk when my robe was in the way. She smiled back at me and sensed my excitement at the day's outing, giving me a reassuring nod as I reached the bottom of the stairs. I felt safe with her beside me and was grateful for a familiar face to calm my erratic heartbeat at the thought of spending time alone with the beautiful Avila. I had no idea what to expect as we rode along in the elaborate carriage. Should I try to engage her in conversation? Should I remain silent and demure, speaking only if spoken to?

My mind raced as I breathed in the exquisite scent of her perfume which wafted throughout the carriage. This woman was magnificent and being this close to her was more unsettling and intimidating than I had imagined. I longed for the easy companionship I experienced with my auntie and had to cut off those thoughts before they overwhelmed my mind with sadness. Misha had recently told me he could sense immediately when I was thinking about my homeland or my family because my whole demeanor took on a heaviness that was painfully obvious. When he told me this, I realized I needed to learn how to hide my emotions better. Now, as I remembered those words, I tried to put a mask on my face that would not allow this woman to see I was terrified to be this close to her.

The ride to the market was not long and the only conversation was a few pleasantries exchanged about her robe and the weather. It was a relief to be out of the carriage and into the fresh air, away from her searching gaze. As we walked side by side through the aisles, she took my arm and linked it to hers, keeping me close as the vendors stared wide eyed and open-mouthed at the two of us. Her jet-black hair gleamed in the midmorning sunshine, her cream- colored robe giving her an air of royalty. In contrast, me with my chestnut hair and deep coral robe made us a picture of beauty, and all eyes were upon us both as we strolled through the marketplace. She seemed to enjoy the stares and kept her head high, with barely a nod to anyone we passed. I, however, had learned to make myself invisible when people stared at my unusual hair color or tried to get a glimpse of my unusual eyes. I kept my head lowered as we stopped at the different booths, though I did smile at the children all around us. I sensed my guide to be a little disappointed that I was not enjoying the attention. I loved seeing the children and my heart was filled with joy when I could give a coin to a person in need. Avila chided me a few times to stand straighter and keep my head up. I did my best to obey so as not to offend her, but the stares of the men were making me increasingly uncomfortable. I began to perspire as the agitation in my heart grew.

We stopped by a spice booth and I could relax a little as I breathed deeply of the aromas from my past. I spoke to the vendor, an older lady with gnarled fingers, who held out some cinnamon sticks for me to smell. I complimented her on the fragrance and the obvious quality of her goods. She then rewarded me with a big smile lacking several teeth.

Our accompanying chaperone purchased some of the cinnamon in addition to a few other spices and we moved along into a stall with beautiful

61

handwoven gowns, robes, and shawls in all the colors of the rainbow. I was treated to a beautiful honey colored gown that Misha's mother said would complement my hair. I thanked her profusely and she waved a hand at me as if to silence me in mid-sentence. Had I offended her? Was it not proper to thank someone who had just purchased an expensive gift for you?

I was lost in thought as we approached the Temple where all manner of men and women gathered, some soliciting, others selling animals. Out of the corner of my eye, I noticed a young girl. She had to be a few years younger than I, and when our eyes locked, we recognized each other instantly. It was my dear, sweet Kiera with the violet eyes and hair the same shade as mine. She was dressed in an elaborate gown with her face heavily painted to make her appear older than her mere nine years. I would recognize those violet eyes anywhere. She caught my attention, and every emotion in me wanted to scream and run to her. I was trapped in the arm of my future mother-in-law, being pulled along. When my neck could no longer hold her gaze, my heart shattered at the realization of what her fate had become. Everything in me wanted to tear myself away and somehow run back to rescue Kiera from the awful truth of the nightmare that she was living. I looked back one last time and saw her wiping a tear from her eye, and my heart shattered a little more. All at once guilt and shame overwhelmed me, and I thought I was going to be sick. Why had I escaped such tortuous circumstances while this sweet child was sold into her destiny as a Temple prostitute? It became hard to breathe and I felt hands on my shoulders as I nearly fainted from the emotions overtaking me.

The chaperones held me with arms around my waist while we were ushered back to the carriage. My eyes strained to search the temple steps, but sweet Kiera had disappeared from sight. I felt my throat tighten. The tears that always followed threatened to pour from my eyes. I then sensed the displeasure of the beautiful Avila; therefore, I swallowed hard to regain my composure. Sitting in the back of the carriage was torture as she questioned me over and over about what just happened to me. I stared at her penetrating gaze and stammered a lame excuse about not having eaten enough breakfast that morning. Though I'm not sure she believed me, she let it pass. For some reason, I knew in my soul that it was not safe for me to share the truth about Kiera and me—the deep bond we shared on the night before I was purchased by Grandfather Jidu.

I closed my eyes and leaned my head back against the cushion, trying to formulate a plan to rescue Kiera from the eternal torment in which she was living. The ride back to the compound was quiet, and my mind screamed with the horror of seeing precious Kiera on those Temple steps. I replayed the scene over and over. As our worlds collided, her eyes bore into mine, and I could do nothing except stare back at her and keep walking. The revulsion and the horror at what I had seen (and understood to be true) in those fleeting seconds of seeing Kiera, threatened to bring up my breakfast. Nonetheless, I sat motionless, trying to calm my stomach.

Soon I would be alone in my room and be able to vent my rage at what happened to this beautiful, sweet little girl whose hair color I shared. Until then, I must be polite and again offer my apologies for cutting the trip short. I would be grateful for the gift of the beautiful gown and excuse myself as soon as was properly possible. I had to think. I had to devise a plan to save Kiera from the nightmare she was living. "God help me," I prayed.

Before I knew it, the chaperone handed me over to Zara and I was in my own room. I did not know who I could talk to about this torment I was going through, so I kept it to myself. I allowed Zara to undress me, wash my face, and bring me something to eat before going to bed.

Long after the door closed and the shadows moved across the floor bringing nightfall, I lay motionless in my bed. The scene again replaying over and over in my mind; her beautiful eyes haunting me, silently screaming *help me* as I tried to push away the reality of what had become Kiera's life. As a Temple prostitute, she would be treated to the finest clothing and even medical care, but beyond that, I could not bear to think of what her days and nights would be.

She was just a child, her tiny frame not even close to becoming a woman. She was supposed to be playing with dolls and running with freedom and abandon, not bearing the weight of a full-grown man and being ripped open over and over again by their evil, insatiable lusts.

"Oh God," I cried in agony. "How could You let something like this happen to sweet Kiera with the lovely violet eyes? Why would You forsake this precious child? If only I could trade places with her, I would."

The tears continued to burn my cheeks while I wept for the lost innocence of my first friend in this new strange life of mine. Had it been almost a year since we sat side by side in the corner eating figs and comparing our hair color? What horror had she experienced at the hands of wicked men? "Yahweh, please help Kiera, and show me a way to rescue her," I prayed.

If I told Misha, surely, he would help me rescue her and she could live here as a servant in the house—maybe even as my servant.

Yes, Misha would find a way to save this precious child from the depths of terror in which was living. As soon as I could speak with Misha privately, I would tell him the whole story. But that would mean revealing the secrets of my past. I would have to tell him how I knew Kiera. The whole story of the darkness of my own mother and father and how they had sold me for a tiny bag of coins in order to buy another bottle of the liquid they loved more than me. I would have to confess how I was stripped naked and roughly washed in front of total strangers. No, I could not bear to see the pity in his eyes and feel the shame of being so worthless to my very own parents. Surely, he would never look at me the same way, perhaps even decide that I was not worthy to become his wife. If he changed his mind about me, I would not be able to help Kiera. I may even be sold or abandoned again, and then what would my life become? No, I could not tell Misha, at least not yet, not until I was secure in his love for me. I had to be certain that he would not discard me like all the others before him. I would have to think of another way to rescue Kiera. "Oh God," I pleaded. "Please help me, I don't know what to do."

The shadows outside my window moved with the breeze that blew the branches back and forth. I sat up in my bed as I heard voices outside my door. I dried my tears as Zara and a man I had never seen before came into the room. Zara carried a light and lit the lamps in the chamber. Another servant carried a tray of cheeses, warm bread, some dates and hot tea. The stranger carried a small black bag.

The man motioned for me to open my mouth and proceeded to examine me to make sure I wasn't seriously ill. I assured him as best as I could in my broken Turoyo speech that I was feeling much better and there was no need to worry. After a few more touches to my head, and feeling my heartbeat, he seemed satisfied with my health and left the room. By this time my stomach was rumbling, and Zara urged me to eat some food.

I was grateful I would be spared having to join the family for the evening meal, though I would miss seeing Misha very much. I needed time to myself to think, to figure out a plan to rescue Kiera. I vowed that even if it took me the rest of my days, I would see her delivered from that awful life. I had to make sure I kept that vow.

I tried not to think of the torture she must be enduring at the hands of countless evil men, but every time I closed my eyes, I saw only the haunted look staring back at me across the Temple steps.

CHAPTER 19

Avila

The Mystery of Myree

REMEMBERING THE DAY, I wondered what had gotten into that child at the marketplace? One minute she was gushing over the new gown I just bought for her and the next she was nearly unable to walk as we passed the Temple. She turned white as a ghost and seemed terrified. Had she made contact with one of the many men who were soliciting and calling to us? Was she being truthful about not having eaten enough and feeling lightheaded? I had thought to try and get to know this future daughter-in-law of mine by inviting her to come along to the market; however, the day had been a disaster.

I had been opposed to father's insistence of finding a wife for my eldest son from the land where his beloved Myriam, my mother, was from. I missed my mother since her passing, but truthfully, it was a relief to not have to compete for my son's affections with another woman. My own mother's desire to take my place in my son's heart had hardened me to her charms. I had long stopped calling her Mother but referred to her by her given name of Myriam.

I was a busy wife and mother attending to the duties of a respected woman in the city. Yes, I had left my children alone with her far too often, but she seemed to relish the times when my son would cry and run into her arms instead of mine. Why did she set her heart on my Misha? Why couldn't she be satisfied to bond with Zain or Jamal? I wanted my eldest son to marry a royal girl from one of my husband's own bloodlines, but after years of conversations falling on deaf ears, my husband agreed with his father-in-law's insistence of getting a wife for Misha from the distant land of Jerusalem.

Upon reluctantly agreeing to a foreign betrothal for my son, I dreaded the day that girl would be brought into my home. My father had made several trips over the last year, always coming back empty-handed, saying he had not seen the *perfect girl* for his eldest grandson. When he arrived back from this last trip, I had been away on business with my husband and the household was in an uproar. When I was told by my father that I would meet my new future daughter-in-law that evening at dinner, I had to hide my distaste and smile pleasantly for all to see. I had to make them believe I was in agreement with this arrangement. Of course, Misha was all smiles as his grandfather told him about the young beauty whom he had found to be his wife. Why couldn't Misha be stronger like Zain, and not always have to appear as a puppy dog wagging his tail at his grandfather?

The fact that Zain was so disfigured was just another disappointment I bore deep in my heart. His features were so similar to mine except for the twisted mouth which gave him the appearance of a mongoloid off the streets. After years of me not even being able to look at his hideous face, he stopped coming around. When he had to address me, I sensed his hatred for me coming through the eyes that looked so very much like my own.

What had my life become? Where was the husband who once doted on me with all the affections of a queen? We had long spent nights apart in separate quarters, but had kept up the appearance of a happy couple in front of family, friends and business acquaintances. I needed to keep my father happy until the day when the family empire would be passed down to my oldest son. When Father finally died, I would be there beside Misha to rule with an iron fist. My husband was not strong enough, but I was, and with Misha under my control, now that Mother was gone, I would finally have my way.

This young thing from Jerusalem was pretty enough—well, if I was being honest—the girl was strikingly beautiful. I had to fight the ugly jealousy that threatened to overtake me when I saw my oldest son's pleasure at seeing her for the first time. It was the same look of adoration that he gave to his grandmother for all those years. Why had he never looked at me, his own mother, with those soft, gentle eyes?

I fought the familiar anger at having to again share my oldest son's affections with another woman. I battled the envy of my lost, innocent youth which was so evident in this Myree. I avoided her as much as possible, being polite whenever I encountered her, but soon realized I needed to get to know her. More importantly, I needed to allow this girl to know who I was, and how I was now the true matriarch of the family. Today's outing was to have been a test for the girl to see how she stood up under my searching gaze. The girl had practically been begging for me to throw her a few crumbs, always staring at me when she thought no one was looking. So, when I approached her in the kitchen a few days ago and invited her to go along to the market, the girl was speechless and then stammered that she would be honored to accompany me. Things were going along just fine until we walked past the Temple. The commotion that is always at full volume when men and women are selling themselves is unsettling, to say the least. It really was a horrifying scene, and I had intentionally led the young girl past it to see what type of response it would illicit in her. There was definitely a response, though I wasn't quite certain what triggered the near fainting spell. I would have to pay close attention to this one. I still had another several months and then my precious son would be off to battle and I would have the girl right where I wanted her. I would then set the stage for how things would be when my son returned home. I had it all planned out, and if I was patient, I would get everything I always dreamed of.

CHAPTER 20

Kiera

The Nightmare Continues

THE TEARS POURED down my cheeks, washing away the layers of makeup that had been painstakingly applied hours earlier when my master's slave had prepared me for my duties at the Temple. I had been unable to feel anything after that first encounter all those months ago with the old man who smelled of rotting fish. At almost nine years old, I had only ever heard the sounds that came from behind the curtain where my parents lay. I did not understand my mother's cries or my father's grunts until I experienced them firsthand.

My own body had been torn open by violent thrusts as the man emptied himself into me. I screamed from the depths of my being as the pain ripped through my young body. From that first horrifying experience, my soul had died, and I rarely spoke. I felt a deep, dark sickness growing inside my heart.

Each day would be the same thing and I had learned to block out the pain in my body, the torment in my mind, and the agony of my soul. I walked blindly through my duties lest I be beaten by my owner. I ate little, kept my eyes closed as much as possible, and wished for death every minute of every single day. Until today …. When I locked eyes with Mary, my heart began to beat again. I remembered the kindness of her arms around me while I sobbed terrified tears on the first night we met. Mary shared her heart and how she had the same fears and dread of the unknown as I did; we even shared the same hair color. But when I was sold off before Mary, I did not even get to say goodbye to my new friend. I had thought of her kindness many times since that night and wondered what had happened to her. Was she being violated by strange men every day too?

The answer came today as the same girl with the same chestnut hair as mine walked right past me on the steps of the Temple. Her robe was clean and obviously expensive, makeup expertly applied. Mary's hair was perfectly braided and falling loosely around her shoulders. Her head was held high as she walked arm in arm with a beautiful rich woman and her chaperones. I could not believe my eyes, it was Mary, I was sure of it. And when Mary saw me and our eyes locked, a whole world of emotions were exchanged between us. But Mary just kept on walking. She did not stop. She did not speak. She did not even acknowledge that she knew it was me, Kiera, her friend. My heart died a little more that afternoon, wondering how it was that Mary got to walk past the Temple with a beautiful robe and perfect hair while I was rotting from the inside out a little more each day? What had I done to the gods to make them despise me this much? What favor had been shown to Mary that she escaped this horror that was now my life? The tears that ravaged my painted face were the last bit of my soul dying, and from that very moment, I vowed to live in the hatred forming in my heart.

Pain gripped my arm as a man known only to me as the Master pulled me behind the curtain and breathed his foul breath in my face. I winced but did not cry out as my new-found hatred stared up at his evil eyes.

"What have you done?" He screamed in my face. "Your makeup is ruined, and you look like a silly little girl crying your eyes out. I should beat you right here, but there are customers waiting for you."

My body stumbled forward as he threw me into the hands of the servant who applied the makeup. The fat girl's hands were soft as she took hold of my arm while the man shouted.

"Fix her face and get her back out there as soon as possible!"

I felt the kindness in her eyes and then turned away as the rage burned inside me again. She too, was a part of this darkness, day in and day out, always gentle with the face paint and eyeliner. Was it pity I saw in her beady eyes, sympathy I felt in her plump fingers, or was it jealousy I sensed as she looked down her large nose at me every day? As she continued to apply more makeup, I looked away quickly and focused on the next object of my hatred: the old man waiting for me to lift up my gown.

Later that evening when I was sold to a skinny bald man, I relished the taste of what my growing hatred felt like, and I gave myself fully to it. I lay beneath his bony body and waited, my mind on fire with the outrage of it all. Never again would I hope for a better life, or trust someone to comfort me in my pain. Never again would I think that someone could be my friend. I would hate everyone, and everything. I would look for ways to punish others until the day I could finally be free from this black abyss, in death. No more tears, no more weakness. I must take care of myself now; no one was coming for me. There would be no escape from this nightmare unless I found a way out. From now on, I would shut down any sliver of hope in my heart and stop feeling sorry for myself. I was not the same child I had been all those months ago before my world turned black. No one was going to help me now; I had only myself to rely on and I would survive any way I could. I would lie, steal, and deceive all of these people who obviously hated me. I would hate them back and someday I would have my revenge, even on that beautiful Mary who had walked right by me today, as if I was invisible. She would pay, they would all pay for what they had done to me.

CHAPTER 21

Myree

Falling in Love

THE DAYS PASSED quickly, and the brisk spring air soon warmed to the heat of the summer. My studies continued and every day was a repeat of the day before. I would get up early for bathing. Next, I had my breakfast before moving on to the school room. After my studies I went into the kitchen and finally on to my favorite part of the day—walking besides Misha in the orchards or vineyards.

I was a quick learner and soon was able to speak the language I was being taught. This made things so much easier as I could now understand what was being said all around me, which was often all about me. I learned to keep silent and listen more than I spoke. I found this to be to my advantage as there was much being spoken about me and the future awaiting me as the wife of Misha.

My betrothed still insisted that while we were alone together, we speak only in my native tongue lest I forget the words of my ancestors. He too learned quickly and became more and more fluent in Aramaic. This, he told, me was a perfect way for us to have our secret language of love that only Jidu would understand. We often walked hand in hand through the gardens, stealing glances at each other and offering one another the bounty of the delectable gardens.

Because I had shared with him the game my auntie and I played, he insisted I play the game with him. I would close my eyes and identify the herbs in the garden by scent or touch. When my answers were correct, he would take my hand in his and bring it to his lips, my eyes still closed. This

72

always brought a flutter to my stomach, and I studied harder to make sure I always got every answer right. We would often walk as fast as we could to try to escape the prying eyes of the chaperones. Sometimes we would break into a run, hide in the orchard and then steal a quick kiss before they could keep us apart.

The first time Misha's lips met mine was like an explosion of color going off in my mind and a jolt of electricity hitting my heart that had stopped beating. Though my mind flashed a brief glimpse of darkness from my childhood, my body betrayed me. Breathless, I felt weak in my knees and I could tell Misha felt it too. We were falling in love with each other, each day a knitting of our hearts together in anticipation of our wedding day. Though we would often speak of our future, neither of us knew many details about our upcoming nuptials. Those were to be decided my Misha's mother. Avila kept herself occupied with the planning day and night, stating that our wedding would be the grandest event of the year.

We both shared a growing excitement about our future together and would speak in hushed tones in the presence of others. Whenever Misha wanted to share something privately with me, he would simply speak my native language which, it seemed infuriated his brother Zain. I pleaded with Misha not to do this in front of his brother as I knew from Zain's reddened face how it upset him. Misha, however, was not afraid of his brother though I was terrified of him.

I tried to express my concern one day over the way that Zain often leered at me when others were not looking, but Misha dismissed my words stating his brother was harmless. I knew in my heart he was far from harmless. It was just like when I was a little girl and had to run away and hide, pretending to be invisible when the men of the village would look at me with those same eyes. I knew Zain was someone that I could never be left alone with. I often felt him watching Misha and I on our walks and took care to never sit next to him at the evening meals. I kept my eyes down and never spoke a word to him, even when he learned how to speak the words, *my little beauty* in Aramaic. The first time I heard him say those words to me, I felt my skin crawl and wanted to run and tell Misha but feared this would only cause more division and strife in the family. Because of that, I kept it to myself and vowed to avoid him all the more.

I tried to win the heart of my soon to be mother-in-law, but after the fiasco at the Temple on our first outing, she never invited me to go anywhere with her again. I was left to smile across the table and make small talk whenever she appeared, which was only on very rare occasions. It seemed that as the wedding date approached, she increasingly avoided me. I found this very curious and lived with the shame that I had somehow failed her and would never be the bride she wanted for her beloved first-born son. Though I excelled in mathematics, science, and art, she would still not grant me the honor of conversation and often left the room when I entered.

The wedding celebration was planned without any consideration for my thoughts or feelings and I sensed her growing disdain for me, though I could not figure out why. I continued to try and impress her with my culinary skills or knowledge of the flowers I would pick and give to her. Still, I got no response other than a perfunctory thank you without even a glance my way.

Oh, how I wish Misha's grandmother was still alive. A woman from my homeland who could provide me with the wisdom and insight as to how to win Misha's mother's heart. Though I tried to speak to Misha about it, he could offer no advice, but simply suggested that I continue to try, always encouraging me with his words of affirmation. He was so proud of the way I had grown in the ways of his culture, language, and speech. Often, he rewarded me with a smile that turned my heart to liquid.

My days were spent counting the moments until we could be together in the afternoons, occasionally going for a ride in the carriage. This was always the highlight of our times together, as we could actually be alone for this brief time. On those rare occasions, I begged Misha to take me to the market in the hopes that I could possibly get a glimpse of Kiera on the Temple steps.

He was always reluctant to take me anywhere near the Temple saying it was a place of pagan worship and great evil. I still had not dared to share the drama that had unfolded months before when I first spotted my sweet Kiera. Therefore, I often urged him to take me to the spice booth, the one closest to the Temple. While there, I would position myself to see the Temple steps, focusing on the women who stood at the top waiting for the men. I scanned the steps each time searching for Kiera, but never saw her. After a time, I began to wonder if I had only imagined those piercingly violet eyes locking onto my own. Had it had only been a vision or even a dream? I prayed it was so and that Kiera was spared the horrifying life of a Temple prostitute. Still, I searched and one day even asked a young, plump servant girl if she had ever seen a beautiful violet-eyed child with hair the same shade as my own. Her expression of recognition defied her answer as she shook her head no, looked away, and hurried off. So, I continued to search, each time coming away more defeated and distressed, knowing I had somehow failed my sweet Kiera, too.

CHAPTER 22

Zain

The Darkness Grows

MY MIND WAS consumed with the Little Beauty and I could not eat or sleep. Often, I felt physically sick when I thought of her. On the rare occasions when I could sleep, my dreams were tormented with sounds of her laughter or the strikingly, mesmerizing green eyes that refused to look at me. How in the name of the gods would I ever survive this agony? I had to find a way to make her mine. I replayed scene after scene in my head, watching that brother of mine take my Little Beauty by the hand and steal a kiss while he thought no one was watching. But I was always watching.

I planned my days around their outings and kept myself hidden behind trees and bushes. At night I found myself underneath her bedroom window listening carefully for any sound of her movements. Oh, to hear the cries as I did that first night so many months ago. The weeping that broke my already shattered soul into splinters. After that, there was nothing left of a heart inside of me, only a cold radiating hatred that burned for all the people in my life who had never loved me. Each day I would pretend to be the loyal, dutiful son that my father required, fulfilling the tasks of taking inventory of the olive groves or reporting the status of the stallions in our stables. I had fooled them all. No one knew I was plotting my ascent to the throne and nothing would stand in my way until I had taken what was truly mine. My father could never look at my twisted face, therefore, he never saw the evil residing within me. My mother was so obsessed with her planning the Hassen wedding of the season, she too ignored the pain that continually poured out of me. I was hated, ignored and treated like a servant, invisible to the world around me. But that was just fine. Being invisible allowed me to put my plans in motion, to have what I wanted and get what I needed. Most of all, I would get what I deserved. Someday I would have it all—the estate, the Little Beauty, the money, and finally the respect of everyone I would rule over. Soon it would all be mine. I just needed to be patient and make sure my plan was flawless. Yes, it was all taking shape in my dark heart, and I knew that I would have my destiny. It was just a matter of time.

As I sat dreaming in the barn one afternoon, the black servant of the Little Beauty came in to gather some of the eggs as she did every afternoon. As she caught a glimpse of me, she quickly turned, pretending she did not see me, as everyone did. But I saw her. And in that moment, a rage ignited in my entire body, exploding in my mind. How dare this slave girl treat me as if I did not exist. I would show her who I was. I called out to her and was at her side within a few strides. As she quickened her steps, I took hold of her arm and my hand clamped down on her mouth to stifle the scream that arose from the death grip I had on her arm. The terror in her eyes only heightened my rage and I whispered in her ear, "If you make a sound, it will be the last sound you ever make."

She clearly understood as the tears fell silently down her cheeks. Within minutes she was lying on the straw in a broken mess of her femininity. I had taken what I wanted, and she was powerless to resist me. The fury within had momentarily subsided and I felt a power that I had never experienced before, something raw and animalistic. The true Zain had now emerged and there was no stopping me. I made sure to inflict a fear in the now broken slave girl that would never leave her. I knew she would keep my secret hidden forever, as she promised she would. If not, I would simply kill her, and I would enjoy that too.

CHAPTER 23
Avila

My Painful Past

THE PLANS WERE coming together very nicely indeed. I would host the party of the season—no, of the year—and everyone from far and near would know the House of Hassen was the richest and most powerful in all the land. It did not matter that I would have chosen someone far better than Jidu had chosen for my beloved Misha. Now it was too late, because that little green-eyed child had stolen the heart of my firstborn son. I could see it every time I looked at him. He was just as lovestruck as his father had been in the first few months of our betrothal.

Our marriage was not arranged just as his father's and his fathers before him. I chose whom I was to marry. Fortunately, Samir was kind and gentle and cared for me while we awaited our wedding day. In him I saw the weakness that love created and I knew I could have whatever I wanted if only I played along with the charade. Our celebration was the event of the decade. Was it only eighteen years ago now? My plan was to have three children, all males to ensure the bloodline would be strong. Sadly, it had already been diluted by my foreign mother whom my father had adored and doted on like an imbecile. Unlike her, who could only produce me, a female, I was certain my children would be male. My heirs would be perfect, strong, and handsome, ready to ascend to the throne where they belonged. When Misha was born, he was everything I dreamed of. As a little boy, he was smart and sweet and, so very handsome—the perfect child.

When my body announced that I was with child again after two years,

I weaned my firstborn and awaited the arrival of my second son. After two days of agony in laboring to bring this baby into the world, I knew that something was terribly wrong. This child was fighting me from the inside, and I began to despise this creature that tortured my body and soul.

When finally, he tore into the world, I could feel the life blood ebbing out of me. His silence was deafening, and as I looked at his face, horror gripped me. His eyes shone up at me, but his mouth was a twisted wound that marred every other feature. I nearly dropped him as the midwife rushed to catch him. A deep fear gripped me from within. How could I have created this hideous creature? How could my body have carried anything but perfection? I felt the darkness closing around me and everything went black. Days passed and my nightmare became my reality. It was true. I had given birth to a monster.

His father was almost as shocked as I was about the deformity, but he assured me we would find the best doctors in all the land and they would fix him. But deep in my heart, I knew that it was more than skin deep. There was something else within the child, a capacity for evil that I shuddered to even think of. Though Samir was gentle with me, I could see in his eyes there was a hint of disappointment, as if I had failed him by producing a child that was so hideous to look at.

I pretended to love the child we named Zain and days later, when my milk came in, I found many reasons why I could not allow that mouth to draw life from me. I gave him over to a wet nurse and secretly continued to nurture my firstborn son with the life milk that my body produced. Misha thrived under my loving attention, and while I tolerated the presence of the child Zain, my eyes could not bear to witness the tragedy that he was growing up to be.

Doctor after doctor tried to help, but it was futile. Zain was destined to be marred and disfigured for his entire life. His father treated him kindly and tried not to show preferential treatment to Misha, the beautiful one. But even I could tell there was a reserve that he showed with Zain he never held with Misha. As Misha turned four, I began to wean him again, knowing that I had given him the best of my body. When I recognized the signs of being with child again, my heart was gripped with fear. What if I produced another imperfect heir? My heart and my mind could not bear the thought. My body took naturally to the life growing inside me.

I was careful to eat only the best food, to make sure I slept at least nine hours a night and was waited on hand and foot. My husband treated me with care and gentleness, desperate for me to give him another perfect son like our Misha.

The birth was a far cry from my second child, and I knew everything was going to be fine. Within ten hours I was holding my perfect baby boy, and all was well with the world. This child redeemed the last two and a half years of anguish and blotted out the memory that I had given birth to anything less than perfection.

In an attempt to keep myself from ever having to produce another child, I moved into another wing of the house and kept my husband away from me by sending him beautiful young servant girls. For all intents and purposes, we had a loving marriage to the outside world. In public, I was sure to be the submitted and adoring wife that Samir had known in our early years. Though he tried to win my affections back, I had erected a wall around my heart that I would not allow him to penetrate. I had given him two perfect sons, and I would never allow myself to become pregnant again. Ours was now a marriage in name only.

As the boys had grown, they played together as children do. Misha with his tender heart seemed not to notice his brother's flawed face, and, of course, little Jamal never knew any different. He looked up to both of his brothers with a quiet adoration. They were inseparable for those early years until Zain began to withdraw from any attention his brothers gave him. He rarely spoke, hating the sounds that came from his ugly mouth and the questions everyone had on their lips when they could not understand what he had said. He seemed to grow more and more aware of his disfigurement with each passing day and I sensed a growing hatred in his heart for himself and me, the one who had created him and sentenced him to a life in the shadows.

By the time he was seven years old, Zain had taken to mean and cruel acts against his little brother. Jamal would follow him out to the barn or orchards only to come running back into the house screaming and bloodied, never willing to explain how he had gotten injured. When asked, Zain would simply stare defiantly at his father and say that he had no idea how Jamal had been hurt. After a time, Jamal no longer followed his big brother anywhere, but quietly retreated whenever Zain appeared. I had my suspicions for a while but knew in my heart the child I had given birth to indeed had the capacity for great evil. I had known it from the very first moments I laid eyes on him, some deep connection between his soul and mine that I could not rid myself of even though I tried with everything in me.

By the time he was around ten years old, I would catch him staring at me, or rather staring right through me. I tried to detach myself from him, but I could not understand the hold he had on me. I wanted to despise him. I had tried in my heart to believe he wasn't even mine. But those eyes, identical to mine, spoke to me and we entered into a quiet game of who would look away first. It was always me and he would pierce me with a distorted smile that said, "See, I am more powerful than you will ever be." It was disconcerting and uncomfortable, but as time went on, I could see how he might prove useful to me in the future. And so, our alliance was born.

I would never allow anyone to see Zain and I together alone in the same room but would take to seeking him out in his chambers or in secret places in an effort to climb into his darkened mind and figure out his thoughts. Rarely would he expose his heart, but the pain in his eyes was as real as his disfigured and twisted mouth. He shared about how he knew he was despised by all who looked at his hideous face and how the pity he saw in people's eyes enraged him. He told me he knew I did not love him, and his father barely tolerated him. He would not speak of his Jidu or his older brother, but deep inside, I knew they were the source of his fury. His inferiority to his older brother, Misha, *The Perfect One*, as he called him, was perhaps the biggest source of his hidden anguish. The way Grandfather Jidu doted on Misha, spoke lovingly to him and practically adored him, was a constant reminder of a pain so deep he didn't even know how to untangle his thoughts. So, he kept silent, locking everything deep inside his darkened heart. I did not know quite what he was capable of, so even in our secret meetings, I kept my distance, remaining only for a few minutes each time. I stayed only long enough to assure him of my devotion, but not long enough for him to cast a spell on me with those haunting eyes that pierced my soul.

CHAPTER 24
Auntie Naomi

Soul Anguish

HOW MANY NEW moons had passed since the daughter of my heart had stood next to me humming the *Love Song to Yahweh*? How many nights had I lain awake replaying the day she was taken from our home, the only real home she had ever known? Seeing the tears in my eyes with each question, my sons had stopped asking when their cousin would return. Now they knew better and would not even mention the name of Sweet Mary when I was present.

One day I watched them talking to their father outside while they tended to the animals. My son Joshua asked, "Papa, why hasn't Mary found her way back to our home in such a long time? She has never stayed away for so long, and I should like to see her again."

My husband was stern and lowered his voice as he addressed his boys: "We must never speak of your cousin again. She has gone home with her parents and that is where she will stay. You are not to mention her name in front of your mother ever again. Do you hear me?"

My three sons would not look at their father and could barely be heard saying, "Yes Abba."

I withdrew to the back room and laid down on the straw where I wept countless tears. I had lain silently as the tears streamed down my face every night since I saw my sister. I was ravaged by guilt for the part I had played in whatever had been done to my Sweet Mary. My sister's face replayed in my mind and my anger turned to bile in my mouth. How could she forget the child at her breast? How could she allow herself to be so controlled by the awful drink and her evil husband, that she would not protect her only child? What had become of her now? I did not know the woman who was curled up in the corner, the one who screamed at me to get out of her home. I prayed through my tears the same prayer I had whispered in the darkness every night since that horrifying day: "Oh Yahweh, please protect my Sweet Mary and bring my sister back from the brink of darkness where she lives." I pleaded over and over with the God of my fathers to have mercy on the child and her mother, to hold them both close and remind them that they are both loved dearly by their family, but more importantly by Him, their Maker.

Each week when we traveled to the market, I searched the faces of every young girl. I tapped them on the shoulder to make them turn so I could look into their eyes, desperate to see the unique emerald green and amber reflected in the sunshine that was my Sweet Mary. Mothers stared at me and pulled their daughters away as my husband shook his head and walked ahead of me. My sons also kept their eyes open to see if they could spot their cousin. It was a promise they made to me as one morning I lay on my bed silently weeping. My husband had gone out earlier in the day to tend to the flocks and my oldest son, Josef, came to me and said, "Ima, please don't cry. We will find her; we will not stop searching for her until we do."

I hugged him tightly and made them each promise this would be our secret—we would keep searching and one day, Sweet Mary would return to us.

Though my husband appeared cold and calloused where Sweet Mary was concerned, I know that he too missed her deeply. His desire to cut her from our memories was his attempt to protect us from the suffering we all faced as one season turned into another and still there was of sign of her.

The village women had also stopped asking what had become of the child with the golden green eyes, as each time she was mentioned, I broke down into tears. My dearest friend, Mary, was the only one who gave me comfort and prayed daily for the daughter of my heart. I knew I could speak freely of my pain and trusted her with my shame of not doing something more to protect her. Always, she would turn me back to our God who knows the path of life and allows not even the sparrow to be harmed without His notice.

She would show me the garments she had woven that week, each one more beautiful than the next, and I would picture Sweet Mary, on the night she had received her precious shawl. It always brought a smile to my lips, and my friend would comfort me as together we hummed the tune of the *Love Song to Yahweh*.

CHAPTER 25

Myree

Time Moves On

I AWOKE BEFORE the sun and lay in my bed thinking. The days had turned into weeks and the seasons went from harvest time to damp frigid mornings where it was hard to get out of my warm bed. Zara would always have a fire lit in the corner oven and the bath water heated to an exquisite warmth that would envelope me in its caress.

In just a few short months, I would be married to my precious Misha. I could barely remember how long I had been in my new world. Perhaps Yahweh in His grace had begun to erase the pain of the nightmare I had lived when I was sold by my mother and father. I still longed for the arms of my tender Aunt Naomi, but my world was now consumed with the long-awaited nuptials of the eldest son of the Hassen family. How was it that I was the chosen one to become the wife of Misha?

I had grown up quickly in the last almost two years, and though I had only almost fifteen turns around the sun, I felt I had aged far beyond what any young girl should ever experience. I had known betrayal and rejection that no child should ever know. Yet here I was, immersed in a hot bath being taken care of by a servant who was also my friend. Every day I received training in the art of becoming a wife. I had begun to bleed several months before, so I knew it would not be long before our wedding day would come. I still did not understand all the political aspects of what my new role would be, but I watched my future mother-in-law every chance I got. I prayed I could be half the woman, wife and mother that Avila was.

As Misha and I grew closer, our friendship deepened, and I knew his love for me was true and genuine. As a man of just eighteen, he was gentle and kind to me. One day on our walk, he told me of his love for me. After kissing me passionately, he shared how desperate he was to make me his wife in every sense of the word. When the shock of what he said registered in my mind, I recoiled as if being burned, and I think he realized that I was still but a child. As I began to withdraw inside my shell, he could sense my fear and inexperience. Though I kissed him with eager lips, I was not prepared to give my body to a man; nevertheless, this is what I knew he and the world expected from me.

He tenderly took my hand in his and lifted my chin, allowing him to look into my eyes when he spoke the words, "I promise to be gentle and kind with you when we become one as husband and wife." The fear inside me would not allow him to say anything more. I tore myself from his grasp and ran away as fast as I could. I knew I was being childish, and my fear was unwarranted because Misha had always been kind to me. Yet for some unknown reason, terror rose inside me whenever the thoughts of our wedding night came to my mind. It always triggered something deep inside that I could not fathom. I had glimpses of horror at the thought of a man touching me, and I retreated further inside myself as the flashes exploded inside my brain. I would push the repressed memories from my childhood deeper into the darkness and pretend that everything would be just fine. I was marrying a man who loved me, and I had nothing to fear.

As I lay in the warm water, I recalled his tender smile and knew I was indeed fortunate to be loved by such a man as Misha. I would continue to grow in my education, in my etiquette, and in all the other ways I would need to become the wife Misha deserved. When he left just two days after our wedding, I would miss him desperately and pray daily that Yahweh would keep him safe and bring him back to me when his year away ended. I would spend the time preparing our home and learning how to satisfy my husband in the kitchen as well as the bedroom. I would be ready for his return and look forward to starting a family, giving him many sons. Yes, this was my answer from Yahweh to calm my fears of having my body taken from me on my wedding night in just a few short months. I was filled with gratitude and heard myself humming the *Love Song to Yahweh* as Zara helped me dress and prepare for the day.

Today I would try to have a moment with Avila and ask her about the wedding feast and what I could expect. I had done all I could to find out about all the details of a Syrian wedding, even consulting the scrolls in the library, but still had so many questions.

Having found little to satisfy my curiosity, I sought out Jidu one morning last week in the courtyard. It was our custom to often retreat to the sunroom and enjoy a cup of tea where he would tell me about his Myriam and ask me all about my childhood. I was careful to only share the beautiful parts, though Jidu knew better than anyone how he had come to purchase me at the slave auction. This was our secret, and it was something we never discussed.

On this particular morning, he welcomed me to sit a while and could sense I had something on my mind. I was reluctant to seem ungrateful to this honored man who had been nothing but kind and generous to me, so, with eyes downcast, I asked him what I could expect on my wedding day. I had so many questions about the ceremony, the guests, and the celebration. He reached down to touch my head and pulled my eyes to his with a smile on his lips. He told me that traditionally a Syrian wedding of this magnitude would be a full week of festivities. However, because of his beloved Myriam and her Jewish traditions which were the same as my own, he had argued with Avila and Samir, and won, concerning the nuptials of Misha and me. The idea that he wanted to honor my ancestors and my homeland touched my heart deeply. He explained the ceremony would be held in the mosque, but he had forbade the idol worship and sacrifices that would normally accompany a traditional wedding celebration. It would be a simple yet elaborate celebration and there would be illustrious guests from all around the region. The ceremony itself would not last long, but the party would go on for days, though Misha and I were not expected to be in attendance for all of that. I was so relieved to know that my part would not require much of me, and Yahweh willing, it would be over before I knew it.

Though I felt far more confident in what was to take place, still I desired to speak with my future mother-in law. Lately, she had paid me no attention whatsoever, even less so than when I had arrived. But perhaps with the date arriving so soon, she might want to include me in some of the details. I longed to ask her what was expected of me, how I should smile, or not smile, what I would wear, and the specifics of the ceremony. It seemed even Misha was being kept out of the details and had no answers for my many questions. I had no one else to ask, so I would try today to get the attention of Avila and find out what I needed to know.

So, on this bright morning, I dressed in my favorite gown—the one Misha's mother had bought for me at the market. I tried to push down the memory of the little girl with the violet eyes and had Zara do my hair a little differently. When I was ready, I left my quarters early and headed towards the atrium where I knew she liked to take her tea as the sun rose.

As I turned the corner, I caught a glimpse of Zain reclining on a couch and stepped back quickly lest he see me. I pressed my back up against the wall to make myself as small as possible. Because it was early, the servants were occupied, and I could only hear the beating of my own heart. I did everything in my power to avoid being seen by Zain. Today was no different.

I was about to leave when I heard Avila's voice and the sound of her laughter mixed with Zain's. I slowed my breathing and kept my head upon the wall straining to hear what it was they were talking about. I didn't think that Misha's brother held the affections of his mother. In fact, I was under the stark impression that Avila could barely tolerate the sight of her second born. In all my months there, I could not recall ever hearing Zain's laughter, so I was intrigued beyond my fear. I only heard portions of what was being said: something about Zain not having to worry and that everything would work out just the way they planned. I was confused beyond reason, and slowly retreated down the hall and back up to my quarters. This was indeed very perplexing, and I would have to mention it to Misha when we were alone again.

CHAPTER 26
Auntie Naomi

Memories of My Past

THE STORM THAT raged outside my window was nothing compared to the storm that battered the walls of my heart and soul. I stared up into the foreboding grey clouds, remembering Sweet Mary and I tried to recall a different time, a time when I was young and free. My mind went back in history to when my sister and I would run and play for hours trying to escape the darkness that filled our childhood home. In the mornings we would wake early to help Papa get ready for his day's work. Our father worked in the fires of his shop, fashioning metal forms for the feet of horses and donkeys. Because he worked so hard, we wanted to get up early and make him a meal to take with him so, if needed, he could stay late to in order to provide for us. We would wash his clothes and make sure he had everything he needed while our mother lay in a deep drink induced sleep.

It was our joy to make him a hot breakfast and see his smile, even if the night before held bitter memories. The mornings were our favorite times because we had Papa all to ourselves. We would pretend we were like all the other families as we waved goodbye to him from our front door.

From then on, we were free to explore the surrounding villages and markets with the few coins Papa had entrusted to us. We knew that we had until the sun was high in the sky before Mama would wake and begin yelling for us to bring her whatever she needed. We would hold hands and skip along the dusty roads as if we didn't have a care in the world. We would giggle and whisper secrets that only we understood.

My sister was 3 years older than me, and Yahweh had blessed her with a startling beauty that captured the stares of everyone, wherever we went. It was my job to keep her from falling prey to the stares of men who would lure her away from the life we both dreamed would one day be ours.

Though I was younger, I was strong. I had an indomitable spirit that did not allow me to falter, even when the hand of my mother would strike me in the face. I would stand as tall as I could and stare into the blank eyes looking back at me as if I was a stranger, instead of the beloved second child of my father.

In spite of my sister being far prettier than me, I was the one my Papa favored. Perhaps because I was small and could still fit on his lap, or because it was me who would run to the end of the lane to greet him at the end of the day. He always had a special smile just for me. And because I was little, it fell to my sister to take care of our mother when she lay sprawled out on the floor of our kitchen.

It was Mira that the villagers would fetch to come and bring our mother home from wherever she went in the late afternoons. I didn't realize my sister envied me in the role of our father's special delight until I overheard her one day speaking to our neighbor when she did not think I was around. She complained that it always fell on her to take care of our mother when she had taken too much drink. She also said she was tired of being third in line for her father's love. Though I knew my sister loved me deeply, the pain in her voice broke my heart and a fear began to grip my mind, wondering what would happen to me if she left. Who would watch over me if something happened to Papa and I was left with a mother who would barely look at me? I tried to push the thoughts away, but as the years went by, Mira became even more lovely and the reality of her departure consumed me. Papa tried hard to keep Mother happy, but the only thing she craved day and night were the bottles she demanded Mira bring to her.

I had long since learned to keep my distance and even found myself in my Papa's shop most days trying to escape the smells and sights of my drunken mother. Father and I would talk and laugh, and he would teach me to soothe the animals in a way that would allow him to get close enough to hammer the metal onto their feet. He praised me and told all his friends that I had a gift with the animals, and he worked far better and faster when I was there to help him.

With Mira left to care for our mother, she became more and more distant from me and Papa. Often when we came home from the shop in the evenings, she would hurry out, saying she was meeting friends. Little by little, she walked right out of our lives and into the home of a man who seemed only to care about her beauty. Though Papa objected, and forbid her to see him, one day she was gone and never looked back.

We heard she married a man many years older who was a fisherman from up north and took her to live in the village of Magdala. He had plenty of money, so I knew she was well taken care of. I know my father's heart was broken for his eldest daughter and that he wished he would have done so many things differently. He confided in me that he never understood Mira and wanted so much more for her. He felt he had failed her by not taking better care of our mother and leaving Mira to take care of his wife.

One ordinary day, Papa and I were working in the fires with the metal while many horses and donkeys waited for us. Suddenly he looked at me, clutched at his chest and fell to the ground, dropping the hot iron in his hand. I rushed to his side and held his face in my hands as he whispered my name and took his last breath. It was that day my world went black. My greatest fears had now become my reality. I was alone, with no Papa or Mira to watch over me. Though I was almost old enough to be married myself, I knew I would now be the only one left to make sure my mother did not drink herself to death. What would the loss of her husband do to her fragile state now? Would she regret all those lost years and vow to begin to live a new life? I could only pray that Yahweh would have pity on me and deliver me from our prison of her drunkenness.

I did not have to wait long to find out because, with the loss of my father, my mother quickly found someone else to keep her company. She stayed away longer and longer, and many times did not come home at night. My world had changed forever and now it was only me taking care of myself. I continued going to Papa's shop day after day, and though his friends had taken over his business, they still requested I come and help with the animals. This was my place of peace and I settled into a new rhythm of life, trusting Yahweh to watch over me. Even if I never married, I would still be okay.

I only heard about Mira on rare occasions in the village market when one of the fishermen's wives would gossip, breaking my heart as I listened to what her life had become. I grieved the loss of my Papa and my sister every day and prayed my mama was still alive somewhere out there.

The years went by and I was surrounded by my father's friends and their families who had taken me in. I had friends who cared about me, and just as I had found peace in the life Yahweh had chosen for me, I noticed my friend Aaron had begun to act differently around me. Where before we had an easy friendship, sharing stories about the animals and our God, now he had difficulty looking me in the eyes. When I asked him about it one day, he blurted out he had fallen in love with me and it was his heart's desire to make me his wife. I was astonished as I had not thought about Aaron in that way, but the idea of becoming a wife and mother had always appealed to me, so I accepted his proposal. After a brief betrothal, we were husband and wife.

He stepped into my Papa's old role as the iron bender, and I continued to help in the shop until I found myself with child. Our life and love grew in the way Yahweh had designed for a man and woman.

The years went by and God blessed us with five healthy boys and a wonderful life I had only dreamed about when I was a little girl.

One day, I caught a glimpse of a woman in the market who looked just like my sister. When I ran to her, she stared at me as if she didn't know me. Though I saw a glimpse of sad recognition in her eyes, she turned away, pulling a stunning little girl behind her. It appeared she had moved back to a village close to ours and her husband had fallen onto hard times. I tried many times to reach out to Mira and the extraordinary little girl that God had blessed her with, but each time she would look at me with longing, give me a brief hug, and hurry away. Sadness and shame written all over her face.

As time went on, Mira would sometimes visit us. One day she asked if Sweet Mary could stay for a night. We welcomed them both into our home, and after that, Mary then came to stay with us more and more often. She became the daughter I had longed for and I knew the best way to love my sister was to cherish, value, and love her daughter. Sweet Mary was an exquisite child with golden, emerald green eyes, and deep, chestnut auburn hair who brought great joy to our lives.

I was startled out of my memories to realize the storm had passed and my boys were now in the house wanting dinner. How long had I stared into my past and the journey that had brought me to this place of loss? Would I never see my Sweet Mary again? Would my sister ever come back from her prison of pain?

CHAPTER 27

Misha

Fear Takes Hold

I HAD ASKED myself a thousand times, how had I stumbled into such good fortune? When Jidu told me he was again going in search of my future bride, my heart was disturbed. Someday soon I would be made to wed a person I did not know—a stranger I did not love, and someone I had not chosen to spend the rest of my life with. This was the third time he had ventured to my grandmother's homeland to find a wife for me, much to my own mother's objections. She would much rather they find me a wife from among the local girls whose family and reputation were of good report, not some stranger whose bloodlines we knew nothing about. Now, as I pictured the lovely face of my beautiful Myree, I was so glad that Grandfather Jidu had prevailed.

The first time I laid eyes upon her, I was struck by the demure strength with which carried herself, as though she had an inner power guiding her. Yet there was a humility that would not allow her to presume she deserved any of life's blessings. When she finally did actually look at me and our eyes locked, I was astonished by the depth of wisdom and pain contained in her striking, golden green gaze. She would not hold my stare, but my heart skipped a beat when I saw the slightest curve of her mouth indicating she was pleased with me as well. From that very moment, I vowed in my heart to win her trust and prayed to my grandmother's God, and to Myree's God, to allow our hearts to be joined in love.

Though I knew little of love, I remember how Jidu looked at my grandmother and desperately wanted the same type of connection with the woman I married. I would often see my own father looking at my mother with the same type of longing. Yet as far as I can remember, she never returned the look, but averted her eyes and made excuses to dismiss herself.

My parents had drifted farther and farther apart, as if the currents of life were raging to take them to vastly different destinations. Mother seemed to retreat more and more after it was finally decided there was nothing more that could be done for my brother Zain. He was destined to live a life in the shadows, trying to hide from eyes that would see his twisted disfigurement. If only he had not allowed the physical pain to enter his mind and heart. If only he did not shut himself off from the love and care of his family. Yes, it was true that some people gasped and turned away when they saw him, but I never did. I wanted so badly to take care of him and protect him from the cruel stares of others, but it was not to be.

By the time he was only five, I could feel his heart growing darker. Though I tried and tried to reach him, he had descended into a place I dared not enter. It was a frightening place where he found his solace in being alone, often in the dark. Many times, I sought him out, only to find him hidden in the recesses of the barn or locked away down in the wine cellar. Though I could hear his ragged breathing, he never allowed me to coax him out.

When I stumbled upon the first bloody mess he had created, I covered up his transgression and explained it was an animal that had killed the hen in the coup. From that point on, there had been a string of so-called accidents which soon became impossible to explain. The grown-ups in our world began to turn a blind eye, as if by acknowledging Zain and his darkness, it would somehow cast a shadow on them. They simply ignored the pain haunting my brother. I no longer knew what he was capable of, yet I still found myself saying things like, *he's harmless* to my Myree, all the while keeping a close watch to make sure Zain was never alone with her.

This is where my fears had taken hold of me. As I prepared for my wedding celebration and imminent departure onto the battlefield, my mind took hold of the reality that I would no longer be present to take care of my soon-to-be bride. This mere child, who had been destined by the gods (or perhaps it was her God who had brought us together) and who was to become the mate for my soul, was my only concern. What if Zain took his rage out on her while I was far away and helpless to do anything? How would I protect her from hundreds of miles away? I vowed to be honest with my Myree before I left and tell her the truth about the darkness hidden inside my brother. I would warn her to make sure to always lock her doors and take care to never find herself in a vulnerable position where Zain was concerned. I would also enlist the help of a few trusted servants to keep watch over my new wife so I could rest assured she would be safe until I returned to start our new life together. Yes, this was a good plan, one I could find peace in as the days of my ability to protect her came to a close.

But what of mother? I had recently seen she and Zain together far more often than I had in a very long time. They would whisper with heads together in the library, or I would find them in the courtyard near the fountains. It seemed they had not only been conversing, but actually enjoying each other's company. Was my mother trying to console herself with her second son, knowing I was soon to be far away? Such a strange turn of events. I had not seen my mother even glance at Zain for many years.

What type of alliance had they forged and why? I pondered this in my heart and wondered if what I was feeling was a hint of jealousy, something I had never experienced in my entire life especially where Zain was concerned.

I tried to be happy that my little brother had finally found a hint of acceptance from our mother, yet I wrestled with something hidden deep inside my soul. A feeling of dread had threatened to take hold of me, and I shook my head and banished the thought. I would not allow my fear to ruin the precious time Myree and I had together before I was to leave.

It was determined Myree and I would spend two nights together after our nuptials. A mere forty-eight hours was all we were given and then I would be taken into a life of war. I knew that father and Jidu would have me well protected while I was on the battlefield. This time away was simply a necessary part of the plan before I returned and assumed my rightful position as heir to the Hassen empire. I had been schooled in commerce and economics, finance, trade and agriculture, yet all heirs to succeed the family patriarch were required to spend one year on the battlefield as a rite of passage. At eighteen, I was ready. I was physically in the best shape of my life and skilled with a sword. If only I did not have to leave my precious, young bride in the hands of my family who I knew had nothing but distain for her. I was grateful beyond words to Grandfather Jidu who had brought her to me. The two of them had a special relationship, and he had promised to look after her while I was away. But would that be enough? I prayed to my sweet Myree's God, that indeed it would be enough, I asked that He would protect her and see her through our season apart.

CHAPTER 28

Myree

This New World

THE FREEZING GROUND was beginning to thaw as the spring rains watered the fields and orchards with the promise of new life. Days turned into weeks and the weeks turned into months. It seemed as if my wedding day was almost upon me. In the quiet of my heart, I begged Yahweh to protect my Misha because, with the arrival of the wedding day, his departure for the battlefield became a stark, cold reality. We would spend two nights together and then he would leave me, his new bride alone with the family I barely knew and was fairly sure did not want to know me. All except Jidu, the one person who could actually speak to me about my homeland, the sights, sounds, and smells of the place where I grew up. I wanted to talk about all of it, except that horrifying day when I was thrown upon the back of a donkey and sold for a few pieces of silver. I wanted to forget my parents the same way they had forgotten me.

I had been taken far away from all I had known, away from my auntie and my five rambunctious cousins—to this place of wealth and indulgence. I rarely thought of that day anymore, it was buried so deep in my heart. Although it had only been a little over two years, I was now a completely different person. I was now Myree, soon to be bride of Misha, and heiress to the Hassen Dynasty.

I rarely saw Samir, Misha's father, except for the rare occasion when Jidu would gather his whole family for a feast in the dining hall. I was so intrigued by my soon to be father-in-law and his devotion to his family and wanted to gather all the knowledge I could so I too, could have the kind of marriage Misha's parents seemed to have. Whenever I asked Misha about his father, he got a faraway look in his eyes and shared very little. I was determined to uncover the story of Samir and Avila and was overjoyed to meet the older gentleman servant who was once Samir's chaperone.

From what I gathered from him and the other servants, Samir had married Avila because of her outward beauty and obvious wealth. He was overwhelmed by the idea of someone as striking as Avila ever giving him a second glance. As the daughter of the Hassen dynasty, she had been the desire of all his friends. Samir had not given much thought to her, believing she would never be interested in him. One day he received a note from a messenger asking for him to meet with Avila the following day at the market where she would slip away from her mother's watchful eye and steal a few minutes to talk to him. Though Samir had only met her once, he had no idea Avila even knew who he was. The idea of coming face to face with her made his heart race. He returned a note telling her to meet him at three o'clock the next day near the cheese vendor and the spice booth. He did not dare to get his hopes up, and part of him thought this might be a joke being played on him by his friends. Though Samir had been told he was a handsome young man and knew girls stared at him, still he had trouble falling asleep that night wondering what this beautiful girl would want to speak with him about.

Being the eldest of a respectable, prominent family had kept him fairly sheltered. Samir had preferred to spend his afternoons with his beloved mother in the library or studying with his chaperone rather than getting into mischief with his friends. Because of this, he rarely gave thought to the idea of girls and was, therefore, quite naive. He was never far from the eyes of his trusted servant who had cared for him since he was a child, therefore he openly told him about the note, and upcoming rendezvous. The wise man smiled at his charge and allowed Samir the freedom he requested but assured him he would be close enough to hear the entire interaction. When the time finally arrived for him to meet with Avila, Samir had tried to portray a confidence he did not feel.

When he caught a glimpse of Avila standing next to the spice booth, he could not believe his good fortune. He moved closer and her beauty took his breath away. Avila must have sensed his insecure awkwardness because she immediately took charge of the conversation, telling him she had wanted to meet, and indeed hoped he would be the one to set up a meeting. She demurely apologized for seeming so forward as to actually reach out to him but said she was getting tired of all the advances of young men she had no interest in being courted by. Avila boldly told Samir he was the one she was interested in and if he would be inclined to feel even remotely the same, she would inform her parents of the idea. Avila was determined to not be married off to a man not of her own choosing and was set on someone handsome and strong like Samir. From that moment on, Samir's life had never been the same and he found himself engaged to the most beautiful girl he had ever seen. He never once gave any thought to the fact that Avila's dowry was something his parents would not even discuss, knowing the wealth of the Hassen family was far greater than anyone in the land.

Samir's father had been skeptical when the messenger came to tell them that Master Hassen was requesting the betrothal of their only daughter, Avila, to his son. Even though Samir's mother had intended he be wed to her best friend's daughter, the sadness in his beloved mother's eyes did nothing to deter him. Samir's father told him he hoped for a bride more like his mother, someone who was not spoiled and indulged as Avila was. When Samir's father had hinted that his beautiful Avila had anything but pure motives and intentions, he stormed out of the house and did not speak to his parents for days. When they realized he was intent upon marrying Avila, they eagerly agreed, thus, the wedding of the season was planned with no expense spared. Most assuredly, Avila was in on all the details and demanded nothing but the best, all for the sake of the family name, of course. The arrangements were made, and they were wed the following spring.

As I watched the rain drench the land, I reflected on the last two years of my life. Jidu had been the best part of this whole experience, next to sweet Zara and Misha, of course. He had been kind and treated me with the love of the grandfather I never knew. I so enjoyed our teatime in the library discussing my homeland. He loved hearing stories of my auntie, uncle and cousins. I described the colorful markets and learning to weave from my auntie's friend, Mary. I spoke of our journey's to Jerusalem for the Passover Feast. His eyes always lit up when he shared about how his sweet Myriam would tell stories of her own Passover experiences. In Jidu's presence, I felt safe and cared for. I knew that as long as he was head of the family, I would be secure in my position as the bride of his eldest grandson.

Spring meant the young men had begun training for battle in the fields which was a day's ride from our land. Many times, days passed and I neither saw nor heard a word from my beloved Misha. Sometimes late at night a note was slipped under my chamber door and Zara would hurry to retrieve it for me. Misha knew I would be holding my breath all day hoping to hear word from my future husband. The notes were more than just words written on a page—they were my lifeline to the man with whom I had fallen deeply in love.

At almost fifteen years old, I really had no concept of what love was, but my heart ached for the touch of Misha's hand in mine and the hours of conversation that flowed so easily between us. I had shared my deepest fears, hopes, and dreams with this friend of mine and he, in turn, confessed how he had no desire to go into battle, and only wished he could stay with me in the security of the palace. Though he was being prepared daily for what lie ahead of him, his heart would remain here with me.

On the rare occasion he was home, we would sneak out to the orchards after everyone else had long since retired. We would lay on the woven blanket Misha had brought and look up at the heavens for hours. Misha would teach me about the constellations, and we would dream together about how our life would be. I would teach him about the ancient scriptures and the scrolls my uncle had taught me to read. I would share about the Shema and before long we were reciting it together as we walked along the orchards or sat under the stars.

He had become an expert on horseback, and had taught me to ride, even giving me a beautiful black stallion as an early wedding present. Our friendship had grown to a place of deep trust, respect, and admiration for one another. We were as comfortable as a brother and sister, yet when Misha reached out to take my hand, I felt as if all the nerves in my body had come to life by his gentle touch. He often treated me as a younger sister—protecting and teaching me— but I could see the love shining in his eyes. Ours was a pure and innocent love, forged out of a desire to actually enter into matrimony with a person of our own choosing, not just an arranged marriage that may or may not have been born of the heart. We both desired to become the best version of ourselves for the other. I often prayed that Yahweh would grant us a marriage like my auntie and uncle, one based on a mutual love for God and His will and plans for our lives. Reading the notes Misha wrote to me allowed my heart to rest knowing he was safe. My affection for him only grew knowing he was thinking about me as well.

Though my nuptials were only weeks away, I still knew little of what the day would contain. I knew Zara and many other servants would prepare me, and I would be taken to the location of the ceremony where my childhood would end. I would be a wife at the tender age of fourteen: and I was terrified. What would Misha expect of me? How was I to become a bride when it seemed that only days ago, I was running in the streets of Nazareth with my cousins. I never had an interest in boys and had hoped to become a famous weaver of the fabrics I had seen so beautifully displayed in the marketplace. Never had I thought I would be married before I turned fifteen years old.

My mind raced ahead to the day when I would have to say goodbye to my Misha. We were to have only two nights together as husband and wife, and then he would go and leave me all alone. Though I had been in this strange land for over two years now, I still felt very much like an outsider. Misha's mother held no warm feelings for me, but instead, barely tolerated my existence. His brother Zain instilled a fear in my heart that I could not escape, and though Misha told me he was harmless, I knew I would have to be ever watchful so as to never be alone with him.

My fondness for Jamal was growing. Though we were almost the same age, due to being the youngest son and coddled by his mother and father, he seemed much younger than me. I had grown up far too fast and seen too many things of the world, and my heart was hardened to the innocence of Jamal.

There were many servants that cared for me, but even Zara sometimes looked at me with envy in her eyes. I knew she wished to someday be free and be married, having a family of her own. Of course, there was Jidu, the beloved grandfather who had bought me for a price to become his grandson's bride. He saw something in me that day at the auction, and I will be forever grateful to him for sparing me from a life of being a prostitute or a slave girl. The thought of being a Temple prostitute pierced my heart and the violet eyes of Kiera burned into my soul. How in the name of Yahweh could I ever help her? Many nights I had lain awake replaying that scene in my head. I should have called out her name; I should have run to her. Why did I just freeze and stare at her while all around us life went rushing by? She would never forgive me; I could not blame her. I left her, abandoned, the same way my mother left me as she watched those evil men take me away. Just as I would never forgive my mother, Kiera would never forgive me. My only prayer was that when Misha returned home and we had a life of our own, we could then go and rescue Kiera. We would purchase her freedom no matter how much it cost, and I would spend the rest of my life making it up to her, begging for her forgiveness.

CHAPTER 29

Myree

The Wedding Day

THOUGH I BARELY slept the whole night, when daybreak appeared at the window, I jumped out of bed to watch all the commotion below. There were carts full of flowers and food and people hurrying through the gates of our villa. Today was the day Misha would become my husband, today I would become his bride. My mind danced at the thought of being married to my best friend. He was the heir to the Hassen throne, the handsome and kind grandson of Jidu, the man who had brought me here. Was it fear I felt in my stomach? Yes, certainly. I was only fourteen years old. How was I going to become all that was to be demanded of me? How would I ever live up to Avila's expectations?

At the same time, the idea of spending two days alone with Misha, where we could talk, and laugh, and dream together seemed too good to be true. Of course, there was also the aspect of being a wife that I could not even bring myself to think of. It was just too horrifying, and I could not imagine allowing anyone, especially Misha, see me undressed. That terrifying picture flashed in my mind before I squeezed my eyes shut and blocked those thoughts from my head.

Perhaps Misha and I could spend the evenings together outside under the stars just holding hands as we had in the past? It was only two nights where we would have a separate villa to ourselves before he would have to leave. Then I would be moved back into my current quarters until his return from the battlefield. It would be a very long year before I would see or hear the voice of the one person whom I had grown to love in a way

I did not know was possible. I looked up to the brilliant blue sky above me and thanked Yahweh for the dream I was living. He had indeed been gracious to me and I asked Him to comfort my auntie with the knowledge I was safe and being well taken care of.

Today my life would change forever. I would be given a new name and a level of esteem which comes from being the wife of Misha. Maybe my new mother-in-law would accept me after I had married her son. Jidu would be the one to hand me over to Misha while hundreds of honored guests would stare at me. I knew I was the envy of many young women in the village and beyond, and though I did not think of myself as anything special, I often heard the whispers about the color of my eyes or the shade of my hair. Misha always spoke of how clever I was and how skilled I had become in the language of his people; or my knowledge of plants and herbs, and how I was able to weave the most beautiful fabrics. Yet none of that impressed Avila. And though Samir seemed to approve of me, Avila's distain was unmatched save for Zain, who I felt desperately despised me for stealing his big brother.

The complexities of the family dynamics were something I would never get used to, and I longed for the simple love and affection of my auntie, uncle and cousins. I desperately wished they could be here with me today and wondered if they even knew I was alive. Did they know I had been sold by my own parents? Did they ever try to find me? Did anyone in the village of Nazareth ever ask what had become of the girl with the golden green eyes and auburn hair? As my former life flashed before my eyes, I felt a tear slip down my cheek and had to close off that part of my heart once again.

I was no longer little Sweet Mary. I was now Myree, soon to be wife of Misha Hassen, who would one day be master of everything before me. As Zara entered the bedroom chamber, a smile found its way to my face as I wiped my eyes. She carried a tray of fruits and cheeses with bread and water as she did most mornings, but today she was humming as she moved, and I could sense her excitement.

Days before, she nervously asked me if I would have any need of her after I was married. I was shocked at the thought of not having my beautiful Zara in my life. I promised her she could stay with me for as long as she wanted and when I was able, I would set her free. I told her the thought of anyone else in my chamber or in my heart made me realize I had grown to love her and wanted her with me forever. Since then, she seemed more at ease. I suppose not knowing what her future held after I was married may have caused her some anxiety. For that I was truly sorry.

She set the tray down and smiled at me as I rushed to throw my arms around her: I hugged her until she squirmed away. A slave was not used to having their masters hug them, but this was no ordinary day. Today was my wedding day, and I wanted to share my joy with the only real friend I had. She motioned me to sit and while I nibbled on some fruit, she unbraided my thick, long hair and began to brush it before she readied my bath water.

Today there would be many servants attending to me, several who would create an elaborate design with my hair using freshly cut flowers. Others would rub oil into my skin until it glowed in the sunlight. Then I would be dressed from head to toe in the most exquisite gown I've ever seen. I knew that this would be the last time Zara and I would be alone, so I turned to her and took her hands in mine. I can't remember when I started to be able to speak to her in full sentences, but it seemed like she had forever been by my side. I told her how grateful I was to Yahweh for her care and love these past two years, and how I cherished her in my heart like the sister I never had. I promised her once again that when I was able, I would set her free and she could have the life she dreamed of.

She stared back at me with tears in her eyes and said, "I believe you, my friend, and until then, I will serve you faithfully as I always have. May you find deep joy in this new season of your life, and may your God smile on you and bless you in every way." I hugged her again and then she ushered me into the pool of warm water.

Before long the room was a frenzy of activity as servants came in and out depositing articles of makeup and jewels that would adorn me. My mind whirled in all the commotion until things suddenly got very quiet and I realized Avila had entered the room. The servants all bowed low to the ground. She barely glanced at them and strode over to where I sat having my hair twisted and curled. Everyone retreated while Misha's mother inspected me from head to toe. I felt like a piece of beef the butcher had just carved and held out before her to approve. I tried to smile, but the fear in my stomach tightened the moment she walked in and I felt as though I might throw up. Oh, wouldn't that be a sight? With this thought, a smile came to my lips and I greeted her with eyes downcast. She barked out orders and the servants scurried out of her reach. I had seen many slaves receive the angry hand of Avila and today would be no different. All the servants knew to keep a wide berth, for no one ever quite knew what type of mood she would be in. She asked me a few questions, which I answered to the best of my knowledge; instructed me as to where I needed to be and at what time, and then she was gone. We all breathed a sigh of relief and the air lightened once again. It was my wedding day, and nothing was going to ruin that, not even the woman I feared would never accept me as part of her family.

Though the sun was barely over the horizon, it seemed like the day had already aged past the noonday hour. The festivities were to begin as the sun began to set in the western sky and would last well into the early morning hours.

I had no idea when Misha and I would be able to escape to our wedding villa, but I feared I would not be permitted to speak with him until that time arrived. Zara fussed over me, insisting I eat the figs and cheese set before me. I nibbled on them but felt as if a stampede of camels were running around inside of me. I could not eat, and a fear began to edge its way into my heart. The questions began to run wild in my mind. What would happen in two days when I no longer had the protection of my Misha? I wondered how I would be able to elude Zain when he knew I was all alone. What would I do to keep myself occupied for an entire year until Misha arrived home? The fear took a strong hold of me when I dared to allow myself to ask the question of what would happen to me if something happened to my beloved Misha on the battlefield.

I began to shiver under the hands of the servants. The woman applying kohl around my eyes looked horrified when a tear ran down my cheek. She motioned to Zara who took me by the hand and led me outside onto the balcony for some fresh air. She wrapped her arms around me and told me everything was going to be all right, commanding me to take some big deep breaths. As I looked up at the cloudless sky, I closed my eyes and prayed aloud, asking Yahweh for strength, courage, and peace. I pleaded with Him to protect my Misha as I had done countless times over the last several months.

As I glanced over at Zara, her eyes were closed, and her hands were folded in a posture of prayer. Could it be possible? Did Zara now believe in my God? Could it be that all those late nights of sharing the stories of my ancestor's faith had finally made their way into her heart and now she joined me in my beliefs? I finished my prayer, and Zara opened her eyes to see me staring at her. A shy smile crept up her face and I beamed at her. I threw my arms around her and we twirled in a circle. She began humming the familiar tune of the *Love Song to Yahweh* and my heart burst with joy as I joined her in song. It seemed the God of my family had opened her heart and found His home inside this beautiful, quiet slave girl. As we stood side by side, we looked down at the carriages arriving and realized we still had much to do, and I was to be married in a short time. We rushed back in and I gave myself over to the care and nurture of the team of women waiting on me.

CHAPTER 30

Myree

The Joining of Hearts

FINALLY, I STOOD before my reflection in the glass and could barely believe it was me, Mary of Magdala. My skin shone in the candlelight, my hair a vision of flowers, and braids encircled with a crown of jewels. The pristine white gown was so bright it was hard to look at, and though it sparkled with gems and pearls that were indeed mesmerizing, it was the face looking back at me that was most startling. The eyes were the same golden green, yet with the deep jade liner, and the gold dust that highlighted my brows, I was uncertain if I truly was the same little girl I had been only two short years ago.

What would my auntie say if she could see me now? And what of the mother and father that sold me to satisfy their wretched thirst? Had my mother ever thought about the day her only daughter would be married to the man of her dreams, or was she so broken she could not dare to think of anything but her next drink? Oh, how my heart ached to have the story of my life rewritten. That story would include the love of a family who would celebrate and rejoice at the good fortune Yahweh had bestowed upon me.

I was startled out of my reverie by the arrival of Avila. She and her entourage entered and looked me up and down from head to toe. Was that a glint of pleasure I saw in her eyes? Perhaps it was envy or just pure hatred. I could not be sure. But as quickly as she had come in, she turned and departed. I stared at her back for the last time as the foreign girl who was purchased for her son. The next time I looked into her eyes it would be as the wife of her beloved Misha. I prayed I would someday see a hint of acceptance on her beautiful face.

I was then set upon a dais and carried down the staircase while musicians surrounded me and serenaded the halls of the palace. They carried me through the opulent gardens, where the scent of lilies and jasmine hung so heavy it was hard to breath. We proceeded to the mosque where hundreds of distinguished guests awaited my arrival. It seems I floated above the earth as I watched Misha approaching me.

Grandfather Jidu stepped aside and then my beloved stood before me, staring transfixed into my eyes. He circled around me three times while I stood frozen in place, my heart pounding in my chest. There were pots of incense throughout the expansive room. Smoke rose toward the heavens as countless servants waved large palm fonds back and forth, up and down in rhythm with the instruments being played. White doves stood in cages waiting for their release, cooing along with the harps and lyres. Dancers floated about the room, while maidens sang with angelic voices.

Was this really my life or was I caught in a dream from which I would soon awake? I barely breathed and dared not blink my eyes for fear everything would vanish before me. I vaguely remember a man reciting words over us, and then the doves were released to cheers and shouts of joy.

Soon we were ushered out into the courtyard where tables and been completely covered in delicacies that smelled heavenly. Cushions and low tables were set all around and people reclined as the servants brought trays to them. Goblets were filled with the finest wines from our vineyards. The music seemed to grow louder as the evening wore on. I barely touched the food on my plate as Misha sat beside me—I was now his wife. Perhaps he was just as nervous as I was, seeing he too, still had a full plate. I longed for him to take hold of my hand or even look me in the eye, anything in an effort to connect us in some way. I felt like an imposter wearing all the makeup and royal finery. So, maybe he did not recognize me as the one with whom he had talked and laughed for the last two years. I dreaded the hours looming ahead of me when I would be taken to our bridal villa. I only wanted to be with Misha, to hold his hand, and talk with him late into the night about all we had experienced during this extremely long day. More than anything else, I felt terror at what would be expected of me on this night.

When Grandfather Jidu finally whispered something into Misha's ear, he nodded his head and took me by the hand. I followed them through a side entrance while the party was in full swing. No one even noticed our departure. My hands were clammy in Misha's, and I was in no hurry to leave. He practically dragged me through our property as we made our way into a carriage that would take us away.

When we reached the darkness of the enclosed quarters, I let out a deep breath, and Misha moved closer to me. He placed his hand on my cheek and felt me trembling beneath his touch. I could not look at him for fear I would burst into tears. We rode in silence, and after what seemed like only a minute, arrived at the luxurious villa that would be ours for the next two days.

The servants attended us as we disembarked from the carriage and led us to the front door. Misha dismissed them all and promptly scooped me up in his arms and carried me up the staircase to claim me as his bride. I shook with fear in his arms and felt like a prisoner who had been taken captive.

As he placed me down on the center of the bridal chamber's large canopied bed, he kissed me passionately and I could not contain the stream of tears that had begun pouring from my eyes. The intricate makeup which had been so artfully applied to my eyes ran down my face and smeared all over my hands as I wiped my cheeks. I fought to gain my composure. Misha stared at me as if I was a stranger, then suddenly he began smiling which then turned into laughter. At this I buried my face in my hands and sobbed. He was still chuckling as he came back to me with a warm, wet towel he had dipped in the bridal bath which had been prepared for us. He lifted my chin and began wiping the black mess covering my face, and in my shame, I could barely look up at him. After he had sufficiently cleansed my face and I was once again resembling the girl he used to know, he went over to the trays of lavish food and drink that had been left for us.

Suddenly I was famished, and though I was exhausted, I willingly shared a meal with my new husband. I was still elaborately dressed in my bridal gown and my hair was still tightly woven with a crown of jewels and flowers. Misha had commented earlier on how lovely my hair looked. That was the only thing I can remember him saying to me throughout the day's events. Surely, he had spoken more to me, but I could not remember any of it. It was as if the last two years of our friendship had dissolved and we were now two strangers meeting for the first time.

While we ate, he commented on the guests, the ceremony and how lovely his mother had looked. I nodded and kept my eyes on the food in front of me, stuffing my mouth full so I would not have to speak. What was happening to me? Why was I so terrified of this man whom I had come to love? As he stared at me, I could see agitation in his movements. He became distant, and though I wanted to scream out that I loved him, my eyes revealed only the terror I felt. After we finished eating, he suggested I bathe first and he would then do the same. He assured me he would give me the privacy I obviously desired. He asked if afterwards when we were both refreshed, we might take a walk in the moonlight, if I wasn't too tired. He called to a servant to help me out of my dress, and after a long time of soaking in the warm water, my nerves were somewhat calm. I timidly entered the bridal chamber only to find my beloved husband sound asleep on our bed. Relief flooded my soul and I tiptoed around the large bed to a chaise across the room and curled up with a soft sheep skin wrapped tightly around me. My wedding night had not turned out like anything I had imagined, and I smiled as I drifted off to sleep remembering that I was now the wife of my best friend.

I woke up to find Misha carrying me to the bed as he whispered for me to remain silent when I heard the knocking on the door. He then went over to open the door, allowing the servants to bring in trays of food for our breakfast. I was bewildered until I realized I had not slept in the same bed as my husband on our wedding night, and the servants loved to gossip about all the comings and goings of their masters. It would be unacceptable for Misha's mother to hear I had failed as a wife on my first night as her daughter-in-law. I knew he was trying to keep me from being the source of ridicule and slander as I had slept curled in a tight ball of sheep skin on a chaise, and not in the bridal bed. I breathed a sigh of relief as I felt the protective love of my husband surrounding me.

When the servants left the trays of food, I smiled at him and said, "Thank you." He realized I understood his actions and smiled back at me. He left me to eat and then came back after he had bathed and dressed for the day.

In the morning light, I was not nearly as frightened as I had been the night before, and I relaxed into conversation with my new husband. Misha could tell I had regained some of my composure. He suggested we go for a walk around the grounds and perhaps take the horses and enjoy a picnic for the day. We had only gone riding a few times and I had so thoroughly enjoyed myself that I was beyond happy Misha remembered how much delight I had upon receiving the beautiful stallion from him as a wedding gift. The idea of going riding could not have made me happier. I willingly agreed to his ideas and gave him a brilliant smile while reaching up to kiss him on the cheek. I could see his face flush and realized this small act of kindness pleased him.

Perhaps marriage would not be as terrifying as I thought. If only we could go back to the way things were when we were comfortable around each other and could talk for hours. What would it take to get back to that place with my Misha? I would do my best to be a good wife to him, and I looked forward to a lovely day together. I had to remember he was leaving very soon, and this was my only chance to prove my love for him before he left.

The day was glorious, and after we walked fairly unnoticed by the people around us, we found the stable. Misha was able to secure two horses for us to be delivered back to our villa after the noonday meal.

The sun shone down on us as we walked hand in hand on the trails beyond the villa. We returned to find a lavish spread of food and ate until we were both stuffed. Misha suggested we rest a while before our ride, but I convinced him I was far too excited to rest and just wanted to get out and explore the beautiful countryside on horseback. He gathered up some food to take with us; though I protested I could not possibly eat another bite. He assured me I would be hungry again after we had ridden for a while.

The horses were saddled for us and we set out to find the back acres of the orchards. Though neither of us wanted to be seen by the family, we dearly loved the orchards and vineyards, and we were certain we could stay hidden among the trees. We had so many fond memories of walking and talking for hours, and, of course, our nights lying under the stars were in those same orchards.

We rode for what seemed to be miles and then walked the horses along the edge of the tree line located at the back of the property. The palace seemed so very far away. It was hard to believe I was now the wife of Misha Hassen, the heir to inherit the dynasty that would one day be his and our children's.

Misha found a secluded place and spread out a blanket. He brought out the cheese, dates, and juice for us, and we ate in the warm afternoon sun. We talked of the wedding celebration and the reality of his departure the next day. I could hardly breathe knowing Misha would be leaving and I took his hand in mine. I looked into his eyes and told him I would miss him with all my heart. He then leaned over and kissed me with passion and longing that truly left me breathless. I tried to return the passion, but felt the same dread and fear rising inside of me again. I pulled back and was saddened to see the confusion on his face. Always the gentleman, he smiled and wrapped up our picnic, then took my hand and led me back to the horses and the open field for our return to the villa. The ride was mostly silent, and though I tried to engage Misha in small talk, he was withdrawn and perhaps hurt by my pulling away from him.

By the time we returned to our bridal chamber, it was nearly dark. I was now the one withdrawn and shut down. Though Misha tried desperately to coax me out of my fears, I could not relax. When he took me in his arms, I tried with all my heart to open myself to him, knowing this was expected of me. He kissed me gently on the mouth, and though I wanted to respond in the right way, when he looked into my eyes, all he saw was terror. I was but a girl of not yet fifteen and he was a grown man of eighteen. I could feel his masculinity and his desire, but I was frozen in my fear. He tore himself away and began busying himself with a pot of tea and cakes the servants had left for us. I went out onto the balcony and lifted my eyes to heaven and prayed for the strength I would need to fulfill my marital duty: to willingly give myself wholeheartedly to my husband. I was desperate for Yahweh to hear me and began humming my favorite song. Soon Misha was behind me, his arms wrapped around me. I loved the feel of him, and when he kissed my neck, I relaxed into him. He picked me up and carried me over to our bed. He gently laid me down and began slowly unbuttoning my robe. I lay motionless on the bed, and when he paused on the last button, I looked into his eyes and saw his love. As he stared at me, the terror rose up again and I began to tremble. The tears slid down my cheeks and he gently caressed my face. He lay down beside me, held my hand, and whispered into my ear.

"My sweet Myree, I know you are not yet ready to receive me as your husband, but I am a patient man. I will wait for you as long as it takes, until you are as eager as I am to be joined together," he paused and then continued. "I want you to be ready and willing to share my bed, my heart, and my body. I will count the days until I return, and then we will truly begin our life together as husband and wife. I love you with all my heart. You are my beloved." My tears continued to fall as I felt the tender love of this wonderful man. Soon, I heard his breathing slow as he entered into a deep sleep.

I lay awake long into the night looking at this gift God had given me. Misha was a gentle friend who loved me so deeply that he would deny his own feelings of desire and be patient with me until I was a little older and a little wiser—a time when I would be able to satisfy him the way a wife should. I knew Yahweh had heard my prayers on the balcony, and I rejoiced that I had some more time to come to terms with what takes place between a man and a woman. I would miss my Misha with every breath I took. While he was away, I would pray fervently for his protection. I would learn and grow into a mature woman, and when he returned, I would open myself to him fully and completely. I would be almost sixteen when my husband claimed me for his own, and that thought filled my heart with peace and ushered me into a deep sleep.

Before I knew it, the servants were back with trays of delicious smelling food. My husband stretched beside me and smiled down at me as he kissed me good morning. He had awakened earlier, covered me in blankets and had already bathed and dressed. The servants giggled at the obvious display of affection. He was gracious and greeted them with a smile. It seemed he was already beyond the disappointment of the previous two nights and had resolved to hold fast to the promise he had given me to come back and then begin our life together in the way it should be.

Was it already the day of his departure? Would I really have to say goodbye to the one person in the whole world I knew really loved me? The thought broke my heart and tears threatened to overwhelm me. I vowed to be strong for my husband, knowing there would be many eyes upon us today as he prepared to leave. The day was already planned and there would be a ceremony of blessing Misha by the elders, and of course, the anointing of his head as the oldest son going off to war. The streets would be lined with people cheering and waving banners. This was no ordinary young man going off to battle, this was the heir to the Hassen throne and many who had attended the wedding would still be in attendance. His mother would kiss him and hold him tight. His father would pat him on the back and tell him he was proud of the man he was becoming. All this had been shared with me by Zara, who had witnessed several men going off to war. I was to dress and be prepared to be the strong and stoic wife, not giving way to my emotions, but holding my head high while waving goodbye with everyone else. I settled my heart and gathered my courage for the day ahead.

Finally, the time had arrived. The ceremony was concluded, and I looked at my valiant husband dressed in his military attire ready to ride off into the sunset. He had spent the whole day with me assuring me of his devotion and commitment to our wedding vows. He held my hand, kissed my lips, and smiled at me, convincing me everything was going to be just fine. He would go off to the battlefield, they would protect him, and he would come home to me so we could start our life together just as we planned. This gave me new confidence, knowing he would greatly anticipate his return home.

When I caught my mother-in-law staring at me throughout the ceremony, I stared right back at her, smiling before she turned away. Everyone was in attendance: Jamal, Jidu, even Zain showed up and though he tried to stay hidden in the shadows of the people—his big brother sought him out and hugged him goodbye. Through lots of cheering and waves, my husband and his company disappeared over the horizon, then he was gone. And just like that, I was all alone again in the world.

CHAPTER 31

Avila

The Jealousy Grows

THE PAIN IN my heart was overwhelming as I watched my son ride off to war. Thinking back over the last two years my anger had grown each day as I watched my firstborn son throw his life away on the pathetic foreign girl brought from the pits of Jerusalem. The anger at my father became a loathing I couldn't hide any longer. To see the way Jidu treated this child, as if he had resurrected my late mother, was too much for me to take. As the only daughter, I was supposed to be the apple of his eye, but instead, I had been replaced by a mere child. I was expected to take this girl into my home, treat her like royalty, plan the wedding of the season, and then just give my son to her. He deserved far more than what this waif could ever give him. Yes, she was beautiful, with her hair and those eyes that flashed with sunlight. I would even have been impressed at her ability to weave, and how quickly she was able to learn our language, had she not been so needy. It seemed at every turn, there she was, trying to speak with me, asking questions, always looking at me with those catlike eyes. I could never seem to escape her gaze. Finally, under duress, I had arranged an outing for just the two of us. I tried to include her in our family, tried to show her how to walk, what type of robes to wear; however, taking her out in public was the deciding factor in me wanting nothing to do with her.

As we walked along the aisles of the merchants, whose voices could usually be heard above the din of the carts and animals, there was a hush in the air. As they stared at me, I stood prouder, enjoying the knowledge that I could still capture the attention of any man I desired. That is, until

I realized they were not looking at me at all. Their focus was entirely fixed on the child who was blossoming into a woman right before my very eyes. The men stared with mouths open and the women fixated with fascination on the unusual hair color that escaped around the scarf, and the eyes that could actually smile. And that is what she did, she smiled at everyone—men and women alike.

She bent down to speak to the children and gave coins to the beggars who dared to approach us. She had created a spectacle in the marketplace, and I was right in the middle of it. When I dared to walk too close to the temple, it was there everything changed. Suddenly, as if she had seen a ghost, the child turned pale and almost fainted right in the street. My drivers practically carried her back to the carriage, and when questioned, she would not tell me what had happened. What in the world had overtaken her, I wondered? I pried and prodded her, all to no avail. It was then I knew she had secrets—deep, dark secrets hidden inside her. I vowed to do everything in my power to keep my son from losing his heart to her.

Since that day, I avoided Myree at all costs. I began taking my evening meals in my chambers feigning a headache or some other ridiculous reason to simply not be in the same room with her. I tried to recapture the attention of my eldest son, Misha, inviting him to go on walks with me, or to escort me to the tea rooms. Sadly, he was intent on spending every waking moment he could with his future bride. It sickened me the way my firstborn looked at this foreign girl, the same way that his pathetic father, Samir, had looked at me on the day I had lured him to the market. At first, it had simply been an attempt to arouse the interest of my own father who barely paid me any attention. However, I found I quite enjoyed being adored by Samir's puppy-dog eyes and knowing he would never meet the approval of my father, Jidu. I had decided this was the boy I wanted to be my husband. True, it was usually the parents who selected their daughters' husband, but I had told my mother I had already given myself to this young man. Therefore, they hurried with the nuptials in case I was possibly with child, lest they be disgraced. I was used to getting what I wanted and with my name, wealth and beauty, it had always been easy.

CHAPTER 32

Myree

Spring into Fall

SPRINGTIME AT THE villa was full of activity. With the planting of the crops, the birthing of all the new farm animals and everything I wanted to do, I had plenty to keep myself busy. I had taken to walking in the orchards and conversing with the servants. At first, they were reluctant to speak with me, but as the days turned into weeks, they became more comfortable with me and would smile when I brought them a flask of water to share. For the most part, I was left to myself. I had moved back into the palace and returned to my old quarters, which were comfortable and familiar. Zara and I had resumed our relationship. Grandfather Jidu often welcomed me to the library for tea.

As I pondered the long months ahead of me, I found myself thinking of sweet Kiera more and more often. I began taking trips to the market, always accompanied by Zara and a couple of chaperons. I would explain I needed some more wool and yarn to weave as I had begun making a beautiful new robe for my husband's homecoming. Many a woman were awed by my skills as a weaver, and I smiled as I remembered the lovely lady who taught me the skill, and whose name I shared.

I had begun teaching myself how to make exotic cheeses, and though I knew Avila held this new hobby of mine in contempt, I enjoyed experimenting with new recipes and could not wait to share the finished products with my husband. For these reasons, I found the need to visit the market at least once a week. On each of these occasions, I would always find a reason to walk past the Temple area where I first saw Kiera on that dreadful day long ago. I kept my eyes and ears open and would intentionally bump into servants asking if they knew of a child with violet eyes who was known to work at the Temple. Most often people shook their heads and turned away, but I was not deterred. Each time I grew bolder and would stay a bit longer at the market.

When I arrived home with my wares, I would share them with the servants who would listen to my stories. My mother-in-law would often question my lack of judgement for going so frequently to the market. She had been told I was seen by the Temple one day and chastised and berated me in front of the staff and family until Jidu intervened on my behalf. I defended myself and my actions by saying I was justified in giving gifts to the beggars who were desperate for a coin. For if not the wealthy such as we were, who would give to the least of these in need? This seemed to please Grandfather and infuriate Avila, even further alienating her from me.

Though I desired a relationship with her, I had given up any hope of her ever accepting me. I was, after all, a lowly foreigner who did not deserve to be married to her son. Because Grandfather defended me at every opportunity, and her distain for him seemed to be growing every day as well. Though I had not yet gotten a glimpse of Kiera, or even heard if she was still at the Temple, my resolve was resolute. I was determined to find her. What would I do if that happened? I did not know, and without Misha to talk to and temper my impulses, I found my newfound freedom as a married woman liberating.

As spring turned to summer and the days got hotter, I could not go as often as I liked to the market; however, I found several willing servants who were more than happy to do my bidding. They were my new friends, and I would make any excuse to converse with them as I often saw Grandfather doing. He saw them as people and treated them with respect. I valued and admired his compassion and grace with those who Avila frequently reminded him were beneath the Hassen family.

Samir was rarely at the table when we dined together which was far less frequently than it had been before Misha left. My mother-in-law made more and more excuses as to why she would not be attending dinner. Whether it was a headache, it was too hot, or she simple refused to come, we dined without her and found those evenings to be far more enjoyable than when she was present. Soon, I realized Zain was rarely in attendance either, which did not disappoint me in the slightest. Grandfather would often invite a learned guest, and we would discuss history, archeology or even the Torah which was, of course, my favorite. They were impressed with my knowledge of the ancient scrolls, and I eagerly shared how my uncle had taught me how to read and write. I told of how I would hide outside the temple when my cousins were in Torah School, listening and learning all I could. This pleased grandfather Jidu, and he would invite me to study and learn in his library which gave me great joy.

We heard very little from the battlefield, only that Misha was being kept safe and was making a name for himself as a strong leader. These messages were brought in and given to Grandfather who would read them at the evening meal. This became the only time Avila was found at the dinner table. When she heard news had been brought from the battlefield, she would impatiently wait for the meal to be served and insist Grandfather not delay but read the message at once. The messages were always over far too quickly, and I was left sitting at the evening meal longing for more news of Misha. Where was he? Was he warm at night? Was he being well fed? Did he miss me as much as I desperately missed him?

Shortly after the words were read, whether it was mid-meal or even as a course was just being served, Avila would excuse herself and leave the table, paying no mind to all of the eyes staring at her back as she departed. Grandfather Jidu was always gracious and engaged each of us in conversation, directing questions first to Samir about the crops or herds, then on to Zain whose answers were usually one or two words. Next was Jamal, who would entertain us all with the stories of his latest adventures. We would all listen attentively as he recounted his ride into the woods, or his encounter with a wolf while hunting with his friends.

Finally, Grandfather would look in my direction and all eyes would fasten on me as I shared about the latest garment I was weaving, or of the newest recipes I had created. I avoided speaking of my escapades into the markets, for fear I would raise suspicions or be questioned about their frequency. I both enjoyed the opportunity to share as well as loathed the feeling of Zain's eyes upon me as if I were his prey and he was the hungry wolf of whom Jamal had spoken.

One day as the mornings had begun to gather dew from the night before, I went in search of Grandfather in our usual meeting place, only to be told by one of the servants that he had taken his tea in his quarters and had not eaten any of the bread and cheese he usually enjoyed. I feared he may have fallen ill and prayed to Yahweh to reach down and touch this man who had become so embedded in my heart. When several days passed and still there was no sign of him, I ventured to his wing of the palace and gently tapped on the door, knowing that to do so would bring the wrath of Avila on me. Still, I feared Grandfathers being ill far more than the berating of my mother-in-law. I had to see for myself what was going on with my dear Jidu. When the door cracked open, a servant appeared. Upon seeing me, the door was closed again, and I knocked harder this time. When the door was not opened—for what seemed an eternity as I stood there, I went in search of Samir to seek the answers I needed. Surely, he would know what was wrong with his own father-in-law. I was told that Misha's father was on a day's journey and would not return until that evening. I would have to bide my time and pray all the more for mercy on Grandfather.

Days passed and still there was no word on why Grandfather had not left his chambers for over a week. No one would talk to me. Samir avoided me and refused to see me when I requested his presence. The servants were whispering in the halls and would not look at me when I passed them. I determined to find out for myself and resolved I would not leave until I had the answers I sought.

I knocked loudly on the door of Grandfather's chambers and did not wait to have the door slammed in my face, but rather entered in boldly when the door cracked open. I moved confidently to where my beloved Jidu lay. At first, I feared I had barged into the wrong chamber, for the man lying in the bed did not resemble Grandfather. Yet upon closer inspection, I realized that my eyes had deceived me. It was indeed the man who had brought me to this place. My heart squeezed in my chest as I looked upon the sunken eyes and skin as pale and yellow as an onion. What had happened to this formerly robust and healthy man whom I had sat across the table from just two weeks ago? His breathing was labored, and as the servants tried to remove me from the room, his eyes fluttered open and he raised one hand as if to halt their treatment of me.

When they released my arms, I quickly rushed to his bedside and took his frail hand in my own. The tears slipped down my cheeks as he tried to smile at me. His voice was but a whisper and I had to lean in close to hear what he was trying to say to me. The only words I could understand were *danger* and *be careful*.

What was he saying? Was he in danger? Was I? Why did I need to be careful? I was desperate to hear more when I felt the strong hands around my arms again pulling me away from this wonderful man who had treated me with such kindness. It was obvious he was near death; I could not bear to leave his side. I struggled to get free, but realized it was no use. I could only shout, "I love you, Grandfather. I love you, Grandfather. I love you Grandfather" as I was dragged from the room.

My own words echoed in my mind and heart as I lay awake night after night. His words of caution to me were a cause of great fear and anxiety as the days wore on. Though I tried many times to see him again, his quarters were heavily guarded. I was told by Avila that in no uncertain terms was I to try and see her father ever again as I had caused him such damage when I had visited him earlier. She tried to convince me I had made his condition much worse and I would surely bring his grey head down to the grave.

She shouted at me, "You had no right to force your way into his chambers. Your actions caused him irreparable harm, and I will make sure my son knows full well of your reckless and selfish behavior."

I was deeply disturbed by her words yet comforted by the fact that if Misha was told his beloved Jidu was sick, then surely, he would return any day. I was confused as to why she was so angry with me, knowing how deeply I loved her father. Her anger seemed strangely out of place and truly misdirected at me. This, of course, only added to my grief and I could barely eat or drink, for fear that Grandfather would leave this world, and no one would even bother to tell me.

Day after day I waited for news of his recovery or his dreaded demise. And then one day, as the leaves began to fall outside my window, I heard the wailing begin outside in the courtyard. My heart sank as I realized my fears had come to pass. My beloved Grandfather Jidu had left this earth. I lay on my bed and sobbed right along with all the others who wailed long into the night. I barely left my room as I knew I was not even a welcome guest in the palace now that Jidu was gone. My thoughts raced around in my head as to what would become of me since it was apparent Avila and Samir had not sent word to Misha, therefore, he would not be returning for another six long months.

I tried to stay sequestered in my rooms. Zara was my only contact with the family outside my chamber doors. Eventually I held my grief at bay and ventured out to inquire of the funeral arrangements. I believe they had all but forgotten about me, or surely did not care if they ever saw me again. However, as I neared the bottom of the staircase, I heard voices in the library and went to seek out whomever was there. Approaching slowly, I heard the muffled voices of Zain and his mother. I did not want to disturb their grief, so I held back and heard words like: "all taken care of, just as we planned." These words were familiar to me and I was reminded of that long ago day when I had heard the same words similarly spoken. What were they talking about? Was it the funeral arrangements that were all taken care of?

I cleared my throat and entered the room. They both turned to glare at me with shock and hatred pouring from their eyes. I knew they barely tolerated me before, but now since there was no grandfather to protect me from their hatred, I felt a fear I had never known grip my soul—I took a deep breath and stood up straighter and simply asked of the plans for the burial of Grandfather. When they had looked at each other again, Avila spoke up and assured me they would not have any proceedings until the spring when Misha was home to attend his grandfather's burial. She then made me aware that it was none of my business, and furthermore, women were not allowed to attend the burial.

I was then dismissed with a wave of her hand as they turned their backs on me. So, it was confirmed. They had not alerted Misha of his grandfather's illness and, indeed, had not even made him aware of his passing. Surely, they could get word to him on the battlefield. I knew my Misha would not like being kept in the dark about these deeply disturbing events. Grandfather's words continued to play in my head; I found myself more cautious than ever before. What danger was awaiting me? How would I survive the next six months until Misha's return?

CHAPTER 33

Zain

The Plan Begins

I COULD FEEL the fury building inside of me. It had been almost six months since I had watched my brother ride off into the setting sun. This began the clock on the elaborate plan my mother and I devised to see to it that all our dreams would come true. One day we would both have what should have always been ours.

My brother did not deserve the rights of the first born. He was always too weak, and too gentle to be the ruler over our dynasty. He should never have been allowed to believe he would one day take the place of the old and feeble man who ran the family empire. The two of them, Jidu and Misha, were cut from the same cloth and neither had earned, nor could handle, the power that came from such an important title.

From the moment the old man brought the Little Beauty into our home, everything had gone wrong. My rage had been boiling under the surface for years, but when I laid eyes on Myree, I knew she had to be mine. I didn't care if she had technically been given in marriage to my brother. Mother promised me I could have her: It was settled. Though I wanted to take her before she had lain with my brother, I was not allowed to take any action. I feared my mother would be angry and ignore me the way she did before the Little Beauty arrived. Since that day, my mother—who could barely look at me since I was a child—had begun seeking me out.

She had taken to sending messages to me asking to meet in the library after everyone had retired or before the sun had risen. She would even come to my chambers on occasion—that is, as long as there was no one around to see her. She and I shared very similar thoughts about the Little Beauty, and the plan for the feeble old man had now been put into motion.

Since our first meeting, we had met often. Sometimes in the barn, sometimes in the wine cellar, but never in plain sight of anyone else. That was fine with me.

Though she treated me with kindness and respect for the first time in my life, I had the feeling she was still ashamed she had given birth to me. I was in awe of her and would do anything to have her look at me and not turn away in disgust. She was truly a genius at getting what she wanted, and her clever plan had worked flawlessly. No one had even the slightest suspicion the old man had died of anything but natural causes. Little by little she had begun slipping just the right amount of the fatal herb into Grandfather's tea. I had acquired the poison for her in the back-alley tea houses where I would often go to soothe my tortured soul. I could buy anything for a price and because I was feared by men and women alike, no one ever questioned my purchase of the deadly herb.

When the time was right, and that brother of mine was safely on the battlefield far, far away—we had put our plans in motion—and no one would ever dare to raise any questions. Now that he was out of the picture and out of our way, we could move forward with the plans which kept me up at night. The promises Mother made to me in order to keep me under control. Promises that gave me the patience to simply watch, listen, and wait for the perfect time. I was content to spy on the Little Beauty from under her balcony. I was at rest getting reports from my servants about her trips to the market, her weaving, and her time spent in the kitchen making her delicious cheeses.

I would bide my time, and when Mother said the time was right, then I would have what I wanted more than anything I had ever wanted in my whole life. Mother promised me that my brother's wife would be mine one day: and I believed her. I just needed to keep my distance from her. I could absolutely not be in the same room with her. I knew if I got too close and got even the slightest hint of her special aroma (the one that smelled like vanilla and lavender) I could feel myself lose control. Yes, I would be patient and not allow my eyes to look upon her silky auburn hair that shone like the sun in the afternoon light. I dare not take in the sight of the eyes that appeared as green and gold as the sea in the distance. I would not—I could not, for fear that my self-control would be lost, and I would do something that would interrupt the carefully laid out plan my mother and I had put into place.

So, I would continue to wait and watch. I would stay at a distance, always concealed in the shadows or behind trees as I had done my entire life. I would position myself underneath her balcony as often as I knew she was in her chambers and I would listen for the sound of her soft humming, or better yet, the sound of her tears falling in grief. That was the greatest sound of all, and I would enjoy the day when she would weep before me, begging for mercy.

CHAPTER 34

Myree

Danger and Caution

WITH GRANDFATHER GONE and Misha away, I had only Zara to talk to and she and I became as close as any two people could be. I would ask her questions about what was happening in the palace, as I rarely ventured out anymore. The time of mourning Jidu was almost over, and we would be allowed to leave the palace again. My heart was so heavy after losing one of the only people who had ever truly cared for me. My eyes would often flood with tears as I recalled our talks in the library or his gentle smile at me from across the table. It seemed I had known him forever, not just the last two years of my life.

I was the wife of the heir to the Hassen throne, yet I was treated as if I were no better than a servant by Misha's family. Would I even have any rights now that Grandfather was gone? Should I not be treated with respect as the wife of the new Master of the palace? Because Avila was the only child of Grandfather and his beloved Myriam, she, alone was in line to inherit the throne; however, since women were mere possessions, the rule would automatically pass to the firstborn son, Misha. All this was so confusing, and I still could not understand the contempt I felt from my husband's mother and brother.

Jamal and Samir spent time together as father and son in the orchards or away on trips, so it was only Zain and Avila left to run the household. As the days began to shorten, I began taking trips to the market again so I could resume my weaving and cheese making. These were the only things that brought me any joy, and I knew I would go mad if I had to stay cooped up in the palace all winter. Zara would secure a chaperon for us and we would take the safety of the carriage, lest I be accused of being a commoner and walking to the market. I again began inquiring about the child with the violet eyes who was seen around the Temple and was always met with the same negative response. I would see the angry man with the black eyes guarding the steps to the Temple, and sometimes catch a glimpse of a girl, but it was never my Kiera.

Days turned into weeks and my efforts had come to nothing. Then one day, while at the spice booth bending down to smell a batch of fragrant spices, I saw the back of a young girl whose hair color was the same as mine. Though her scarf was wrapped around her head, ours was such an unusual shade, I recognized Kiera instantly. Before I knew what was happening, I had dropped the bag of spices, and called out "Kiera!"

Her head turned and I looked into the same eyes of the little girl who sat had next to me huddled in the corner those two plus years ago. They were the same color, only now they were different. They stared into mine with a pain and darkness I did not recognize. Could this be the same girl? The years had not been kind to her and the scowl on her face distorted her features into a twisted sneer.

I tried to push through the crowd to get closer to her. She turned and disappeared up the Temple steps behind the man with the black eyes who dared me to approach. Now people were starting to take notice as Zara was pulling on my robe to follow her back to the marketplace. I had no choice but to allow myself to be led away.

At last, I had seen her. She was alive! And she had seen me as well. Perhaps she would realize I had not completely abandoned her but had thought of her day and night and was still searching for her. My heart was heavy as we entered the palace that afternoon. I went directly to my chambers, telling Zara to take my purchases to the kitchen. I would usually enjoy sharing my treasures with the staff and telling them about a new spice I was going to blend with the goat's milk to make a new type of cheese. But today I did not have the energy for their questions and simply needed to be alone to ponder the change in my little Kiera's eyes.

I stepped out onto the balcony, watching the slowly setting sun. I wondered what horrifying fate awaited Kiera on this night. My mind had to shut down to the darkness which overtook me. Shame and guilt overwhelmed me for allowing her to remain in that awful place this entire time. I should have told Misha about her immediately after I had seen her the first time over two years ago. Surely, he would have taken pity on me and paid to have her released to him. She could have at least been brought here to work as a servant. Even that would have been a far better life than the one she was living.

The tears slid down my face and I wept for the little girl whose innocence had been stolen from her. I wept for all the lost dreams and for all the girls who were sold at the auction that day. My sobs came harder; I allowed my pain and loss to escape. I wept for my Misha and wondered if I would ever see him again. I wept for Grandfather and for my own mother who had agreed to sell me to strangers. I wept for the feel of my auntie's arms wrapped around me and for my cousins who would tease me.

Suddenly, directly below me, I heard a noise. Was that laughter I heard? Someone was in the bushes directly below me. Who was out there? Who would be so cruel as to interrupt my grief with laughter? I knew of only one person, and as I quickly retreated into the shadows of my room, I was certain Zain had been below me. I was sickened to think this was not the first time he had positioned himself there to be able to spy on me. Grandfather's words of danger, and his cautioning me to be careful came to my mind. A chill took hold of my whole body. Did Zain have others watching me? Was I being followed each time I went to the market or for a stroll out in the orchards?

I resolved to be more diligent in my movements and to keep a closer eye on who went with me on my outings. It would not do for my mother-in-law or brother-in-law to know of my searching for Kiera at the temple. Surely, that would give them all the more reason to hate me. Fear wound its ugly fingers around my heart, and I knew I was truly alone in this world once again. The terror of the sound of his laughter beneath me kept me awake until the sun rose when, finally, I drifted off into a fitful sleep.

CHAPTER 35

Naomi

The Search Continues

THE DAYS OF the harvest were upon us and the pain in my heart was still piercing as I thought of my Sweet Mary. It was always this time of year when we would celebrate the day of her birth and my eyes welled with tears as I separated the wheat from the chaff. She would be growing up, now a young woman of striking beauty. Where on earth had she been taken? If my sister knew, I had not been able to get her to tell me the truth about her daughter. Every time I traveled to her village to find her, I was more and more devastated at the life she was living.

In the last two years, there had only been one time I had seen my sister when she had not been too drunk to speak. When I questioned her, she began sobbing and screaming at me to leave, to get out of her house, out of her life, and never come back.

What nightmare thing had she done that haunted her so deeply? Her husband had stopped coming home and I heard the women in the village use deplorable language when speaking of my beloved sister. They told me there were men who came and went from her home, and all they needed to do was bring her a bottle of drink and some bread and she would welcome them in. That explained how she lived without a husband to support her. My heart raged between tender compassion over her brokenness and blinding anger at the mother who would let go of her only daughter.

Secretly, I continued to search for my Sweet Mary every chance I had. At the market, I would search for the auburn hair, and look into every young girl's eyes, hoping to catch a glimpse of the golden emerald color so unique to my niece. I had to be careful as my husband had long since forbid me to search for her, and even the mention of her name brought a dark scowl to his handsome features. My boys were growing up and they often left me to tend to the animals and harvest as each pursued their studies and chosen careers. My oldest was now almost twenty-two and thinking of a family of his own.

My days were filled with washing, baking, and carrying water from the well. It was there that I would meet with my treasured friend, Mary. I trusted her like a sister, and I felt safe sharing my deepest fears and secrets with her. She had showered my Sweet Mary with love and kindness while teaching her the intricate craft of weaving. Mary had a deep affinity for the child who bore her name and had created the most beautiful shawl for her. She told me often, as she had woven the beautiful colors together that were so close to the shade of Sweet Mary's eyes and hair, she had prayed over the garment and had asked Yahweh to protect and keep its wearer safe from harm. I remember seeing my Sweet Mary's eyes as my husband handed her the robe my friend had created especially for her. She clung to the fabric and held it to her face astonished something so beautiful was now hers. She never took that shawl off and even wore it underneath her plain, everyday robes, telling me that when she could feel the soft fabric against her skin, she felt special and cherished. What had ever become of that priceless gift?

I asked Yahweh again and again to keep her safe in His arms, to protect her and remind her of all the words of the Torah we had taught her. She had been a truly remarkable child, learning quickly and hungering for more instruction and knowledge even at a young age. I was grateful for the years we had to teach her and love her, and I prayed she carried all of that in her heart, no matter where she was.

Did she even recognize she was turning another year older as the harvest was collected? Oh, how my heart longed to see her face again, to hold her in my arms, and to hear her humming beside me our favorite *Love Song to Yahweh*. Though my faith was strong, and I believed that the God of Abraham, Isaac, and Jacob was all powerful and could part the seas, I also knew there was great evil in this dark world. I tried not to lose hope of ever seeing the beautiful child again.

CHAPTER 36

Kiera

Power in Hatred

AS I SAT on the cushioned chaise, waiting for my next customer, I had another message from a servant to tell me about the beautiful young woman with the golden green eyes and hair the same shade as mine asking about me again. I had lost count of how many messages I had received in the last several months. I knew she was out there searching for me. Just last week, I had heard the name by which my parents called me shouted over the throng of the marketplace. I recognized the voice of the one person who had shown me kindness before I entered into my own personal living hades. That had been two long years ago, and though I had thought of her often after the first time she saw me on the Temple steps, I had shut my heart off after that and buried the idea there was any good left in this hostile world. From that day on, I had vowed to protect myself from the evil raging around me and I killed off the last part of my heart which held any emotion, becoming a hard shell of a human being.

As a child of barely eleven years old, I had grown up fast. I did what I needed to do in order to survive, often stealing from the men who visited me as they slept. I became the most sought-after girl in the Temple and began insisting I be granted more freedom and privileges. I could do no wrong as long as I commanded the high prices the rich men would pay. My skills were now becoming well known, and as one of the youngest, my future was secure. I had my master right where I wanted him. Before long I would find a way to rid the earth of his vile body and take control of the girls who would soon be under my care. Until then, I would enjoy the stature I had achieved in the two short years I had been here, and I would continue to relish the idea of plunging a knife deep into the master's black heart.

I would then dream about how I could take revenge on the one I knew only as Mary, who did not even bother to look my way as I was dragged away kicking and screaming off the stage by the evil men who had destroyed my life. She was just like everyone else who made me believe they loved me, and then left me all alone.

As my mind drifted back to that horrifying time, I allowed myself to remember when we left the tent after I had been sold. A big man dragged my kicking and screaming body while holding his huge hand over my mouth. When I bit down on the flesh, I was struck so hard I only regained consciousness many hours later. I awoke to realize I was locked in a dark trunk that smelled like the breath of the man who had struck me. The darkness surrounded me so close even my screams went unheard to my own ears. I was alone and more scared than I had ever been. Even back home when my father beat my mother, sisters and me, I had never been this frightened. I wished only to die and be with my beloved grandmother. I don't know how long I banged my fists on the sides of that trunk; however, I could smell the blood dripping down my arms. After what seemed like forever, I was so hungry, it was only when I licked the blood from my arms that I felt sustained. I was so weak I simply went to sleep and hoped I would never wake up.

Suddenly there were rough hands all over me and I was being lifted out of the trunk. My body was so limp I could not stand and had to be carried. I heard voices telling them to bring food and water. Someone was going to save me. I was not dead and maybe someone would be kind to me and give me something to eat. I was weak from hunger and so exhausted, I blacked out and fell onto the floor when they put me down.

I awoke to find myself naked and in a warm bath. Hands were washing my hair and tending gently to my still bloodied hands. Someone else was pushing grapes into my mouth and I almost choked on the delicious fruit. I became aware of my surroundings and realized I was in some sort of a palace. I was being tended to as if I were a princess and the mean man who had struck me was nowhere to be seen. In my little girl embarrassment, I tried to cover my nakedness, but it was no use. These women were skilled

at bathing young girls, and though they were gentle, they kept a firm hold of me. After I had soaked the dirt away, my hair was washed and rinsed over and over again. I was lifted from the tub and oils were rubbed all over my frail little body. My hair was covered in an ointment that smelled of everything beautiful. My hands were bandaged, and I was dressed in a soft golden robe. I was taken to a room where I was told to eat and sleep, and then I was left all alone, again.

When I awoke, I was ravenous and greedily ate everything left for me: the meat, figs, bread and cheese. I sucked down all the water in the pitcher. I looked around the room and climbed back onto the big bed and fell asleep. The next several days were the same—someone would bring me food and water, change the bandages on my hands, and then leave again. I could not understand the language they spoke and had no idea where I was, but I was getting stronger every day. Surely, someone would come to get me and maybe take me home to live with them and I could be a little girl again … at least that was what I dreamed would happen.

I began to recognize the same people whom I had come to think of as my guards. Every day was the same, and though I tried to talk to them, they ignored me. They would not allow me to leave or even look out the windows. I was a prisoner, and I had no idea what my fate would be. I don't know how many days and nights I was kept in that room, but after what seemed like a very long time, I was taken by one of my guards, given over to a man, put into a carriage and then taken to what they called the Temple.

At the Temple, I was met by a mean looking man who took me into a large room with lots of other girls, some my age, but most were older than me. They were all dressed in beautiful robes and had makeup all over their faces. They looked at me with blank eyes and paid no attention to me as one after the other left the room. I became frightened when I began to hear screams coming from the rooms surrounding us. I retreated to a corner of the room where I curled myself into the smallest ball I could and tried to disappear.

I was shaken from my memories by the sound of the door opening. I stood up and wiped the tears from my cheeks that I had not realized were there. I greeted the old man in front of me. It was time to go to work.

CHAPTER 37

Myree

The Nightmare Begins

THE LEAVES HAD all fallen from the trees and the orchards looked barren and desolate in the distance. The balcony had always been my favorite place, but now I was so cautious, always wondering if someone was watching me. All the joy had been gradually draining from my life and the fear and anxiety I lived in was what I carried around with me day and night. There was no place I felt safe anymore, knowing I had no one left to protect me. I would wake up with every little noise, wondering if someone was in my room; and therefore, I always felt tired as I slept so fitfully.

A cold wind came up and the clouds on the horizon were ominous. It looked like a storm was coming in and I wrapped my robe a little tighter around my shoulders. I didn't like storms and knew that tonight I would not sleep as the thunder crashed and the lightening lit up the skies. Perhaps Zara would agree to sleep in my room with me tonight.

Though she was just down the hall, if she were with me in my room, maybe I would not feel so frightened and could get some sleep. This was strictly forbidden, as slaves were never allowed to sleep in the masters' quarters. But Zara had become so much more to me, and no one need ever find out. About a year ago, when I was very sick, she had slept in my room beside my bed. Misha had insisted upon it even though his mother protested. I was sure Misha would allow it for tonight as well, just because of the storm. I would speak to her when she brought in my evening meal. This thought gave me some peace as I moved into my chambers and closed the doors on the cold wind and approaching storm.

My mind always traveled back to Misha. He was always close to my heart and I missed him so much. I loved him even more than I ever thought possible when I considered the way he treated me with such kindness and tenderness on the two nights after our wedding. He had every right to take what was his, but he loved me and wanted our union to be beautiful and special. So, understanding my terror, he was willing to wait until he came back to truly be my husband. I had assured him before he left, I would be the willing bride he wanted upon his return. I would count the days until we could be truly together as husband and wife. The thought still made me uncomfortable, but I vowed to be the wife he deserved and would do whatever it took be make him happy.

All I knew about mating was from the sheep and cows my uncle had raised. I can still remember how my cousins would laugh and my auntie would cover my eyes in the barn when it was that time of the year. I had no idea what to expect but I knew my Misha would be sweet and gentle with me.

As night began to fall, Zara came in, lit the lamps and made sure there was a fire going in the hearth. She even brought in some hot rocks to place in my bed to keep my feet from freezing. As I sat down to eat, Zara prepared the room and laid out my bed clothes. When I had finished eating, she pulled all the drapes closed as it had begun to rain. She then helped me out of my robe. As she took all the pins from my hair, she began brushing it in long even strokes, knowing this always relaxed me when I was anxious about anything.

She knew quite well my anxiety about storms, so in order to distract me, she chatted on about the servants and what was happening in the kitchen. When I asked her about sleeping in my room, she laughed and told me she could not, for if it was ever found out, she would be beaten, and she did not want to take that chance. I pleaded with her to take pity on me and promised I would take the blame, but she looked me in the eyes and we both knew that would not be how it would play out. I would not be able to cover for her. She promised to bring me a cup of special tea which would help me to relax a bit and bring sleep to my eyes, then agreed to stay with me until after I fell asleep. I would have to be content with this.

When Zara left my chambers to get my tea, I felt even more jumpy than before. The storm was rattling the windows and the drafts that came in the cracks blew the drapes around. I knew I would never sleep tonight and decided to get out the parchment paper and write a letter to my beloved Misha. Even though I knew my letters would not be in his hands until he came home, I had taken to writing him almost every night. I shared my thoughts, hopes and dreams, but never my grief, fear or the dread which had taken hold of my heart.

I settled in to write and did not realize how much time had passed. My eyes had grown heavy and when Zara came in, I was just finishing up my letter. I was glad to have her back, but when she placed the tray on the table, I saw her hands were shaking badly. I asked her what had her so distressed, but she just averted her eyes. I took hold of her hands and made her look at me and tell me what had happened to upset her. She said that Master Zain had been drinking and had confronted her in the kitchen, asking her all kinds of questions about our trips to the market. He told her he knew about the questions I had been asking about the girl at the Temple and was angry I had disgraced the Hassen name by inquiring about a Temple prostitute. She stammered that she was only able to break free when another servant came into the kitchen and interrupted them. She ran out as fast as she could and had to hide until the master left. She then gathered the tea and came directly here.

She broke down into tears and I took her into my arms and let her cry. I knew she was even more frightened of Zain than I was, though I never knew quite why. This was so disturbing. By now I was wide awake. I paced the floor wondering what to do now that Zain (and probably Avila) knew everything I had been doing. He had been spying on me all along. I should have been more careful. Grandfather's words came back to haunt me again … danger … be careful.

Now that I had stirred up the wrath of Zain, what could I do to protect myself and Zara? I felt horrible that my actions had affected her in such a negative way. I could lock my door, but that would be no defense for someone who had a key or who could break it down, if he so desired. The rain beating against the windows did not help our state of mind, and I insisted that Zara share my tea and we both try to get some sleep. She composed herself and was again the dutiful servant, making sure I drank the majority of the tea. She ushered me into bed, tucking the blankets tightly around me because of the stormy night. I made her promise to lay down too, and I yawned as the tea took hold of me.

My eyes flew open as I felt a hand clamp down over my mouth. I was startled wide awake, but my head was foggy because of the tea. Where was

Zara? Was this a nightmare? The dark reality of Zain's hot fetid breath in my face brought the nightmare into focus. Zara was gone and Zain was on top of me pouring out all the rage he had kept inside for so long. I tried to fight, but it was no use. The thunder crashed outside, and rain beat against the windows. All the horror I had imagined in my mind could never compare to the evil that was unfolding before my very eyes. He was raging at me, his twisted mouth spewing hatred and filth I could not comprehend. He pulled me up by the hair, tore the blankets away, and then ripped my nightgown off of me. I screamed with all the terror within me. The thunder crashed and the lightening lit up the room. I saw his smile and heard his laughter as his twisted mouth came down hard onto mine. I tried to fight but it was no use. I clawed at his face with everything in me. I felt the full force of his hand hit me so hard my neck snapped back. I cried out to Yahweh and fell back into blackness.

I don't know how long I lay unconscious, but when I awoke, he was gone. Only the pounding of my head and the pain between my legs told me it had not been a bad dream, but a true living nightmare. I rolled off the bed, pulled a blanket around me, and crawled into the farthest corner of my dark room. I curled into a ball and sobbed as the reality of what happened to me slammed into my brain. My body shook uncontrollably. My face was bloodied from the place where the ring that Zain wore on his left hand had opened my cheek. The rain still beat against the window, and I wanted to run out and jump off the balcony to end the scenes that kept replaying in my mind. Over and over, I saw the horror, heard the laughter, and tasted his ugly breath as his mouth came down on mine.

I squeezed my eyes shut as I tried to stop the images, but still they came. My whole body was wracked with sobs and my teeth chattered as the tears fell hot on my cheeks. Daylight was starting to seep in under the drapes. When I heard the door open, I shrank further into the darkness of the corner, fearing he had returned. Smaller and smaller I shrank into myself as I heard Zara's voice searching for me. My muffled sobs alerted her to my location in the corner, and she rushed to my aid, wrapping her arms around me and breaking into sobs of her own. When I looked at her face, I saw that she too had been beaten and my heart shattered all over again. It was not only me who had been the victim of Zain's evil wrath, but I had brought pain upon Zara as well. I don't know how long we stayed huddled together in the corner weeping. By the time light began filling the room, we had cried all the tears we had. Zara then slowly got up, went and locked the door, and then moved a heavy piece of furniture in front of it.

It was not yet daybreak, so the house was quiet after the storm. I knew no one would bother to come and check on me even after such a stormy night, so I felt a measure of safety with the door locked and barred. Zara took me by the hands and helped me up. She led me to the chaise lounge, placed a pillow behind my head, and wrapped a heavy woolen blanket around me. She then went to run a bath for me. Unable to think, I complied with her instructions. How was she able to perform her duties knowing what had happened in this room? It was all so confusing to me. When had she left? Was she still in my room when Zain came in? Is that why he beat her? I had so many questions, but my mouth was bruised and swollen, and I could not speak. My mind was still blurry from the effects of the tea I had been encouraged to drink the night before. I could not bear to look into Zara's eyes for all the shame and disgust I felt for myself. I was no longer pure and undefiled for my beloved Misha. Everything had been stolen from me by the monster who was his own flesh and blood. The sobs engulfed me again as I fell to the floor in anguish.

Zara let my tears flow and then half carried me to the bath. The water was warm and inviting, but I hid myself and shivered from the cold which had taken hold of my heart. Zara gently washed my hair and tended to my wounds, not thinking about her own bloodied face. I then took the towel from her hands and gently washed the dried blood from her broken lip and cheek. She allowed me to tend to her and we both cried tears of humiliation and shame.

She seemed to understand the depth of my pain, and I wondered if this was why she had always shown such terror in the presence of Zain. Had Zain violated Zara in the same way he had tortured me last night? We never spoke any words, but our hearts were knit together in an understanding that went beyond anything spoken.

She helped me to get dressed, stripped the bloodied sheets off of the bed, and braided my hair before she made herself presentable and went to get my breakfast. I held her hand hoping she would not leave. She promised to return and told me that everything was going to be just fine. She had a confidence and a fire in her eyes, but I knew in the depth of my being that nothing would ever be fine again ... ever.

CHAPTER 38
Zain

Power Unleashed

I AWOKE FROM the sleep of the dead that often accompanied one of my episodes and shook my head to remember the night before. Slowly, I began replaying the events of the stormy night. The fierce winds had come in suddenly, and with a ferocity I had not seen in my seventeen years. Only once had I experienced that kind of wild tempest, with thunder and lightning, wind and rain so powerful it took my breath away. I loved the power of the storm and sat enjoying the memory of the flashes of bright light that lit up the darkness. The rain had pelted my face as I stood outside and willed the wind to sweep me up, up and away into the dark clouds that had always surrounded my daylight.

Sitting in the dawn of the new day, flashes of my victory replayed in my mind. I was tormented by black shame and the equally exquisite feelings of remembering my Little Beauty's body beneath my own. I had finally taken what was rightfully mine. She had always been mine from the first time I laid eyes on her. Never mind that Jidu had brought her from a faraway land to be the bride of my brother. When I caught a glimpse of her and saw the way the sunlight danced in her silky hair and how her eyes shone with a purity that contrasted my own depravity; I knew she would be mine. I had waited patiently, I had allowed my brother to have his time with her, knowing she was already mine in my heart and soul. And even on their wedding night, I waited as I drowned my anguish with heavy drink and banished the ugly thoughts from my mind of him lying next to my Little Beauty.

A smile formed on my twisted mouth as I remembered the deeply satisfying feeling of victory when I realized my big brother had not yet tasted of the first fruits of his own bride. The power that surged through me as I rightfully claimed what had always been mine was intoxicating. I remembered fighting off that dark-skinned vixen as I entered into the room and the feeling of my fists connecting with her face as she came after me again and again. I dragged her out of the room and left her bleeding and unconscious in the hallway. I needed to be alone as I fulfilled my long-anticipated dream. I don't recall making my way back to my own quarters, but I knew I was still fueled by the storm that continued to rage outside.

I must have fallen asleep at some point and here I was, tucked safe and sound in my own bed caught in between the state of sleep and waking, piecing together the previous night's events. As I stretched and allowed myself to enter into the reality of daybreak, I caught a glimpse of my hand and reached for the ache that had formed on my face. I touched a gash and recalled the pain of the slave girl's claws as they raked down my cheek just before I beat her unconscious. My body still bore the evidence of the terror I had visited upon both the dark-skinned slave and the Little Beauty. As I allowed myself to remember the events of the night before, my wet clothes on the floor confirmed that all the images I had so sweetly been savoring. They had indeed been my reality.

I had finally risen to my rightful place within my family. I had taken what had never belonged to my brother and now I could live in the sweetness of my own power which would now forever be mine. I would laugh in the face of my brother when he valiantly returned from the battlefield knowing the secret would remain forever between me and my Little Beauty. Myree would never bring shame upon herself or her beloved Misha by sharing the truth of what had taken place between us. No, my secret was safe; it would be our little secret to guard together, and no one would ever know of our night of passion.

CHAPTER 39

Myree

The Agony Continues

I DID NOT dare to leave my chambers. Zara always kept the door locked and the armoire pushed in front of it; hoping that would stop any evil from again entering my prison. We had a special knock she would give to alert me of her presence. She remained sequestered in my rooms with me most of the time unless it was to retrieve our meals or to do my bidding.

I had not tended to my weaving or stepped foot in the kitchen in weeks. I had not seen another person besides Zara, and I was beginning to receive questioning messages about my health and well-being from my mother-in-law. I tried to assure her I was just feeling a bit under the weather. I had no intention of ever leaving my room, lest I encounter the darkness that had overtaken me on that one stormy night. As I retreated further and further into myself, I realized I was barely living, but rather simply existing, day to day, wondering why I was even alive.

Surely it would be better for me to end my own life than have to face the searching eyes of my Misha when he returned in just a few short months. How would I ever be able to hold his hand or allow him to kiss my lips when I was filled with dark shame and such a deep self-loathing that I could not stand my own reflection? I had not slept or eaten much, and my pathetic reflection showed me how disgraceful I truly was. Only Zara kept me alive and I know the reason she spent so much time with me in my chambers. It was to prevent me from doing something that would have eternal ramifications. She would force me to eat a few bites of food between my tears, trembling and constant nausea. She made sure I bathed every few days, and in an attempt to get me to relax, she brushed my hair every single night.

As night fell, my anxiety rose. I would pace the floor with a wild look in my eyes wondering if tonight would be the night when evil would again enter my bedroom. I desperately wanted to run away, but where would I go? I had no way to support myself and part of my heart—the part that was still beating—still longed to see my husband again. With every new winter storm, my terror rose until I was like a caged animal, unable to think or feel until the dawn broke, and the light entered to push away the shadows.

One morning after the full moon, there was a firm knock on my door and a rattle on the lock as the guest tried to enter. I held my breath while Zara went to the door to inquire whose presence was demanding entry. I heard the voice of Avila say in her stern voice, "Open this door at once, I will not be denied entrance into my own home, no matter who resides within."

Knowing I could hide no longer, I nodded to Zara as she half carried me to my bed. I had not touched the bed since the night of terror, but instead I had slept curled into myself far in the corner of the room. I knew I needed to be sick in order for Avila to leave me alone. As Zara moved the chest and unlocked the door, my husband's mother strode into the room looking around for I don't know what. When her eyes finally landed on me, she visibly gasped. The shock on her face registered in my heart that I must truly look as dreadful as I felt, and just as well, I may as well play the part. Through my barely opened eyes I watched as she moved closer to the bed. I thought I saw a hint of compassion in her eyes as she looked from me to Zara, and seeing I was in no condition to answer any questions, she began interrogating my trusted servant and friend.

Avila demanded, "How long has she been like this? What is wrong with her? Why didn't you alert me so I could bring the doctor?" Zara stammered her answers as best as she could trying to hide our secret, but it was of no use. Avila surveyed the room. She noticed the position of the chest and pillows on the floor in the corner where I had made my bed. She stared hard at my pathetic frame and strode out of the room without a backward glance.

I did not know what to do, but quickly motioned for Zara to close, lock the door and place our fortress in position. I crawled out of bed and retreated to my corner of safety, pulling a blanket over me, for the chill had taken hold of me again, and I began to shiver uncontrollably.

The sight of Avila brought all my fears to life as I wondered if she had any knowledge of her son's actions. If she did, was she a party to my terror? It seemed she was genuinely shocked at my condition and I detected no condemnation or hatred—only pity. It had been well over a month since I had left my chamber, and much longer since I had caught a glimpse of my mother-in-law. What would she do now? Was I to be forced to rejoin the living as part of the household? Would she make me resume my former hobbies or attend family meals? The thought of seeing the face of my evil brother-in-law again brought a convulsion to my stomach and I rushed to the basin to spew its meager contents.

I did not have to wait long until the answers to my questions came, as later that afternoon another knock came to the door. Avila's voice demanded entry and Zara quickly ran to the door. I almost felt a hint of a smile seeing her growing strength as she adeptly moved the chest and opened the door to a parade of strangers. I barely had time to pull the covers over me and close my eyes before there were hands on my head. I shrank back at the nearness of the stranger whose touch made my skin crawl. I knew I needed to cooperate, lest he determine something was really wrong with me. After forcing my mouth open and looking into my eyes, this man whom I assumed to be a doctor, then pulled the covers back and touched my stomach. I tried to fight him, but it was no use. I had to suppress a scream when his hands moved over my belly. He then covered me back up and requested a conversation with Zara and Avila outside my door. I knew Zara would be questioned at length and hoped she would not allow our dark secret to be exposed. I heard the footsteps retreating and knew things were going to have to change if I were going to survive.

CHAPTER 40

Avila

The Dark Truth

HEARING THE DOCTOR questioning the slave girl, it became apparent that he had a suspicion Myree was with child. Pregnant? But how could that be? There was no indication of this at all. Her body showed no signs and it had only been in the last two months she had been in seclusion. Misha had been gone for nine long months at this point; surely, she would be close to giving birth by now. I knew nothing of any rumors circulating amongst the servants about her not having her cycle for the last seven months. This pathetic waif held no resemblance to the striking bride who married my Misha last spring. She now had dark circles under her eyes, which appeared hollow and vacant. Her skin was sallow and translucent.

Surely the doctor had it wrong and Myree was not pregnant but had indeed contracted some deadly disease. This made absolutely no sense at all. I tried to recall the last time I had seen her. It seemed I could always catch a glimpse of her in the kitchen or in the library working on her weaving. Was it only the last two months when she had just disappeared from sight? Then it hit me: with a wave of nausea, I had to sit down. Glimpses of the blankets on the floor in the corner and the chest placed in front of the door flashed through my mind. This girl was not sick at all but filled with terror. Watching as she shrank back and visibly flinched at the doctor's touch, it was obvious she had not contracted an illness but had been terrorized by a man. I knew only one person capable of such horror. Could it be that her deterioration had come at the hands of my son

Zain's evil heart? My mind whirled and I had to steady myself to figure out what to do.

I had to summon Zain and get to the bottom of this, to see if he had any part of this awful scene unfolding before me. Was he capable of raping his own brother's wife? The question did not settle in my mind before I knew, without a shadow of a doubt—he was more than capable of such evil. If the girl was indeed pregnant, there would be no way we could pass it off as Misha's baby. He would be home in a few short months, and if he ever found out what his brother had done, there would be a fierce battle and one of my son's would die.

If only I could speak to Samir about this, but because of his disdain for his second son, he would no doubt side with the girl and banish Zain forever. Then what would we do with the bastard illegitimate child? Surely, Misha would never accept the child of his brother as his own flesh and blood.

My mind reeled and my thoughts tumbled together as I scribbled out a message for Zain to join me in the wine cellar after dark. I placed the note in the hand of my trusted servant and wondered if anyone else knew of what was unfolding upstairs in the chambers of my daughter-in-law. This was a dark secret that needed to be kept silent. Anyone who was privy to it could not be allowed to remain. Of course, the girl's slave, Zara, would have to be maintained, for it seemed she was the only one Myree would allow to come near her. She had been caring for her night and day for the last two months and was the only one she trusted.

No, I could handle this on my own. I would get to the bottom of this mystery and then devise a plan to put in motion that would take care of everything. No one need ever know anything about what I feared had come to pass. I would create a story that would surely bring out the truth in Zain. If I knew my child at all, there would be no way that he would allow my story to be told. He would take pride in breaking the soul and body of his brother's beloved wife. I would hear, firsthand, what his part in this whole nightmare was. My heart was again gripped with a new level of revulsion for the child I had brought into this world.

Later that evening, in the dark and dank light of the wine cellar, I had my answer. Upon seeing the look on my middle child's face, as I subtly brought up the subject of his sister-in-law, I felt a new kind of cold grip my heart. I was overtaken by the evil that surrounded me and realized what I had known from the moment I had given birth to this child—there was indeed a monster living inside of him. Trying to hide my fear and revulsion, I let it slip how I feared the girl had somehow taken a lover and become impregnated by him. I explained my calculations and how I came to this conclusion, watching closely for his reaction. I shared my disgust for this girl. How dare she bring disgrace upon the Hassen name. While I was still talking, fury erupted before my very eyes and Zain took hold of my arms demanding I not speak another word. He ferociously defended the honor of his brother's wife and told me that not only had she not taken a lover, but she had not ever even consummated her union with her husband. In triumph he declared that he, and he alone, was the only man she had ever been with. He declared she was a pure virgin when he had taken her, and that was the way it would always be. She was his and he would never allow anyone else to touch her again as long as he lived. He shouted in my face and shook me until I was about to faint.

He released me and grew more and more agitated as he paced length of the cellar floor like a caged animal. He began crying and raging, begging me to help him figure out a way to make her love him the way he loved her; the way he had loved her from the very first moment he had ever laid eyes on his Little Beauty.

He took hold of me again while I stood frozen in terror as he screamed in my face. His hot breath came faster, as his tears continued to flow. I felt his strong hands wrapped hard around my frail arms. I feared for my life if I did not agree to his sick and twisted plan. I knew he had lost whatever sanity he ever had, and that I was dealing with a madman.

I regained my composure remembering he was the son who would do anything I wanted and all I needed to do was convince him we were in this together. I was his ally, not his enemy. I began speaking in soft, hushed tones, calling his name over and over again, knowing I would have to wear long sleeves for the bruises that were already forming on my arms. Slowly, I felt his grip on me loosen and the shaking ceased as he realized it was his mother in front of him.

The rage subsided and he looked deep into my eyes before falling at my feet in agony, wailing his apologies and begging for my forgiveness. I stood absolutely still, and though I desperately wanted to run as far as I could from this demon who had inhabited my son, I remained and found myself lifting him from the floor and comforting this tortured son of mine. I promised him everything would be all right and I would take care of all of it. I told him that someday soon I would make sure she was his, but until that day, he just needed to trust me. I looked into the eyes, so like my own, and shuttered as I extracted a promise from him that he would not go near her until I told him he could. He uttered the promise through the twisted mouth which had so contorted his whole being, and I knew I had regained control of this son of mine.

The power surged through me and I began formulating the plan that would bring resolution to all the problems that girl had brought upon this family since the first day my father had proudly introduced her as my Misha's future bride.

I would get what I wanted, Zain would be vindicated, and Misha would have the wife he truly deserved—the wife of *my* choosing. Yes, the plan was coming together in my mind, but would have to be carried out quickly as Misha was scheduled to be coming home in a few short months. I would take care of everything, and I would soon reign in my rightful place as the true heir to the Hassen Kingdom. A slow smile spread across my face as my son lay whimpering in my battered arms.

CHAPTER 41

Zara

Horror Revisited

THE THOUGHT RACED through my mind for the millionth time ...
I should have killed him in the barn that day after he violated me. I should
have taken the opportunity to rid the world of his evil, but instead, I had
allowed him to remain, only to visit his evil upon my mistress, the kindest
person I've ever known.

Day by day, I had watched her beauty wither away as the light in her
eyes dimmed. She still had not spoken except for the one time she screamed
at me in terror, even though the attack was several weeks prior. I could not
coax her back to life. All joy and peace had been drained out of her on that
dark night. I still bore the scars on my face but tried to pretend I was just
fine. Though I was haunted by the memories of his fists slamming into
my jaw, nose and mouth, I still smiled when I caught a glimpse of the scar
forming on his face due to my clawing his face with all my might.

I was surprised when I awoke alive in the hallway and felt the pain
radiating through my head. I had fought with every fiber of my being to
protect my gentle Myree. Long ago, she had woven her way into my heart,
treating me with respect and kindness, like an older sister instead of the
slave girl I knew myself to be. I treasured her above myself and vowed to
keep her safe ... but I had failed her. It was my fault she was now dying
a slow death right before my very eyes. I would never forgive myself and
would spend the rest of my life devoted to her safety and well-being, even
if it meant giving up my own life to save hers, or ridding the world of the
evil that would dare to come near and harm her again.

If only I could will her to live again, but if I dare mention the name of her beloved Misha, she would collapse into sobs of pain and regret. I had once thought to hum the *Love Song to Yahweh* as she had called it, thinking it might revive her spirit. Instead, she had screamed in fury at the top of her lungs, "There is no such God as Yahweh! He was just a fairy tale I was deceived with as a child."

Since then, her silence permeated every inch of these chambers, and I had all but given up the idea of her ever speaking again. Sometimes I felt a chill run down my spine as I would catch her staring blindly at nothing for long periods at a time. I longed to be able to wrap her in my arms, but she would scarcely allow me to get near her except when she would retreat into the silence of the bathing water I would often run for her. I always had to stay close, for fear she would submerge herself into the pool and never come up. Often, I would find myself wrestling with her as she coughed and sputtered on the water she wished would take her life and put an end to her misery. She would look at me with those beautiful eyes that were now dead and vacant, and the tears would fall afresh. I could rarely get her to eat a bite, though I brought all of her favorite breads, pastries, cheeses and fruit. She was withering away from the inside out and I could do nothing to bring her back to life.

When I changed the sheets for the second time and still did not see the bright color of her cycle staining the bed, I began to fear my own worst nightmare had now been visited upon this girl: she had been impregnated by the demon who had taken her soul. When she began to wretch into the basin each morning, my fears became a reality, and I knew deep in my heart she would bear the illegitimate child of her husband's brother. She had conceived in her body the demon seed of a violent and evil man, and her world was about to get even darker than it already was. How could I bear to bring her the news which would likely be the final blow sending her over the edge into oblivion forever?

I did not have to wait long to find out. Before I knew it, the queen of the house herself banged on the always locked door and demanded to be allowed in. When I recognized the voice and looked at the huddled figure in the corner, I knew my secret was about to be revealed. I quickly dragged her waifish form and lifted her into her chamber of torture, covering her body in heavy blankets. I hurried to push the chest away from in front of the door to allow Avila entrance. She barged in as I unlocked the door and stood there surveying the room with its furniture in disarray and the makeshift bed still lying in the corner. Perhaps she would simply believe that was where I had been sleeping. When she continued her inspection and her eyes landed on the shrunken frame in the large bed, I thought I may have caught a glimpse of compassion. Or was it simply horror as she viewed her daughter-in-law for the first time in weeks? Seeing her face pale, I knew in my heart what I had been witnessing was indeed true, Myree was gone and Avila did not recognize the form lying in the bed. After questioning me, she turned and left without another word.

Later that afternoon, Avila returned again. Banging on the door, she demanded to be let in. She then motioned to the hallway and pushed open the door while the room filled with a medicine man and his associates. My mistress laid tensely in the bed, eyes half-closed and when the doctor approached the side of the bed, she visibly shrank further into herself. I rushed over and allowed her to hear my voice and feel my presence as the man reached out his hand and placed it on her forehead. Her eyes shot open wide as if she had just been touched with a hot fire poker. Her terror was palpable in the room as the doctor asked her to open her mouth. I feared she might bite down on his fingers as he looked down her throat. When he tried to remove the blanket, there was a low growl coming from deep within. She fiercely held the blanket tightly before I could pry her hands away and allow the man to touch her stomach. She looked pleadingly at me, begging for protection, but there was nothing I could do. I was helpless to come to her aide once again. Suddenly, as if she could bear the scene no longer, Avila turned on her heels and rushed out of the room, followed by the man and his team. I was then called by Avila to join them outside the door and had to assure Myree I would return quickly.

As I entered the hallway, Avila told me to close the door, and I knew this was the beginning of the end. The medicine man began to question me. Out of my deep love for my friend, I felt obligated to share the truth, for fear I could no longer help her. Moreover, I needed someone to tell me what to do. I could see Avila was unsteady on her feet as she began to hear the answers I gave as the questioning continued. Though I always tried to hide my face by keeping my eyes downcast, I was commanded by Avila to look up when I spoke. In doing so, this allowed Avila a glimpse of my still bruised face and the deformed nose that had been broken on our night of terror.

She began to sway, causing one of her servants to take hold of her and lead her to a bench. The facts had become obvious to her upon seeing my disfigurement. She then dismissed everyone and remained sitting where she was. I hurried back into the chambers and was not surprised to see no body lying in the bed where we had left her just moments earlier. My poor Myree was beyond frightened. She lay trembling on the floor in her corner, and I feared that her frail frame could not take anything more. I sat down next to her and tried to soothe her with words of comfort. Eventually, she fell asleep and I sat motionless on the floor next to my precious friend, wondering what would become of the two of us.

CHAPTER 42

Myree

The Torture of Living

DAYS TURNED INTO nights as I relived my horror over and over again. Sleep only brought the nightmares closer. Even in the light of the brilliant sunshine, the images continued to flash before my eyes. My body, too, bore the effects of the devil's torture upon me. I could not eat or sleep; therefore, when Zara insisted that I put on a clean robe, or immerse myself in the warm water, I did not recognize my own body. Then I began to feel the nausea that controlled both my days and nights. I felt it was a fitting punishment as my body was filled with revulsion and wanted to expel everything deep inside me. The retching lasted until I was spent and could no longer hold up my head. I would drift off, not knowing the difference between when I slept or woke.

Life had become a never-ending nightmare and I was desperate to end my continuous torment. I would then think of my beloved Misha and weep uncontrollably for the life that would never be ours. I desperately wanted to see him again, to be held in his arms, and to pretend everything was as it had been before he left. I dreamed of his return, and how we would begin our life together as he had promised me.

But how could I ever look into his loving eyes again without exposing the blackness that had taken over my soul? Surely, he would know something was terribly wrong with his beloved wife. It would be a lie I could not perpetuate, and yet, if I did expose the truth, his honor would not allow his brother to remain alive. He would be forced to choose between me and the brother he had once loved so deeply. Of course, if

Avila ever became aware of the truth, I would be the one not allowed to live. She would convince Misha I had willingly given myself to his brother out of loneliness. Would my Misha ever believe such a blatantly evil story? My mind would spin out of control at every scenario which played itself out before my eyes, and I would drift into a fitful sleep, awakening again to the retched sickness that had taken hold of me.

When my mother-in-law came into the room and brought the medicine man with her, it was then I knew my story would not (and could not) remain Zara's and my secret. She would know something terrible had happened to cause me to be this sick. Was it sickness of mind, heart and soul? Or had the evil one infected me with some horrifying disease that had taken over my body? After the terrifying exam, Zara was summoned outside with Avila and the medicine man. When Zara returned from the inquisition, she began acting strangely around me.

I was still locked inside the prison of my mind and had not spoken to my friend, except to scream at her once, and then I again retreated into my silent world. She tried harder to persuade me to eat the dates and cheeses she brought to me, insisting I take several bites every few hours to regain my strength. I had no will to resist her but complied with her requests when I was not spilling my guts into the basin. I feared something was terribly wrong with me and waited for death to overtake me.

I had not thought of the God of my auntie since He had abandoned me on that dark and stormy night. And even when I felt the words of the Shema rise up in my heart, I pushed them down into my pain and refused to believe in a God who would allow such horror to be visited upon an innocent girl. Surely there was only evil in this world where parents sold their only daughter and young men raped their brothers' wives. No, there was no God in this world, at least not one who loved me.

One morning, several days later, Avila banged on the door again and shouted at Zara to prepare me for an outing. I was to be dressed and ready to go within the hour. It seemed I had not left my chambers for months, and fear tightened every muscle in my body. I had no desire to go anywhere with anyone, lest I come face to face with evil again. I was not willing to get up and refused to be dressed. I shook my head violently at Zara. She left the room with my explanation as to why I could not leave my sickbed and came back quickly stating I did not have a choice. If she did not have me ready to leave, Avila would send in other servants who were willing to do her bidding.

The hours passed in a blur. I was dressed and ushered down the stairs and out of the house. I was so weak I could barely walk. I had to be carried in the arms of a servant I had seen before but did not know. His arms wrapped around me triggered explosions in my mind and I was transported back to that night. I wrestled to be free, but to no avail. Holding me tightly, he pushed me into a carriage where Avila waited. Zara was allowed to accompany me, and I held tightly to her hand with all the strength left in me. By the time we were underway, I had drifted off to sleep up against Zara who positioned herself for my comfort. Avila would not look at me, which was just fine, for I feared her almost as much as her son.

I had no idea where we were going and how long we would be gone. I woke only to wretch and then slept for what seemed like hours when finally, by nightfall, we stopped. In my mind I wanted to believe my mother-in-law was truly concerned for my well-being and was taking me to a place where I could rest and regain my strength. After all, it would not be good for her son to come home to find his beloved bride a mere shadow of the wife he had left just twelve months before. Just being away from the property and knowing I was safe from my tormentor had surprisingly lightened my heart. Although I was still so weak and nausea was my constant companion, I somehow felt a little better.

I was helped inside and taken to a small room where I was told to rest and eat. Food was brought in and I forced down some fruit and a little bread. Zara was my ever-present source of comfort and courage. Although, she too, was bewildered as to where we were or what was taking place. We both lay down and then were awakened to voices outside the door.

I don't know how long I had slept, but the commotion outside the door had startled both Zara and I wide awake. I could hear Avila's voice along with another voice that brought chills to my whole body. I did not know why or how, but somehow, I knew that voice and it instilled fear in my heart. I sat up and curled into myself as Zara took a protective stance against whatever it was on the other side of the door. I held my breath waiting for someone to come in, but after a moment, it was quiet, and I sat back in my exhaustion.

Zara made me eat a bit more and just when I started to relax, the door burst open and there before me stood a face I recognized, and eyes so mean I could never forget.

Suddenly, I was transported back in time two years to the night I had been ushered into a room full of girls who were about my age. I relived the scene while my mind replayed my rage and indignation at what had happened to all of us. I remembered the sound of my own voice escaping from my lips as if I had no control over what had been growing inside of me and had to be let out. And just as if it were yesterday, there she was: the mean old woman with the evil eyes. I could feel her hand connecting with my face, her disgusting spittle running down my chin, and the sound of her cursing at me in some language I did not understand. Now, our eyes locked, and at the exact same instant she recognized me as well. A slight smile played on the corners of her mouth. Zara had no idea what was taking place, but then I knew. This was not a nice place where my husband's mother had brought me to grow stronger. This was the place where my nightmare had come to life after being sold by my parents.

Fear gripped my heart and again I knew there was no God in heaven watching out for me. If He did exist, He had turned his back on me and left me to die a slow and agonizing death. Why was I here? What did this woman want with me? What evil was I to endure now? Her eyes went back and forth from Zara to me and then she turned and left the room.

I was shaking so hard that Zara wrapped her arms around me to still the tremors that wracked my body. Though it was not cold, I shivered in the morning air. Before long, others entered the room and Zara was commanded to come with them. She held fast to me and was then forcibly removed from the room as I heard the cries from my own heart echo off the walls. The mean old woman approached me, her evil eyes silencing me with one look. I was picked up by a man and was unable to fight the strength of his arms around me. I was taken to a room with a table in the middle. The man deposited my weak and frail form onto the table. I was powerless and my fear was suffocating me. The smell in the room was strong and pungent as I lay on the table willing myself to disappear. He held me in place with his strong arms while the mean, old woman forced some horrifying liquid down my throat. I wished for death once again, and I felt my life could not become any darker— that is until the woman reached her hand between my legs and I felt a searing pain tear open my insides. Blackness overtook me and I welcomed the dark.

I was burning up and felt the grip of death clawing at my body. I could hear Zara and Avila talking out in the hallway, and when I opened my eyes I was back in the place of my torture, in the room and on the bed where the original nightmare had begun. I would hear Zara calling my name over and over as I gave in to the darkness again. The next time I awoke, Zara was hovering over me and wiping my forehead with a damp cloth. Opening my eyes brought the recent events to my mind and I could not recall much of anything except traveling and the evil eyes of the mean, old woman. After that, everything was too difficult to remember.

Zara was holding a cup to my lips and the cool liquid tasted of honey and lemon. I drank greedily as she helped me to sit up. I felt a warmth between my legs and as I pulled back the blankets, I was greeted with a bright red stain on my undergarments. I was so weak, I could not sit up by myself and my beloved friend helped to get me cleaned up. There was a knock on the door and my terror rose. Zara opened the door slightly and I heard Avila's voice. I watched as Zara left the room and I closed my eyes to the pain of my existence.

It seemed that days turned into nights. I would sleep, wake, and sleep again. Finally, one morning, as the sun streamed through the drawn curtains, I opened my eyes and realized I had not been allowed to escape this life but must remain here in this prison of torture. Something inside of me had died, and the only part of my soul that felt alive was filled with something I barely recognized. All that was left inside me was a deep burning desire to inflict as much pain as I had endured on all the people who had made my life into this endless, living agony. I wanted everyone to suffer, starting with my pathetic mother and worthless father, then onto the mean eyed old woman, the demon Zain and his wicked mother Avila; each person who had treated me as if I was simply a piece of refuse to inflict injury and pain upon.

This burning fire of rage had turned into hatred. A feeling so foreign to me that I did not understand it. Yet, somehow, it gave me a measure of comfort against the terror I had been existing in. Inside me, a deep desire for revenge was threatening to take root in my heart. It consumed my mind, allowing me to escape the darkness which had taken hold of me. I was tormented day and night. I was no longer able to close my eyes due to the horrifying images playing out over and over. Daylight only brought more torture as I walled myself inside my own prison.

Zara was always close, feeding me and making me drink some potion or another. Somehow, the nausea that had gripped me for months was no longer present. I was able to sit up in bed and though the sun was shining brilliantly, I was still living in the shadows of fear.

I hated the weakness inside of me and vowed to rise above it, move forward, and endure this life that had been forced upon me. I had no choice and resolved to begin living again. It was my only option, or else find a way to really end my own life. Though death seemed preferable, I knew my faithful companion would not allow it. I opened my mouth and found my voice for the first time in what seemed like forever.

Zara rushed to my bedside with tears streaming down her face and tried to take me into her arms. I could not allow her to touch me and resisted her embrace, much to her shock and dismay. I asked for a bath to be drawn, some food to be brought, and for help to get out of this torture chamber. I softened a little when I saw the hurt in her eyes and took her hand and held it in mine. She searched my eyes as I began asking questions. When I sensed her reluctance to speak the truth, I demanded she tell me everything and spare no details. Over the next several hours as the horror unfolded, I realized I had lived through unspeakable trauma and had somehow survived. Zara told me what I already knew in my mind, and I felt my heart shrink and harden a little more. As the voices inside my head grew louder and louder, I retreated back into my silent world of pain and darkness. I locked any trace of hope deep down where it could not be battered again. The voice of Hatred convinced me to somehow repay all the evil that had been inflicted upon me.

CHAPTER 43

Misha

Months on the Battlefield

IT SEEMED LIKE forever since we rode off into the setting sun. We were surrounded by the sounds of cheering and the waving of banners. I could not help the feeling of pride that had taken root in my heart. I was finally of the age to go off to battle. I was the firstborn son of a very wealthy family. I had a stunning young wife who adored me and the whole world was at my feet. There was an excitement buzzing in my mind as I remembered the months of training I had endured to be prepared for what lie ahead of me. The friendships had been slow in forming; I had to prove myself as one of the troops just like each of them. Yet, I was not like them at all and they rarely let me forget it. Though most were men closer to my father's age and seasoned fighting men, some were just a little older than I was. I tried to get them to see me for the person I really was, Misha, the warrior, not Misha the heir. The latter was not easy to overcome as I was delivered to the training grounds in a carriage instead of on horseback like everyone else. My armor was new and shiny while theirs was worn and bore the scars of previous battles.

Life on the battlefield was hard and the months dragged on. Spring had turned into scorching heat on the sands of the desert. I was ready to fight, yet I was not allowed to get near any of the action. I had a protector that Grandfather Jidu had assigned to not leave my side. He was to make sure I never got close to any fighting. This I only learned after months of him preventing me from doing what I thought I was supposed to do—fight.

159

Every time we moved to a new location, I was treated with the care of an heir apparent which included the finest treatment, tent and food.

Though I was not allowed to go too near the battles, I would hear the stories of the men coming back from the frontlines. We were, by far, the superior fighting force, so there was never really any doubt of our victories. I got the feeling these battles were more for show than anything else. There were a few casualties, but not on our side. I would hear the men celebrating how they had taken the spoils of a raid, but not of the deaths inflicted. The armies we faced were few as we advanced each week. I heard stories about how we had invoked fear upon the surrounding smaller nations as they heard of our conquests. Most of them had fled long before we arrived. I felt the distain of the other men in our troops who thought of me only as the pampered son of a wealthy dynasty. Though they treated me with the respect I deserved, I still wished to be allowed to fight alongside them to prove my worth.

At night I would retire to my quarters earlier than the others who remained sitting around the fires. I would think of the only thing that kept me alive: my sweet Myree, and how we would start our new life together as husband and wife upon my return. I dreamed of the new role I would play at Grandfather's right hand, shaping and directing the future of our family.

How would I endure the remaining long months without my beautiful bride? My mind would recall our conversations, and I could still hear her laughter in my ears. I feared as the time went on, that I would begin to forget. Would she also have trouble remembering my face, my voice and my love? I prayed her heart would not grow cold and that Grandfather was keeping her safe.

I wondered why I had not heard any news from home. I had sent many messages, yet still I received nothing in return. Many nights when sleep would not come, I would go outside and lie under the stars as she and I had done so often together. I would speak softly into the night sky, asking Yahweh to remind her of my love. I prayed He would hold her in the palm of His hand and bring us back together once again. On the rare occasion she was allowed to visit my dreams, I could see her golden emerald eyes lit up with sunshine and her glorious locks of dark chestnut hair that I longed to run my hands through. She was so close, and I could hear her voice and smell the vanilla and lavender scent that clung to her young body. I dreaded the sound of the men outside my tent who would pull me from my dreams and awaken me to the hard reality which was to be my life for many more long months.

I still had to endure the frigid nights of the desert winter and feel the ground thaw beneath my feet before I would hold my bride in my arms. Until then, I would work hard to gain the real respect of the men, and I would earn their trust as I served them on the battlefield or wherever I had the occasion to find myself in their company. This time was meant for my good. It was to strengthen me to return and assume my rightful place at my Grandfather's right hand until he finally passed the throne to me. I vowed to use this time to the best of my ability, to become the leader I knew was deep inside, to return and make everyone at home proud of me, especially my beautiful Myree.

Until then I would listen, watch, and learn about everything going on around me. I would devise strategies and plot out the course for our army to pursue and instill fear in all the other nations around us. I had acquired the respect and friendship of one of the couriers who would carry messages back and forth from the battle lines. I told him to keep his eyes and ears open as he travelled and report to me any activities that would perhaps give us any advantage over our enemies. He spoke of others he encountered on his treks and would tell me of the stories they would talk about around the fires at night.

One tale the courier shared involved one of the leaders of a detachment of soldiers who talked of routing us by camping in the mountains and ambushing us as we moved forward without any knowledge of their whereabouts. Upon hearing this, I set my mind to learning if there was any truth in the words spoken by this young messenger.

Having access to the horses and not having much responsibility, I rode out one evening as the sun was setting, keeping myself out of plain view. I searched the horizon and spotted a small army of soldiers making their way up the mountainside. From my vantage point, I was able to remain hidden and watch while they built a wall of boulders and debris which they would use to camouflage themselves. As night fell, the entire detachment disappeared into the landscape of the mountainside. I rode back to our base and located our leader, requesting a meeting with him that very night. To my surprise, he agreed, and I shared with him my findings. He questioned me at length, then, seeming impressed with my suggestions, he took my words to heart causing him to change the tactics for the morning's ride. He ordered a small troop to ride behind the enemy encampment before dawn. The goal was to surprise and engage them at first light of day. By early morning, our men had returned with a new victory and more spoils of war. There were treasures of weapons, plunder and unique delicacies which were now shared with me. I was then given the role of Sunset Scout and would bring back any news of the enemy's movement. This garnered me the favor of the men, and even the leaders finally accepted me as one of their own.

CHAPTER 44

Zain

Living in Confusion

IT WAS ALMOST time for that big brother of mine to return. Had it already been almost a full year since I had been free from his presence? If only he would have been killed in battle, but I knew that would never be allowed to happen. He was the chosen one and probably had not even been allowed to pick up a sword, much less enter into battle. I knew this because I often spied on the men when they returned from their training exercises. I also listened in as closely as I could to all of the old man's conversations when he spoke to my father and his military men. Though I was often present, Grandfather Jidu never paid me any mind, and truthfully, I believe he and the others had grown to see me as invisible, though I was anything but. Now that the patriarch was out of the way, Mother and I had been able to live far more freely without fear of his disapproval. We should have taken care of him long ago, but when we had finally conceived the perfect plan, Mother assured me everything was right on schedule.

Though she had not spoken to me since our encounter in the wine cellar, I knew she was still moving the plan forward. I continued to enjoy the memories of my night of love with the Little Beauty, but Mother made me swear to never speak of it and to avoid any encounters with her. In fact, she forbade me to have any contact with her whatsoever. This was not difficult as she had not left her chambers for months. I was told by my trusted servants she was ill, and they had even feared for her life. This news made my heart beat a little faster. If she died, then my brother would never have her. She would go into her death having only been loved by me. In the next breath,

I would feel tears running down my face at the thought of never seeing her again, of never hearing the angelic voice, or seeing her mesmerizing eyes.

I was tormented by the thought of her and equally tortured by what I had learned from the servants just this week. They told me my mother had taken her away for a couple of days. When she returned her sickness had spread and she was now the cause of them having to scrub the sheets free of the stains of her crimson blood. There were rumors of the cause of the blood, but I quickly pushed them from my mind. Surely, Mother would never be party to terminating her own flesh and blood. No, I refused to listen to these lies and had the servant beaten for even uttering such ugly tales. Mother and I were of one mind. She promised me everything would be just fine, and I believed her.

But what would happen when the chosen one returned? I had come to believe Mother was going to take care of him while he was away just as she had taken care of Grandfather. Still, the messages continued to come week after week. I was made to endure hearing the tales of victory and the endless reports written by the hand of my big brother.

Mother seemed to enjoy hearing from her eldest son which made me doubt her allegiance to me. If ever I questioned her about the future, she would assure me that it was all under control. I hated to think she had more control than I did, yet I knew I needed her to make sure the plans went forward as she told me they would.

I had to bide my time and be obedient to her orders, though it made my heart ache to not be able to catch a glimpse of my Little Beauty. When I would sit under her balcony at night, I rarely heard any voices, but still I sat and listened, night after night.

Once in a while I would see Myree's dark-skinned slave as she hurried from the kitchen or laundry. She kept her head down and refused to look at me whenever I tried to address her. One day, as she rushed down the stairs, she did not see me until I met her halfway up and she raised her dark eyes to mine. A chill ran down my spine as I viewed the hatred radiating from her. I feared for a split second she might rush at me and push me to my death down the staircase. Just as quickly the fear returned to her face. She simply avoided me and ran the rest of the way down the staircase. A thrill of power coursed through my veins, and I knew—with every fiber of my being—I was meant to rule this house and everyone in it.

CHAPTER 45

Myree

Hatred Grows

I FANNED THE fires of Hatred in my heart and his awful voice consumed any trace of love that had once resided there. I hated my life, my flesh, my past, my present and my dreaded future. I rarely slept for the demons that visited me in the dark were far more terrifying than the ones I lived with during the daylight hours. Time passed and I felt the warmth of spring on the horizon. Spring meant Misha would be returning soon, unless he was already dead, and I had not been informed. That would not surprise me. Nothing could shock me at this point.

I never saw anyone in the household. They all knew that coming near me meant to risk receiving the wrath of my smoldering anger. Zara tried repeatedly to converse with me, but I had only silence for her now.

At night I would stare out at the blackened sky cursing the God who had made me. In the morning, I would fall into a fitful sleep full of darkness and terror. I rarely ate and hardly recognized my reflection in the mirror. Avila came to my chambers once to see how I had recovered, and the sight of her brought screams from the depths of my being. Her shock was evident, and I enjoyed watching her squirm as I ranted unintelligibly at her. She tried to tell me that Misha would soon be returning and how I needed to regain my strength so I would be ready to welcome him home.

While I paced the length of the chamber, Zara ushered her from the room, explaining how she would help me regain control and have me healthy by the time Misha returned. I heard their voices outside the door and listened as that vile woman dared to tell my maid how she better be able to make me presentable in a few weeks' time or else she would be severely punished. Avila went on to say, "If you can not get her to cooperate, I will make both of you suffer in ways that you have not yet experienced."

What did that even mean? Would the evil in this house never end? Surely, there was nothing more she could do to further destroy my soul. What could she possibly be talking about? Rage built inside me, and I desperately wanted vengeance.

How would I ever be able to look into the beautiful eyes of my husband again? Surely, he would see the darkness in me which boiled just below the surface. How would I ever be able to hide the shame, the disgust, and the hatred I felt for myself and everyone else in this world? If he would not have abandoned me like everyone else, I would not have fallen prey to his devil brother and been inseminated with his spawn. I would not have had to suffer the agony at the hands of the wicked Avila, her medical men, and the evil woman who tore my insides out.

I knew Grandfather had fallen at her hands; I was convinced she had murdered her own flesh and blood. I should have run away as soon as Misha left, knowing I would not be safe in his absence.

As thoughts of his gentle eyes flashed in my mind, I wrestled with trying to hide the darkness from him. Would it be possible to fool him into thinking I was the same pure virgin wife he had left behind only twelve short months before? Could I remain calm when he tried to touch me? Would I become unhinged like a wild animal, clawing and fighting the way I had on the night my dreams ended? I did not want him to suffer, but I knew that one look at me and he would know everything had changed. There would be no hiding the truth from him.

As these thoughts raced around and around in my head, I became more and more confused and began hearing voices in my head. Then I would answer the voices out loud. I rehearsed every scenario over and over again and found no viable way to stop the spinning in my mind. In one scene, I ran to Misha, and as he wrapped me in his embrace, his breath became the hot horrifying breath of Zain and I screamed in horror!

In another scene, the entire family stood in a line outside as the army rode on horseback into the walls of the compound. Beside me stood Avila on one side and Zain on the other, daring me to make a move or utter one word to incriminate them. I screamed in terror as Misha rode right by me without even looking my way.

On and on, my mind spun in circles as I tried to figure out how to escape the reunion with my husband. I had a couple of weeks left and a plan began to form in my mind. If I could just steal a horse and ride off into the night, no one would ever find me, and all my problems would be solved. Yes, that was the only reasonable answer to end the nightmare I had endured at the hands of these wicked people. But where would I go? I had no one to turn to, I had no way to find my way back home. I knew only of one little girl with violet eyes and even she could not bear to look at me. I would take some provisions and ride as fast as I could, as far away as the horse would take me, and I would be free. I began making the plans and would leave as soon as the full moon waned. The darker the better and the more lost I would become. Into oblivion I would go and everyone would be better off.

The day was spent rehearsing the plan in my mind. I paced the room and Zara could do nothing to calm my nerves. When at last she took her leave and went to her own room, I snuck down the back staircase and slipped out the door into the cover of darkness. I ran to the barn and silently saddled up the beautiful black stallion my husband had given me. I threw myself on top of him and kicked him forward with my heels.

Into the night we sped, out through the vineyards Misha and I had walked in for miles together. Memories flooded my heart. I felt the cool air hit the tears as they poured from my eyes. I wept as I rode into the night, grieving for all the losses I had suffered, knowing Misha would soon forget about me and move on with his life … without me. His mother would find him a more suitable wife now that Jidu was gone and they would be allowed to live happily ever after.

I spurred the horse on, mile after mile, and as I saw the beginnings of daylight, I knew I was headed east. My horse was tiring after being pushed so hard all night, so I slowed as we neared a forest of trees. I got off the horse and walked until my weary broken body would not go another step.

I found a stream and let the horse drink while I sat for a few minutes. I must have closed my eyes because it was almost dark when I awoke to a cool breeze blowing through the trees. I didn't know where I was going but wanted to get farther and farther away from where I was, so I rode deeper into the forest.

It was pitch black as the night descended and I wondered what kinds of animals would like to have me for their dinner. I pictured myself being torn to pieces by a pack of hungry wolves; however, I savored the thought of finally being delivered from this walking death.

I rode on until the horse could go no farther and knew I would have to wait for daylight to keep moving. The forest was so thick that even the stallion could not navigate through the trees. I was tempted to leave the horse and keep going, but sat down instead, pulling my cloak tightly around me and fell asleep quickly. Being far away from my prison gave me a sense of elation and peace. I realized I had not really slept in months.

The chill of the morning awakened me, and as my horse grazed nearby, I stretched and felt the emptiness of my stomach. I fed the horse some oats and chewed on a piece of bread and some cheese while I surveyed my surroundings. I had no idea where I was. Being completely lost and alone in the middle of the forest elicited no feelings of fear or concern. My only need was to keep moving and lengthen the distance between where I was and where I wanted to be.

My mind played tricks on me as I walked and pushed my way forward. Tree limbs grabbed hold of my robe and pulled at my hair. I heard noises to my left and right, behind and before me. I stumbled and fell, scraping my cheek on the way down. My own blood felt warm to my touch and I licked the red from my fingers. I didn't know if I was walking in a straight line or in a circle. I was only certain there was no end to the dense forest.

The voices inside my head kept me company, accusing and tormenting me with thoughts of death. If only I was brave enough to wrap my belt around my neck, climb up into a tree and fly away from this dark world. In my fifteen years I had seen more evil than I had ever dreamed possible. I felt hot tears running down my face, thinking of all the things I would never get to experience: the love of my husband, the feel of a baby growing inside me, my purity and innocence, and the faith I had in a good God which had been so violently stolen from me. I dried my tears and vowed to never be weak or vulnerable again. I would live my own life on my own terms and never be beholden to anyone ever again. I had no idea how I would survive, but knew I had to make a way.

As my thoughts raced around in my head, I heard sounds coming from the way I had just travelled. I heard dogs barking and men shouting, and

I knew I had been found. I mounted my horse and tried to urge him on, but the forest was just too thick, and he could not get through. My only hope was to run as fast as I could and try to escape into the woods. I ran with the branches tearing at my arms and face, the barking dogs getting louder and louder. I could climb a tree, but then I would be trapped. My mind was frantic. I ran until my lungs burned and my arms and face were bloodied. I had no place to hide. When I got tripped up over a rotted log, I flew facedown into the hard brutal forest floor. My mind spun into a million different directions, and then went black.

When I awoke, my hands and feet were tied, and I was on the back of my stallion being led by a line of men. Flashes of a time years ago being led on the back of a donkey flooded my tormented mind. Leading the way was the devil himself. I squeezed my eyes shut to block the sight. There was a cloth stuffed into my mouth and my screams were only muffled cries which brought about laughter from my captors. I was a prisoner again, and I longed for death more than the air I breathed.

CHAPTER 46

Zara

The Escape of Myree

ON THE MORNING I arose to find Myree gone, I was terrified. What had she done? Where had she gone? Would I find her cold, lifeless body lying somewhere? I searched the palace and the barns only to find her beloved black stallion was nowhere in sight. When I realized she had run away, I was desperate to find her in an effort to spare her more harm. If Avila were to become aware she had fled, we would all suffer her wrath. I tried to pretend all was well and went about my day as usual. Since Myree had not been seen by hardly anyone for many months, it was not hard to keep her secret. I only hoped she could get far enough away before anyone learned of her absence.

On the second day, there was a knock at the door and Avila tried to enter. I always kept the door locked; however, she insisted on coming in and continued to bang on the door. I tried to tell her Myree was not feeling well, but she demanded I open the door. When she stormed into the room and searched the chamber, she realized her plan to present her subdued daughter-in-law to her soon-arriving son was unraveling. She then unleashed a barrage of questions on me. When I honestly stated I did not know where Myree was, she slapped my face again and again as if the pain would bring forth the answers she wanted. She left the room in a rage and called all the servants to the foyer.

When the commotion rose to a fevered pitch, I saw Zain come from his chamber and take his mother by the arm. He then gathered a team of men together and they all rode off towards the orchards.

I rushed back to my room and collapsed onto the floor sobbing and begging Yahweh to protect my sweet Myree, who had already endured such extreme torture at the hands of these people. When another night passed, I had hoped perhaps she had escaped once and for all. But I knew the evil one would never allow the one he called his Little Beauty to leave him on her own terms. He would find her and punish her in his own way, and she would die another slow death upon her return.

I kept watch by the window, straining to hear the sound of horses' hooves beating on the ground. When, on the third day, I saw a line of horses coming toward the palace, my heart sank as I recognized a body tied and thrown over the back of the stallion. Was she free at last in death? Part of me prayed this was true, but when they stopped and tried to lift the body, I heard the muffled primeval scream I knew to be my Myree. What had she now lived through that would torture her mind and fill her vacant eyes with terror again?

She was brought kicking and fighting to her chambers where I was told to get her bathed and cleaned up. One look at her told the story of her escape. Her arms and face were torn to shreds and her hair was matted and wild. Her eyes still held the previous torment, but now there was a look of defeat and detachment that had not been there before. How would I ever reach her when she had retreated so far inside herself? I tried to comfort her with words of how happy I was to see she was alive, but she turned away and curled herself into a ball in the corner of the room. I tried to get her to let me help her into the bath, but she resisted me and remained withdrawn and silent.

When Avila banged on the door several hours later, I knew there would be a price to pay. I had not been able to get her cleaned up and knew I would be severely punished. Upon Avila's entrance, I braced myself for the stinging blows, but instead was met with a soft voice and the appearance of the medical man carrying his worn leather bag. Avila told him to do what he needed to do; therefore, he approached the body in the corner. He tried to coax her to respond, but instead, we heard a low growl come from her throat. Avila clapped her hands and two male servants rushed in and came to the aid of the doctor. They must have had this plan formulated before they arrived because the two servants held Myree's arms while the doctor inserted a tube into her mouth and forced her to swallow whatever liquid was in the tube. Myree fought for as long as she could until all the fight went out of her and she was subdued. I was told to get her bathed and cleaned up immediately.

I don't know what they gave her, but she was calm and quiet for the next several hours. I was able to get all her cuts cleaned and bandaged and her hair washed and combed out without any resistance. This was not the Myree I had known for the last several months, and though I was grieved to see the light completely gone from her eyes, I was glad she had found some peace, even if it was a drug induced peace. Before bed, the same team entered the room and repeated the process of flooding her body with something that took control of her mind. The morning found the same people entering the room and I had to stand by and watch as they administered the liquid which had given Myree a night of dreamless sleep.

Day after day this went on, though they must have begun reducing the dosage because Myree was at least able to focus her eyes and was compliant when I asked her to eat. Her wounds were beginning to heal. The days were counting down until her beloved Misha returned. There was now a guard stationed outside our chamber's day and night. Avila and Zain would not risk the possibility of Myree running away again or something even worse happening that they would have to explain to Misha when he arrived home. Because of her drugged state, I was more free to investigate what was going on and how Avila planned to present this shell of Myree to her returning son. I listened as closely as I could to every conversation and finally began to see how their plan was going to be played out.

By keeping her drugged, she would be compliant and subdued and not in her right mind; therefore, anything she said would not be taken for truth by anyone, much less Misha. Avila and Zain had devised a story about how Myree had been inconsolable for months after Misha left which attributed to her rail thin body. She would not sleep or eat but would only cry day and night, wailing how she missed her beloved Misha more than life itself. When the doctor finally diagnosed her with having had a breakdown, and what seemed to be an evil spirit; he gave her something to help her sleep. After months of taking the sleeping potion, she became irritated, irrational, and prone to screaming fits and rages. The doctor had to change the medication, and he declared this was the final picture of how Myree would remain for the rest of her life.

They planned to sell this story to Misha and quietly remove Myree from the home while bringing in a lovely replacement wife who would take care of Misha's every need. Zain told his mother how she did not need to worry about Myree ever becoming a problem to their family again because he would take her far away and she would be his wife then. This seemed to satisfy Avila, thus, the plan was set.

As the whole household prepared for the hero's homecoming, I was confident Misha would never let go of his beloved Myree. I knew he would love and care for her as long as he had breath in his lungs, no matter what state she was in. There would be a real battle which would take place when Misha saw the condition of his beloved bride whom he had entrusted into the care of his family. Of course, he did not yet know that his dear Grandfather Jidu had passed away, so that grief would be the first blow. Then seeing this unrecognizable girl he loved: this would be his undoing. I prayed to my mistress' God for this family and what would take place under their roof in the days ahead.

CHAPTER 47

Myree

Locked Inside My Mind

MY EYES WERE open, but I could not see clearly; my ears were hearing sounds, but I could not understand them. My body lie motionless on the bed, and I longed to find my corner where I could curl up and disappear. My arms and legs were so heavy I was unable to lift them, much less try to get out of bed on my own. Each time I did, Zara was there to catch me as I began to fall. I wished for death, but only sleep came to me, which was only a temporary escape. I had glimpses of the dark forest and could hear the sound of dogs barking as they got closer and closer. I recalled the taste of the horrid liquid being forced down my throat while men held my arms with a viselike grip, unable to resist them.

I gave up the will to live. Each day was the same. The man with the black bag would come in and I simply opened my mouth to welcome the potion that allowed me to escape into oblivion.

At times I would wake myself screaming out in the night as the shadows chased me deeper into the darkness. Often, I would see the eyes of the evil one himself staring at me. Other times I would try to open my eyes, but the dreams were relentless in their pursuit. My dressing gown would be soaked with perspiration, urine or both. Zara would then lift me shaking and sobbing from the bed, and gently set me down in the warm waters of the bath. She would stay close by as I often slipped beneath the waters seeking my own death. Never would she allow me to remain under the water. Then I would feel her gentle hands lifting me out of the water and wrapping me in a soft towel. She would rub oil into my skin as I lie on the bed and the room would fill with the scent of lavender and vanilla. I would then, once again, fade back into the dark shadows of sleep until I awoke once more.

I didn't know if it were days, weeks or months I remained this way, but one day I woke up and could see without the blurry haze that had been constant before my eyes. I heard the birds outside my open bedroom window, and I was able to rise without the help of my beautiful friend. My head was still very cloudy, and I could not form a coherent thought. I only knew that I was very much alive, though I still wished for death to take me. My body ached from lying in this torture chamber, but when I looked out the window, the bright pink of the blooming cherry blossoms greeted my eyes. The sky was a clear brilliant blue, and the sun danced off the pools of water in the distance.

It seemed like spring had finally arrived, and with it, the sounds of lots of activity around the villa. There was something trying to wake up in my brain that kept rising, but I could not follow it to remember what it could possibly be. Something about spring stirred up my heart, and at the same time, my mind would close down and bring darkness. I went to my corner and sat down trying to clear the fog, wanting—yet not wanting—to see clearly again. I blinked and must have fallen asleep because there were now voices just outside my window. This made me sit up and listen. It was that woman's voice, the one who never accepted me and was so cruel to me. I shrank back down, hoping my dark-skinned friend would come in soon and give me something to eat. I could hear her raised voice harshly shouting orders to the servants: "You there, take this and place it over there, bring that over here."

The courtyard was filling up with containers of blooming hyacinths, and hibiscus, roses and carnations. Through the open window, as the breeze filtered into the room, the sweet scent of jasmine filled my nostrils. I wanted to take in a deep breath and enjoy the delicious smell, but the darkness inside of me would not allow myself such a pleasure. Instead, flashes of evil flooded my soul. I placed my hands over my ears, curled up into a ball, and wished for the liquid that made the darkness go away in sleep.

Soon Zara's hands were upon me and I was in the water again, her strength lifting me easily in and out of the pool. The food was placed on the table and I was instructed to eat while she combed the tangles out of my waist length hair. Maids were bringing in clothing, dresses, robes as well as scarves which came in every shade imaginable. I wondered what strange thing was going on that I should need any new clothing at all. I certainly did not want, nor did I have, any reason to change out of my dressing gown. This had been my attire for as long as I could remember, and if I never had to don another dress or robe in my godforsaken existence, it would be too soon.

The noise and activity continued throughout the day. After I had eaten and Zara had dressed me in one of the new gowns, I was told we were to venture outside for a walk in the courtyard. *No, no, no, I will not leave my chambers. I am not going anywhere,* my mind shut down as I tore at the robe fastened around me. Zara tried to quiet me down, but I felt my heart racing and feared the demons inside me would fly out of me if I kept my mouth open. The voices inside my head grew louder and I began screaming. Soon, the man with the black bag was rushing at me. I welcomed the potion he offered and drank it down greedily. The voices then quieted down, and I was able to find my corner to close my eyes and end the chaos.

Each day, Zara bathed, dressed me, and brushed my hair. Day after day she tried to coax me out of the room, and every day I would simply scream until my savior arrived with the liquid that took me away from it all. Often, I would hear raised voices in the room: that of the evil Avila and sweet Zara. I could catch bits of what was being said, but not enough to make sense of it. If Avila came near me, I would simply bare my teeth and emit a low growl from deep within me until she slowly backed out of the room. The fear I sensed in her gave me great pleasure, and I relished those rare appearances of her in my chambers.

Later that night, while Zara was gently brushing my hair, she spoke the name I had not heard in quite a while. Misha—the name that once evoked joy and pride to swell in my heart now only brought shame and grief pouring from my eyes and running down my face. Zara told me he was due to arrive home within the week. She had heard earlier in the day about how he had been delayed in returning from the battlefield but would be home soon. She also told me of the plot Misha's mother and brother had concocted. The scheme was to convince my husband I had lost my mind after he left, stating the doctors declared there was no hope I would ever return to the person I had once been. They would simply send me away and find a new bride for him within the month. My beloved friend, Zara, tried to assure me I had nothing to worry about because my husband loved me deeply and would never let me go.

As I heard those words spoken by my servant with such tenderness, my whole body began to shake involuntarily. I wished only to run and jump out the window to escape the thought of ever having to see the one man who I believed had truly loved me. But I was no longer that girl. There was now no trace of the sweet Myree left inside of this frail and gaunt body of mine—the one with the hollow eyes staring vacantly back at everything.

Zara continued the long strokes of the brush and began softly humming a familiar tune. My breathing returned to normal and the shaking subsided. She tried to get me to lie down in the bed, but I still preferred the safety I felt curled up in my corner. As I laid down, I wondered what this all meant. Surely Misha would take one look at the remains of what I had become and run as far away from me as he could. What would happen to me then? Would I be cast out into the barren desert to die of thirst, or discarded into the forest to be eaten by wild animals? Would they just kill me and dispose of my body in a shallow grave? Perhaps they would sell me again, this time to the traders who would turn me into a slave, another wife of an old man, or even a Temple prostitute. An ache began in my heart, the same heart that had died the night I was raped by my brother-in-law. I wept for all I had lost. I sobbed at the thought of Misha seeing me like this. I knew he would look into my soul and see the depths of evil that had been visited upon me. It was too much for my frayed mind to take in.

What had I become? What had they turned me into? Avila and Zain had killed grandfather Jidu and were now going to convince Misha that his beloved bride had lost her mind. They would tell him I was no longer willing or able to be the wife he needed beside him as the new head of the Hassen Dynasty. Indeed, I was not the wife he had said goodbye to all those months ago; I hardly recognized myself in the reflection pool. My mind could barely form a coherent thought, and my speech was slurred most of the time. How could I even look him in the eyes? How could I allow him to see what I had become? He deserved so much better. My eyes closed on this reality and I welcomed the darkness taking over my frightening thoughts.

CHAPTER 48

Misha

The Return Home

DAYS TURNED INTO weeks and the sun began warming the tents earlier and earlier. It was now springtime on the battlefield. Soon I would be released to return home to my rightful place in my family. As the eldest heir of the Hassen Dynasty, coming in from the battlefield, I would return to a hero's homecoming with parades and trumpets. Jidu would be there, as would Mother, Father, Zain and Jamal. And of course, the one who was never far from my thoughts, my beautiful beloved Myree would be there waiting to greet me.. Oh, how I longed to get lost in her eyes and run my hands through her hair, finally becoming one with her as her true husband in every sense of the word. It is what had kept me going every day of this last year and now it is only days away.

The delay of our return both frustrated me and heightened my desire to depart once and for all. The smile on my face had all my fellow soldiers envious, as they knew exactly what I was thinking. If they had ever caught a glimpse of my bride, they were smiling in agreement with me, for they too, knew I had the most beautiful wife to ever walk the face of the earth. I only wished each of us could go home to our families and end this constant lust for more territory, more loot, and more power. When I became head of our family, things would change, and these men would be treated with the respect they deserved.

Since I had achieved the status of Sunset Scout, I had earned the respect of the men and the leaders. In turn, I showed them the same. The leaders were not as happy with me at first, for it was not dignified for the heir to the throne to help around the camp, earning my keep like all the other men. However, when the atmosphere in the camp changed and there was more laughter and cooperation from the troops, they began to recognize servant leadership as a positive means to produce a cohesive and efficient army. I was sought out by the elders more often than not and asked my opinion on decisions that were being made. I had become a valued member of the army, and I was actually going to miss some of the aspects of being on the battlefield.

Those thoughts were quickly dismissed when my mind conjured up the picture of my bride on our wedding day. She was dressed in a pristine white gown which hugged her perfectly shaped hips—the slightest revelation of tender young breasts giving way to her slender neck, and the face of an angel with a smile that lit up the heavens. With the sound of a symphony playing softly, birds rejoicing in song, the waters rushing over the rocks in the fountain, and the sun gleaming shadows down through the canopies; our wedding day could not have been more perfect.

Reliving the day kept her memory alive in my heart. The feasting, dancing and celebrating were only a blur, for all I longed to do was be alone with my radiant bride. Late into the night while the last guests were still celebrating, we were finally alone in our villa. I could not wait to take my love into my arms and show her the extent of my affection. At first, she was shy, but then as I kissed her deeply, I could sense her trembling in my arms. I suggested we eat some of the delicious foods that were brought into our chambers earlier. After that, I scooped her up into my arms and laid her on the bed to begin removing her bridal gown. She said nothing, but kept her eyes turned away from mine. When at last I placed my hands beneath her chin and lifted her face to mine, it was then I saw the tears glimmering in her eyes. Soon they overflowed onto her cheeks and all the heavy makeup began running down her face. I smiled and went and got a towel dampened with water to gently remove the streaks of kohl on her beautiful face. I wiped away her tears and recognized the girl beneath the elaborate costume she had worn for the day. She was a frightened, fourteen-year-old girl: I was a strong young man, ready to take what was mine.

With every ounce of my restraint, I withdrew from the bed as she looked at me with eyes wide with questions. I suggested she take a warm bath to ease her nerves, to which she readily agreed. When I was startled awake, it was to knocking on the door. I realized I was still fully clothed, and my bride was curled up fast asleep on the chaise across the room. I bid the servants to wait, and brought my sleeping wife to the bed, covering her with blankets as I took off my shirt. I wanted to cover her in every way possible and knew the servant's gossip would soon reach my mother's ears if they witnessed the actual scene in our room. My beloved was startled but understood my actions as the servants entered with breakfast trays. Shy smiles played on their lips as they snuck glances at my bride with the covers pulled up to her neck in our bridal bed.

They left as fast as they arrived. I went to bathe and change, and upon my return found my new wife fully clothed, eating breakfast and ready for the day. We ate in silence at first, the previous night's embarrassment still fresh in our minds. Slowly she warmed to me and I suggested we might have the kitchen prepare a picnic lunch and take the horses for a ride out into the orchards for the day. This seemed to please her, and we began our first day as husband and wife. I reminded myself throughout the day about how she was still a young girl—although stunningly gorgeous, well-spoken and intelligent—she was still barely more than a child. I would need to be patient and win her love and willingness to truly become my wife. I thanked Yahweh for the gift she was to me as I rode behind watching her hair fly in the wind and catching the sound of laughter coming from her beautiful lips. I vowed to be patient and wait for as long as it took for her to be ready to become my wife in every sense of the word.

That evening, as we returned to our villa, I pulled her into my arms, desperately wanting to be with her. Again, when I pulled back to look at her, I saw the tears flowing, sensing her fear as she trembled. I asked what was wrong and if I had done something to hurt her. She only shook her head and cried harder. I ran a bath for her and assured her I was a patient man, and I would wait for as long as it took for her to be ready to receive me. I told her we would have a whole lifetime ahead of us to share and enjoy the pleasures of married life. Though God knew I certainly wanted it to begin then and there, He gave me strength as I lay down on the bed. I believe He put me into a deep sleep as I did not hear when she climbed into bed beside me.

Before I knew it, daylight had come, and the servants were knocking on the door to bring us breakfast. This was the day of my departure to the battlefield, and though it was not the honeymoon I had anticipated, as I looked at the lovely Myree, my heart swelled with pride knowing she was all mine and always would be. I would be back before I knew it and we would then start our life together as a true husband and wife.

Thinking back, it felt like it was just yesterday that I looked back to see her smile and wave as I rode off into the sunset. At the same time, it felt like an eternity as well. I wondered if she would even remember who I was, or if she would be ready to be my wife upon my return. It would not be long now, just days, and she would be in my arms again. After all the welcome home celebrations, the ceremonies, pageantry, the feasting with my family, then—and only then—would we be allowed to be alone. My whole body was tense, and I set about my tasks for the next few days, willing them to pass as quickly as possible.

CHAPTER 49
Avila

The Plan in Motion

SO MANY PREPARATIONS had to be made before the long-awaited return of my firstborn son. My nerves were on high alert. Trying to keep Zain in check and working hard with the doctors and the servant girl, Zara, to make sure Myree was presentable for Misha's arrival was proving to be all but impossible. Zain was barely able to keep his emotions in check knowing that upon his brothers return he would once again be relegated to the position of second born son. He had been enjoying the pleasures of my company while Misha was away far more than he ever had in his entire life. Part of that was my unrelenting fear he would again do something irrational and bring more shame upon his own head and the Hassen name.

So far, I had been able to cover all the tracks we had taken to ensure our plans moved forward flawlessly. But my nerves were frayed beyond the breaking point. I feared he would somehow betray the trust I had given him in our complicit arrangement of getting rid of Grandfather. I did not know if Zain realized I had taken care of his indiscretion with his brother's wife. I didn't care a thing about her. My only concern was that my beloved Misha came to his senses and recognized she was not the right one for him to fulfill his duties and carry on the Hassen family name.

With the pitiful state that Myree was in at this point, I could almost guarantee he would realize his error in judgement and now allow me to choose the best woman to rule beside him when he took his rightful place as the leader of our family. It would take some convincing, but when we told him the story of how his fragile wife had lost her mind after he had left, he would have no choice but to allow her to disappear into oblivion and move forward with his life. With the potion the doctor was giving her, she was in no condition to be coherent enough to tell any of the events that had transpired. Even if she did, no one would believe her.

Myree had become no more than a stark raving lunatic in a skeleton's body. Long gone was the stunning young girl he married just one year ago. Oh, how things can change in the passing of just four short seasons. With that imbecile grandfather out of the picture, Zain under my control, and the woman of my choosing beside my son; I would finally have the power I deserved all along. I should have been allowed to reign as a woman, but these men, with their antiquated ideas, would not see the strong, intelligent person I was. They felt I was only good for one thing, and that was simply procuring an heir to the throne. I would show them all: and very soon. My husband was away most of the time now, which was fine by me. He would no longer be a problem either. But for now, I needed to focus on reestablishing my relationship with my beloved Misha.

The homecoming ceremonies would last for days, and when my son got a taste of the power and influence which was now his, he would soon forget all about Grandfather Jidu and his foreign bride. The reports from the field had proven to me that my firstborn was indeed the prized possession of the Hassen dynasty—the man I always knew he would become. He was a natural born leader, insightful and creative, strong and brave, rising among warriors twice his age and experience. He was his mother's son and together we would reign and have everything I ever wanted.

The last time I looked in on that wife of his, I was appalled by what I saw. When I heard the low growl come from within her, I was more convinced than ever that my plan was, and had always been, in the best interest of my son. She certainly was not fit to stand beside my beloved Misha and rule in my place. Though I had not planned on it unfolding in this way, Zain's indiscretion proved to be an act of the gods in crushing her spirit. Then with the tragedy of her conception, I knew I needed to take matters into my own hands and make sure Misha never found out what his brother had done. It was not my fault the girl had lost her mind after the procedure to rid her body of Zain's child. She had since refused to leave her chambers, speak, eat or take care of herself. The stupid girl's failed attempt to run away had proven the perfect opportunity to keep her under control with the concoction the doctor had come up with. She was beyond hope, and if not for that black slave of hers, she would be dead by now; however, that would never do. Misha would have to come to the conclusion on his own—Myree was not a fit wife for him. And after taking one look at her now, he would surely come to the same determination. Yes, everything was falling into place and all my dreams were about to come true.

CHAPTER 50

Naomi

The Endless Loss

IT HAD BEEN a full two harvests since I had seen my Sweet Mary girl after she was taken from my home by that wretched father of hers. Not a day had gone by when I did not whisper a prayer to Yahweh to watch over her. Lately my spirit had been so disturbed, as if somehow, I could sense something was very wrong with the child whom I had come to think of as the daughter of my own heart. I had no idea where on this earth she was and my attempts to question my sister had proven pointless. Mira was in a prison of her own making and I could not reach inside to break down the walls she had erected around her. Whether it was guilt, shame, regret or all of the above, my sister would not speak to me. She would not even look at me when I tried to approach her but rather, she screamed at me to leave her alone. My husband had long ago forbid me to speak of either my sister or my niece in his presence. Even my sons had given up hope of ever finding their cousin. Sometimes at night when I lie awake, I can still feel a deep ache where she once lived in my heart. I prayed she would be safe, but I had a terrible sense of foreboding that told me something was very wrong, and she was not okay.

She would be barely fifteen years old now, and I feared day and night for her safety. Where was she? If only I could track her down and bring her back to the love of the people she had come to know as her real family. If only I had one more day with her to share my heart and tell her how beautiful she was: not just on the outside, but on the inside where it really mattered. She had been given a wonderful gift of being remarkable to look at with her golden emerald green eyes and deep auburn hair, but I feared those very things had also been a curse to her. I knew what could happen to young girls who would sell for a high price to men that were filled with darkness and evil. I'm sure my husband feared the same thing, and that is why he forbade us to speak her name. Pain was etched on his face, too. Even after long two years, he knew I would never stop yearning for her, and he would turn away from me when I wept in the darkness of night. My only solace was my friend Mary who carried around her own sadness locked inside her heart. She would hold me as we grieved together for the loss of the beautiful child who bore her same name. We would try to comfort ourselves with the words of the Torah and prayed often together for the safety of the children we loved. I lamented about the darkness in the world, and the evil in men's hearts. My friend would listen and agree, sharing how we could not understand the ways of the Lord, and we had only to trust and believe His ways would accomplish His will. I admired her faith and prayed I could be more like her. But each day when I thought of my Sweet Mary, the fear lodged in my heart grew a little stronger.

I relived the horror of that day which was so deeply etched in my brain, and I could not stop the pictures flashing over and over in my mind. I could still hear her father's voice shouting to bring his child to him, smell the putrid stench of his breath, and see my sister's shame in her stooped shoulders and downcast eyes.

If only I had refused to allow him to take her, or if my husband had stood up to him. We had practically raised her in our home. Did that not give us certain rights to protect her and keep her safe? Again, and again I dragged my mind out of the pit of guilt I often found myself in. I begged Yahweh to heal my heart and forgive the sin of failing my precious Sweet Mary. Still, my heart ached as I sensed in my spirit she was in trouble. I felt her heart crying out to mine in the dark of the night. I prayed earnestly for God to spare her life and somehow bring her back to me and to the family who loved and missed her still.

CHAPTER 51

Myree

A New Plan

DAYLIGHT BROUGHT MORE activity again into the courtyard. My eyes were forced open from my drug induced slumber to see bright blue skies and hear shouts of workmen among the singing of the birds in the trees. Zara was up and busy with the running of the bath and my preparations for the day. Each day she would try to coax me from my self-imposed prison of silence in order to get me to speak, to get dressed, to eat a bit more, or perhaps go outside for a walk. I wondered how many more days it would be before my Misha returned. And for the first time in a very long time, I felt a warmth in my heart at the thought of my husband who loved me. The man who was so kind and gentle with me. I struggled to remember the beautiful promise he made to me on our wedding night. I could barely picture his gentle smile telling me he was a patient man and how we would have a lifetime together. Just as quickly my mind went dark. What would he think now when he saw me again? With that thought, I was overwhelmed with shame. I wish Avila had just killed me or allowed me to kill myself in order to spare Misha the agony of seeing me like this.

As I lay in the loathsome bed, I stretched out my frail and weakened body. Each night I would curl up on the floor in my corner, and each morning I would find myself back in the confines of this giant bed that threatened to swallow me whole. I slowly moved to sit up and found my head was not spinning as it usually did upon waking. Zara rushed to my aide and I allowed her to help me to the chamber pot. I passed my reflection in the looking glass and wondered if Mary was still anywhere deep inside the reflection looking back at me.

A new plan was forming inside my cloudy mind. I would have to open my mouth and find my voice to bring it to life. I cleared my throat and mumbled to Zara that I would have my tea before eating or bathing. She shook her head in disbelief, shocked to hear my voice again, a big smile playing on her lips. I told her that when the man with the black bag came in, I would need her assistance to reject the foul liquid he forced inside my mouth. She wholeheartedly agreed to assist me in whatever way she could.

As the sun rose high in the morning sky, I scrambled to believe there might be a way to face my Misha once again. In all my darkness, he was the one ray of light which lit the corners of my mind. Then in the same thought, a shudder would rip through my body, the voices would scream in my mind, and I would remember I was damaged goods. I was no longer the virgin bride he promised to wait for, but rather a broken and ugly remnant of my former self. Of course, there would be no way to avoid him upon his return. I would have to face him sooner or later. When he looked at me with disbelief in his eyes, his mother and brother's voices would be the ones he would hear telling him the lies they had concocted to turn him against me once and for all. Would he believe I had lost my mind to grief at his departure, and that was what had brought me to this pathetic image of my former self? Surely, he had more confidence in who I was and would refuse to accept this story. I was certain he would insist that I tell him the truth of what had really transpired while he was away.

My shame and self-loathing overwhelmed me once again: I felt the tears slip down my face. What choice did I have? Could I summon even a shred of courage from my shattered heart, and perhaps convince Misha he needed to release me and allow me to return to my homeland? Would Avila and Zain agree to send me away in disgrace? It was always what my mother-in-law had wanted, and with Grandfather Jidu gone, there was no one to defy her. But my husband's brother was another story altogether. If Misha would be so kind as to discard me, and even escort me back to Nazareth, I feared the evil that lived in Zain would track me down, claim me for his own, and never give up what he had so brutally taken on that dark and stormy night. I could still hear his voice whispering in my ear when he found me in the woods. "I will never let you leave me. I own you;

you are mine forever." My tears fell harder as my mind spun wildly out of control.

In the warm waters, I wondered if there was any way I could pretend none of my torment had ever really occurred. Was there any way to erase the darkness, put a smile on my lips and face my beloved husband as if he had just left? Could I still be the anxious bride awaiting her groom's return? A glimpse of the hatred I felt in my heart sparked to life again. A feeling I had forgotten in my drug induced state now returned as I had not allowed the poison to enter my body since the night before. The desire for revenge rose up inside me and I relished the feeling of life, as dark as it may be. I was still alive, though I wished it were not so. I had to come back from the edge and figure out a way to walk through the next several days when I would be expected to stand and greet my hero husband upon his return.

I allowed Zara to braid my hair, and though it was dull and brittle and so much thinner than it had been, it still remained my best feature. I would have to will the life into my golden green eyes that stared blankly back at me. If I allowed the anger I felt for all the people who had betrayed me to ignite the fires of hate buried deep within, I just might be able to find my way back home. Back to my auntie and the only people who ever showed me what love really looked like.

Home ... returning to my auntie had been my prayer to the God who had forsaken me. I was truly alone in this world. I had only myself to rely on and only my survival instincts to carry me through the days ahead. Perhaps with some skillful makeup application and some camouflaging robes, Misha would not be as shocked to see that I was no longer his beloved Myree. I would have to stay away from him and not allow him to take me in his arms, for then he would clearly see and feel how I was a mere shadow of my former self. If I could convince him I was no longer in love with him and he would be better off with a bride of his mother's choosing, he would have to let me go.

Yes, the plan forming in my clouded mind might just work. Over the next several days, I would have to fortify myself, keep pretending to be under the influence of the drugs, and convince Avila to think her plan was about to suceed. I needed the assistance of Zara and I knew she could be trusted. So, I shared with her the thoughts swirling around in my mind, hoping she could shed some light and clarity while helping me move

189

forward in my dream of returning home. I would gain as much strength as I could, still giving the illusion to Avila and the doctors that I was under the control of the mind-numbing liquid.

I would wait until the proper time when Misha and I were alone. I would plead with him to release me from our vows and grant me passage to return to my homeland. I would convince him I did not love him so he could move on with his life and be the ruler he was destined to be. After all that had been stolen from me while he left me to rot in this god-forsaken place, it was the least he could do for me. I would have to be quite the actress, but at this point, I would do anything to escape this prison I had been sold into less than three short years ago.

CHAPTER 52

Misha

Almost Home

THE TIME HAD finally arrived. Tomorrow we would break camp and cross the last of this barren desert to reach my homeland, my family, and my beautiful bride. I could not sleep for all the thoughts rushing through my head. Though the spring weather had made it quite pleasant in our tents, the feathers in my cot had been crushed over the months of moving from site to site. Each time I moved I would feel a poke, not allowing me to get comfortable. The night air was still except for the crackle of the fires which were tended all night by the watchmen. Occasionally an owl would screech in the darkness as it found its prey.

I allowed my mind to wander in anticipation of what the morrow would bring. I thought of the homecoming we would receive, the instruments playing, the girls dancing, the lavish feast which would be set before us. Of course, most of it would be for the return of the heir to the Hassen Dynasty, but I wanted my fellow soldiers to be celebrated as well. My wishes were made known in my last letter home. I was still perplexed as to why I had not heard back from Grandfather in these last several months, but I anticipated his broad smile and welcoming arms as much—or more—than anyone's, save my sweet Myree. My heart felt as if it might explode inside my chest. I still had not allowed myself to imagine what it would be like to take her in my arms again. My dreams were about to come true.

I allowed myself to again think back to our wedding day, and how radiant she was as I walked toward her, the shy smile playing at her full lips. I hardly recognized my child bride with all the womanly makeup, jewels and crown she had been adorned with, but her eyes spoke volumes to me. She was still my precious Myree, the one I longed to spend the rest of my life with. Though I had confided most all of my deepest secrets to her, I knew in my heart she carried a very heavy burden which she refused to share with me. Grandfather had never spoken of how he had acquired her, and being she was so young, I fought what I knew must be the truth: somewhere, there was a family that must be missing this sweet, kind and beautiful young lady. Someday, when we were settled in as a married couple and I was established in my rightful place, I would make sure to find out the truth and perhaps even be able to re-unite my bride with a family that surely loved and prayed for her safety. I vowed to do whatever was in my power to ignite and restore all the joy and light which would one day shine from within her.

I could hear the low whispers of the men as the watchmen changed shifts. Their voices hinting at their excitement to sleep in a real bed and to feast on the banquet I had promised would be laid out for them. These men had become like my brothers, and I would make sure they were compensated for their sacrifices and hard labor over the last year.

I thought of my own brothers as I lie on my back, staring up at the darkness and somehow the night seemed to grow colder. I pulled my cloak tighter around me, as Zain's face filled my mind. Why had he been punished with such a cruel disfigurement, while Jamal and I were spared? Yet, it wasn't only his mouth holding the pain. Somehow his eyes had turned dark and I had not been able to see the light that had once been his as a little boy—before he realized his own burden. I recalled trying to say goodbye to him as I was about to leave, wondering if that might be the last time I saw him. Though I sought his once familiar eyes to wish him well, the person staring back at me was a complete stranger. When had this happened? There was a time when he had trusted me, dare I say even loved me, but that was no longer true. It had not been true for some time.

I often caught him looking at my Myree when he was not aware I was watching him. I wondered what he was thinking. Did he question whether he would ever be loved by someone like her? Did he long for a friend and companion to share his pain with? The chill penetrated my bones, and I prayed my brother would someday know the love of a woman and somehow, he too would experience what I had found in my Myree.

Jamal's young face then filled my heart and I suddenly longed to rekindle the relationship that had been ours before I left. At fourteen years old, he would be a young man now. I desired to have this little brother of mine by my side when I took my rightful place as the heir. Jamal would be a fine leader, as he was kind and smart. Though Zain had tormented him on many occasions, I had intervened often enough that he respected and valued my company. Yes, I should like very much to invest in my relationship with Jamal. Though I would still try to break through to Zain, I feared there was little hope of ever truly connecting with him.

The night dragged on as I thought of what awaited me. First, there would be the parade we would have to endure, then the long lines of well-wishers who had come from miles to celebrate our victories. After that we would feast in the courtyard with family, close neighbors, and friends. I would then be taken by Jidu into his study to commend me and to receive the blessing from his right hand. Father and mother, Zain and Jamal would be present, but my Mryee would not be allowed into this inner-circle ceremony. I would have to wait long into the night, until after the guests had gone home, to return to my bride waiting for me at our new villa.

I would walk in and stare deeply into her eyes before taking her in my embrace. Then she would open herself to me and give me what I had been so patiently waiting for. It wasn't that I wanted the physical union only. I wanted us to be joined together as one—in heart and soul as well as body. She was my best friend and my trusted confidante. I longed to share everything with her. After our love was made complete, we would sit and talk until the sun came up. Perhaps we would take a walk through the orchards and then return to continue our exploration of one another. Yes, this was my heart's desire, and I thanked Yahweh for keeping me safe and allowing me to live this charmed and privileged life.

It seemed forever that I had been dreaming about our homecoming, but soon the day had come to life and the men were breaking camp. I stretched my body, and though I had barely closed my eyes, I felt as if I had slept a full twelve hours: so excited was I to begin our final journey home. Since I had insisted on doing my fair share of work around camp for the last several months and had not allowed the men to treat me differently than anyone else, I would be expected to pack my own gear. Therefore, I set about the tasks in front of me.

Breaking down camp was always much easier than setting it up, and I was quite comfortable with the precise way everything fit together like a puzzle. One wrong fold or an object out of place and everything would have to be brought back out and repacked. It was a good thing I had studied each and every item in my tent and knew its exact destination on the carts and horses. Soon, I was finished with my gear and was helping the other men whom I had come to cherish as brothers.

My mind went—as it often did—back to my own brother. If only he would accept my help and allow me to come to his aide, but it had been years since Zain had sought me out, and almost as long since he had even really spoken to me. Though I tried to engage him, it seemed in the last two years he had slipped further and further into his own darkness, barely acknowledging I even existed. I vowed to work harder to break through the walls he had erected around his heart and include him in my new world with my wife. Soon he would be an uncle, and I wanted both of my brothers by my side to share in the joys of my marital happiness.

Finally, we were on our way home. The sun was overhead, and the fields of wildflowers were paving our way. All the men were in good spirits because most of them would be allowed a well-deserved rest before returning to the battlefield.

The journey seemed endless until, off in the distance, we could see the signs of life in the city. It was all I could do to reign in my horse and not kick him into a full gallop the rest of the way. It would not be dignified for the heir to the throne to be seen riding like a madman into the village square. No, I would restrain my desires and allow this day to unfold in the way I knew it would. I would be patient and participate fully in all the festivities until I could have my heart's desires.

CHAPTER 53

Zara

Hope is Born

MY MISTRESS SEEMED to be coming back to life. Just this morning, she spoke for the first time in many months. She had also ravenously eaten the food I brought her instead of picking at each bite. I had to remind her she had not eaten much in several months and she may want to slow down. Though her eyes were still wild with pain, anger, and terror; she was alive. I feared for her sanity, because she had become dependent on the liquid to keep the voices in her head quiet. How long would this version of my friend stay present? I wondered at what these new changes meant. I did not have to wait very long at all before she began sharing the thoughts running franticly around in her head. She knew it was just a matter of days before she would be forced to face her husband; it would not do for him to see her in this condition.

I had been able to keep Avila away, but seeing the days drawing close to Master Misha's return, I knew we could expect a visit from her any time. Avila would want to make sure her plan was on schedule to force my friend out of her home and out of her son's life. I had told Myree what I had overheard, and we talked through the morning and into the long hours of the afternoon. All the while, the arrangements for the returning troop's arrival was going on just below us. My beautiful friend was still locked inside of the shell of her body, but I was overjoyed that she was venturing back into the land of the living. I told her all about how her mother-in-law had a plan in place which entailed her still being very much out of her right mind. So, as she began to share her scattered thoughts, she told me her resolve was to convince her husband she did not love him anymore. She hoped he would soon release her into freedom and allow her to return to her homeland. I could scarcely believe what I was hearing. Her self-loathing was clearly evident and was causing her brain to be confused. She was not considering the fact that though everything had changed for her, nothing had changed for Misha.

Myree's clouded mind was obviously very unclear about how Misha felt about her. I knew in the deepest part of my heart, even if he knew everything that happened to his precious bride, he would still love her fiercely and try to win back her heart. Perhaps if he were to know the real truth about the torture she had endured at the hands of his evil brother and mother, he would feel differently (not about Myree, but about them). Surely there would be anarchy within the family if the truth ever got out. But how would this frail thing ever be able to convince her husband she did not truly love him? Her thought was to tell him she only realized this while he was gone, and after she had time to think about who she really was. She would explain how she was not fit to be the wife of a ruler and had no love or desire to remain his wife. The anger and hatred which consumed her would be the resolve she needed to accept nothing but his agreement of her departure.

Her heart's desire was to go back to her auntie in Nazareth and live a quiet life, away from all of this. She would tell him that if he truly loved her, he would release her and find another woman who was more suited to royalty, since she was just a peasant girl from a small village who had a family that undoubtably missed her. Myree and I had vowed long ago to never reveal the true origins of how she had become a part of this Hassen clan. Long ago, I had buried the sight of her on the slave auction stage deep in the recesses of my memory.

One day when she had found me crying for my lost mama and family, Myree had shared her deepest darkest secret: her own father and mother sold her to strangers for a small bag of silver just so they could have the drink they craved. She wept with me on that day, and we had vowed together to go to our graves bearing one another's pain and shame.

If we could convince Avila that Myree was still under the influence of the potion the doctor supplied daily, and if she thought there was no threat remaining, Myree might be allowed to have time alone with Misha.

Of course, she would need plenty of time to convince him she did not love him. If she could play this role, would Misha—the returning war hero—perhaps be willing to let her go?

Undoubtedly, Avila would fill her son's mind with all kinds of stories about what had transpired while he was away. Such as how Myree would scream and rant for days at a time; how she was insane and had lost her mind. Avila would then bring in the doctors to verify this diagnosis. If Myree could put on the show of her life, her plan just may work. However, if Misha were to be able to break through the wall of hatred she had built around her heart, he would find only a broken, tragic soul who had suffered through unspeakable agony at the hands of his family. May God help them all if Misha discovered the truth of what had been done to his beloved bride.

We had only a few short days to prepare everything, and I needed to get Myree as strong as possible and back to her former self as much as I could. Surely if Misha was allowed to take his frail wife in his arms, the story would unravel; therefore, Myree knew she would need to keep her distance ... and that suited her just fine.

When she caught me humming the tune of our old favorite song, she took hold of my arm and forbade me to ever sing that around her again. The pain in my arm was shocking, but more startling was the anger in her eyes when she hissed, "There is no Yahweh, no love and no Savior." She released my arm and turned away from me as tears formed in my eyes. I trembled at this person I no longer knew. I kept my distance from then on, wondering where Myree had gone, and if she might ever return. I grieved the loss then, knowing the sweet girl I knew had died on the night she was brutally raped by her brother-in-law.

I feared Myree was gone forever. All the horror which had followed that dark night had drained the very life from her soul. Surely, no one could survive that depth of torment and ever be the same again. I wondered where our God was now. Why had He allowed such horror to be visited on this beautiful child? I broke out of my reverie and set about putting the plan in motion which would possibly set her free. I prayed it would be so.

CHAPTER 54

Avila

The Return of My Son

COULD IT BE I was only days away from holding my oldest son in my arms? Misha would be back from the year-long treacherous battlefield excursion his grandfather and father had insisted he experience. They believed it was necessary in order for him to assume his rightful place as the next heir apparent to the Hassen Dynasty.

Had it only been twelve months since I kissed him goodbye? Often, it felt like a decade had passed when I considered all of the trouble his hideous, imbecile brother had created in the last six months. True, it had been my plan to make sure that the feeble Jidu was out of the way before my firstborn returned. Zain was only too grateful to be included in the plan, which had made it easier to execute the slow poisoning which made it appear Jidu had simply taken ill and never recovered. However, it seemed with my delusional second son beholden to me and my secret, Zain had taken advantage of his power and did whatever he wanted which meant almost ruining everything I had so carefully put in motion.

The little, wretched foreigner Jidu had bought for my son had never been good enough for my beloved Misha, so maybe it was just as well that Zain had destroyed her. After I figured out what happened, and realized Myree was with child, I knew what I had to do.

Misha could never know what his brother had done, for his honor would not allow his brother to live. Though I cared little for my second son, it would not bear well for our family name if one brother killed his sibling. It seemed Myree had truly gone out of her mind after her attempted escape, which sealed her fate. I could not allow her to remain even the least bit capable of telling the terrible tale of what happened while her husband was away. I needed only to prove she was demented, and she had made that clear with her endless wailing and raging. The doctors had been able to keep her in a drugged state of confusion in which she was either sleeping or barely coherent. Surely, when I told my son how she had been inconsolable when he left and had slowly lost her mind over the months he had been gone; he would see for himself that she was not the right woman for him as the new leader of our family. He would see my side of everything and allow me to bring him just the perfect new bride who would meet all his needs and truly fit into our family.

Upon his arrival, there would be days of festivities and obligations which would keep him away from his bride. I needed to keep Zain out of the way. I knew I could only allow the girl to be glimpsed from afar by Misha so he would think she was indeed the same as when he left. But then I would eventually have to break the crushing news to him about the death of his grandfather and share how his death had played into the demise of his wife. Yes, she had been fairly attached to Jidu, so this added a nice accent to her inconsolable grief and derangement. With the power he would receive from his father passing him the birthright blessing—which should have been given by my dead father—he would forget all about this waif and assume his authority as the head of our family. I would then have her taken away in the night, and no one would ever know where she had disappeared to. Yes, all my plans were coming together nicely and soon I would have it all.

The servants were working frantically to create the perfect atmosphere for the hero's homecoming. The tables were set up, the musicians were there, the food had been brought in from all around the region. Even now I could smell the roasting meat. I needed only to check on the girl and make sure she was at least presentable, and somewhat coherent. I would keep her sequestered, until I had time with my son. Though I knew he would want to see her immediately, I would tell him she had sent word that she was feeling a little under the weather and would join him later in the evening after all the festivities had quieted down.

When I checked on her earlier in the day, she was just as I had hoped: sitting up in bed barely able to form a sentence. Her hair was no longer the luxurious mane it once was, and even her startling eyes held a vacancy, giving her a haunted look. Her once lithe body was now a mere skeleton of skin and bones protruding at sharp angles at her shoulders and neck. Surely, my son would not even recognize this person as the wife he had thought to love at one time. So much can happen in just twelve short months. I would have him fully convinced, so by the time he got to see her, he would have to come to the same conclusion, which was that she was not fit to be his wife. I needed only to let him know I would take care of everything and then he would take solace in the comfort of his mother's arms. I would have my son back and everything I always dreamed of.

CHAPTER 55

Myree

The Plan to Go Home

I WAS GETTING stronger by the day, and as Zara had tended to my hair and skin, I felt a little more like myself. I was barely able to keep my burning hatred locked deep inside me. Thanks to one of the other maids, we had word of Avila coming to check on me, and I was able to put on quite the show for her. If she wanted me docile and drooling, that is what she would get. Though, when she got close enough to look me in the eyes, I desperately wanted to tear her face apart with my bare hands. If ever there was a reason to despise a person, my mother-in-law had given me every right to want her dead.

The doctor continued to come and administer the liquid poison, and thinking I was the compliant creature I appeared to be, he paid no attention to me. I quickly spit the vile liquid out of my mouth as soon as he turned to leave.

This had been going on now for almost a week and my head was fairly clear at this point. I knew I was no longer under the spell of the potion because the voices of burning rage and hatred had returned. I was consumed with the need to be free from this place and everything associated with it—including the husband I once thought I loved. My mind had convinced me that if he truly had loved me, he would have never left me. The horror I had experienced in his absence would never have happened, therefore, even he was to blame for the black nightmare my life had become. All of them, even Jidu, who had purchased me as a slave, was evil in my mind. What kind of man purchases a child bride for his

201

grandson? Only the worst kind of person would do that—the same kind of people who would sell their only daughter to evil men for a few silver coins.

And God? Well, He was the real one to blame for all of this. For if he was truly the God of Abraham, Isaac and Jacob, and had a plan for his chosen people; I certainly wasn't one of them. He too had abandoned me into the hands of pure evil, turned His back on me in my greatest hour of my need, and ignored the endless cries of the one He was said to love. No, there was no God, and I would do well to remember that. My only solace in my darkness was the thought of returning to Nazareth, to my auntie's home and her arms of love. On my way back to my hometown, I should like to stop and take revenge on the people who brought me into this world and watch them suffer the way I had for these last three years. They deserved to rot in hell and get a taste of what it feels like to know true torture and torment; the same kind they had inflicted upon me.

What would my auntie think when she saw me from afar walking down the dusty road toward her home? The last time I heard her voice, she whispered in my ear how she loved me. She was the only one who had ever shown me true love and a tiny part of me longed to feel her arms wrapped around me once again. But what would I even say to her? Would she question me endlessly about where I have been? Maybe she would see the emptiness inside me and simply love me back to life? I would have to wait and see how it would all unfold. For now, I must convince my husband that I am not the same person he used to love, which is true in every way. I must make him see I did not care for him at all. And though it would be difficult, I would only have to summon just a sliver of my rage and unleash it on him to get him to see it was over between us. He would then tell his mother he was sending me away and it would all be over. Then I would be free.

CHAPTER 56
Misha

Return to Loss

HOME! I COULD see the rooftops, hear the music playing, and smell the aromas of the delicious food being prepared for our homecoming. The men were almost as excited as I was to be home, but no one could be even half as excited to see their bride as I was. A love-starved man who had left his beloved wife without ever fully knowing her. That was all going to change as soon as I could extract myself from all of my duties to the men and the responsibilities to my family. I had waited a full year; I could be patient for a little while longer. If only I could catch of glimpse of her, my heart would be at peace. I knew what was expected of me and I would fulfill my obligations first, and then find my wife.

Would she be on the balcony of our new villa or would she be waiting for me in her chambers? My mind could barely focus as the voices of cheering got louder and louder upon entering the city gates. Music played and barely clad girls danced with tambourines and cymbals. There were shouts of victory and banners waving high in the air. My eyes searched for my beloved, but she was nowhere to be seen. Soon I could see my beautiful mother, my regal father, and my two brothers waving at me as I rode into the crowded streets. But where were Jidu and Myree, the two I had missed the most and longed to see most desperately?

As I rode high in the saddle of my stallion, something struck my heart, and I had a foreboding in my soul that I could not shake. I smiled and waved, trying to push the feeling down, but it persisted. We were escorted around the village and the cheering continued, as well as the waving, shouts of accolades, and the dancing girls.

When finally I was allowed to dismount, my mother was in my arms kissing my face. I longed for my bride, but it was my mother who took me by the hand and ushered me into the courtyard where dignitaries stood awaiting my arrival. I knew what was expected of me and I played the part. My father took his place beside my mother and brothers. Still, there was no sign of Jidu or Myree. My heart beat loudly in my chest and yet I continued with the ruse. I accepted the plate of food and the goblet of wine that was handed to me and watched as the young girls danced in front of me—my mind a million miles away. More guests came and were introduced as visiting royalty from nearby cities, they were eager to make an alliance with the new heir to the throne. I studied each of them and filed their names and cities away in my mind. I was extremely weary from lack of sleep and the full days ride. I wanted nothing more than to extricate myself and go to my wife wherever she was. I knew my mother had a ceremony planned and it would be hours before I would be together with my bride.

As soon as I had a brief moment, I turned to my mother and father and questioned them about the whereabouts of Grandfather and my wife. The look upon my father's face could not be disguised. When I looked at my brothers, they quickly turned away. My mother assured me she would explain everything when the time was right, but for now, I needed only to fulfill my duties. I had a sinking feeling in my chest and felt trapped by the role I was forced to play in the charade which was now my life. My mind ran through frantic scenarios over and over again, and by the time the food had been eaten and the guests were beginning to leave, I was overcome with anxiety and fear.

Finally, I was led to my grandfather's library. A deep dread had taken hold of me. My mother sat down and indicated I should do the same. I stood as the questions began pouring from my mouth. She simply held up a hand to silence me. I demanded answers to my questions. To which she simply lowered her head and would not look at me until I calmed down. The tension in the room was palpable. When at last she raised her head, there was a sheen in her eyes. She then calmly told me that my beloved grandfather had passed away six months prior. She explained, with little emotion, how he had fallen ill. She stated that though she had wanted to alert me of his condition, knowing how much he meant to me, Grandfather had demanded I not be informed.

I listened from a distance as I watched the woman who gave birth to me talk about how her father had declined over time and then one morning, he was no longer with us. The grief ripped at my heart and I felt a loss like I had never felt before. This was the man I had loved like a father when my own father had been absent. He was the man who taught me to ride, to laugh, to learn and how to love deeply from the heart. I could not restrain my pain and I wept unashamedly in front of my family who sat coldly staring at me from across the room.

When I had composed myself, my father decided that now was the time to bestow on me the rights of the firstborn. I could not have been more disgusted at these people who seemed to care so little for my obvious pain. I rose to leave and find my bride when my mother's voice halted me at the door. I turned to see all of them staring at me, and I felt my world crumbling around me. She rose and placed herself between me and the door and said she needed to tell me some sad news of Myree. She would not allow me to leave before she did. My legs gave way beneath me and Jamal's arms were around me guiding me to the chair where I had been sitting moments before.

Was Myree dead too, I wondered? I vaguely remember my mother's voice telling me how my bride had been despondent and overcome by sadness at my departure, rarely venturing from her room for months at a time. She told of wailing, weeping, not eating; how she was not able to sleep and was given to fits, and outbursts of rage. Then, with the death of Jidu, she had turned morose, unable to be consoled or reasoned with. My mother spoke of Myree trying to end her own life on several occasions and how they had done everything possible to help her—even consulting doctors who were able to aide her by giving her something to help her sleep.

My mind spun out of control as I staggered to the door. I would not be held back by my mother's pleas for one more moment. I raced up the stairs and banged on the locked doors—the fortress that kept me from my sweet Myree. I stood for an eternity until I heard the lock unlatch and Zara peeking through the crack of the door. I pushed past her and allowed my eyes to adjust to the darkness, as the hour was late. My eyes went directly to the form that lie motionless in the bed. Though I wanted to scream and rush to her side, I slowed myself and forced my breathing to steady, as I had so many times before going into battle.

Where was my vibrant bride? Was it true she was no longer the same beautiful creature I had waved goodbye to all those months before? How could I have allowed myself to be so far away when the people I loved the most,, desperately needed me? So many questions assaulted my heart as I stood shaking beside her bed. I ordered Zara to light the lamp.

Her eyes were open, and I saw a glimpse of my beloved before she closed her eyes again. When they opened back up, there was a stranger lying before me. She had become a mere shadow of her former self. It appeared everything my mother had said was true, and yet my heart resisted believing her words. How could my strong and vibrant wife be reduced to this shell of a person?

I heard voices behind me, and I ordered everyone to leave me alone. My family had followed me up the stairs and spoke in hushed whispers at the entrance of the room. My mother's words tried to comfort me but ended up feeling shallow and empty. She tried to persuade me to go with her, to allow Myree to sleep, saying she needed her rest. All I knew was that I was not leaving my wife's side ever again. What she needed was me, her husband, to love her back to life once again. I then turned slowly and demanded everyone leave the room, immediately.

I sat and stared at the woman I loved, and the tears began to flow. I wept aloud, torrents of tears I had held back for an entire year. I allowed my grief to pour from my heart and mourn for all I had lost in the last twelve months. I wept for the men I had seen die on the battlefield. I grieved for the grandfather whom I never got to tell how much I loved him. I sobbed at the sight of a barely recognizable Myree, whom I had forsaken for some rite of passage as the eldest son. My heart shattered while shame and guilt wracked my body. I had failed those I loved the most. I would spend the rest of my life making up for it. I would serve and love the one person who had captured my heart—the lifeless creature before me. My exhaustion overcame me and I succumbed to it. I laid myself down on the floor next to my wife and allowed the sleep to overtake me.

I awoke to a small hand upon my shoulder and eyes that I used to know so well staring back at me. I sat up and tried to form the words I had rehearsed in my head for so many months. All those words of love, hopes, and dreams for our future together. I opened my mouth, but nothing would come. Instead, I took her fragile hand in mine and again could not stop the torrent of tears flowing down my face. I wept anew for the lost days, for all her pain, and for the fact I would never again hear my grandfather's voice.

Silently, she walked away from me as I sat in my grief. I could not find the words I needed to say, and it seemed as if we were nothing but two strangers together for the first time.

From across the room, she rang the bell for the servants to bring breakfast, and I watched as she opened the curtains to let in the light of day. Was it sadness? Anger? Or was it pity I saw in her eyes as she glanced at me? I was still fully clothed in my uniform have just arrived home the night before. I felt shame and embarrassment over my display of emotions and told her I would go change my clothes, then return so we could talk. Without uttering a word, she nodded her head and dismissed me with her eyes. Who was this person? Had my mother been right in her assessment of her mental state? Where had my Myree gone and how would I get her back?

Upon leaving the room, I encountered Zara and asked to speak with her privately. She averted her eyes, slipped past me without responding and closed the door to her mistress' chambers. I knew she was loyal and had cared for my bride for these last three years. If anyone would know the truth about what happened, it would be her. I vowed to speak with her before the day ended so I could get the answers I desperately needed.

I bathed, ate a hearty breakfast, and returned to the room where I had last seen my beloved. Passing a man with a black bag who must have been the doctor caring for Myree, I knocked on the locked door. I was allowed entrance by Zara. My wife sat motionless near the window, not even turning at my approach. She sat stiff and upright with the angles of her shoulders sharp beneath her robe.

I knelt before her and tried to take her hand in mine, but she pulled away from me. I begged her to look at me, and when she did, the eyes that used to look so adoringly up at me, now stared right through me. I was shocked but kept my composure, trying to be strong when I actually wanted to collapse into tears again.

My heart was broken as I sat on the floor at her feet. I promised myself

CATHERINE L. TERRIO

I would be patient and give her all the time and space she needed. I would show her how much I loved her and win her heart once again. I began by telling her of my shock over the news of Grandfather's death. I told her I had no idea that he was even ill, and of my intense grief that he was gone. I shared the hurt and anger I had towards my mother for keeping such news from me. I wept while telling her I would have returned immediately had I know she was hurting so deeply.

I asked her why she had never written back to me after all the letters I had sent her. At this, I thought I saw a flicker in her lifeless eyes and then her blank stare returned. Had she received any of the letters I had written to her over the last year? Pages and pages of declarations of my love, of my dreams for our future together; our children's laughter and joy. I continued to pour my heart out apologizing for not being there for her when she needed me the most. I begged her to forgive me and allow me to make it up to her. I vowed to love her until the day I died, declaring how she was my whole world.

I was not prepared for the silence I received in return for the outpouring of my heart, and when I asked if she would please talk to me, she stated she was tired and needed to rest. I tried to help her up, but she turned from me to Zara and reached out her needy hand to her servant. I watched as my beloved bride walked away from me and furthered the distance that seemed to grow greater now—even more than when I was hundreds of miles away on the battlefield. I was again dismissed by my wife and my bewilderment increased every moment. It seemed she was locked inside herself, unable and unwilling to allow me access to those parts she once freely shared with me. Her frail form broke my heart and again, I promised myself I would be strong and patient with her.

A knock on the door sounded and I went to answer it, only to see my mother standing there wanting to come in. I blocked her view, exited the room, and took her by the arm looking for answers I could not find anywhere else.

208

CHAPTER 57

Avila

My Lost Son

THE PLAN I had spent every waking moment of the last six months rehearsing in my head was not unfolding the way I had imagined. As my distraught Misha encountered me at the door of Myree's chambers, it was clear everything was unraveling in his heart. As we descended the stairs, he began to question me ceaselessly. I had to wrench my arm free from his agitated grasp. By the time we reached the library, I let him know I did not appreciate his accusatory tone, and though I understood his confusion, wasn't he now convinced this girl had never been the right one for him after all?

I will never forget his next words: "Do you really understand, Mother? I dare say you know nothing of true love or the agony of grief as you have allowed your heart to grow as cold as a stone." The sound of my hand slapping his cheek echoed off the walls of the large halls as we both stood silently staring at one another. My quick reaction was proof that my nerves were stretched tightly over my aged skin. I was shocked at myself and at the man who stood before me hurling vicious words into my face. Why did I respond so passionately? Was it because I knew in the depths of my being, his words rang of a truth I did not want to acknowledge? When had I allowed my heart to grow as cold as a stone? My mind rewound to the early years when it was just the three of us: Misha, our only beloved child, and my husband who once adored me. Memories flooded my mind: laughter, silly games of hide and find, of walks in the orchards where we would lift Misha high in the air between us; memories of making love to my husband to create another new life … Zain … that was when my heart had begun to freeze over. The pain of this child's disfigurement banished me into a shame-filled seclusion. I was never the same. Even after the redemptive birth of my third son—perfect in every way—there were scars which were already too deep, and I was too lost in the world of my own self-pity.

Time stood still as I raised my hand to his now reddened cheek. The revulsion in his eyes shone brightly, and he recoiled at my nearness. "What have you done, Mother? What have you done to my beautiful wife? I knew you were not pleased when Jidu brought her to us. You have barely been able to conceal your distain, but what are you capable of?"

He continued shouting, "How does a brilliant, vibrant young woman just disappear in the span of twelve short months while under your supervision? I vow with every breath I take, I will not rest until I find out the truth of what went on in this palace over the last year of my absence." With that, my eldest son turned and stormed out of the room and possibly out of my life forever.

Tears stung my eyes, but I quickly blinked them away as my mind ran frantically ahead at the possibilities. If my son ever found out what had truly taken place here, he would surely kill his brother with his bare hands, and possibly even his own mother for what I had done to my own grandchild. Regret and remorse were emotions I did not entertain. I must simply move forward in making sure the truth remained hidden forever. I should have made sure there was no trace of our actions long ago. It would have been so easy to dispose of the young girl when I had the chance. I chastised myself for my failures and shook off the last vestige of my humanity as I plotted the demise of my daughter-in-law once and for all. Yes, the doctor would play a convincing role in this plan unfolding in my mind. I would simply make sure the next dose of toxic potion she received would have a lethal effect. Soon, Zain and I would rest easy knowing the truth went with her to the grave. Of course, her slave would have to go as well, but that could be an easy accident. No one would ever be the wiser.

Though my son would grieve deeply at her death, in time he would come to see it as a blessing in disguise. He would then be able assume his rightful place as the head of our family. It might be a while, but eventually he would forget all about the idea that I had something to do with the poor girl losing her mind, and we would go back to being a family again, the way I had envisioned us. He and I would rule side-by-side and begin acquiring the territories around us as our empire grew in wealth and power—the way it should have been all along.

CHAPTER 58

Myree

My Husband Misha

OH, HOW MY heart seized within me at seeing my beloved Misha. I had forgotten how handsome he was, and it seemed his time on the battlefield had only increased his beauty. He was stronger, and yet, as he sat and wept at my bedside, it took everything in me to not break down, weep with him, and allow him to take me into his arms. Although he was the same man who left a year ago, I was not the same girl he had married. I was no longer worthy to be his bride. I was broken, empty, and so desperately lost in my torment. Seeing his face again caused me to recall every single conversation we shared—especially those early walks in the orchards together where he would try and speak in my native tongue. I wanted to relive each moment we spent together and cherish it in my heart, but my heart was beyond shattered and would hold no memories of the hope, love or joy which had been lost to me forever. I felt only a deep simmering rage which consumed me and allowed me to remain frozen and detached from this man I once loved. I could see the confusion in his eyes as he stared at me, as if he did not recognize the woman he had left in the hands of his evil family.

Should I be the one to tell him that his own mother and brother had murdered his beloved Jidu? Would revealing the truth place more of a wall between us than I had already been able to erect? I knew I must continue to remain locked inside myself, pretending to despise this man before me. I could not allow myself to even look into his eyes, for fear he might see the anguish that still tortures me day and night.

I knew I must remain stoic and eventually he would tire of the pathetic thing I had become. His words of love and promises to be patient with me were similar to those he had whispered to me on our wedding night. Oh, if only I had given myself to him on that beautiful night as his bride and of my own free will. At least he would have tasted my innocence before having my purity violently taken from me by the devil himself. No, there could never be any thought to us having a life together. I was empty, dirty, consumed with shame-filled self-loathing and I would never be a proper wife: the kind of woman he deserved. His mother had been right all along. I was never good enough to be in this family. I was nothing but a foreigner rejected by her own parents. It was best to stay with the plan my mind had created and persuade him to send me away. It may take some time, for he seemed unwilling to forget the sweet times we had shared in another lifetime.

I could not allow myself to recall the memories of which he spoke. Instead, I had to remain rigid in my stance of pushing him away. Surely the sight of me, emaciated and frail, would be enough to deter his affections. I must keep myself locked away inside my mind, isolated and shackled by my grief and rage. These were my only companions at this point in my pathetic existence. If only I had been successful in ending my own life, I would be free in the darkness of death. Why couldn't I have run farther when I had escaped? But where would I have gone? I had no one in this world except Auntie who was so very far away. Perhaps now, with Misha and all his resources allowing me to leave—even making sure I arrived in Nazareth safely—I may have a chance at starting over.

I would go back to the only home I had ever known and pretend I was okay. I would make them all believe there were no demons chasing me relentlessly day and night. I could sit at Mary's feet and learn how to weave in the same way she did and maybe even support myself and my auntie.

I knew I would never marry, for there was no man who would ever want such a damaged and defiled woman. I was now unfit and incapable of giving or receiving love in that way, but perhaps I could find some measure of peace in the fabrics I would create. Yes, this would be the only way my life would ever make sense again. I desperately needed to flee this place with all its evil that had been visited upon me. It took everything in me, as my mind had begun to clear from the awful liquid I had been given, to stop dreaming of visiting violence and torture upon those who had turned my life into a living torture chamber.

Seeing Avila in my chambers made my skin crawl and my heart race with thoughts of scratching the beauty from her face with my ragged fingernails. I had not seen my husband's brother since that fateful night so many months ago, but I knew if and when I did, I may not be able to control the rage burning inside of me when I thought of his twisted smile above me. Yes, this was the place I needed to stay in order to remain locked inside my darkness. This was the safe place where hatred lived, and I could not hear the shattering of my own dreams in my husband's voice. I dared not think of his words, his tears, the letters I had never received, or the softness of his touch as he tried to coax me out of my prison. For him and for his future, I must believe this was the only way. Someday he would rule, remarry, have children, and live the life he was destined to live before I was ever brought to this godforsaken place.

As Zara entered the chamber with a tray of food, she told me she had seen Misha ushering his mother downstairs and he did not look pleased. A slight smile pulled at the corners of my mouth, and I was satisfied for a brief second. I wanted him to hate her as much as I did. The doctor came in as usual, and as I lay catatonic in my bed, he simply put the device in my mouth and pushed the vile liquid in as he had done every night and morning for these last several weeks. I was slowly becoming an expert at fooling those around me, even the doctor. I quickly spit the poison into the chamber pot beside my bed. Though I needed Zara to aide me in my plan, no one would ever know the depths of blackness consuming me. I had sworn her to secrecy, and she vowed with an oath to take my secrets to the grave with her.

Perhaps I would ask Misha to send Zara away with me when I left. I would then be able to give her the freedom she so longed for. Yes, that was a good addition to the plan, for then she could never be forced to confess all she knew about me. It was frightening to think of all the horror she had witnessed on my account, as well as her own experiences with the evil brother-in-law of mine. I shuttered to think how she too shared my own personal nightmare. As soon as possible I would set her free to live the life she always dreamed of: a life with a family of her own. As she helped me into the warm bath water and gently took care of me, gratitude welled up in my heart. An emotion I had not allowed myself to feel in a very long time. She had been so good to me, right from the very first day when she took my small hand and escorted me into this new world. She had barely left my side over the last three years, and I wondered what our lives might have been like had we been born to other people in another time.

By the time I had bathed, dressed and eaten, the sun was high in the sky. I sat like a statue near the window, thinking Misha would return soon. As I sat, with the breeze blowing the scent of jasmine through the open window, I caught a glimpse of two figures down below in the courtyard. Both were easily recognizable, and my heart was torn in two with the powerful emotions of love and hate. It was my Misha walking beside the evil one and having what appeared to be a heated discussion. I could not decipher what was being said, but only that Misha's body language was full of passion while his brother remained aloof and disinterested. I bid Zara to come and perhaps go down and see if she could hear what was being said. However, before she could leave, Misha stormed off in the direction of the house. Surely, now he would come to me and try to get me to open up to him once again. I waited patiently for his footsteps and remained motionless when he entered the room.

CHAPTER 59
Zain

My Brother's Return

IT HAD BEEN days since we celebrated the heroes' return from the battlefield. Several days since my mother had even glanced my way as our mealtimes had resumed in the lavish dining room. It was strange to see my mother sitting in the place where Grandfather Jidu once ruled and reigned—the head of the table with the special chair that had a throne-like appearance to it. My father sat mutely across the expanse while my little brother and the chosen one sat side by side as if they were the only two in the room. As much as I loathed to admit it, Misha was still my mother's beloved favorite son, even after all we had been through together in the last year. Though I had done everything in my power to win over her heart and had proved myself loyal beyond words, still, I could barely get her to look at me, much less steal a few minutes of her time. In my blackened heart, I knew she still despised the twisted mouth that mocked her for producing such a monster. She had been waiting for the return of her firstborn. From the time we were young, the one thing she had always longed for was only to see his perfect face smiling back at her.

Yet, in the days since he returned, he did not seem to be the adoring son he once was. He seemed agitated and was not eager to speak to her when she addressed him, even risking her wrath when he did not acquiesce to her demands. I knew he had taken the death of his beloved grandfather Jidu very hard and dared to question both her and me extensively about the circumstances surrounding it. Mother and I were absolutely united in our stories of his untimely death and could recite it backward and forward

216

with no hesitation whatsoever. That is what we did day after day when he had approached us—both together and separately. We conferred often to make sure the other would not falter under the weight of his interrogation and seemed to have passed the test.

It appeared he had moved on and was consumed with understanding what had happened to Myree while he was away. I overheard him questioning her several times about the state of my Little Beauty. My mother was a master at feigning indignation as to her having anything to do with the demise of his precious bride. As I walked into the library, I almost applauded her performance. Instead, I settled for a secret smile we rarely shared after my brother stormed out of the room. She breezed past me without a word, and I was left once again with the crumbs my brother had left for me to survive. Oh, how I hated Misha and all of his beautiful perfection. Even in his state of grief, he still remained civil to everyone he came in contact with, winning over the affections of the staff and visitors who came to our home to pay homage to the new ruler of the Hassen household.

I longed to be in my mother's favor again, but even my little brother, Jamal, got more of her attention these days. Avila was once again using the power she had inherited by ordering the slaves around, showing complete disdain for my father, and pretending as if the year of secrets we shared had never transpired. It seemed as if the plan I had conceived in my head would never come to pass. It was the beautiful plan of my mother and I ruling together with the Little Beauty right beside me, smiling up adoringly as my wife. I should have known she would never consider ridding the earth of her firstborn son and allowing me to rule in his place.

How naive I had been to trust her words that "everything would work out perfectly for both of us." Now here we were: I was back to being the invisible son, overshadowed by Misha, the perfect one. Nothing had changed. I had been an imbecile to believe she and I were on the same side and were together in our thinking of the future. Though I had told her through my tears over and over that I needed the Little Beauty to be mine once and for all, she still allowed my brother to go to her chambers upon returning home.

My brother would not utter a word regarding the condition of his beloved Myree, but I knew the servants were whispering about how he

217

was overheard weeping in his room at night. This was the only thing that brought consolation to my heart. It would seem I had stolen my brother's wife's soul, along with her body, and she no longer belonged to him. There was still hope alive in my heart that one day she would be mine. I still sat under her window at night hoping to catch a whisper of her voice or see her shadow cross the room, and this was the topic of my brother's confrontation with me that morning.

Misha strode towards me in the courtyard as I returned from the stables and took my arm in his hand. I could see the rage in his eyes when I looked at him and the thought of his tortured pain made me smile. He shouted at me and demanded to know what I had been doing sitting below his wife's window night after night. Some wretched servant must have reported this news to him, and I vowed to severely punish the one who had betrayed my secret hiding place. Wrenching my arm free, I brushed off his touch and calmly stated it was none of his business where I sat, what I did, or with whom I did anything.

I told him I was no longer intimidated by his position and frankly enjoyed life far more when he was not around. This seemed to infuriate him all the more, and I took a step back when he leaned his face towards me and snarled that he would get to the bottom of what had happened while he was away. Furthermore, he whispered through clenched teeth, "If I find out you had any part of the demise of my wife, I will kill you with my bare hands."

It seemed life on the battlefield had changed my big brother into someone I had never seen before. Though a chill ran down my spine, I simply smiled at him as he turned and strode off towards the house. I felt the grip of fear take hold of me for the first time in a very long time; and I did not like it one bit. I must prepare to be on guard at all times, just in case Mothers' plan was flawed and I needed to take matters into my own hands. Yes, there could be another way I could achieve my desires. I must devise a new plan on my own which included getting rid of anyone and everyone who stood in the way of me getting what I needed, and what I truly deserved.

CHAPTER 60

Myree

Secrets Revealed

WEEKS HAD PASSED and still, day after day, he came to my chambers. Sometimes he'd bring wildflowers; sometimes books he would read to me. I sat staring blankly out the window waiting for the hours to pass so that I could finally curl up in my corner and weep the hot tears that burned in my throat the entire time he was with me. I had told him countless times I was not the girl he once knew, and how it would be far better for him if he were to allow me to leave as soon as I was strong enough to travel, so that he could get on with his life. He seemed unfazed by my words and refused to entertain the idea I did not love him anymore. He would pour out his heart hour after hour, reminding me of the dreams we shared of our future together. He was determined to win my affections and was relentless in his pursuit of my heart.

It was becoming more and more difficult to avoid looking at him while he read or even dozed in my presence after a long day of attending to family business. I was weakening in my resolve and I knew he had caught me gazing at him while he read. I had been captivated by the sound of his voice and before I could quickly avert my eyes, I caught a flash of his beautiful smile. I knew the only thing that would gain me my freedom was to convince him I could no longer share his heart or life, and all I needed for my happiness in this life was to be set free.

One evening, while I was preparing for bed, Zara had allowed him entrance while she went to get me some hot tea. I was surprised to see him in my chambers in the soft light of the candles—he rarely came to me in the evenings. I was tired and unsettled in my spirit, for my commitment had started to weaken in the last few days. It was harder and harder to maintain my façade. The hatred and anger fueling my resolve had begun to waver under the love of my husband. The horror I had been living was replaced by a stirring in my heart each day for the man I used to love with every fiber of my being. When I realized my servant and the protector of my secrets was nowhere to be found, I trembled at the thought of being alone with my Misha. I tried to conjure up images in my mind of the torture I had endured while he had been away, but all I could see before me was this beautiful man with so much love in his eyes.

I rushed towards the door but realized I had nowhere to run. I walked to the window and told Misha I was not feeling well, and it wasn't a good time for him to be there. Before the words had barely left my mouth, he was behind me, so close I could feel the heat emanating from his body. He did not touch me, but softly whispered my name, declaring his love for me. "Myree, my sweet and beautiful Myree, please come back to me. Please, my precious beloved bride, don't leave me. I can't bear to think of life without you. I need you," he whispered in my ear.

Then his hand was on my arm, gently turning me to face him. I wanted desperately to run, but I was paralyzed by his nearness. He lifted my chin to look into his face and the tears began to pour from my eyes. He took my face in his hands, and as I looked up, I saw tears running down his face. We wept together for the loss, for the pain, for the grief we shared. I was then in his arms, clinging to him with all I had. As his lips met mine in a tender kiss, my mind exploded with the horror of the last time a man's lips had been pressed to mine. Taking a step backward, I screamed a bloodcurdling sound that pierced the silence of the night. I could not see the man before me, but only the devil himself on top of me growling and pouring his rage into me as he ripped me open. I was blinded by the sight and ran forward with teeth bared and hands curled in order to defend myself from my attacker. "No, no, no!" I wailed in a frenzy, rabid as a caged animal. "You will not hurt me again. Misha will kill you if you ever touch me again. I will kill you before you hurt me again."

I tried to claw at his face, but he easily held me at arm's length. My voice was not my own coming from my mouth as I unleashed the horror and rage from the depths of my soul. I don't know what I said, but I could see only my tormentor' face as I backed away and shrunk into my corner. Misha stood frozen in the middle of the room and watched as I curled myself into a ball and rocked back and forth with my hands around my knees, exhausted and spent.

The servants were then surrounding me, and Zara's face came into view. The commotion had aroused the entire house. Even Avila was at the door. Misha shouted for everyone to leave save Zara. He cleared the room and slammed the door in the face of his whining mother. I don't know how long I sat tucked into my corner—the place I had found safety for so long—but I could hear Zara weeping and Misha's voice questioning her again and again as she tried to protect my secrets. My eyes had cleared, however, my head pounded through the fog.

Misha was on his knees before me, sobbing in between his words. "Please forgive me my beautiful Myree, I should have never left you. I was not here to protect you from the evil of my brother. I never thought he would be capable of such horror. I should have known. I should have stayed. It's all my fault. I am so sorry. Please forgive me. I will not rest until this crime is avenged. My brother and mother will pay for their sins. They will pay for all of this!" Then he stormed out of the room and was gone.

And I was left there alone … cold and trembling.

The night air blew a chill through the open window as Zara tried to coax me from the corner. I sat motionless reliving what had just transpired. I had let my guard down and allowed Misha to take me into his strong arms. Then my mind went black as a force greater than I could imagine took hold of me. I don't know what I had done or what I had said. Zara's face was etched in grief as she unfolded the tale to me.

I had given Misha reason to question her about what had happened to me and what Zain had done to me. Zara poured out the whole story to him, all of it, including the pregnancy, killing of my child, and how his mother and brother had murdered his beloved grandfather. That explained the rage I saw on Misha's face before he left my room.

As the night grew colder, we heard a commotion down below in the courtyard. Voices were shouting and people began gathering to see what was happening. I rose from my corner wrapped in the blanket Zara had given me. We looked down into the lighted courtyard to see Misha and his brother standing face to face screaming at each other. All the years of envy and hatred spewed from Zain's mouth as Avila rushed forward yelling at him to be silent and not to say another word. Misha stood frozen in place, as the devil himself raved about the night he raped his own brother's wife, simply for his own desire and lust.

As Misha wept tears of outrage, we all watched as he lunged at Zain, wanting only to punish him for the evil he had committed. As a soldier, Misha was trained in hand-to-hand combat, but because of his blind fury, he had entered into this battle weaponless. His brother, however, had kept a dagger tucked into his belt, hoping to have an opportunity to use it on anyone that should cross him. Tonight was the night.

When Misha got within inches of him, Zain pulled the dagger from his belt, and I saw the glint of metal in the silvery moonlight. He plunged it into the middle of my beloved Misha and did not stop. In his madness, Zain continued to plunge the knife into his brother's body over and over again. The screams that rang out in the night came from all directions. Avila dropped to her knees as she watched her depraved child kill his own brother. The servants wailed as they witnessed the horror of evil pouring from the master they had hated for years. Zara, too, let out a sound that came from deep within her. I remained silent as I watched the life of the one person I had ever truly trusted, bleed out onto the cobblestones of the courtyard. His body lie lifeless as hysteria broke out in the whole village, who, by now, had gathered and witnessed the horror. Avila's wailing voice rose above the others as a mother's grief was awakened.

Somehow, Zara had the sense to know we could not stay for another minute. Misha, our protector was now dead, and both of our lives were now in danger. She gathered some supplies into a bag, threw a dark cloak around my shoulders. She covered herself and dragged me down the back staircase into the servant's quarters. We rushed out the side entrance and into the darkness and ran to the barn where she saddled a horse. We flew off into the night, with me clinging to her in shock. We rode long and hard for what seemed like hours. We finally arrived at the one place no one would ever dream to look for us. In the light of the early dawn, we climbed the empty steps and knocked on the door of the Temple where I had last laid eyes upon my precious Kiera.

CHAPTER 61

Kiera

Unwanted Visitors

I WAS DEEP in a state of slumber when my ears heard the commotion coming from far away. It had been a long night and my body lie exhausted beneath the cool sheets in the pre-dawn twilight. I remained still, not wanting to awake fully. But before I knew it, there was a knock at my door and one of the girls timidly poked her head into my room. I sat up wondering what could have possibly given her the boldness to approach my room. I bid her enter as I wrapped my robe around my tired body. Though I was a mere twelve years old, I had lived a lifetime and earned the title of Goddess of Love in the ranks of the Temple prostitutes. After the first two years of torment, I began to understand the ways of evil and started to use my young body as the weapon it could be. The price had risen for my services and I could now demand anything I wanted to keep the money flowing into the high priests' greedy hands. My violet eyes, auburn hair, and the now famous title, Goddess of Love, caused men and women to travel from all over the region to be with me. Once I realized my value, I vowed I would use it to my benefit. My master had given me his approval and the authority to rule over the other girls—though most of them were older than me—as long as I played my part in all of the darkness living in the Temple.

The young girl stood stammering at the door muttering about some visitors who had come to the entrance to the Temple. I could barely understand her ramblings and slapped her face to bring her to attention, demanding she tell me about the visitors. Through her tears, she stated that one of the visitors was a young black slave and the other had hair the same shade as mine with eyes as green as mine were violet.

My memory took me instantly back to the night before I was auctioned off at the slave trade to the one person in whose arm's I had found comfort. Mary, her golden emerald eyes beckoning me to sit beside her as I crawled toward her. I reached out to touch her hair, which was the exact same shade as mine. The pain in our eyes was a mirror reflection of each other, scared and helpless in a place we never should have been. But then I was taken away, and she never even said goodbye to me.

Over two years ago, when I saw her face across the marketplace, I am sure she recognized me, our eyes locked before she turned away, just like everyone else had done to me in my pitiful life. I shut the last part of my heart down that day. I was on my own in this dark and evil Temple, and there would never be anyone whom I could count on except myself. I was alone and I would do whatever it took to survive in the nightmare I was living.

I told her to take our visitors to the waiting room while I took my time dressing, deciding what I would say to the person who had betrayed me and never looked back. By the time I entered the room, the light was beginning to shine through the windows, and I caught a glimpse of the hair which was indeed the same shade as mine escaping from the dark hood that hid the young woman beneath it. My voice was calm as I said just one word: "Mary." Her head rose and her eyes met mine in a blank stare that startled me.

Had she gone mad in the years we had been apart? Was this the same beauty who had brought a hush over the crowded auction hall? And what was her slave doing bringing this pathetic creature to the door of the Temple in the dark of the morning's dawn? The questions tumbled around in my head before I told one of my girls to bring hot tea and cakes for our guests. I needed a moment to formulate my thoughts and decide what I would do as they were obviously seeking refuge from some form of threat. I carefully regarded the two and decided they could both play a role in the life I lived. I would see to it they felt welcomed and secure as I groomed them both into the beauties that lie deep within each of them. Perhaps this day would turn out to be a promising event in the light of my precious sleep being disturbed.

I would need to tread carefully. I could see the fear and distrust in their eyes, yet their desperation was obvious considering they had ridden a horse into the night with nothing but a small bag of supplies for both of them.

Why come here unless they were desperate, hiding and never wanting to be found? I was in a place of authority and the power I had to protect or reject them coursed through my veins. Perhaps with her beauty, the men might take their eyes off of me, and I could generate some income from her. Of course, I would have to keep her in my sights, convince her I was her only friend, and I could be trusted. Just as they had done with me, causing me let down my guard, I would do the same to her. I would treat her with care and respect before I demanded payment which would eventually suck the very soul from her (that is, if she still even had a soul).

I had my doubts as I walked around the room asking questions that only the dark-skinned slave girl would answer. When I commanded Mary to speak, this apparently mute girl stared again at me with vacant eyes looking right into my soul. This plan of mine may take some time to allow this girl to return from whatever horror it was that had driven her here. Surely it could be no worse than the misery I had lived through, and look at me, I had risen above it all and now lived like a queen.

The days passed and I made sure the slave Zara and her mistress Mary were both sequestered away in safety, forbidding anyone to speak a word of the two new visitors. I went often to check on them and still there was no change. Mary remained locked away in a catatonic state. When I questioned the slave girl, she gave me perfunctory answers that made no sense. She simply said they had traveled a long way escaping from an evil master. If that was true, how was it that when I laid eyes on this girl, no more than two years ago, she was in what appeared to be perfect health—a thriving woman of stature in society? I wondered what had transpired in less than twenty-four months that had crushed this one-time beauty into the mute, tormented waif she now was. Had I misjudged the possibilities when I agree to give them refuge? It seemed she may be beyond repair, driven mad by demons only she could see.

I would give it time, and if I did not see any changes soon, I would turn them both out into the street to fend for themselves. I was living in a world where men's lust and women's desire for reproduction would make them pay anything to be in good standing with the gods; not running a charity for runaways. It might take time, but I could be patient, for I knew the worth this one could bring with her eyes the color of the deep sea in sunlight and hair thicker and richer than even mine. She would pay for the right to be in my world, and I would see to it that she indeed did pay. I would allow the slave girl to serve me closely so I could get to the bottom of the mystery. When the time was right, I would put them both to work.

Life in the Temple was a world in and of itself, and my time was consumed by demands from high paying clients, tending to the Master's whims, and making sure all the other girls stayed in line. The new slave girl was proving to be valuable as she anticipated my every need. The loyalty and fierce protection she showed for her mistress was admirable. The girl had still not shown any signs of returning to life but seemed to be slipping further away. Every once in a while, I found myself looking upon her in pity. What happened to the beauty who had once taken control over sixteen hungry and scared girls on the night we were taken into captivity? Over and over, my mind replayed the scenes that had transpired on that dark night. The awful night we spent together as she told tales of her God who had rescued a girl named Esther, and another woman named Ruth who had left her foreign heritage to become one of the Israelites, only to be married and become the great grandmother of a King. What had so destroyed that young girl, turning her into this mere shell of a human being? Many mornings I had reports about screaming and wailing in the middle of the night coming from the rooms on the other side of the Temple where I had hidden them away.

Recently there had been rumors at the marketplace of a hunt for a runaway slave and there was talk of every house being searched. Surely, they would not go searching house to house for a mere slave girl. This had to be more about whatever these two were running from and I decided I would need to find out more. I sent my servants out into the marketplace to find out what they could.

When they returned, they were accompanied by several men who appeared to be very wealthy. They inquired about whether we had heard of two females who were in trouble and needed to be brought back to where they belonged. When I caught a glimpse into the eyes of the one who spoke, the one with the twisted mouth, my heart seized and I quickly looked away. I had seen evil in the eyes of men—many times—but this was different. This man looked to be the very definition of evil. With his deformed mouth and eyes that blazed red, he could have been the devil himself. A shutter ran down my spine as my master told the man he knew nothing of stray females. Before he shut the door in his face, my master stated that he kept his women under tight control, and the man should try and do the same.

Weeks slipped into months and still no change in the one I once knew as Mary. I was able to put the slave to work and she earned enough to pay for the both of them. Unfortunately, the plan I had told my master about, my plan to get them both working the way all of us did in the Temple, was proving harder to make a reality.

Mary was weak and fragile and had a haunted look about her. She was jumpy and her eyes darted about as if searching for someone who would do her harm. I could not imagine the horror she had witnessed, even though I had lived my own horror for the last three years. I would have to continue to tell my master how the girl would eventually have value, and he just needed to be patient and trust me. I was desperate to know what it was that had turned this once confident and beautiful young girl into this pathetic creature.

I questioned the slave girl, Zara, as often as I could and little by little the story was unfolding. Mary had lived a sheltered and pampered life for the first two years since we had been separated, this much I had gathered. But when her beloved husband went off to war, everything changed. That was when the trauma occurred, but I still had no idea what it was that had so dramatically changed her. Every so often, I would hear her slave refer to her as Myree. Apparently, that was the name which had been given to her by her new owners. I would only call her by the name I knew to be hers. She usually looked at me with eyes that said she recognized the name, but that person no longer resided within her.

She was docile for the most part. But one night I heard what sounded like a wounded animal screaming in pain and went to see what was happening. Upon entering, I could hear the slave girl, Zara, talking in soothing tones to one she called Myree who was hunched down in the corner of the room. The screams were being ripped from her throat in obvious torment and did not seem capable of coming from one so frail. Was this the demon calling to be freed from within her soul? Were there many who would long to be freed from her small frame, or did they reside within her only to continue the torture that had so obviously gripped her mind? When I spoke her name, there seemed to be a recognition in her eyes, and with one final wail, she dropped to the floor and lie exhausted and weeping.

I could not bear to witness such agony and fled from the room to the safety of my own walled fortress within my mind. I needed to be strong, for I could not allow myself to show any weakness in front of the other girls. I had fought hard to get where I was, and I would fight to stay there. I vowed to show no mercy as I wiped away the tears that had wet my cheeks.

As the seasons changed, life went on as usual, but it was becoming more difficult to pretend that one day Mary would work as we all did—pleasing the men who came to pay for some favors from the gods, or just to satisfy their own filthy lusts. Though she was getting stronger physically, she trembled in the presence of my master and his patience was wearing thin. I tried to keep her out of sight as her beauty was undeniable, even in her weakened state. I decided that Mary would join Zara, and they would both be my chamber maids. I knew keeping her close to me would be the safest thing I could do for her. I had cut off all her auburn hair, and told her to keep her eyes downcast, lest anyone see they held both startling beauty and tortured anguish.

I determined that her mental torment had definitely been created at the hands of men, because she became visibly agitated whenever she had any encounters with men of any age. I tried to keep my emotions walled tightly inside my heart, as I did not want to feel anything but anger and hatred for her. However, pity and compassion are closely knit together, and I found myself protecting her far more than I should, for reasons I didn't quite understand. I knew I needed to send them away to fend for themselves, but I feared for their lives. I was told by my sources that the hunt for the runaway slave was still being conducted in the villages by the man with the twisted mouth.

CHAPTER 62

Zara

Refuge in the Temple

WHY DID I ever think coming here was a good idea? The thought which had plagued me for the last five months must have tumbled out of my mouth. From across the room where she sat doing her mending, I saw Myree raise her eyes to me. Thinking back to that horrifying night, I had no choice. We had nowhere else to turn, knowing both of our lives were in danger since Master Misha was dead. Though I heard the hunt continued for the two runaway women, we had been safe here in the Temple for all this time. This is where we needed to stay.

My sweet Myree was gaining in strength, but still she never spoke, even when the young Kiera demanded she say something—anything at all—her tongue remained silent.

The screaming terrors of the dark were still frequent. Other nights I was awakened mostly by her flailing and moaning throughout the long hours of darkness. I tried to stay close, so I could wake her quickly before she awakened the entire wing of the Temple. Thankfully, Kiera had seen to it that we were sequestered in a vacant area of the Temple where no one ever dared to venture. We were told to remain out of sight and not to make any noise. Sadly, screaming at any time of the day or night was not an uncommon sound throughout the Temple. Unfortunately, there had been a few occasions when I could not rouse Myree from the grip of her sleep-induced horror, and I had to resort to throwing cold water on her face to wrestle her from the demons chasing her.

On several of those occasions, we were visited by Kiera. She was beyond angry upon arriving but seemed to take pity upon her long-lost friend when she saw Myree curled in the corner sobbing and soaking wet. My new mistress would order me to clean Myree up, keep her quiet, and then quickly leave. I don't know how many people actually knew about our presence. There were many young women living in the Temple where we knew all sorts of evil to be taking place at all hours of the day and night. I am not sure Myree was even aware of where we were. Perhaps if she knew, she would be driven further into her madness. But so far, we had been kept safe. The other girls, who would bring us meals or whom I occasionally encountered while serving as Kiera's chamber maid, seemed to pay us no attention. It seemed as if everyone had their own troubles and could not be bothered with ours.

Never in my wildest dreams would I think this would be our place of refuge. Perhaps Myree's God had led us here, and He would protect us and keep us safe until we could figure out what to do next. I know Kiera had originally thought we would both be put to work as Temple prostitutes as soon as we were able, but because I made myself so indispensable to her, she thought it wise to keep me as her own personal servant.

As far as Myree was concerned, it became quickly and painfully obvious to Kiera that she was in no condition to be working, especially because she still would not speak, and trembled violently in the presence of any man. Her frustration had been evident for the first few months, but if I wasn't mistaken, I could have sworn I sometimes saw a glimmer of compassion in her violet eyes.

Kiera found work for Myree in mending garments, and when she arrived with shears in her hands one day, I feared for our lives. But then she told me to hold Myree still and she began cutting off all her gorgeous locks, stating now she would not garner as much attention. I still longed to know the connection between the two of them and thought perhaps, one day in the near future, I might attempt to ask my new Mistress about how she and Myree had come to know each other. Of course, the striking beauty of the hair color they shared would be an immediate source of bonding. I could only figure it happened some time when they were both being sold at the slave auction—as I vaguely remembered the stunning child with the violet eyes.

As the days wore on and the seasons changed, the daily routine became as normal as my previous life as a slave. I found myself humming the familiar tune I had learned from Myree years ago. The *Love Song to Yahweh* was once Myree's favorite. Before that dark night of her soul, she often prayed to her God and told me of the many adventurous stories written in the scrolls of her people. She loved to share about Noah, David, and the people of Israel who had escaped my homeland where they had been enslaved for 400 years before fleeing from Pharoah into the wilderness. I had come to enjoy our times of storytelling and missed them terribly. I feared I would never hear my friend talk about her faith again. I doubted she would ever find her way out of the darkness.

If only her God would bring the healing to her mind she so desperately needed. Sadly, before this could happen, she would have to believe once again that He even existed. My sweet friend Myree had told me long ago to never again speak of Him in her presence. So, in the quiet of my nights, I would silently hum the words in my head and pray this God, whom she used to love, would set her free from her prison. I had seen so much pain in my own life, yet something about her stories had given me hope. I still believed in her God and prayed He would still believe in her—in both of us—enough to somehow get us out of this place and into a new life.

I desperately wanted to take her away, back to her homeland and the village of her auntie, where she had been loved and cherished as a little girl. I dreamed of a place where both of us could be free. A place where perhaps if God would smile on me, I could still have a future and a family of my own. But how could this ever be, when we were at the mercy of Kiera, the Goddess of Love, who held our very lives in her hands?

CHAPTER 63
Myree

The Madness Grows

BLOOD, ALWAYS SO much blood running down the street where my beloved Misha lie while his evil brother held the dagger over him sneering his victory smile. Then I was running, and he was chasing me—closer and closer so I could smell his breath, feel the weight of him on top of me and hear my own screams so loud I would wake up myself and everyone else. Other times I would be running in the courtyard where the brothers were fighting, and I would throw myself in front of the dagger meant for my husband. Now the blood would be mine, and I would hear my beloved Misha wailing as he held my face in his hands. The sobs which tore from my soul would cause Zara to shake me violently. She lived in fear that my cries would wake the others and alert them to our presence.

I didn't know how long we had been in this place. Most days I vacillated between terror, anguish, torment and deep debilitating shame which did not permit me to really live, but instead, kept me in a state of silent fear, barely breathing. I would not speak. I was imprisoned inside my mind by pictures of my past replaying over and over. I was the little girl on the back of a donkey riding away from parents—the mere child who had been sold for a bag of coins. There was the devil with the twisted mouth always around every corner, ready to rob me of my childhood virginity. Avila was inside my head as well. The beautiful woman who hated me from the very first day I arrived, plotting my demise from the moment I was brought into her home. I could not forget the evil woman who slapped my face, and then loomed over me with a metal tool as they held my legs open before

232

my world went black. And always, I saw Misha's blood running over the cobblestones as I screamed his name from my bedroom window. Over and over these scenes played before my eyes, relentless to leave me alone, until I could no longer hold my eyes open. Only to have them visit me in my sleep. I was living a never-ending nightmare that I could not escape no matter how hard I tried.

Zara was a constant companion and when she was called away to serve the beautiful young Kiera, she would leave me hidden in a dark corner of a small room—covered by blankets and surrounded by the musty smell of things cast off long ago. I was only too happy to stay in this secret place, away from people where I could allow my mind to torment me with all that I deserved. I was the reason my beloved Misha was now dead. It was all my fault, and had I never been born, he would still be alive and married to one who was worthy of his love. If only I had been able to convince him to let me go, but he was relentless in his pursuit of my heart and I had been weak. He would not stop until he knew the truth of my brokenness. I should not blame Zara, though in my heart I did, knowing that had she not shared the truth, he would not have gone after his brother. But it was my fault, mine and only mine. I was to blame, and it should have been me lying on the stones with my life blood leaving my body. Oh, how I wish it would have been me. Even now I wished for death, every day and every night. But it never came, and my well-deserved torture continued.

Lately I had found myself with robes in my hands, mending material, or hemming the lengths. I don't know how I knew how to do this sewing, but it came naturally for me. I was able to escape for a few moments of time into the steady moving of the needle going in and out of the garment. Once in a while I had flashes of another time long ago when I was a small child, sitting at the feet of a beautiful woman who was at the loom weaving lovely colors into stunning robes and shawls. I would see a glimpse of light as the sun shone in the window. I could get a glimpse of her smile before the blackness descended again, and I was sent back into the torture chamber of my mind.

I did not mind the work, and I got better and faster with the fabrics each day, knowing this would at least keep Zara and I away from the other side of the Temple where the men came and went. She would keep Kiera well taken care of, as she had me for those years, before everything changed. I would sew as fast as I could, earning a smile from whomever put the garments in my hands. I kept my head covered and my eyes down, grateful I was no longer an object of attention. When Kiera came at me with the shears, I closed my eyes and wished for death, but only felt the pull of my long hair as it hit the floor in front of me. I cared nothing for my once beautiful long locks, and was happy to be rid of one of the things that drew people to me. Now if only I could gouge out my very own eyes, I would be rid of the unique features that made me different, and I would be just like everyone else. But I was too much of a coward to even do that.

PART TWO

10 YEARS LATER

CHAPTER 64

Myree

The Return Home

THE DAYS HAD turned into weeks and then months and years as Zara and I found our place in the new home, which I had come to learn was the Temple. The place where I had seen the lovely Kiera so many years ago, standing on the steps before strong arms had roughly taken her inside the heavy doors. I recalled it had been my mission to rescue her from her prison, and the irony of her being my rescuer was almost too much to fathom. My mind had returned to me in bits and pieces for stretches at a time before I was swallowed up again by the demons. Many times, in my clarity, my fragmented mind shocked me into remembering all that I had endured during my years as the girl who had married Misha.

It was a sweet time before he went away to war, but then everything changed. I knew I needed to quickly shut my mind down at that point, for one of the demons would always come in and take me away.

Sometimes, I welcomed them as they would consume me and the trauma I had lived through. Each one was a different, dark companion. I had given them names, or rather, they had given themselves names and would take over when I felt tired, sad, or just when I allowed my mind to wander. Their voices were constant and kept me company through the years.

In the beginning, the voices would appear mostly at night, whenever I would fall asleep. However, after months of no sleep, they became my constant companions. Day and night, they were always present. Whether it was the one called Death, or Rage, Hatred or Fear; each would settle in and transport me in time to a place with which I may or may not be familiar. These pictures in my mind were always related to the face of the evil one I used to know as Zain, my husband's brother, who stole my soul one dark and stormy night; or the evil old woman who tore out my insides until blackness overtook me. I never knew what I was capable of during these episodes, but always Zara was close by, shaking me and calling my name until they were driven away for a while. Other times, the ones called Suicide, Addiction, and Shame would take over, and I would find myself covered in my own blood, having sliced into my flesh trying to feel something other than the dark emptiness. After the first time Zara found me in a bloodied state, she kept a close watch over me whenever I was taking care of the mending of the garments. For if I had anything sharp in my possession, it quickly became a weapon the demons would use to convince me to harm myself.

For a long time now, I had found glimpses of peace in the herbs which one of the girls shared with me when she could no longer tolerate my nightly screaming. Zara had not been aware of what the girl had given me. It was a green powder wrapped in one of the garments that I was to mend. Upon placing it in my hands, she told me to mix a little with my nightly tea and I would sleep like a baby. I recalled the doctor coming into my room and giving me a potion that would take hold of my mind and allow me to sleep, and I welcomed whatever it was this girl gave to me. Longing to be free from my tormented dreams, I did as I was instructed and every night I was able to escape into a world of colors and visions where nothing made sense.

Each night I would anticipate the escape and find myself floating into the skies or dancing on the clouds. My secret was safe with the girl who brought the powder, and she seemed happy to give me the one thing that allowed me to rest in peace in the darkness of night. Zara was completely unaware, until one night she found me wandering the vacant hallways of the Temple and had to practically carry me back to our quarters. She then searched my belongings and found my special herbs, finally understanding how it was that I was suddenly not screaming through the night. She thought it prudent to allow me to keep taking my little secret, however, she insisted on administering it to me, lest I take too much and not wake up in the morning. Now I require the beautiful green powder to even think about sleep as my body craves it like the air I breathe.

Keira had become our protector, and as long as she was in charge of the Temple prostitutes, we were safe. In my moments of lucidity, I realized Kiera had saved our lives and we were deeply indebted to her. While Zara served her during the daytime, I stayed hidden in my dark corner where I was safe and could sew and weave the garments I was given. They had brought me all the tools I needed to create beautiful garments, though someone always watched over me as I made myself useful. The girls would beg me to weave them a robe or a shawl. With stacks of fabrics and wools, I had plenty to keep me busy. My mind was able to direct my hands as I got lost in the beauty of the colors and textures. Apparently, we were both worth keeping around.

As the years passed, I saw kindness in Kiera's eyes and heard a softness in her voice when she would call me Mary and try to coax me out of my silence. I don't know how long it had been since I heard my own voice, but I vowed to remain in my own self-imposed dungeon of quiet, content to be told what to do and when to do it. As long as I was given the green liquid, I could remain still and quiet, but when it wore off, I could not be held responsible for my actions.

Sometimes I would let my mind rewind in time to when I was a little girl, and in the recesses, I could catch glimpses of my sweet auntie, hear her soft voice and smell the heavenly aroma of unleavened bread baking over the fire. Whenever I allowed my mind to go there, I knew there would be suffering. I was punished by Shame or Rage or Hatred when they snuck in and reminded me I was not worthy of those memories. I was not that little girl anymore, and I had no right to the beautiful images. My mind would begin telling me that if my auntie and uncle had ever really loved me, they would have fought to keep me, and taken me from my drunken parents. If I ever meant anything to them, they would have tried to find me. But they didn't. To them, I was just a worthless excuse of a child whose own parents hated her so much, they resorted to selling her to strangers. Always nearby, Hatred and Rage would then come to life inside my mind. In the darkness, they would take possession of me. I despised myself and still wished for Death, once and for all, to take me down to the grave where I could finally rest in the pits of hell where I knew I belonged.

One spring morning there seemed to be more commotion outside of our vacant section of the Temple. Kiera rushed in demanding Zara hide me in a place where I could not be seen or heard, and would not be found.

"Quick, take Mary and hide her in the back of my closet, and give her something to keep quiet. There will be trouble if the new master sees her and her unique beauty," she ordered.

The fury of panic that surrounded me brought in Fear. I began to moan and wail uncontrollably. Kiera demanded I be quiet, slapping my face in an attempt to control me.

"Mary, you must stay silent. I cannot allow them to find you!" Kiera breathed into my face. But it was too late. Fear already had his claws deep in my troubled mind.

Zara quickly showed me the little green potion that I greedily drank and soon slipped into oblivion. I was dragged into the recesses of Kiera's own dark closet and locked inside the darkness where I could fade away in the colors of my tortured mind. Soon there were voices outside the door— men—several of them with raised voices causing me to shrink farther back into the darkness of my fear-filled mind.

The people outside my hideaway moved about the room for a while, before leaving me to my beloved silence. I must have fallen asleep for it was dark outside when I tried the door and ventured out of the closet. Kiera and Zara were together occupied with what seemed to be packing a trunk. They spoke with quiet voices in hushed tones. When they noticed me standing there, I felt hands guiding me over to a couch where Zara sat me down and gave me something to eat. Ever gentle, Zara spoke tenderly to me and explained that it was time for us to leave. We could no longer stay in the safety of the Temple because a new master had come in and Kiera was no longer able to protect us.

"Myree, I need you to listen carefully to me and we need you to do everything we say. Can you do that?" my sweet friend whispered to me. We were to leave that very night under the cover of dark. Kiera had arranged for a transport to take us back to my homeland, back to the village of Nazareth where my auntie was and where my family lived. She had made all the arrangements and we were to leave within the hour. There was no time for my mind to unravel. I was told to take my garments, keep my hands busy, and my mind occupied. In my lucidity, I felt a glimmer of hope. I was going home, and Zara was coming with me.

But what of Kiera? Would she not accompany us and leave the living hades she endured every day? With eyes that pierced my own, she stared at me deeply for a long moment before taking my hands into hers and allowing a tear to slip down her cheek. "Please do everything that Zara tells you to do," she urged me. "She will keep you safe until I can find you once again." She assured me she would stay until our safety was guaranteed and then she would follow when the time was right. Kiera promised she would see me again. This brought comfort to my troubled mind and I embraced her as the tears flowed from both Zara's and my own eyes. The night became darker as we gathered our meager belongings, and then it was finally time to leave the home I had known for many years. What would happen now? I dared not allow my thoughts to wander but kept them safe in one area of my heart. I held tightly to this, the one dream I had kept alive for so long; I might see my beloved auntie once again.

The transport was pulled by two horses and driven by one man, a trusted servant of Kiera's. I heard him promise his mistress he would deliver us to our destination or give his very own life trying. Soon we were jostling around on the long journey south, back to my homeland. Zara held my hand, squeezing it tightly so that I would stay present with her in the carriage.

Morning came and we were allowed to get out and wash by a stream while the driver watered and fed the horses. We ate a few bites of cheese and some figs, though neither of us had much of an appetite. Soon we were traveling again, and the sun was high in the sky before we stopped once more.

We drove through the night and slept fitfully, even as we were bounced around the carriage. The diversion of being in the back of a carriage was just enough to keep my mind focused and contained as we continued onward. Since I had no idea where my family actually lived, the next day, as the sun was setting, we were let off to find our own way at the edge of the village called Nazareth. We had arrived safely. Our guide bid us farewell before leaving us in a place that looked vaguely familiar to me.

Smells of lamb roasting on a fire stirred our stomachs as Zara took my hand and led me along the road. I kept my head down and my eyes focused on taking one step at a time through the dusty street. I heard the language of my childhood spoken and my thoughts began to whisper in my mind. I could feel Zara squeezing my hand harder to focus me as the moans began to escape from my lips. She pulled me aside where prying eyes could not see us and slapped me hard on the cheek to awaken me from my fear-gripped thoughts. I looked at her as she hugged me close and then we continued on until we found a place where we could lodge for the night.

Zara paid the innkeeper as I kept my head down and my mouth closed. We found our way to a small room in the back where we could find the privacy Zara had insisted she needed for her friend who was ill. We ate a bit of bread and dried meat that had been packed for us. In my somewhat lucid state of mind, this sweet woman, who had been my constant companion, spoke in hushed tones that soothed my soul. She reminded me of all the ways my auntie's God had protected us for these many years, and how it was His hand that had brought us here, back to my homeland where I had family and people who loved me.

She made me look deep into her eyes and recited the words of my childhood, the Shema: "The Lord, the Lord is One. You shall love the Lord your God with all your heart, all your mind and all your strength." A peace washed over me as I heard the familiar words. She then began humming a tune that was locked so deep within me, it had to fight to get out. She held my hands as I allowed the tune to wash over me, cradling me in the beauty of the melody. Afterwards, she stood and went over to our lone small trunk we had carried with us. My friend brought out a small wrapped package, one I had not seen before. As she held it tenderly in her hands and gently began to unfold the paper, I caught a glimpse of the golden and crimson threads woven together along with a soft emerald green color. The tears broke forth from deep within me as I reached to touch the sacred garment I had carried with me from my auntie's home all those years ago. The memories flashed of the beautiful Mary weaving the colors together, her voice telling me as if it were yesterday, "Mary, this is a very special garment. The colors are of the sea at sunset and remind me of the same beautiful shades of your eyes and your hair."

The night she delivered it to my uncle's home as a priceless gift to me, was a night I will never forget. I had not seen this precious robe for all these years, but Zara had kept the treasure safe for such a time as this. I wept deep cleansing tears and wondered if perhaps there was a God in heaven who was still watching over me.

I slept without the potion for the first time in I don't know how long. I awoke feeling scared but also hopeful that perhaps my life was not over, but just beginning again. The demons were battling for a place in my mind, but as long as I heard the soft humming of the *Love Song to Yahweh*, they were kept contained.

Zara stayed close to me and explained we would stay in for a day or two, and when I was feeling strong enough, she would go in search of my auntie.

"I will take your beloved shawl and go from door to door to see if anyone might remember a woman named Mary, the weaver of beautiful garments who was also your auntie's best friend." She would then track down my auntie and use the robe as proof of my identity, bringing her here to the safety of the inn. This seemed wise to me. The thought of venturing out filled me with anxious thoughts, and I longed for the peace I had tasted the night before. I kept busy with my sewing and Zara kept up a constant song, filling our small room.

Another night passed and the dreams and demons were kept at bay. My mind was filled with dreams of what it would be like to see my auntie again. What would she think of the woman I had become? Shame and Death always taunted me when these thoughts filled my head, and I would begin to rock back and forth, back and forth to soothe my troubled mind. I had to banish them quickly, lest they take control and I lose myself completely. Just thinking about the feel of her warm arms wrapped around me and the smell of lavender clinging to her, brought a timid smile to my lips.

I heard Zara reciting the Shema under her breath since we had arrived and though part of me wanted to join in with her and find comfort in the familiar refrain, my heart would not allow me to think of the God who had abandoned me at such an early age and left me to die a thousand deaths at the hands of cruel and wicked people. I fought to block out the words. Rage and Hatred were always close by reminding me that my only goal was to get revenge on the ones who had caused me such anguish. My heart would start beating faster and faster and I would begin to pace the small room, before Zara would give me a small dose of the green potion, keeping me from going mad. Her eyes always showed me only kindness and pity as she took care of me, and I had to battle the thoughts that always returned: she would be so much better off if I was dead.

Part of me was desperate to leave the confines of the little room, and another part wanted to curl up in the corner and give in to the self-loathing that had consumed me for so many years. I could hear the sound of the animals on the streets, the commotion of carts going by the small inn. I smelled the aromas of my childhood and wondered if my cousins might be somewhere just outside the window which brought in the morning sunlight.

Was my uncle still tending his sheep in the fields? Was Mary still weaving the beautiful shawls for the women who walked by on the dusty roads? With thoughts of the people from my past, Death then appeared and told me they were all dead. No one cared about me. And if I were to leave the small room, my own dreaded father might see me and take me prisoner and sell me once again for a few coins. I could hear my mother's drunken voice hissing in my ears, "You're old enough now to be of some use to us."

The voices got louder and louder as the walls pressed in. I bolted for the door, only to have Zara's firm hands wrapping around me and pulling me back to the bed of straw on the floor. She gave me a good dose of the magical liquid and soon I was in my own little world of color and clouds. Days passed with little change, and I despaired of being here, of living, of having any hope that Zara would ever find my family.

One day, when I had just woken up from a mid-morning nap brought on by the heavy dose of potion Zara had given me earlier, I heard voices outside the room. Soon Zara rushed in and closed the door behind her. My mind was clouded, unable to remember where we were or how we got here. Zara spoke softly to me, and I wondered if Kiera was outside the door. But surely, Kiera would have rushed in as well if she were here.

Zara reminded me that we had left the Temple several weeks ago. We had traveled to my homeland and were now in the village of Nazareth. "Remember," Zara explained, "I have been searching from house to house for your family ever since we arrived." Her voice came from far away, and my mind fought to focus on what she was saying and what all of this meant. Then I heard the voice, just outside the door, the one I had cherished in my heart for all these years.

"Mary, my Sweet Mary. Is that really you in there?" Zara looked at me and told me she had found Mary, the woman who had created my beloved shawl, and her best friend Naomi, my beloved auntie. They were now living together after both of their husbands passed away. These two women were now just outside the door and wanted desperately to see me.

Zara hurried on, "I have told them as much as they need to know about the last thirteen years. I have shared with them how your heart is very fragile, you don't speak, and you sometimes become agitated. They assured me they did not care about the past, but only wanted to see you and shower you with love. Can I please let them in?" Zara begged.

My thoughts were tangled and flew around in my head as I slowly nodded. My heart pounded and my throat was dry as these two beautiful women slowly entered the small, shadowy room. Paralyzed in confusion, I sat curled up, motionless on the straw bed unable to raise my head. Then my beloved auntie was on her knees, weeping and saying the words, "Mary, my Sweet Mary" over and over again. She dared not touch me but sobbed unashamedly while I sat, eyes downcast. With tears running down her face, my auntie cried, "Please, you must know that every night since you were taken from me, I have prayed to Adonai to protect you. I have been desperate to know where you were. I despaired that you were even still alive. Everywhere I went, I have searched the streets and the marketplace for your unique hair color. I have turned the faces of young girls to look into their eyes, praying to catch a glimpse of you my precious, Sweet Mary. For all these years, I have not stopped searching for you. Now, here you are, and I praise our good and gracious Yahweh who hears the cries of His children and answered my prayers to bring you back to me."

She praised her God over and over and poured out her soul while weeping tears of gratitude to Him for allowing her to see the beloved daughter of her heart once again. Finally, I raised my tear-streaked face, and I was enfolded in the same sun-kissed arms that held me as a child. Grief and unimaginable joy overwhelmed me. I collapsed into her chest and allowed her to stroke my hair and whisper my name while I cried years of unshed tears onto her shoulder.

Then another woman, Mary, came over and sat next to us, praying softly, and thanking Jehovah Jireh, the God who had provided a way for us to all be together again. Zara also joined in the blessed gathering, and wept quietly, as if she did not want to disturb this holy reunion.

There seemed to be a bright light in the room as if I was in the presence of holiness, of angels, or of God Almighty Himself. These two women were the same two who had loved me, nurtured me, taught me, and mentored me as a little girl. I don't know how much time passed while we sat there. I could not fathom I was finally home. For what seemed a brief moment, I was able to forget the utterly pathetic sum total of my life. While sitting there with these women who loved me, I could feel their strength, yet I could also feel the battle beginning to stir within my mind, my heart and my soul.

I began to rock: back and forth, back and forth. Moans began to escape from my lips. From a distance I could hear my name being called over and over, "Mary, Sweet Mary. Don't leave us. Please stay with us." The room began to close in, and I could not fight the demons off any longer. I heard a scream being torn loose from my throat and then I was alone on the cot. Zara's strong hands were holding me down and forcing the green liquid into my mouth. The women stood in the corner looking at me as though I was a wild animal, confusion written all over their aged faces. I growled at them from the corner to where I had retreated, as Zara ushered them out the door.

CHAPTER 65

Naomi

Prayers Finally Answered

MY MIND WAS weary, trying to process what happened on this day. I could not believe that the one thing I had prayed about for so many years had finally arrived: I had held my Sweet Mary in my arms. Lying awake, reliving the day, joy was mixed with a pain squeezing my heart until I could barely breathe.

The knock on the door in the early morning hours was a surprise to both my friend Mary and I. We had no idea who this young dark-skinned woman was standing before us. In a language that was obviously not her own, she rushed to tell us her story.

We invited her into our home as she tried to explain how she had wandered all over the streets of Nazareth for the last several days searching for one called Mary, the weaver of beautiful garments. She described how a woman at the well told her about someone named Mary who was a weaver and lived with Naomi at the edge of town. Her excitement grew as she looked to me when I told her my name was indeed Naomi. She then took out a carefully wrapped package, and with gentle, loving hands; revealed her prize to us.

Both Mary and I gasped aloud as we recognized the one-of-a-kind garment which my friend had woven all those years ago for my Sweet Mary. It was, without a doubt, the very same garment. In my shock, the questions started flowing at the same time the tears did. "Could it be that my Sweet Mary is still alive? How did you come into possession of such a garment?" I asked.

My friend Mary had to reach out to touch my arm to stay my tongue and calm my beating heart. I took a deep breath and lifted my eyes to heaven, silently pleading with my Abba Father to give me some answers to the questions that had now plagued me for what seemed a lifetime. The woman told us her name was Zara, a longtime servant of a woman named Myree. She shared how they had traveled a long way to come back to the homeland of her mistress who grew up near here but was raised by her loving auntie and uncle who had five sons. My tears flowed faster now as she spoke, and I just wanted to scream out, "Where is she?"

Zara explained in great detail that the years had been unkind to her mistress, and how she had suffered a great deal at the hands of evil men. She went on to tell us how her friend Myree had not spoken a word to anyone in over ten years and often would fall into spells in which she was not herself. When I finally interrupted her and demanded she take us to my Sweet Mary, she lowered her head. I immediately felt ashamed of myself for raising my voice. This woman obviously loved her mistress and friend very deeply to have taken care of her all these years. I apologized for my outburst and humbly asked her to continue.

She told us of the early years when Myree was young and still believed in the God of her Auntie Naomi; how she had taught her the *Love Song to Yahweh* and had shared the stories of faith past down from her ancestors. When she described how Myree had learned the Shema from her uncle and how she would recite it every day, my heart leapt. I knew this was, indeed, my Sweet Mary she was talking about. I could barely contain myself, but my friend bid me to take a deep breath and consider what this woman, Zara, was trying to tell us. Yes, it seemed it was the same person, but no, she was not the same person at all. Mary told me I would do well to heed Zara's words before barging into the world she had lived in, a world of which I knew nothing about.

My heart shattered again to think of the pain, the years of isolation, the anguish she had endured. All I wanted to do was to show her how much she was loved. I wanted to bring her home and make up for all the lost years. The sadness in this precious woman's eyes told us more than we wanted to know. I would have to pray and seek the wisdom of the Lord so I could get to know my Sweet Mary once again.

It was decided we would accompany her back to the inn where they were staying. Zara told us if Myree agreed to see us, if she was in the right state of mind, and if she was not too agitated; we would be allowed into the room for a brief visit. These restrictions were hard for me to accept, but I prayed the entire time we walked through the village and my soul had found peace by the time we arrived.

Though I thought I had prepared myself, what I saw when I entered the dimly lit room, devastated my heart. My legs went weak and I felt my friend's arms around me giving me strength. The woman curled up on the bed, who would not raise her eyes to mine, was not my precious, Sweet Mary. Her eyes darted about the room as she held her knees to her chest. The hair and eyes were the same unique shades, but time had ravaged her, and she was barely recognizable for a woman of only twenty three years. Her face was sunken, and her skin hung loosely on her frame. For a moment, I thought I was looking at my very own sister who had been dead for many years. The tears started streaming down my face as I gently called her name over and over again, begging her to look at me. When at last her eyes looked into mine, the tears were flowing down her cheeks too. All I could do was sob as I gently touched her hand.

I praised the God of Abraham, Isaac and Jacob for bringing my Sweet Mary back to me. I told her over and over I had never stopped looking for her, that I had lain awake many nights praying, thinking, and wondering where she was. When I uttered the words, "I lost a part of my heart that day, and I have missed you with every breath I have taken for all these years," she reached her arms out and collapsed into my embrace. We clung together as my friend, Mary, praised God. It seemed time stood still. I was ready to take her with us back to our home when suddenly she began to rock back and forth, back and forth. Then a sound came, at first low and quiet from the depths of her throat, then louder. While I watched in horror, her eyes rolled back into her head. I released my hold on her and slowly backed away as Zara came in between us and began shouting in a language we did not understand. She held my Sweet Mary's arms tightly and pulled a vial of something from the pocket of her own robe, forcing the liquid down my niece's throat before telling us it was best we leave right now.

I could not stop weeping as my friend and I walked the long road back to our home. Her arms around my shoulders were the only thing guiding me as the tears blurred my sight. My heart was both elated and devastated, if that were possible. Seeing my beloved Sweet Mary sitting on the cot was like a dream come true. For so many years I dreamt about what it would be like to hold her in my arms, to stare deeply into her golden green eyes, and once again hear her voice lifted in praise to our God. For many years now, it was something I rarely allowed myself to do: to believe she was even still alive. Now, it seemed my worst fears had come true, for this was not the beautiful, vibrant little girl I once knew and loved. It broke my heart see her locked deep inside of herself, head downcast, and eyes barely looking our way. Her friend, Zara, told us she had experienced a lot of trauma since I had seen her last, but I was not prepared for this. I shuttered and could barely catch my breath to think of the evil that had fallen upon her since the last time I saw her all those years ago.

As we reached the home we now shared together, Mary put on a pot of tea and insisted I sit down so we could figure out a plan to help Sweet Mary in her distress. It seemed as if she were no longer in control of her own mind and there were other dark forces which had the right to appear whenever they choose.

"She did seem to recognize both of us for a few moments, don't you think?" Mary questioned, as she offered me some steaming tea. I held the warm cup in my hands and gained a measure of comfort from my beautiful friend's words.

What would I have done without my beloved friend Mary, I wondered, lost in thought. When my Judah got sick, it was her and her family who surrounded me and my children. Although my sons were a source of strength, they all had families of their own and soon I found myself alone—day after day, night after night. It was then when Mary suggested I sell my place and come and share her home, which was much larger than mine. It seemed like a good plan, and my sons were eager for me to find my own way and not be a burden on them, though they would never voice such a terrible thought.

Mary had been widowed several years earlier and I had tried as much as I could to be a good friend in her time of need. I had no idea what she was living through until I, too, had experienced my own deep grief at the loss of my husband. I realized that together we could serve God and the other widows of the community. I had found a new hope in my sadness. Both of us were blessed with wonderful sons, daughters-in-law and grandchildren. However, having each other to lean on was a gift from Yahweh Himself.

"Naomi," I heard my name being called and realized Mary had asked me a question.

"Yes, I do. I do believe she recognized us," I stammered. "She clung to me as she had when she was but a child of six years old. Her eyes still held the same color, didn't they? I asked my friend. "But there was no life in them. Sweet Mary stared vacantly at both of us as we tried to remind her of our love for her. It was as if she wanted to believe us, but something inside of her would not allow it." I paused in thought, then continued. "When she started to rock back and forth, the hair on my arms stood up and I felt a chill run down my spine. I sensed the presence of evil in the room. Did you not feel the same?" I asked.

Mary took a long sip of her tea before her eyes met mine and she whispered, "Indeed I did. The darkness that took over your precious niece was strong and powerful. She will need a tremendous amount of prayer and fasting to be delivered from that force." She took my hand in hers as the tears slipped from my eyes.

Oh, my Sweet Mary, what has happened to you? Where have you been and how will I ever see you returned to me? In the silence of the late afternoon, with our hands joined, we sank to our knees and pleaded with our Jehovah God to hear our prayer and deliver my precious Sweet Mary from the grip of the evil one. We prayed and wept until the room grew dark. We then rose to prepare our evening meal and formulate a plan which would include getting others to join us in prayer. We would visit Sweet Mary every day, and when she was strong enough, she and Zara would come and stay with Mary and I. We would care for them as the daughters of our hearts, and God would bring the healing they both needed. With resolve, we vowed to be faithful and trust Almighty God with her soul. Now, as sleep overtook my weary heart, I rested in His sovereign care for my Sweet Mary.

CHAPTER 66

Zara

Sacred Reunion

WHAT GOOD FORTUNE! What a miracle it was! I had found the beloved Auntie Naomi and her friend Mary, the weaver of beautiful fabrics. As I lie on my cot, hearing the fitful breathing of my mistress, I thought back over the last few weeks. It had been days of going out very early in the morning while Myree was still deep in her drug-induced sleep. I had resorted to giving her an ample dose at night so I could find my way to leaving her alone for a few hours each day.

In the mornings, I would go to the well where the women came to draw their water for the day. Most times they ignored me and my questions, only to whisper to themselves and laugh as they cast their glances at me. As a foreigner, I knew my speech was sometimes hard to understand, but I worked hard to master the language of my mistress. I had to hide my injured pride as I arrived each morning, knowing it would be the same thing.

Sometimes I would give Myree a little dose in the afternoon as well so I could go house to house asking if anyone knew the woman named Mary who was the weaver of fine garments. I despaired of ever finding either her or the famous Auntie Naomi until one day I saw a young girl, no more than fifteen or so, who looked similar to me. I wondered what her story was as I tried to entice a smile out of her. She obviously belonged to someone, and so it was difficult to get close enough to ask her a question.

Then it happened. On a morning while her mistress was gossiping with the other women, she stole away and got close enough to tell me there was a woman named Mary who wove beautiful garments. She lived out on the very edge of town, a half a day's walk. I was so happy, I wanted to hug the young lady. Instead, I smiled as brightly as I could and asked Yahweh to bless her. With this, she beamed and slipped back to the well, unnoticed by her owner.

With this new-found information, I had to formulate a plan that would allow me to travel the half day's journey to the edge of the village and find this woman who may have information about Myree's auntie. I had been able to pay the innkeeper in advance for the days we had stayed at his abode. I wondered if I might take advantage of his wife's kindness to keep an eye out for my mistress while I was gone. I had explained to them that she was ill, and I had tried with all my might to keep her quiet. Still, I feared there may have been a time or two when I was not able to silence her before her moaning or screams reached through the walls.

After much thought and prayer, I realized I had no other choice but to ask for help. It would be disastrous if Myree were to wander into the streets unaccompanied, for her fears would be triggered. And without me to keep her focused, she may very well do something we would both regret. Yes, I had no choice than to ask for some aide and trust that Yahweh would watch over my beloved friend.

So it was when I went out early, before the sun rose, and found my way to the edge of town. I went from house to house asking if Mary, the weaver of fine garments, resided there. When at last, to my shock and elation, I was invited in by two beautiful women, each old enough to be my mother's age. I poured out the story while they waited impatiently. I then produced the beautiful treasure I had carried with me. They both gasped in awe upon seeing the shawl and then the one who I believed would be called Auntie—in her excitement—yelled at me to take her to her niece. I knew I must make them understand. I sat silently with eyes downcast, and she humbly apologized, begging me to forgive her zeal to see her long lost niece.

After I had told them as much as they needed to know, we began our journey to the inn. We hurried along and when we arrived, I bade them to wait outside, praying Myree would be in a good place. I poured out the story of finding her long-lost auntie, asking Myree if I could invite them in. She stared at me without blinking and nodded that yes, I could allow them to enter. I held my breath and watched the scene unfold.

Naomi went directly over and knelt before Myree who was curled on the cot, locked inside herself. She was gentle and kind, not touching my mistress, but only weeping and whispering words of love while the other Mary stood and prayed silently to herself. Finally, it happened: the words of love she was pouring onto her niece had unlocked the door to my Myree within. She raised her head, tears streaming down her face. Timidly, she allowed herself to be enveloped by her beloved auntie who praised God over and over. Mary and I approached, and together we sat weeping at this beautiful reunion. Sadly, this only lasted a few moments before I heard the sounds, and saw the rocking begin. I knew it was only a matter of minutes before Myree would be lost to us once again. I inserted myself in between all of them and held my friend's arms while her beautiful eyes rolled back and disappeared. I rushed to get the potion into her mouth. Then she was gone. The liquid took a few moments to enter her system, and while she emitted low growls from deep within, I held her down and motioned to these lovely women that they should leave—and leave quickly.

That had been weeks ago. Each morning, just as the sun was rising, I would hear a soft knock on the door, and there they were, holding baskets of fresh fruits and bread. Every day they brought more: a tea pot, cups, and fabrics. Our tiny room was now filled with beautiful robes, shawls and blankets. We were now surrounded by familiar foods, scents and beauty. With each visit, Myree, whom they called Mary, would allow them to stay just a little longer before the demons overtaking Myree would demand they leave. We would eat, drink tea, and sing the *Love Song to Yahweh* while Auntie Naomi shared tales of my friend's childhood. We were captivated by the stories of how Naomi's own sons would watch over their young cousin, and how her uncle spoiled her with extra portions of meat. She shared how her little niece, Sweet Mary, used to sit attentively drinking in every word as she listened to her uncle read from the ancient scrolls of the Torah. Myree would remain still until she could no longer fight off her demons and the rocking would begin. They would then pray and take their leave, assuring us they would return in the morning. Each day would begin again with their gracious and patient hearts knocking on the door.

As I drifted off to sleep, I asked the God of Abraham, Isaac and Jacob once again to have mercy on my friend and bring her the healing we all so desperately longed to see. I prayed for freedom and deliverance from the horror and trauma that were Myree's constant companions. Perhaps tomorrow would bring the miracle we were all seeking.

CHAPTER 67

Beautiful Mary

Weaver of Fine Garments

IN THE DARK hours of the night, I prayed and recalled the events of the day. One look at the young woman curled up on the cot and I knew. Deep in my spirit, I knew that my Son was the only one who could bring healing and deliverance to this tortured soul. As I stood and paced the small, darkened room, I prayed seeking Adonai. There in that place, I felt His Presence in my spirit. He was in the room with us. He had not forgotten this child, and though the world had brought pain and darkness, nothing was impossible for my God.

Since the time I was but a child myself, I had experienced Yahweh's miraculous grace and mercy in my life. At only fifteen years old, the angel's visitation had changed my life forever. Watching my miracle child come into the world, I treasured every single word I had heard. I carried those words deep in my heart, holding tightly to the promises I was given. My child would be the Son of God, and He would save His people from their sins. It all seemed like another lifetime ago. Since Joseph's passing, I had only my own memories to ponder and pray through. I had only shared portions of my story with my best friend, Naomi. No one else would ever understand or believe me. Surely, they would think I had lost my mind.

The last time I had seen my Yeshua was at the wedding celebration in Cana. It was there when my motherly instincts had risen up in me. I felt it was time to release my Son into His destiny. "Do whatever He tells you to do," I told the servants. I knew He had been reluctant to enter into the full scope of His power, but when my friends had run out of wine early on in the festivities, it was a miracle they needed. I knew of only One who could do the impossible, and I felt it strongly in the depths of my heart—it was time for my precious Son to become my Lord and Savior.

Since then, I have not seen Him. However, I heard the reports from other people who attended the wedding and had witnessed the miracle first-hand. They had followed Him and watched as His ministry began to take shape. The stories were nothing short of astounding: the healing of a royal official's son, a deaf and mute man who had been set free to hear and speak again, the leper who had been cleansed. I prayed fervently for my Son, for His protection, and for His health. I knew someday a sword would pierce my soul, just as Simeon (the old man in the Temple) had told Joseph and I when my baby was only eight days old.

Yeshua's travels took Him all over the region, and though my heart physically ached to see my firstborn, it had been months since He had returned from His journeys. I never knew when to expect Him and prayed my God would send Him home soon. I was confident that He could bring deliverance for Mary from the oppression by which she was imprisoned.

Though I often tried to send word to Him, I would never know when He would surprise me with His hearty "Shalom Ima!" Lying on my cot, I prayed my Father in heaven would send His beloved Son to His earthly home to Nazareth on behalf of this desperately broken woman whom I had looked upon today.

Just hours ago, I had stood in the room, reciting the words of the Shema, humming the *Love Song to Yahweh,* and trusting the mighty power of Adonai. Before I knew it, Mary was in the arms of her auntie, weeping as my friend held her niece and I praised our good and gracious Father for returning her Sweet Mary to her. I approached the cot and joined in the celebration with Zara. We all sat together in a reunion celebration, crying and thanking Yahweh for His abundant mercy.

Within moments, the atmosphere changed. I could sense the presence of darkness as the tortured Sweet Mary began to rock back and forth, back and forth. Naomi tried to hold the frail hands of this beloved child, but she had wrenched them free and we heard a sound which came from deep within her. It was not a sound I had ever heard, an anguished guttural sound that was not of this world.

And then Zara was flying about the tiny room, placing herself in between us and her mistress, inserting a vial of liquid into her closed mouth. Zara had to hold her hands down and practically sit on top of Mary to subdue her enough. She then looked our way and urgently told us it was time for us to leave. And leave now! Stunned, we stumbled towards the door, and just as it closed behind us, my friend immediately broke down into sobs that wracked her entire body. All the years of hoping, praying, and dreaming of this reunion were shattered in the span of a few moments.

I took her by the hands and turned her away, lest she be tempted to run back in and make matters worse for these two beautiful women. It was evident Zara had encountered this situation numerous times, and I reassured my beloved friend that we would return tomorrow, and everything would be better. It would take time for Mary to remember she was loved and cherished, and I reminded Naomi we just needed to be patient.

Tossing and turning on my bed, I wondered about the pain and torture Mary had suffered and what type of demons had taken over her soul. Surely, my Yeshua would know how to banish these spirits and restore Mary to her right mind. As I prayed, I remembered the words of Anna the prophetess, the old woman at the Temple who had told everyone about my child and the redemption of Jerusalem. Certainly, this word was meant for souls like Mary who were imprisoned in the grip of the enemy. I wrestled with whether to share my heart and hope about my Son with my best friend. I longed to be able to assure Naomi that He would indeed be able set her Sweet Mary free, but I did not want to step into the territory reserved for God alone. To even hint that Yeshua would be coming to redeem her life would mean getting my friends' hopes up.

What if that was not Yahweh's plan for Mary? Who was I to question the mind of God? Having surrendered my desires and made my peace, I resolved to trust in the perfect and sovereign will and timing of God. I thanked Him for His provision and care.

Sleep was nowhere to be found this night, and I could hear my friend tossing and turning across the room. I was certain she had not slept either.

"Naomi, are you awake?" I whispered in the darkness.

"Yes, my friend," she replied sitting up. "I have not been able to sleep all night, for the pictures keep replaying in my mind. The elation and the shattering of my heart continues over and over again as I come to realize the woman we saw today was not my Sweet Mary anymore." She then confessed, "Fear has taken hold of me, yet my faith is desperately trying to remember that Elohim is mighty, and He is able to bring the healing she needs."

I rose and tucked my robe around me in the chill of the early morning hours. I stoked the fire and heard my friend light the oil lamp as neither of us were getting any sleep this night. After we had brewed some strong sweet tea, we knelt together to pray before we made the long journey back to the other side of town where we would shower these women with the gentle and powerful love of God Almighty.

CHAPTER 68

Zara

Hope Stirring

WEEKS HAD PASSED and every new sunrise had brought a knock on the door. Mary, as I had now come to call her, would awaken early in anticipation of our visitors. Her heart was full of torment as she longed to be able to control her mind for even a few more minutes each day. Her auntie, the beautiful Mary and I had prayed together often when my mistress was lucid, and her mind would allow it. Though she remained trapped in silence, I could sense she enjoyed when the three of us hummed the *Love Song to Yahweh*. Some days our guests were allowed to stay for a few hours before the tormentors returned. Other days it was only several minutes before the moans began to escape from her lips. Try as she might, my friend was powerless to drive the demons away once they decided to invade her mind. We had now established a routine, and on many occasions they would quietly leave, and then return after a short time when Mary was calm again. They brought such peace and joy to our little room that I was deeply saddened whenever they were forced to leave.

I wondered how long they would continue to make the long journey from the other side of the village every day, and I prayed they did not tire. I hoped that after seeing the beauty in my friend's heart, they would remain committed to us both. These women were so kind and gracious to me. They treated me like a daughter, though I was merely slave girl. I had never experienced this kind of love, and I could certainly see why my mistress held so tightly to the dream of returning to her Auntie Naomi's loving care.

The money that Kiera had so generously given to me on the night of our departure from the Temples was proving to be a gift from God. It allowed me (with the help of the ladies) to keep Mary safe and well fed. Kiera had also entrusted me an extravagant gift that night, which I prayed I would not have to use until much later.

"Take this bottle of perfume," she urged, placing the bottle in my hands. "It is very rare and most costly. It will provide for you when you run out of money." I wrapped it gently and placed it safely in a box at the bottom of our trunk. I hoped I would not have to use it, but rather one day, be able to place the gift into Mary's hands as a reminder of her protector's love for her. The innkeepers were kind as well, pretending they had not heard the commotion which often came from our room. I was feeling more and more at home here in Nazareth and hoped this would be the place of refuge my mistress and I had needed for so long. If only God would have mercy and bring deliverance for my friend once and for all.

One early morning, while I was gathering water at the well, I heard the women speaking of a Healer, a miracle worker who had made the lame walk and the deaf speak. I pondered over these words, and though I was desperate to know more of this man of whom they spoke, I was still an outsider and would not be spoken to even if I did ask a question. I vowed to listen more intently for news of this man, who may very well be the answer to all of our prayers for my beloved friend, Mary. Day after day, I tuned my ears to hear of any words spoken about the man who could do miracles. One day, I heard He was heading back to his hometown, this town of Nazareth. I could not believe what I had heard and quickly ran back to the inn to await the arrival of our guests. I was anxious to see if they might know anything of this miracle worker I had been hearing of.

When Auntie Naomi and Mary arrived, I could barely contain myself with the excitement I felt. Upon entering, I began questioning them about what I had heard. My words were barely out of my mouth when the beautiful Mary began smiling from ear to ear. I could not understand her joy, until she bade me to sit while Naomi made tea and we could all share something to eat. Only then would she begin telling us all about the Healer that I had been hearing about. Our Sweet Mary was in good spirits this day, and so, as we all gathered together in a circle on the rug, we joined our hands and prayed. Mary prayed a blessing over the food, Naomi prayed for her niece to feel the love and peace of God, and I prayed the miracle worker would indeed be the answer to all our prayers. As we broke bread together, Mary told us all about her family, her beloved Joseph, who had been gone for nearly ten years now, and about her five sons and two daughters. My Mary's eyes opened wide when she heard the names of the boys. I placed my hand on hers, reassuring her that she was fine. I urged beautiful Mary to continue. She continued on, declaring how she loved all her children equally, but how her eldest, Yeshua, held a special place in her heart. As she began to share of what a special child He had been, Mary began to rock back and forth, and I knew this story would have to be continued later.

"We would love to hear more of your story," I insisted. "Perhaps I could get Sweet Mary calmed down and then you could return in a few hours?" The disappointment on Naomi's face was almost as great as mine; however, we all knew Mary was our first priority and would do whatever was necessary for her peace of mind.

"Of course," they graciously responded. "We will go to the market and return for an afternoon visit before making our journey home." Naomi quickly prayed a blessing over her niece and the room was quiet, all but for the low moaning coming from the lips of my friend.

I wondered about this strange turn of events. What was the connection between the miracle man and the beautiful Mary? Could it be that the one she spoke of as her son, Yeshua, was indeed the same person the women at the well had spoken of? Was He the one who healed the sick and caused the deaf man to hear? If that was true, where had He been all these weeks? Why had not Mary summoned her son to come immediately to help her friend's niece in her affliction? So many questions were running through my head that I had to pause and take a few deep breaths. If Mary's son was indeed the Healer, He would come when God deemed it the right time and not a minute before.

Being surrounded by these two faithful women of God, my own faith had grown considerably in the last few weeks. I had learned and been challenged in my understanding of a God who could part the sea, but would often remain silent to the prayers of His children. I still had so much to learn. However, I felt a growing peace inside my heart which allowed me to rest in the God who had the love and adoration of these women I respected so much.

I had given Mary a small dose of the liquid that brought her peace and she had been resting comfortably for a few hours when we heard a knock at the door. I rose quickly to allow them to enter, anxious to hear the rest of Mary's story and how her family might be connected to the Healer of whom the women at the well had spoken.

They hurried in and I could sense Mary and Naomi were bringing good news. I urged them sit and could hardly wait for the tea to brew. I begged them to tell me more of the story Mary had begun earlier and how it all related to the miracle man that everyone was talking about.

Mary calmly began where she had left off. She spoke of her firstborn son Yeshua and the circumstances surrounding his birth being extraordinary. She did not go into detail but said He was indeed set apart and sent by God to bring healing to all mankind. I could see Naomi was impatient, urging her friend on when finally she cut her off and blurted out "He's coming! He's on his way and should be here any day." Naomi rushed on, "The stories are true! He has healed the sick and made the blind to see. People have testified, and Mary has confirmed that when she was with Him a few months ago, He actually changed water into wine at a wedding in Galilee."

Breathless, Naomi got up and paced the room, trying to contain her excitement while her friend sat smiling. Our Sweet Mary sat unmoving her eyes downcast. I looked in awe at Naomi and then back to Mary again, who was the actual mother of the one they called the Healer. My mind raced. Would He come and set my beloved friend free once and for all? Do I dare to dream He could be the answer to all my prayers?

As my mind went from one question to another, Mary continued talking about how kind and gentle He was. She stated how because of His remarkable birth, she had known from before He was born that God had a plan, and now that plan was unfolding right before our very eyes. I wanted to jump up and down and scream in my excitement. Then I saw Mary beginning the slow rocking back and forth, and I knew she had experienced enough stimulation for one day. As I gave her a dose of the green liquid, I urged her to lie down and rest while I ushered the ladies out the door.

When we had all stepped outside and the door was securely closed, I took Mary's hands in mine and dared to ask the question that was beating out of my heart. Looking deeply into her warm brown eyes, I pleaded with her, "Would you please ask your son to heal my sweet friend? I beg you, please. I have been praying for this for so many years. I believe the God I have come to know and love would be gracious enough to find it in His heart to heal my precious Mary. Can you bring Him here, please?"

The look in her eyes was one of compassion and love. I know Naomi, like me, was praying the answer would be yes. Holding both our hands tightly, she looked from Naomi to me. With tears glistening in her eyes, she whispered, "We don't know the mind of God and what His plans are for Sweet Mary. We can pray and seek His face, and when my Son arrives, I will share with Him all that I know. I will do everything in my power to get Him to see Mary." She went on to say, "Perhaps God will be gracious and show us a miracle. However, we must never put our God to the test." She warned, "His will is good and sovereign, no matter what happens. Can we all agree to trust Him for Mary's healing, however He will bring it about?"

Both Naomi and I nodded our agreement as tears slipped down our faces. As we clung together, Naomi prayed for her niece, asking the God of Abraham, Isaac and Jacob to do what only He could do and to have mercy on her beloved, Sweet Mary. I kissed them both and bid them a safe journey home.

CHAPTER 69

Myree

The Torment Continues

MY MIND WAS trying to make sense of all I had heard. What was all this talk of a miracle worker? A Healer? A man who could lay hands on the sick and make them well? One who could give sight to the blind? I was stunned to think that this same man was the son of auntie's friend, Mary, and He was actually coming to Nazareth.

When I heard Mary speak the name Yeshua, something stirred in my heart. I dared not allow even a glimmer of hope to enter my mind. The voices were always nearby, ready to punish and rob me of any moments of peace I may experience.

I battled the confusion every day when my auntie and her friend visited. I wanted so desperately to hate them both and to scream at them to leave me alone. Yet, somewhere deep inside of me, there was still a tiny sliver of my heart that longed to be loved and cared for. Each day when they arrived, I experienced their compassion in the ways they cared for me. My mind would be at rest for a short time, and I could fight off the demons for a little while, but when I could fight no more, my mind was taken from me.

Beyond my control, the whispers would start and then get louder until I could think of nothing but the green liquid that allowed me to escape from the voices inside my head. Of its own accord, my body would begin to rock back and forth to the rhythm of the lies that consumed my tortured mind. It was Hatred who reminded me of the evil man with the twisted mouth who had taken my soul. Then Rage fueled my dreams of punishing the woman who was my mother-in-law. Afterwards, Shame always crushed me with scenes of the old woman holding the tool, forcing my legs apart. The images played over and over in my mind. Suicide convinced me I was better off dead, but day after day, I found myself trapped in this darkness. I was controlled by Fear who told me the evil people were still out there searching for me and would never give up. The agony of Death was always reminding me convincing me that had I never been born Misha would still be alive. Hatred shouted at me—I could trust no one—especially these women. I knew I was not worth the trouble I was causing Zara and now my beloved auntie and her beautiful friend Mary. I wished for death constantly.

If not for Zara and the green potion, I may have attacked these two women. I would have clawed at their faces and pulled out their hair. I didn't want to think those thoughts, but always after they had been with us for a short while, after we had eaten, and they sang and prayed; it was then the darkness would creep in and visions of seeing them lying bloodied on the floor would fill my mind.

Though I tried desperately, I could not escape the visions. When my body would begin to rock, I knew I had lost the fight. Strange sounds would escape from deep within me. After that, because of Zara's intervention and the green liquid I craved, I would find sleep—sweet freedom from the torture for a little while. It was just a matter of time until the voices returned, for they always returned. I could only be grateful for these precious moments when I was able to think clearly and to wonder if there was such a man who could heal the sick. What would happen if such a man would come to visit me? Would I ever be able to find my voice again?

Searching my mind, I went back in time to a circle of people sitting around a fire underneath a star-filled night sky. I was possibly seven or eight years old and I had attended a Passover celebration with my auntie, uncle and cousins. On the journey home, a boy was lost. His parents were franticly looking for him. We camped for three days while waiting for the family to return. When they did, the boy, who was maybe twelve or thirteen years old, was scolded by all the adults. That night around the fire was one I will never forget. This boy told us the story of his three days in the Synagogue with the priests; of how he had questioned them and discussed the Scriptures. Thinking back, my mind locked onto a moment in time when his eyes caught mine from across the fire. I saw a look of kindness and heard gentleness and compassion as he spoke. Was this the same Yeshua my auntie and all the others were talking about? His mother and father were my auntie and uncle's friends, Mary and Joseph, who had traveled with us for the feast. After all these years, I wondered if this could be the same person? I knew of Him as a child, but would He remember me if He saw me now? I was not the same little girl anymore, in fact, there was none of that little girl left in me. The only thing which remained and would possibly give me away were my golden green eyes and auburn hair.

Going back in time made me think of my cousins. I wondered where they were, and what happened to my uncle. My words were still locked inside of me and the only sounds I had made for years were that of the animal I had become. I doubted I would ever speak again but would simply remain imprisoned in silence for the rest of my days. It was times like these—when the memories came, and the questions started—I began to feel the weight of my worthlessness. Death would always beckon me to find peace in his arms.

CHAPTER 70

Naomi

Hope is Kindled

NIGHT AFTER NIGHT, I tossed and turned on my cot. The anguish of my heart was my constant companion. Weeks had passed since the first day I had laid eyes on my Sweet Mary. Day after day as the sun was rising, my friend and I made the long journey across the village to the inn where Zara had kept my niece. And *kept* is exactly what this kind servant had done for so many years. It seemed that Sweet Mary had lived in this state for over ten years now—silent and withdrawn, fighting the demons who tortured her soul. Oh, how I longed to hear my Sweet Mary's voice raised in song to Yahweh. But the only sound that came from her did not sound anything like the little girl I remembered. No, indeed, the sounds she made left me shaken and filled with fear that my Sweet Mary might be gone forever. After living locked inside the prison of her mind for so long, was there any hope of her ever being set free? I knew our God was mighty, but today I had begun to despair. Day after day, and we still saw no change. It was always the same: at first, she seemed happy to see us and would eat and drink with us, even look me in the eyes. Sometimes she would allow me to hold her hands while we talked, prayed and sang songs together. But before long, always far too soon, the movements would begin, her body taking on its own rhythm ... and the sounds—the awful, soul-piercing sounds that came from deep within her. Always, Zara would quickly take over and we would scramble to get out of her way. Some days we would be welcomed back in after a time of rest, but it would not be long before Sweet Mary would disappear again, and Zara would quietly ask us to leave.

What a precious young woman Zara was to have taken such good care of my Sweet Mary for all these years. I was truly indebted to her for her love and service. I prayed that one day we would all be able to live lives of freedom: Mary from her demons, Zara from her commitment to care for my niece, and my friend Mary from the sadness she always secretly carried in her heart. All the years of pleading for the life of the daughter of my heart, and here we were, together, yet separated by a chasm I could not seem to cross.

As I lie in the darkened room across the hall from my snoring friend, I wondered how she could possibly sleep after hearing of her beloved Yeshua returning to Nazareth. Wasn't she excited to see the first-born child whom God had given her before she and Joseph had ever lain together? She had told me the story many times and still I fought to believe the details. How could a virgin be with child? I knew my beautiful friend was a gift from God to me and to many others. Truly Yahweh had favored her with grace and compassion; however, my doubting heart struggled to believe.

I had known her since our children were small. We would walk together to the well to fill our jars with water for the day ahead. Thinking back, I tried to recall the young boy Yeshua. Was it possible that He was the Healer? Could the stories that He had changed water into wine and restored sight to a blind man possibly be true? I wanted to believe, but I feared getting my hopes up that perhaps my Sweet Mary could be healed as well. I wrestled with my thoughts, my disbelief, and my doubts. Finally, I rolled out of bed and found myself on my knees begging Elohim, the Lord God Almighty, to give me faith to believe. I prayed for the faith that Ruth had when she told her mother-in-law she would leave everything and follow her and her God to whatever future awaited them. I pleaded for the faith of Deborah who went into battle trusting the Lord would give them victory. I needed my sleeping friends' faith who always reminded me—with God all things are possible.

When Mary stirred at sunrise, this is where she found me: on my knees with my face to the ground, agonizing in praying. Helping me to my feet, she embraced me and helped me over to the table to sit down. She then made us tea before we started out on the long journey to see my precious niece. I dared not ask her about her Son, the Healer, for I did not want to put pressure on her or our beautiful friendship. The peace that filled my soul this day was a gift from my God, and I would trust Him to take care of my Sweet Mary, knowing she was safe in His hands.

It had been several days since we heard the women talking about the Healer coming to Nazareth. Many of them knew He was the son of my friend and had tried to get an audience with her every day while we walked. We were often surrounded by people, as they first knocked on our door each morning, and then accompanied us on our long journey. I had begun to lose hope about this man, Mary's Son, the Healer, ever returning to our village. I desperately tried not to put all my hope in Mary bringing her Son to visit.

CHAPTER 71

Zara

The Healer Arrives

ON THIS MORNING, like all the others, when I heard the knock on the door, I rose quickly to allow the women to enter. But this time upon opening the door, I saw a man standing with them. He was a tall man with very gentle and kind eyes. He resembled Mary when He smiled. This must be the Son she spoke of, the one everyone was talking about. Could it be that He was here to see my friend? I lifted my eyes to heaven and offered a silent prayer before welcoming them all into the room. When my precious Mary looked up from her place on the cot, she quickly backed into the corner of the room and began moaning and rocking back and forth.

After Mary introduced her son, Yeshua, to me, He asked if we would mind if He spent some time alone with my friend Mary. I looked at my mistress and went to her side speaking softly to her. "Precious friend, this is Yeshua. He is Mary's son and has come to visit you," I explained while she rocked back and forth, a low sound coming from her throat. "He has been called a Healer and we are going to step outside while He speaks with you. Please don't be afraid." I assured her. "He won't hurt you. Just know that we are right outside the door." The distressing sounds continued, and I did not want to leave, but I felt Naomi's hands upon my shoulders and these two precious women leading me out the door.

I could not hear what was being said inside, but I heard the familiar moaning growing louder and the deep voice of authority speaking in low tones. I heard commotion, as if something was overturned. I heard a crashing sound, but I felt hands restraining me from rushing back inside to my friend's aide. My fear was rising. Soon, beautiful Mary's voice was raised in song while Naomi prayed fervently for her niece's deliverance. I could do nothing but join my heart with theirs and trust God was in the room with the Healer and my precious friend.

I don't know how long we waited outside, praying and singing, but soon a few others had gathered with us. Together, we trusted that whatever was going on inside the room, God was at work. We believed He would hear our prayers for this tortured woman.

When I thought I could not restrain myself for one more minute, the door finally opened. There stood my mistress—calm and in her right mind. She had a smile on her lips, and sunlight sparkled in her emerald eyes. I had not seen this woman for over ten years, but there was no mistaking it, this was my Myree, the girl I had known so long ago.

Time stood still. She looked at me and Mary, and then her eyes fixed on Naomi. She opened her mouth and said one word: "Auntie." A sob broke from Naomi's lips and then she was holding her niece in her arms and dancing around. God had heard the cries of our hearts and we knew we had received the miracle we prayed for. Tears of joy were flowing down our faces as we encircled one another, laughing and praising God for giving us back this beautiful woman. I had not heard her voice lifted in laughter or song in so many years. All I could do was lift my hands in praise to El Roi, the God who had seen my friend and delivered her from her darkness. The celebration continued and I barely noticed the departure of the Healer.

Yeshua had brought us a gift and then silently made His way down the road as people had begun to gather. I wanted to run after Him, but as if He sensed my desire, He looked back at me with His kind, gentle eyes and smiled. I lifted my eyes to heaven and mouthed the words "Thank You." Then He was gone.

My attention returned to the joyful praise that filled the air as many had gathered and begun asking questions as to what we were so happy about. The four of us had a secret. We joined hands and we walked back inside together. The place had been transformed into a brightly lit, perfectly ordered room with a pot of tea waiting for us to sit and enjoy. We had so much to talk about. I could not contain my tears, looking at my friend who was serene and full of peace for the first time in so very long. At this moment, all my doubts and wavering faith had been washed away. My faith was real! I was now a devout believer in the One True God, Jehovah Raphe, the God who heals, and in His Healer Son, Yeshua.

Now, hours later as night was fast approaching, and we had to say goodbye to Mary and Naomi; I was uncertain about how to care for my precious friend. I did not want them to leave, fearing this was all a dream. For so many years I had taken care of my mistress' every need, trying to keep the demons away. Now, as I busied myself about the room, I wondered if this was all too good to be true.

Could she really be set free? Delivered from the torment that had plagued her for so long? I was shy and did not know what to say or how to act around this woman who now had not experienced an episode for several hours. I was startled when she spoke my name, for I had not heard it come from her lips for so long, and I was not used to her voice breaking the silence in the room.

"Zara," she said. My Mary came and took my hands into hers and looked deeply into my eyes. "I know this is all very hard to understand, and I cannot truly believe it myself." Her voice caught, and she continued. "From the moment I laid eyes on Yeshua, I knew everything was about to change. We have both had a very long day, so let us prepare for bed and tomorrow we will have more clarity. For now, let us be thankful for what has taken place today and worship Yahweh in prayer, shall we?"

She led me over to the cot, and knelt down while I followed, barely able to speak. And then the most beautiful sound came from my friend's lips as she prayed.

Good and Gracious Adonai, You are *worthy* of all my adoration. You are faithful and loving, kind and generous, merciful and patient. You are sovereign and all-knowing, all powerful and ever present. You have been so faithful to me, and I am overwhelmed by Your mercy. You are the light in my darkness and the Prince of Peace in my troubled soul. I don't even know how to pray after all these years, but You have never left me and never forsaken me. Everything I need is found in You. All I could ever want is who You are. You are my hope and strength, my peace and joy. You are my ever-present help in times of trouble.

When I was afraid, You came near and held me in Your strong arms. You provided for me, Jehovah Jireh, You guided me in the path of Your righteousness. You brought us here to this place and You reunited me with my family. You are my Healer, my Helper, and my Lord. I am never alone, for now I know Your Presence is more real than the air I breathe. I can never express the depths of my gratitude to You for what You have done—for delivering me, redeeming my life from the pit and for crowning me with Your sweet love and compassion. My life is now worth living again because of You. You are so good. Who am I that You, the God of the Universe, would take notice of me? I am astonished that You love me unconditionally with an everlasting love, and my only response is to give my life back to You in complete and total adoration ....
Thank You for sending Yeshua to me today, and for His hand of healing that has set me free. I am now Yours forever. Amen

Tears were flowing down my cheeks as I listened to her pouring her heart out to her God— to our God. I was undone and could only weep as she finished praying. She turned to me and lifted me by the hands. After kissing me on both cheeks and embracing me, she looked long into my eyes. She then whispered, "Thank you, my beautiful friend for everything you have done for me. I will be eternally grateful to you."

She led me to my cot and urged me to lie down and get some rest. The peace that filled the room was tangible. I knew I was on holy ground, and as I laid there, my only thoughts were, thank You, God. Thank You, God. Thank You, God. I continued thanking Him until deep, sweet sleep overtook me.

CHAPTER 72

Beautiful Mary

My Son Arrives

THINKING BACK OVER the last 24 hours was like living in a dream and I had to pinch myself to believe it was all really true. Lying on my cot, my mind raced to recall each and every beautiful moment.

My Son, my precious beautiful Son had come home! I could barely believe my eyes when He stood at our door just last night in the dark shadows of the setting sun. He said He had just left His friends and made His way to find His mother, apologizing for the lateness of the hour. Naomi greeted Him with an embrace, and we ushered Him into our home. It had been so long since I had held His face in my hands and kissed his weathered cheeks. I had kissed those same cheeks a million times when He was a baby as He lay in my arms. He was the miracle infant sent into my body from God above.

Oh, how I wished Joseph were still alive to see the man his son had become. Yeshua was so loving, gentle, kind and gracious—just like His earthly father. Though there were none of the physical traits of Joseph, His heart mirrored the man who had raised Him. Many times, Joseph and I had stared in wonder at the gift God had given to each of us. We often talked late into the night about the visits from the angels we both had received. We spoke of how our baby Yeshua had narrowly escaped the sword of the madman King Herod. Because he was so threatened by the message of the visitors from the east—the message of the birth of a new king—he had ordered the death of all male children under the age of two.

It was Joseph who had awakened me in the middle of the night, shaken to his core, and insisting we leave immediately to flee for our lives. I knew to trust the man God had given to me and hurriedly packed only that which would not slow us down on our escape to Egypt. It was reminiscent of our travels to Bethlehem two years before, when I was heavy with child. Only this time it was Joseph leading me on the donkey while I cradled our squirming toddler son in my arms.

Staring at His face brought tears to my eyes as He lovingly smiled at me from across the table. Though I loved each of my children, Yeshua was the child of my heart, the boy whom Simeon spoke of, whose life would pierce my very own soul. He had been such a compliant child, unlike James and His brothers, never selfish, always the peacemaker, which got Him into trouble with his younger brothers and sisters.

Oh, but He was so clever, and wise beyond His years. Whenever anyone would try and take advantage of His kindness, He would ask them questions in His gentle but authoritative voice that would always make them stop and think. He would speak to them about Torah and what Adonai would desire of them. I would smile as I watched Him school His siblings without them ever knowing He was teaching them about character, honesty, and integrity.

I fussed over my Son, making Him comfortable while Naomi made us tea and laid out a spread of date jam, cheeses and warm bread. She knew how He loved to eat and had gathered all of His favorite things in preparation of His arrival. We had been waiting so long since we had heard that He was traveling home. And now He was finally here. Though both of us wanted to pour out the story of Naomi's tortured niece and beg Him to travel with us to see her first thing in the morning, we held our tongues as my Son ate His fill and leaned back with a contented sigh.

Without us having to say a word, He told us He would gladly travel with us in the morning to the edge of town to visit the young woman. But for now, He just needed to get some sleep. As He stretched out on the mat, I quickly got him a blanket and covered Him up. When I bent down to kiss His cheek, He was already fast asleep. Naomi and I could barely contain ourselves and I knew we would get very little sleep. She hugged me tightly before going to lie down on her cot. Neither of us could dare to speak what was on our hearts—the questions that filled our minds—and so each of us lay awake until the early morning hours before we finally dozed off.

Before I knew it, I smelled the delicious aroma of warm bread. My Son was up and cooking breakfast in our kitchen while Naomi and I scrambled to dress and ready ourselves for the day. I'm sure we were a sight, having not slept much of the night, but my Yeshua smiled as He greeted us and busied Himself by serving us breakfast. We were both told to sit down and drink our tea while He laid the plates out upon the table. When did my Son learn to cook eggs and bread, I wondered, speechless as I drank my tea? Naomi was too nervous to speak as well. When He took both of our hands in His and lifted His eyes to heaven, we bowed our heads in prayer. We ate the most delicious meal ever, and then we walked together across the village. Soon, many others joined our journey.

I had met many of His friends at the wedding we attended together in Cana several months before. Many of them were among the entourage who followed us to the inn where Mary and Zara stayed. Zara would not be expecting so many people, and surely Mary would find all this excitement too much for her. We knew we would not be able to stay long before she became distressed.

I wondered what would come of this day and prayed silently while holding Naomi's hand in mine as we walked. She, too, was lost in thought as we traveled. Both of us were content to remain quiet and tried to focus on what Yeshua was speaking to His friends about.

When we arrived at the inn, my Son had the discretion to ask His companions to go and get some supplies and then meet Him back here later. Soon Zara was inviting the three of us into her room and there was Mary on the cot, wanting to greet us, but immediately wary of the strange man standing in her room.

I introduced my Son to Zara while Naomi went over and sat next to Mary. The air seemed to buzz with electricity as Mary sat warily on the cot. A low growl was heard, and I feared we would have to leave before Yeshua could even speak with her. Zara was anxious and tried to soothe Sweet Mary, but she would have none of it. When Yeshua spoke her name, the room went silent. Mary backed into the corner, curling herself into a tight ball, knees under her chin, arms wrapped tightly around her legs. And then she began rocking back and forth. When my precious Son asked us if He could speak to Mary privately, I could see the alarm in Zara's eyes, but as Naomi and I nodded to her, she allowed us to lead her out of the door.

We heard the crashing of cups and plates and sounds that were not of this world. We had to restrain Zara from rushing back into the room we had just left. The tears were flowing down all of our faces as we huddled together on the ground and joined hands in prayer. We sat and prayed and then stood and sang the *Love Song to Yahweh* over and over so as to drown out the noise coming from behind the door.

I don't know if it was minutes or hours, but time stood still. Suddenly we realized that all was silent, and we could hear voices inside. Voices, as in two people talking together, which was not possible because Sweet Mary did not speak, unless …. With eyes fixed in anticipation, we held our breath as we saw the door open and Mary standing with a smile on her face. As she looked at each of one of us with love and peace in her eyes, she opened her mouth and spoke just one word: "Auntie." Naomi rushed to wrap her Sweet Mary in her arms, weeping while praising Jehovah and dancing around her niece. I, too, could not stop the tears from flowing as Zara and I held each other and watched the two women share a long-lost love story.

Soon Mary, Zara, Naomi and I were all wrapped together, our arms entwined, our feet moving as we laughed, cried, and worshipped our great and magnificent God. From the corner of my eye, I saw my precious Son slip out the door and out of sight as the crowd began to gather around us, wondering what all the commotion was about. We had no idea how to tell of the miracle we were holding in our arms. Sweet Mary's smile radiated from her beautiful face. Zara then led us back into the room, away from all the prying eyes.

Because of the excitement of the day and the lack of sleep the night before, Naomi and I were exhausted. Though we longed to stay and hear every single detail of what had transpired in that room, we were content to simply sit together and praise our great and awesome God. Before long the shadows were falling, and we had to drag ourselves away so we might make it home before nightfall. We promised to return first thing in the morning, and as we each embraced one another for the final time that day, Naomi offered a sweet prayer of gratitude which had us all in tears once again.

As we made our way across the village, we were met and escorted by my Son and His friends. They had appeared out of nowhere and made the long trip seem easy and light. They parted ways with us at some point and Naomi, Yeshua, and I continued to our home.

I felt a peace in my soul I had not experienced in a very long time as I listened to the rhythmic breathing of my Son and my best friend. I had witnessed my precious Yeshua perform another miracle. I smiled and thanked Adonai again before my weary body drifted off into a deep sleep.

CHAPTER 73

Mary

Healed and Set Free

I OPENED MY eyes. My mind was clear, and my heart was at peace. My body lie still and calm on the cot, as I relived yesterday's events. The morning had dawned just as every other morning of the last ten years: dark, agitated and restless. I wondered when the voices would begin torturing me. Zara and I prepared for our visitors just as we had each day since they had arrived several weeks ago. It was always the same. I began the new day with a tiny sliver of hope, longing to see my beloved auntie and her beautiful friend Mary. Then shortly after their arrival, my tormentors would begin assaulting my mind.

Death was the voice that told me I should not be wasting the time, effort, and love these women were pouring out upon me. He whispered into my ears that I would be better off dead; so they could get on with their lives.

Shame then battered my soul with the reality of how I had ruined Zara's life. Fear taunted me, reminding me that I was too much of a coward to even end my own life. I had welcomed the voice of Suicide for so long. I was eager to take my own life on many occasions. My body would then remind me of the power of Addiction. I needed the green liquid to release me from the long hours of fighting with my demons. I craved it more than the air I breathed. I battled Hatred until I fell into an exhausted dreamless sleep. Each day I would wake to another day of eternal punishment.

But this day was different. The man, Yeshua, had entered our room and my world would never be the same again. At first, I felt the enemies of my soul rising up inside of me, but when He spoke my name, I was gripped by the sound of His voice alone. When the ladies left the room, all the demons broke loose inside me, and I had no control whatsoever. My body threw itself against the wall as He spoke my name over and over again. My throat uttered sounds that were not of this world as I thrashed around the room trying to escape His presence, but there was nowhere to run. So, I overturned the table, threw the chairs, and tore at my robe.

Finally, when I fell to the ground, paralyzed and spent, He bent down and touched my head. The feeling of light and warmth radiating from His hand was unlike anything I had ever felt. It was as if the brilliance of sunshine had begun to fill my mind, warming the cold recesses, chasing out the darkness until it then flowed down into my body. When the light reached my heart, there was an explosion of love, shattering the walls and consuming the Hatred, the Rage, the Shame, the images of Death and Suicide, the chains of Addiction; even the Fear.

The light was so bright that nothing but peace could remain. My body tried desperately to resist, to hold onto the darkness, clawing at the dirt on the floor, but I could not move. It was as if a beautiful weight was pressing all the toxic poison out of my body, freeing me from the chains that held me imprisoned for so many years. Though my mouth tried to scream, no sounds were allowed to exit. Finally, though I had no sense of time, I opened my eyes.

His hand was in mine lifting me from the ground and leading me to sit opposite Him at the table which now held a steaming pot of tea and two cups. My eyes were blurry at first. I could not get a sense of where I was or who this man was. As He spoke, wave after wave of gentle grace washed over me, and then He smiled at me. It was the most beautiful, radiant, gentle smile I had ever seen. And I knew—I knew this man had delivered me. He had set me free. This Healer had been sent from Yahweh to redeem my life from the pits of hades. He had given me a new life. Peace and gratitude flooded my soul as I wept deep tears of joy. The voice I had not heard in over ten years whispered the only thing present in my mind: "Thank You," I said. Tears flowed down my face while I laughed in amazement at the sound of my own voice. My Redeemer told me Adonai was not finished with me yet, and there was work to do, for the Kingdom of God was at hand. I simply nodded my agreement, knowing that although my whole world had just been radically transformed, this was just the beginning.

As I looked around the room I had shared with my precious friend, Zara, for these last several weeks, I remembered being frightened earlier when she, my auntie, and Mary left me alone with Yeshua. Now, all I wanted at that moment was to see these beautiful women, who had loved me so well, and to share this miracle with them. As if knowing my thoughts, Yeshua stood, took me by the hand, and led me across the room. With a gentle touch on my shoulder, He smiled and urged me forward to the open door. Though I wanted to stay in His presence, I longed for my auntie's embrace. Knowing this was only the beginning of my new life, I felt courage well up inside my soul.

Standing in the open doorway, I caught sight of the three women huddled in what appeared to be prayer. As if drawn by an unseen force, all eyes were then upon me, staring in disbelief at the smile on my face. When I opened my mouth and said the one word that had been locked deep inside of me for so long, "Auntie," a sob broke forth from each of them. I was caught up in familiar, strong sun kissed arms, enveloped in a fragrance of lavender, and held by a love so fierce it took my breath away.

Then Zara and Mary were surrounding us as we all laughed, danced, and praised the God who had delivered me. I glanced up just in time to lock eyes with my Healer. He passed behind us, and in that moment, I knew He was my destiny.

The celebration continued for hours as we sang, prayed, and worshipped together. I knew I was free, once and for all. The past was but a memory and my future was waiting for me to discover.

Last night, I was awake for many hours hearing all the sounds outside the window. I wondered of this new life and all that lay before me. I worshipped my Lord God Almighty and offered Him my every breath, every beat of my heart, and every ounce of my mind from this moment forward. Incredible peace overwhelmed my soul, and I drifted off into a heavenly slumber.

The new morning had dawned bright and clear. I heard my precious Zara humming the *Love Song to Yahweh* while she prepared our morning tea. I remained still for a few more moments as the reality of what had transpired yesterday flooded my soul. I was awake and my mind was clear.

My heart was at rest. It was true. I was free! It wasn't a dream my mind had tricked me into believing. It was real. As I stirred, Zara looked over at me with anxious eyes, the questions frozen on her lips. I rose and went to her with outstretched arms. She wrapped me in her embrace as salty tears ran down both of our faces. It seemed impossible and too good to be true. But it was real. Before another moment went by, I took her by the hand, and we knelt down beside my cot to pray. She readily joined me as we both bowed together in prayer.

> Lord God of the Universe, we come as your beloved daughters, on our knees in humble gratitude for all you have done. Thank You for sending Yeshua to save me and redeem my soul. I can hardly believe the unconditional love I feel flowing in my heart. Today, I offer myself to You as Your servant. May You be pleased to use me in whatever way You desire and may my life bring glory and honor to Your name. Thank You for my beautiful friend Zara who has loved me so well for all of these years. I pray You would bless her with the desires of her heart as we begin this new journey together, walking in Your love. Thank You for my beloved auntie and her best friend Mary who have believed in me and loved me for so long. May they know how deeply I love and appreciate them, and may they be blessed for the blessing they are to so many. Adonai, we adore You and commit this day into Your loving hands …. Amen.

Before long we heard the familiar knock and chatter at our door, and our beautiful friends entered to embrace and sing and dance around our little room as we all continued the celebration from the day before. As we sat and shared some breads and cheeses with our hot tea, we spoke of the miracle and the Miracle Worker who had delivered me from my darkness. I asked His mother question after question about His life, His ministry, His friends and His plans. Mary was patient with me and answered as many questions as she could, sharing from her heart the pride and adoration she had for the Son she had given birth to. After a time, we went out for a walk and I was astonished at the clarity of vision I was experiencing. It was as if I was seeing the brilliant aqua blue color of the sky for the very first time. My ears were hearing birds singing songs in the trees we passed under. Little children were laughing as they ran through the dusty streets and I had never heard such glorious sounds. People smiled as we passed by and exchanged greetings, and I could not help but hum a song of worship and gratitude as I walked along, marveling at the incredible grace and mercy of my God.

When we returned to the inn, my auntie looked at her beautiful friend and nodded as they exchanged a smile. We sat down on the cot together and Auntie began to share of the hopes and dreams they had prayed about for so many years. The dream of her and her niece being reunited once again after so many years and how that niece would come to live with her again, once and for all. As Mary nodded, she looked at Zara and whispered, "We would love it if you and Sweet Mary would come to live with us in our home. We have plenty of room, and it would bring us such joy to have you both under our roof. Besides," she laughed, "this place is too small, and we don't think we can make the long journey across town one more day. Will you please come with us today and be our guests for as long as you would like to stay?" She asked while looking at both Zara and me.

The quiet in the room was broken by the laughter that burst from Zara's mouth. She looked at me, I nodded and said, "Yes, yes, a thousand times yes! We would love to come under your covering and join our hearts to yours."

We all laughed as the tears shone in our eyes and we began immediately making the preparations to end our stay at the little inn. We had very little of our own things to pack. I had dressed just that morning in the exquisite shawl that had been woven for me all those years ago. There were the lovely robes and blankets Mary and Auntie had brought for us, baskets of cups, dishes, and small gifts. I knew of only one more article that we would treasure and take with us as we left for our new home: the beautiful and priceless bottle of perfumed oil given to Zara by Kiera the night we left the Temple. Zara had showed it to me on a few occasions when I was in my right mind. I have always treasured its beauty, carefully placing it in the ornate box in which it traveled. We had been wise with the funds

283

that Kiera had entrusted to us and had not needed to sell the bottle which would have given us more riches than we knew what to do with. As we joined our hearts in prayer to give thanks to Jehovah Jireh, who had so graciously provided for us over and over again, we worshipped the God who had woven our lives together and laid out a path for all of our futures.

As we traveled along the dung-filled road through the village, I marveled at the reality of how these two elderly women had made this long arduous journey twice every day for the last several weeks. *No wonder they were anxious to have us under their roof,* I mused to myself as we walked along through the village. Some things looked familiar to me, as I took it all in. My eyes were open and scanning the crowds, hoping to catch a glimpse of my Redeemer. I wondered if He would appear again, and I prayed that I might have the opportunity to share my deepest gratitude with Him. I had asked Mary of His whereabouts and her words were poignant: "I never know when He will arrive or depart." She answered truthfully. "I have come to the conclusion that He is not mine to wonder about anymore. My God has much bigger plans for Him. So, I take whatever time is given to me and cherish each moment I have with my Yeshua."

I marveled at the unconditional love of this beautiful mother. I remembered sitting by the fire all those years ago, wondering what it would be like to have parents who were so worried about you that they would search for three days to find what had been lost. I did not know what my future held, but I now knew who held my future and I was committed to serving and following the Savior who had set me free.

As we walked along the road, I prayed for God to show me the path He was laying out before me, and I vowed to live my life for Him alone ... whatever that looked like.

CHAPTER 74

Zara

Prayers Answered

IT WAS A dream come true! My prayers had been answered and my mistress had been delivered from her demons. I walked along the road to our new home and into our new life with my feet barely touching the ground. I kept glancing over at my transformed friend. It was hard to reconcile this beautiful woman with the tortured soul I had cared for over the last ten years. This was the same girl I had met all those years ago with fire in her emerald green eyes and hair that glowed brilliant in the sunlight. I battled the thoughts in my mind telling me this wouldn't last. I feared she would enter into an episode again and this dream would end.

I prayed for a deep faith to rule my heart, and for complete trust in the future that lay ahead of us. Were we truly to come under the care of these glorious women of God who had opened their hearts to us? To me, a foreigner and complete stranger?

As if sensing my doubts, Yeshua's mother came alongside me and took my hand in hers as we walked. She did not release it but held tightly and smiled at me along the way. She was a gift from above; a mother figure that any girl would dream of having in her life. And here she was, holding my hand, reassuring me everything was going to be just fine. Peace flooded my soul and the fear fled as we walked. I felt her love flow into me as she held my hand. She didn't need to say a word, but her gentle smile told me everything was going to be all right. When we finally arrived at the home of Mary and Naomi, I was overwhelmed. It was more than I could have ever dreamed. The house was lovely and spacious with a lush garden out back. Across the courtyard there were a few chickens, a goat and what appeared to be a very healthy cow. We were shown to our room which overlooked a peaceful stream and mountains in the distance.

While I was taking all of this in, I heard a commotion at the front door. Boisterous greetings rang out in hearty male voices. Mary and I had just gotten our things settled and had to leave the beauty of our new surroundings to see what all the noise was. Could it be the Healer had come to visit His mother? What would Mary's reaction be when she saw the One who had delivered her from her torment? I did not have to wait long for my answers as I watched her shyly move forward and bow low to the ground in reverential honor before Him. He gently took her by the hand and helped her up, smiling with the most brilliant, joy-filled expression on His face.

Soon the room was filled with others who had experienced the Teacher's wisdom, His touch and His light. It was as if He glowed from the inside out, His smile lighting up the room. Yeshua's mother and her friend, Naomi, were busy in the kitchen and I joined them while more people gathered in the living space. Some brought food to share, others just wanted to hear from the Master, as I had heard Him being called.

I was in awe of this man who seemed to love each person genuinely from his gracious heart. He embraced His mother often as she brought platters of bread, cheeses, meats and fruits to set before her Son. He shared joyous laughter with His friends, from roughened fishermen to a well-dressed tax collector. It seemed that even a couple of His siblings had heard of His arrival in Nazareth and had come to share in the love of family. I was introduced to Simeon, Jude and Jacob—three more of Mary's sons. Deborah, Yeshua's sister, had also come and brought her infant son who was at her breast. Mary was delighted to have her family under her roof and could not stop laying her hands on her children and grandson.

I watched and listened while I busied myself with the fire and keeping the water pitchers filled from the large pot sitting outside the back door. Mary had brought in juicy, red tomatoes and crisp green beans from her garden. There was a light-hearted feeling of celebration in the air. We had so much to celebrate, though the only ones who knew of our miracle were the few with whom we had shared the good news. Yet even they could not possibly know the extent of the life altering deliverance my Mary had experienced. My friend was at total peace. She had a serenity which radiated from her whole being. She smiled at the stories being shared and kept to herself as she basked in the presence of her Deliverer. Her auntie stayed close to her, hugging her every chance she got, whispering secrets in her ears causing Mary to beam with joy.

For me, this was a taste of heaven and I felt so blessed. I could hardly believe this could be my new life. Never in my thirty-two years had ever I felt so free and so secure. I lifted my eyes to heaven and thanked Adonai over and over again. Almost as if on cue, Yeshua commanded the attention of everyone and asked us all to bow our hearts in thanksgiving for the bounty of blessings we were about to share. Silence penetrated the room. Yeshua addressed Yahweh as Abba Father and spoke as if God Almighty Himself were right in the room with us. He thanked and praised Him for the beauty of family and friends and for the gracious provision before us. It was as if we were all standing on holy ground, the Presence of the Lord so powerful and real. I could do nothing to keep the tears from escaping my eyes in sincere and humble gratitude.

When He finished praying, a hush held in the room until He smiled and said, "Well, this food is not going to eat itself." Everyone laughed and began passing the trays around. After the meal was finished, someone posed the question to the Teacher saying, "Master, John and his followers are declaring the Kingdom of God is at hand. What must we do to prepare our hearts?"

A silence settled over the room. All eyes turned to Yeshua, and everyone eagerly waited for the wisdom He would share. People sat on the floor and crowded around Him as close as they could get to hear what He would say. Mary looked at Him with hungry eyes, leaning forward in anticipation to hear every word. He began to teach us about the Law and Torah. Together we recited the Shema and then sang a few songs. He spoke of the need to have a heart fully devoted to El Shaddai, the Lord God Almighty, who was a jealous God and demanded we follow Him with all of our heart. He spoke of El Roi, the God who sees each one of us and loves us as if we were the only person on the planet. He talked of the need for cleansing, explaining the symbolism of baptism and how it was an outward profession of an inward transformation. He encouraged everyone who wanted to wholeheartedly follow the Lord Adonai, to express their devotion through baptism.

I had heard of the one they called the Baptizer and wondered when and where I could tell the world of my love for Jehovah Rophe, the God who heals. I could tell my Mary was thinking the same thing as our eyes locked across the crowded room. As if reading our hearts, Yeshua told about John the Baptizer and even of His own followers who were baptizing in the Jorden river day after day. He explained how we need only to follow the lines of people into the waters to have our hearts washed in the ceremony of baptism. He shared of His plans to travel to the same region of the Jorden River in just a few days. The people were nodding and murmuring about how they would all travel to the river as well. I knew Mary and I would be among those first in line.

We sang and lifted our hands in praise together. We laughed, danced, and continued feasting on the delicious delicacies on the tables. It was very late before all the people began to make their way home. Though Mary tried to persuade her son to stay with us, he politely declined and kissed His mother goodnight as the last one to leave. Where would he go? I felt terrible, as if we had displaced Him from His own mother's home. Mary assured me that He rarely stayed with them and had more than enough offers from grateful people who would take Him and His friends in for the night.

It was the best night of my life: sitting on the floor, hearing the truths of the God I had come to know, being surrounded by new brothers and sisters who were just as hungry as I was to know more of this Abba Father of whom Yeshua spoke. Sweet Mary was beaming as she hummed while getting ready for bed. We were both so filled; we just wanted to share and relive the beauty of this night. Naomi and Mary were radiant as well, though both of them declared they were exhausted and needed their rest much more than we did. My mistress and I talked and giggled like teenagers while planning our journey to join Yeshua and the others, where we too would be washed in the Jorden River.

CHAPTER 75

Mary

My New World

WHEN ZARA AND I finally laid down to rest after another evening spent in the presence of my Deliverer, I was still buzzing with a sense of purpose and excitement. The last several evenings had been something I never dreamed possible. Night after night people crowded around the Master, listening to His teachings, His stories, and moreover, hearing His heart. The room was full, but the air was sweet to breathe. It was as if we were all desperately hungry for whatever it was we would be fed. It was our souls that were starved, not our bodies, nonetheless, the food was piled high on platters night after night and everyone feasted until their bellies were full.

Until a few days ago, most of these people were complete strangers to me except, of course, Auntie, Mary and Zara. However, after just a few nights of sharing in prayer and worship to Adonai, the others now felt like family. Yeshua was a brilliant Rabbi, and He taught with a wisdom from above, with humility and passion. He was not like the teachers I remember from my childhood when I used to listen from behind the door. His truths came in the form of stories, about fields and farmers and sheep that needed their Shepherd. Our hearts were now knit together because of Him and the love He spoke of—a love so real and powerful, one would be willing to give their lives for it.

Each night was the same: more people crowding in to hear the wisdom of the Master and to share in the beauty of the fellowship of believers. Our voices raised in adoration, our hands lifted in prayer, our knees firmly planted on the ground in reverent submission. It was a taste of what it would be like in heaven. Yesuha taught about the beginning of days and how evil mankind had become. He explained how it was necessary for God to wipe them all out with a flood to begin again with Noah, a righteous man, and his family. His wisdom knew no limits and each question asked was gently taken, thoughtfully considered, and thoroughly answered. People were amazed and could not get enough. It was difficult to get them to leave each night, many times long after midnight.

After four wonderful nights, we rose after having only a few hours of sleep, too excited to stay in bed a moment longer. This was the day we would all start our journey to travel together to the Jorden River and be baptized into the family of God. We could barely contain our excitement as we dressed and kept our voices to a whisper, trying not wake our beloved auntie and Mary. But we were not alone in our excitement. They were already up, preparing our tea and meals for the adventure ahead. They too, would be traveling with us to the Jorden to see what all the excitement was about. Mary told us she barely slept a wink as she was desperate to see her long lost relative, John the Baptizer. He was the long-awaited son of her cousin Elizabeth and Zachariah, the priest. It was Elizabeth's home to which Mary had fled when she found herself miraculously with child, confused and afraid. She told us of how when she first entered the home of her aging cousin, she received a greeting that startled her and was forever written on her heart.

Her cousin Elizabeth had declared, "Blessed are you among women, and blessed is the child you will bear. But why am I so favored, that the mother of my Lord should come to me?"

Mary told us she was shocked beyond words and had to sit down with the realization that Elizabeth already knew she was pregnant, though she had not uttered a word to a soul. She continued sharing what her cousin said to her: "As soon as the sound of your greeting reached my ears, the baby in my womb leaped for joy. Blessed is she who has believed that what the Lord said to her will be accomplished."

Mary continued sharing that Elizabeth was already well past child-bearing age when John was born, Zachariah, too, was well along in years. Mary told us how she was mesmerized as they recounted the visitation of an angel and how Zechariah was struck mute while he was ministering in the temple. A tale that was hard to believe but had proven true when Mary later learned Elizabeth had given birth to a son. At that time, while still mute, Zechariah wrote on a tablet, "His name is John." This was the name the angel said the child was to be given, and Zechariah was then able to speak once more. We all sat in rapt attention while Mary shared the circumstances surrounding the miraculous births of her son, and His cousin, John the Baptizer. I took it all in. It was as if my vision was getting clearer each moment and my destiny had already been determined for me. The next few days would change my life forever—of that I was certain.

We traveled with dozens of other pilgrims the many miles to the location of the Jorden River where John was baptizing. We stayed as close to Yeshua as we could while He gently led His mother along the road. There was laughter and song, and we stopped every few hours to rest and share our food and drinks. The trip would take us many hours to travel and we were prepared to camp overnight, if necessary. It reminded me of the days of my youth when we all traveled to Jerusalem for Passover.

The air was full of celebration and the people were devoted to following the teachings of the one we called Master. I was blessed beyond my wildest dreams and my auntie was never far from my side, holding my hand and telling me of her love for me. With Zara lying beside me at night and looking into the star-filled sky, I had to remind myself that I was not dreaming, and this truly was my new life. I was free, healthy, whole, in my right mind—my God had delivered me from the grip of death and insanity. How could I ever repay the One who had set me free? I knew only that my life was now in His hands and I would follow Him to the ends of the earth if I could.

The next day dawned bright and early. As we packed our belongings, there was talk of the river in the distance. This was the day we would reach our destination and celebrate with other fellow believers of this new Way. As we marched forward, singing and praising Yahweh, the atmosphere was electric, charged with expectation and excitement. There was talk of miracles and healings the Master had performed. I smiled, knowing in my heart that I was a living, breathing, walking, talking miracle, saved by the hand of my Deliverer.

I too, was anxious to see John the Baptizer and his followers who preached that the Kingdom of God was at hand. What would it be like to step into the waters and be immersed into new life? Though my life had already been made new from the moment that Yeshua entered our little room, I wanted all He had for me. I wanted to be washed clean, to grow, and learn everything I could about the Torah, about prayer and fasting, about the Kingdom of God. I had lost so many years and I had so much life yet to live.

Zara too was more excited than I had ever seen her, barely able to contain herself as we walked alongside the followers of the Master. Mary and my auntie were steadfast as they sang songs and told stories about when Yeshua was a boy. Everyone was eager to hear the stories. I could remember glimpses of the pictures she painted of a boy who was wise beyond his years—the one who stayed behind in the temple with the priests for three days while his parents were frantically searching for him. His only explanation being "Why were you searching for me? Didn't you know I had to be in my Father's house?" This brought laughter from the people and even a smile to Yeshua's face as Mary recalled taking him by the ear and dragging him all the way back to Nazareth.

Finally we arrived at the river, surrounded by the disciples of John and the hundreds of people going into the water and coming up again with faces glowing like the sun. I was desperate to join them as well but had to wait my turn like everyone else. Soon Yeshua's disciples were in the water also and began baptizing people into the Kingdom of God. When my turn came, I recognized the man who beckoned me to him. He was one of those who had been with Yeshua each night, the one they called John, though not the Baptizer. Zara was beside me and urged me forward. The water was waist deep and flowing one way, so I had to carefully make my way. Step by step, I went into this new life I knew I was called to live. It was as if everything was getting clearer and brighter and, as I went under the water, my old life disappeared. I emerged a brand-new creation. Gone was the residue of any of my former self, and in its place a new confidence that I was exactly where I was supposed to be. Yahweh had redeemed my life from the pit and I would spend the rest of my life serving, following, and loving the One who had delivered me from the grip of Satan himself. Zara and I locked eyes. I knew she felt it too. We were both radically changed forever, and our lives would never be the same.

We camped by the river for several days. Each day more and more people came to be baptized, to hear the Teacher, and to experience the miracle of His Presence. People were bringing their sick to Him. He would touch them, and they would be healed. Miracles were happening all around us and there was singing and dancing and praising Adonai day and night. I was hungry to hear every word He spoke, so Zara and I stayed as close as we could. We cooked and cleaned along with Mary and Auntie and made sure the Master had plenty of food and water to drink.

Mary hovered around him as the adoring mother she was. Soon there was talk of moving on, and I could see the sadness filling her eyes. Zara and I had decided on the night we were baptized that, as much as we loved Mary and Auntie, and as difficult as it would be to say goodbye; our new life was now forever devoted to being followers of Yeshua. The thought of being separated from my beloved auntie once again almost broke my heart, but I had never been more certain of anything in my life. I prayed that she would understand.

When we found them by the fire late that night, tears were shining in my eyes as I looked at the woman who had loved me so well for my entire life. This beautiful woman who never stopped praying for me and had kept me alive in her heart for all those lost years. I could barely look at her, so she simply reached out her arms to me, and in a warm embrace, told me she knew I was destined to remain with the Master.

As the tears fell down our cheeks, she smiled and told me not to be sad. "My Sweet Mary, this has always been the prayer of my heart for you all these years. I prayed for Yahweh to hold you close in His arms and allow you to know how priceless you are to Him and to me. We will never have to say goodbye again, for our hearts are joined together in the Lord Yeshua."

I sobbed as I held her tightly. Soon, Mary and Zara were enfolded in our embrace and we all rejoiced while grieving at the same time. These godly women held us and laid their hands on our heads, as my auntie prayed that we would be set free to live in the fullness of who Elohim had created us to be. Mary continued praying for us to be used mightily by Jehovah Jireh, and that He would set our lives on the path He had laid before us, following the Teacher for all our days on this earth. The tears dried up and a peace settled over us as together we quietly sang the *Love Song to Yahweh* for the last time. Mary made us promise to take good care of her son and to try to get him to come back to Nazareth as often as possible to see his mother. We laughed and promised we would give our lives to being a blessing to him and his cause. It was a beautiful way to begin a life of adventure we could never have even imagined in our wildest dreams.

Each day was filled with people, always so many people wanting to be near to the Master. They would bring their sick and broken to Him, desperate for a touch from the Healer. Zara and I tried to make His life as comfortable as possible, for we knew that His body could only take so much. He needed to eat, sleep, and get away by Himself for times of solitude. As we served Him, He would often smile at us in gratitude, knowing we were sent by His mother on a mission to keep Him well fed and cared for.

Days stretched into weeks and months as we traveled with our band of brothers. Through the dusty streets of Cana, up to the coast of Tyre and back to the mountains of Korazin, His teachings and healings brought thousands of people from all over the region.

One day, the Master had been teaching for hours and it was getting late in the day. We were a long way from any towns and when Philip urged Yeshua to send the people away, the Teacher replied, "You give them something to eat." The disciples were confused and looked to one another for answers before Andrew brought a young boy to Yeshua. "Here is a boy who has two small fish and five loaves of barley bread," he stammered, "But what good will they be with so many people?" The Master told us to have the people gather together and sit on the grass. He then looked up to heaven, gave thanks and then began breaking the loaves and giving us the food to distribute. We knew better than to question Him at this point, so we did as we were told and we kept handing out more fish and more bread as the hours stretched on. There had to be at least five thousand men, plus women and children who were fed that day. We could not explain how the dried fish and the bread would not run out, and watching each person eat their fill, gave me a whole new love for Jehovah Jireh. He was the God who would send His Son to the earth to supply the very essence of life to the world that was so desperate and hungry to be filled.

There were times when we could sense the heavy burden the Master carried on His shoulders as He taught us about His mission saying: "My food, is to do the will of Him who sent me and to finish His work." We could sense His frustration when He taught in the Temple and called out the Pharisee's and Teachers of the Law saying:

> If God were your Father, you would love me, for I came from God and am now here. I have not come on my own; but He sent me. Yet because I tell the truth, you do not believe me! Can any of you prove me guilty of sin? If I am telling the truth, why don't you believe me? He who belongs to God hears what God says. The reason you do not hear is that you do not belong to God.

Strong words but always delivered with a heart of love desperately longing for all people to know the Father and do what is right. We all grew strong in His teachings and lived to share the message of truth and love with the whole world. As we traveled from place to place, we could sense the load the Master was carrying got heavier and heavier. He was passionate when He told us the fields were ripe for harvest and the harvesters were few. Zara and I knew we were part of a much bigger plan, and we too were the harvesters Yeshua spoke of.

When our friends Mary and Martha led us down to where they had laid the body of their brother, Lazarus, three days earlier, we grieved deeply. The sadness was almost more than we could take. When the Master told the men to roll away the stone, there were tears falling down his cheeks. The sisters protested, fearing the odor of the dead, but then He stated, "Did I not tell you that if you believed, you would see the glory of God?" At this point, we were becoming accustomed to the miraculous and had no doubts our friend might be raised from the dead. However, to hear the Master shout the command: "Lazarus, come out!" And then seeing a dead man wrapped in burial clothes walking out of a tomb; this was far beyond what we had ever imagined when we signed on to be his followers.

We fell with our faces to the ground and worshipped Yeshua, rejoicing with Lazarus' sisters and all our friends. The party in Bethany that night was one of praise and adoration for the Son of God whom we followed. From then on, it seemed the opposition grew, and we had to be more careful wherever we traveled.

In order to help support our Master, Zara and I had finally sold the beautiful bottle of expensive perfume which Kiera had given to us on the night we departed the Temple. It had provided well for our small band of disciples while traveling together. We often thanked Yahweh for Kiera, praying that we would indeed someday be reunited.

Thinking back, it was then the Teacher began telling us of his earthly departure saying, "We are going up to Jerusalem, and everything that is written by the prophets about the Son of Man will be fulfilled. He will be handed over to the Gentiles. They will mock Him, insult Him, spit on Him, flog Him and kill Him. On the third day He will rise again."

I knew my heart could not dare to begin thinking of life without my Deliverer. I tried to ignore those teachings, wanting desperately to deny what He was saying. I prayed He would stay with us forever. Many of us talked late into the night, long after the Master was asleep, trying to understand what he was teaching us. In our hearts, we refused to believe there could ever be a life without Yeshua, our Messiah.

The week we traveled to Jerusalem for the Passover was full of teachings and quality time spent together. It was as if the Master was longing to infuse us with all the wisdom of heaven that He could possibly pour into us. Our last supper together was both beautiful and brutal all in one evening. Our beloved Yeshua identified one of our own as His betrayer.

The events quickly unfolded after that and are still a bit of a blur which my heavy heart tries desperately to forget. It began in the garden where he was arrested. I was later told by Peter and John of the abuse that our Messiah suffered at the hands of what appeared to be obviously drunken Roman soldiers. Then the mockery of a trial where He was falsely accused and condemned to die. I wailed along with the other women as we walked alongside Him on the tortuous road to Golgotha. He fell many times under the weight of the heavy cross—His back bloodied, His body beaten and spent.

We stood at a distance from His cross, weeping tears of deep anguish and intense sorrow. Zara, Salome and I held onto Mary, Yeshua's mother, and my beloved auntie, who had joined our caravan several weeks before. We could not leave, and we could not get close enough to Him; however, I know He knew we were there.

At one point, He looked at his mother and said, "Dear woman, here is your son" and then He told John, the beloved one, "Here is your mother."

We wailed all the louder seeing Mary collapsing to the ground writhing in pain. We all fell to the ground beside her, clawing the ground and throwing the dirt in the air to cover our anguish. The darkness in the sky mirrored our hearts: we watched the Son of God leave this earth.

The ground shook and our hearts shattered further as at last He uttered, "It is finished."

In our agony we pleaded with the man Joseph of Arimathea, who had become a disciple after Lazarus was raised, to use his influence with the council and ask for the body our Lord. Because of his standing, Pilate agreed and ordered Yeshua's body be released into his care. We wept and wailed as we followed them to the new tomb where they placed the body our Messiah.

It was two days before we women could go to the tomb to give Him a proper burial. We wondered how we would ever be able to roll the giant stone away from the entrance. When we arrived at the place where Joseph and the others had laid Him, to our surprise, the enormous stone had been rolled away. Two men in clothes gleaming bright as lightening stood beside the opening. As we peered in, they asked us, "Why do you look for the living among the dead? He is not here. He has risen!"

We immediately ran as fast as our feet would carry us back to the disciples to tell them the news. Together, we all rushed back to the tomb. John arrived first and dared not go in. Instead, he stayed outside trembling. When Peter arrived, he rushed in and it was just as we had said. Yeshua was not there. Our hearts were as confused as our minds as we wondered where our Lord had been taken. Long after the other disciples slowly filed away, I was left alone in my grief—my tears falling on the ground where I sat unmoving and bewildered. A man came up to me and asked me why I was crying. Through my tears, I begged: "Sir, if you have carried Him away, tell me where you have put Him, and I will get Him." Then I heard the voice of the One who had delivered me, the One who had loved me, set me free and taught me— the One who had radically changed my life simply by saying my name ... "Mary."

I knew it was the Lord. "Rabbi!" I cried out, trying to reach out and touch him. He spoke to me then saying, "Do not hold on to Me, for I have not yet returned to My Father. Go instead to My brothers and tell them, 'I am returning to My Father and your Father, to My God and your God.' "

Days passed, and we experienced the risen and resurrected Yeshua over and over again. Our hearts were strengthened with the mission He had given us when He said, "All authority in heaven and earth has been given to me. Therefore, go and make disciples of all nations, baptizing them in the name of the Father and of the Son and of the Holy Spirit, and teaching them to obey everything I have commanded you." The words that He spoke next will stay with me forever, imprinted deeply on my heart: "And surely I am with you always, to the very end of the age."

As we stood surrounding Him, He reached out His scarred hands and blessed each of us, and then He was taken up into the cloudless blue sky and disappeared from our sight.

I don't know how long I stayed there staring up at that brilliant blue sky. It seemed like forever as my whole life had flashed before me as on a scroll. Standing there alone, after everyone had departed, I fell to my knees and raised my hands in worship. I knew this was not the end, but only the beginning. The calling the Master had placed on my life that day, only three short years ago when He delivered me and set me free, was sure and strong. I was to live out the abundant life He had created me for, proclaiming Him as Lord and Messiah. I worshipped and prayed, committing my life once again to serving my risen Master and Savior, Yeshua, and the Kingdom of God for as long as I had breath in my lungs.

THE END

Dear Reader,

Thank you for taking the time to journey with Mary to her place of healing. I want you to know that I have experienced the healing power of Jesus first-hand in my own life, and so can you. If you have struggled in this life with pain and suffering, Jesus gets it. He loves you, and He wants to meet you right where you are. All it takes is a willingness to fully surrender and allow the Healer into your heart, mind and life. He is real and He wants to walk with you on your journey. Though there is no secret formula or magic words to say, it begins with a conversation that might sound like this ... "Lord Jesus, I believe You are real, and I though I don't fully understand how You work, I come to You with my heart in my hands admitting that I have made a mess of my life. I really need a Savior to bring me the peace, strength and joy that I am searching for. Would You forgive me for all the ways I have failed, sinned and fallen short, and come into my heart to live forever? I surrender my past, present and future and give You my life. I want all that You have for me. Be my Healer, my Savior, and my Lord. Please show me what abundant life with You looks like. I ask this in Your mighty name...amen."

If you just prayed that prayer with a sincere heart, the Bible says that there is a celebration in heaven happening right now. You are now a new creation, the old is gone and the new is come. Your name is now written in the Book of Life for all eternity, and your salvation is secure.

Please tell someone you trust about this life changing decision and find a good Bible believing Christian church to get plugged into. Your journey is just beginning, and Jesus has a brand-new life for you, starting right now. Don't turn back but follow hard after the One who has been waiting for you. Welcome to the family of God!

DISCUSSION QUESTIONS

1). Beauty in most all cultures is considered to be a blessing. But it can also be a curse. The Bible tells us in Proverbs 31:30 that charm is deceptive, and beauty is fleeting, but a woman who fears the Lord is to be praised. How did you see Mary's beauty being a curse for her at a young age? Discuss the ways we can empower the young girls in our lives to be safe within their true identity as children of God.

2). Often the dynamics within our families are very complicated. How did you see the relationship between Naomi and her sister Mira (Mary's mother) unfolding when they were little girls?
* For further discussion- How does that compare to the sibling rivalry of Jacob (whose mother favored him) and Esau (whose father favored him)? Discuss how each of them could have allowed the other to be their ally instead of their enemy.

3). As children we are often exposed to religion in some form or another. How did Mary's exposure to the God of Abraham, Isaac and Jacob at a young age help and hurt her on her troubled journey in life? How has religion affected your life either positively or negatively?

4). Zara was Mary's faithful companion, protector and friend for over thirteen years. How did her self sacrificing love impact her own life and the life of her mistress Mary? Was her decision to take Mary to the Temple a positive decision or a negative one?
*For further discussion- In what ways did her love for her friend compare to the self-sacrificing love that Ruth in the Bible showed to her mother-in-law Naomi?

5). Kiera's was a life that was sacrificed on the altar of beauty. How did you see her role in Mary's life?
*For further discussion- In the same way Esther's beauty led to her rise, discuss your thoughts on how Kiera handled the life that she had been chosen for her?

6). Two brothers born to the same mother, one viewed by the world as "perfect", the other born disfigured and left to live a life in the shadows. Discuss how Zain's life could possibly have been redeemed if his own mother would have seen him differently? What is our role in the lives of people that seem different from us?
*For further discussion- What similarities do you see between Cain and Able, and Zain and Misha?

7). Trauma has played a devastating role in Mary's life, indeed in many of our lives. How did the enemy of Mary's soul exploit her vulnerabilities? How did the abandonment by her own parents at such a young age impact all the other trauma that followed? What do you think was the breaking point for her? How do you see the hand of God alive in Mary's life throughout her journey?

8). When Yeshua walks into the room and Mary sees Him, the evil in her comes face to face with Immanuel, God with us. With one encounter with the Savior, Mary is delivered and set free. Describe the emotions she and the others must have been feeling as she spoke the word "Auntie" for the first time in over ten years? Have you ever come face to face with the Healer in your life? If you feel comfortable, share a time in your life when you experienced a touch from the Master.

9). Mary's life was radically altered when she was healed, and it led her to commit her life and future to serving her Master. After Jesus ascended to heaven, discuss what you think her life would have been like. Do you think it is possible to be completely content in devoting your life to the service of the Lord?

10). What do you feel is the main theme of the book? How would you summarize that theme?